The
Kingdom
of
Kandy

Colin Hodgson

Published by C E Hodgson
Colchester,
United Kingdom

First edition August 2012

ISBN: 978-0-9569498-5-1

ACKNOWLEDGMENTS

Many thanks to the people of Wikipedia. A true fountain of knowledge and resource.

Cover designed by Colin Hodgson, loosely based on the Champaner Fort Walls in Gujarat, India

Contents

Colin Hodgson

1 -- COLONY

April 1971, the mining colony of New Bury, around the camp fire.

Stumpy continued his tale. "And the entire race of intelligent bacteria had dwindled down to just a handful. The once-endless queues were almost depleted. But one of the survivors stood up on his orange-box and addressed his fellows. 'Friends, Bacteria and countrymen, lend me your ears. Our communistic, bureaucratic and destopian ways have destroyed us. Before we are totally extinct, I'm gonna throw away my contraceptives, take that girl at the back who I fancy, and we're gonna have children, and we're gonna go into the World and explore and discover, and make a new World with schools and holidays and even shops, and we'll start a new beginning. And I'll call us the Uman Wace, and I'll be your dictator, and you my servants. Follow me to beyond the new horizon.' And so the intelligent bacteria realised the errors of their ways, and decided to become un-equal and multi-structured, each fitting into his most appropriate slot, and they chose to stop waiting for our daddy's body to be accessible. They would instead go yonder in search of other food."

"Is that it?" asked Peter. "A strange ending." The fourteen year old human looked at Stumpy and raised his eyebrows.

Stumpy, a strong and handsome green lad, just cuddled tightly up to his little twin brother and they both chuckled.

Peter sat beside Stumpy, his alien friend who was indigenous to the New Bury Colony. He held his own frail, deformed sister, Katie, as they all watched the twin moons creeping across the skies. The fire warmed their faces and the white-hot embers sent sparks into the skies, which floated up but died long before they could take their places with the other stars. The two marooned humans had been listening attentively as their very good friend told his tale, and while Peter gently brushed Katie's long blonde hair away from her green eyes, he again asked, "Well, is that it?"

Stumpy calmed his giggles and then concluded his story about the Uman Wace. He laughed, "Haha, not quite the end, so…. And while the intelligent bacteria had been waiting for millions of years for their only known food-source to become exposed, that's my father's body, they'd lost their way. They'd spent their entire existence arguing, meeting, discussing, convening, reconvening, presiding, minuting and eating each other. They didn't even notice when our daddy's tomb became eroded by the wind and rain, nor when he sat up and proudly looked around at his domain. So, after having a really good stretch, Daddy stepped out of his tomb, right on top of the Uman Wace. They were all squashed!"

Peter and Katie joined in with Stumpy's laughter.

"That can't be a true story," Peter jested.

Stumpy pumped his chest out, and proudly stated, "It is, I made it up myself, and that's the truth." Their laughter rang around the Colony. But Mo, his little twin brother, suddenly wept as he clung around his neck. Stumpy's twin brother was dying!

Peter, a million miles from home, looked at the little green lad across the burning embers, and then whispered to Katie, "Mo will soon die. What can we do?"

The eight-year-old replied quietly with slurred speech, "Whatever happens they must make the decisions. Any decision on their future must be theirs, else it won't help us." Katie brushed her long blonde hair aside. "But soon we'll all die, and I'll never reunite with Catherine."

As the four of them kept themselves warm around the camp fire, the rest of the colony slept. They all knew that the corrosive gas was wafting its way around the globe, destroying everything in its path and continually propagating, and when it had travelled full circle around the planet, it would all be over. A sombre mood began to fall on the camp.

Mo, with a shake in his voice, asked, "When will you tell your story, Katie? Tell us your story, please, before I die."

Her twisted face pushed against Peter's ear. "Can you get my book, please, pumpkin?"

He set the book in front of her and she fingered through to a section titled 'The Kingdom of Kandy' but to her horror it was blank! She forced a look of fear. "There's no story to tell. I'm so sorry." Her delivery was morose. "I'll have to make up a story, just for you, Mo." And she put her mouth to Peter's ear and whispered, "Peter can tell my story."

He began to convey her whispers. "This is Katie's story. It's all about a time when God went missing." His sister just whispered, and whispered. Peter continued. "Sometimes, God has to leave his throne and his children, and go out in search. And we all suffer."

But Mo interrupted, pushed himself away from Stumpy's neck and kissed Katie on the lips. He held one of his spindly hands on her forrid and stroked it with his razor-like nails. "I'll give you, when the time comes," he gasped, struggling for breath.

She knew what he meant and she answered with a loving smile. Her future was assured.

Looking into her face Mo slowly pleaded, "Tell us your story, Katie, before I die." Little Mo's breathing was strained as he pulled himself back around Stumpy's neck.

Stumpy enquired, "Is it a long story?"

Peter looked at the book. The pages, previously blank, were suddenly packed with pictures and narrative, and Katie twisted herself around to give Peter a big kiss on the lips, then whispered, "It is now."

"Yes," replied Peter, "very long." He could not stop grinning.

Stumpy joined him, flashing his white teeth under the twin moons. With renewed boast he stated, "Then, Peter, I'd better tell you what we've agreed. Mo is going to give himself to your sister when he goes, not to me. We've agreed, and so has our daddy, so, no arguing. Now you can begin."

Peter was shaking with the promise of Stumpy's and Mo's gift. Stumpy was to give up his life as a God, by giving Katie his inner strength and knowledge; by giving her his own twin brother, Little Mo. Katie was to go home.

With the book perched on his knees and Katie whispering constantly in his ear, Peter began Katie's story of The Kingdom of Kandy.

"This is the *true* story of the missing God, and the return of the Qeervis. Now listen very carefully. Back in the seventeen hundreds God worked with her earthly project team, the Qeervi Royal Family, to study man's ability to be good to each other. A secret society was formed, and it set about its business helping others. With the British East India Company as their chariot the benevolent society began to spread throughout the trading world. But their plans changed when the naughty Mother of God decided that she wanted to go home with her Lamma. As a result of her connivance the Qeervi family were ceremoniously crucified by a scholarly sect from Nepal, the Chi Bantri. Nobody knows why but the family dispersed, as God went back to her throne, and the others went elsewhere. They were lost, and God was alone, and very, very desperate. But the daughter of God, just thirteen years old and who had just begun her confirmation period of suffering, showed her undisputable strength and took up the challenge of proving her thoroughbred. She refused to die.

"After a few years the Chi Bantri saw the light and stopped trying to torture the poor girl to death; instead they adopted her as their earthly idol. So she became the spiritual foundation of the sect, guiding them towards the good and charitable, in the memory of the formidable Queen Maya, the naughty mother of God. But one terrible day in the lord's year of eighteen fourteen, the new Monsignor of the Chi Bantri met with his inner court. They changed direction. The Chi Bantri condemned their own members in the Kingdom of Kandy to an horrific death, to begin their two hundred year reign of terror. They became the malevolent society which ultimately influenced all the governments and powers into perpetrating in the interests of the Chi Bantri. Every act of genocide and most scenes of suppression has had the Chi Bantri behind it, reaping the worldly benefits of inhumanity. Anyway, the daughter of God, her eyes blinded by the torture, kept the tabs on the vile sect by her spiritual influence, knowing that one day her family would return and they would, as God's earthly project team, destroy the monster which they had created. And she would then sit her final exams to complete her two hundred year apprenticeship."

Peter turned the page of Katie's book, 'Unknown India', and the story continued.

Colin Hodgson

2 -- THE GREEN EYED GIRL

This is Katie's story of the missing God. Now listen carefully.

Late September 2008, Boxted Airfield, Station 150, Langham, England.

The long, straight runway is one of the few remaining remnants of this Second World War airfield, which played a vital role in the struggle for democracy and freedom, more than seventy years earlier. Time had hidden the reality of war from the flat Essex countryside.

"Lest we forget", a memorial had been erected at the entrance to the runway. Consisting of a 'v' shaped white brick wall which pointed along the runway, it remembered the bravery of the Royal Air Force and four American Air Groups which flew from Boxted during the Second Word War. Many concrete bollards sat like sentries along the road, which cut across the end of the runway.

The runway had a well trimmed, three metre high hedge along one side, a remnant of another, more humane, era from the region's past; apple growing. The orchards had since all been removed, leaving little evidence of the area's fruit farming industry during the latter half of the twentieth century. The trimmed hedges were all that was left. They had been grown to protect the apples from the winds which cut across that flat countryside, and on that day they sheltered another "industry", the boot sale.

It was a bright autumn day and many people wandered up and down the runway, some aimlessly, some deliberately. Stalls of all shapes and sizes were lined up and the quiet was slightly disturbed by the distant sound of country and western music ringing from one of the stalls. With the hedge to the left and the stalls and car-parking to the right, the whole scene was sombre, almost sad. People desperate to sell, people not wanting to buy, and many just wondering why they had even come at all.

Like many of the other householders trying to turn their rubbish and excesses into cash Robin stood alone, behind his wares. He had been given two to three hundred books by a local group who could not sell any of them at a church bazaar, and it was probably easier for them to donate them to Robin's cause rather than to take them to the refuse tip. But Robin believed he could sell them and raise loads of money for polio children!

Standing in front of his car, with the hedge on the opposite side of the runway, he had laid down a blue plastic tarpaulin and the books had been carefully spread across it. Amongst the books he had placed two green charity collection tins, for Polio Children. The lady on the next stall was selling a bit of everything, from children's toys to garden tools.

"Hello. I'm Glennys" she said as she caught Robin's attention.

"Hi. I'm Robin. Hoping for a good day?" he asked.

"Hope so. Need to raise some Christmas money. It's pretty tight at the minute." She shrugged her shoulders.

Robin stuttered a little as he asked, "Do you come here often? If you know what I mean."

She smiled and quietly replied "Most weeks. I lost my job a couple of months ago and my husband doesn't earn enough by himself. And it gets me out."

Robin briefly looked at his feet in embarrassment then slowly said "Sorry. You mentioned hubby, I wasn't trying to chat you up."

"So what's wrong with me?" she laughed. "Only joking. I'm happily married with two daughters. Does that mean you're single?"

"Yes. Well, divorced. Been divorced for about ten years now. I'm fifty four and left on the shelf, I think." His shaved, bald head shone a little in the autumn sun.

Glennys paused for few seconds. "Well old man, your 'bootie' luck might be changing." She pointed to the other end of the book-spread where a young boy was looking at a briefcase, overseen by his dad.

Robin paused for a few seconds, and then tried to act like the market trader. "That would be perfect for school. I got it from a friend who works for DFDS. It's brand new."

The dad asked "How much?"

Robin was caught out. Thinking quickly he replied, "It's all for Polio Children, so put in the pot whatever you think."

The man looked across at Robin, grabbed the boy by the hand and walked off down the runway.

With a confused frown Robin asked Glennys, "What was that about?"

"Don't know" she replied. "You just have to put up with the weirdoes. Try giving a price next time."

Over the next hour Robin sold a few books, priced at about fifty pence each. Then another man, with his daughter, took an interest in the brief case. He picked the case up and inspected it.

"How much?" asked the man, holding the case towards Robin.

"Well it's brand new and unused. Must be fifteen pounds in the shop. Say, one pound fifty?" He waited in anticipation.

The man just put the case back down on the tarpaulin and walked away with his daughter. The little girl looked so disappointed.

Robin was beginning to realise that a sensitive dreamer like himself was not going to enjoy the boot sale environment. Everybody seemed to speak a different language, even the English, and lived by a different set of morals, and simply valued everything at very close to zero. In the twenty-first century desperation still prevails!

Fussing about a few pennies was alien to him, spoiled brat springs to mind, but everything he had ever had was worked for and paid for. I do not think he had any true idea of just how desperate the world really was.

Sometimes people can have visions which take them off to far away lands or distant times, where they see what they want to see, but they don't often see what they need to see. Robin was one of those dreamers with countless visions in his head, which are always being selected to suite his mood. As he watched the people walk straight past his 'Polio Children' collection tins he began to wonder if he was really among his own kind, or maybe they were all ghosts from the airfield's darker times. It had been part of a death culture during the Second World War, killing as many of the opposition as they were able. And there he was, standing right there on the runway. He wandered off to a time past, and dreamed about standing there, watching, as a Marauder bomber approached the airfield to land. It swung around in preparation, and approached the main runway from the south, still flying at one hundred and fifty miles per hour. Those bombers were nicknamed 'widow makers' since they crashed so often at take-off and landing. This time the plane touched down, bounced along the runway for a while, then settled and slowed safely to a halt in front of Robin. Sitting on top of the fuselage, just in front of the dorsal gun turret, was a young German mother and her three little daughters.

"Are we there yet?" asked one of the daughters.

"I need a wee," said another.

Mummy just looked down at them and calmly said, "No, we've got a little way still to go. We're still bleeding and are not dead yet." The third daughter just cried.

Mummy and her three daughters lowered their heads in shame as the crew climbed out of the plane. The airmen had survived another mission, successfully killing and maiming the enemy, while the young mother and her family just sat on top of the plane, waiting at the gates of heaven.

The hedge returned, the plane went back to nineteen forty three and Robin stood looking at the people milling up and down past his book stall. He looked over to Glennys and said "I don't think I want to stay here. I'm gonna put fifty pounds in the tins, and get rid of the books. I'm going home."

Glennys looked around and said, "Don't give up. There are some nice people here as well. You've been unlucky. Anyway, you're blocked in so you're here till we all move out!"

He looked around him, and she was right. With his car completely hemmed in, he was going nowhere, until at least midday.

"Do you know how much a cup of coffee is here?" asked Glennys.

"I would guess about a pound" he replied.

"No. One pound fifty. Same as your brief case. And three times as much as you're selling the books for. Try something." Glennys reached down beside her car and stood up with a piece of card. She rested the white card on the bonnet of her car, took a marker pen out of her pocket and wrote 'FOR POLIO CHILDREN -- ALL BOOKS £1'.

"If they really want your books they'll pay a pound for them."

She handed the sign to Robin. He lodged it upright between two large books, stood back then put his hands on his bald head and said, "Let's go for it."

People wandered past for a while, and then a young couple stopped at the stall. They pulled the books about, came out with four books and then dropped four pound coins into one of the boxes. Four pounds in one sale, almost doubling his takings! Several people then bought books and Glennys stood behind her stall with a smug look on her face, and Robin thought, 'Pity she's married'.

As the morning moved on, the wind became a little stronger, causing the large leaves on the hedge to first look one way along the runway, and then follow the swirl to look round the other way. Robin studied the movement and wondered if they were looking for something. Maybe they were expecting somebody from the past! Waiting for the next bomber to come in with the "good" news?

Glennys whispered, "Robin. Wake up. Are you anywhere nice?"

"Oh. No, just daydreaming. I was wondering what the leaves are looking for. Look. They're looking that way." They watched for a few seconds. "Now they're looking up the other direction."

Glennys cast a very old fashioned look at him.

"Sorry," he said, "just daydreaming."

Robin's dreamy gaze was attracted to a group of four children standing almost opposite, as if they were sheltering under the hedge from the light wind. They were about eight years old and three were boys, and one a girl. Their clothing was inconspicuous but clearly a school uniform, with light blue-grey overcoats, just revealing grey short trousers, and the girl had a grey pleated skirt. They were discussing something and rather shyly passing half-glances towards Robin. The little girl, who had shoulder length blonde hair and a cheeky grin, seemed to lead the glances.

Robin noticed their attention and was suddenly aware that they were talking about either him or his books. He felt a little uncomfortable. They were just children, but he oddly felt very self conscious, so he set about rearranging some of the books which had been shuffled about by the customers, and while he was bent over he felt safe, as he managed to avoid the children's eyes.

Suddenly, a pair of tiny feet in white ankle socks stood underneath his sightline. He looked up to find the little blonde girl staring him in the face and smiling, biting her bottom lip nervously. The stare was intense. Big grey-green eyes pierced his defences. He was under attack, and felt vulnerable.

"Wotcha, mate" she said. "Me an' me mates wanna buy a book." It was a soft voice but a rough, strong South Essex accent. "'ow much?"

"A pound each." He looked across at the notices which Glennys had made.

"I *know*. But we ain't *got* a quid." She carried on staring into his eyes.

"Ok. How much have you got?"

"I've got firty six p." She shuffled her feet around a bit. "I'll see what me mates've got."

As she turned and plodded over to her friends, Robin felt a sense of relief. Escape. The eyes were hypnotic, and they were beginning to get hold of him! He watched the children turning out their trouser pockets. Each boy handed something over to the girl, and then they searched their other pockets. One boy carried a satchel, and he tipped out the contents on to the runway, and then returned them. Huddled around each other they counted the money which they had collected. Back came the little girl, and her eyes recaptured Robin. His escape was short-lived.

"We've 'ad a whip an' we've got forty eigh' p."

"Is that everything?" he asked.

"Yeah, that's it. Honest." She again began biting her bottom lip.

"I believe you. Honest." He smiled, and she stopped biting her lip. He said, "Do you a deal. As you're willing to give polio children *all* your money, forty eight pence, I'll let you have *all* my books. And, listen on, you. You can have a free brief case worth one pound fifty! Bargain of the century."

She started giggling and walked to the end of the stall and back again, then looked over to her friends, raised her thumb to them then turned back to Robin, still giggling. "That's daft. We couldn't carry 'em all." She carried on giggling. "But the one we want is still 'ere. Give ya forty eigh' p for it. Me mates all agree." She bit her lip again. "Can we 'ave just the one for forty eigh' p?"

Robin was a little confused. He asked "Is it a special book?"

The girl shrugged her shoulders then, quite unexpectedly, said "I'm Caferine. I'm named after a saint. She's in India. Calcu'a. You 'eard of 'er?" Catherine waits for a few seconds. "Cat got yer tongue then?"

"Don't get cheeky." He was falling in love! "Sorry. Yes. I've heard of a Saint Catherine. She's a Catholic saint, isn't she? She rolled down the road tied to a cartwheel, burning."

"Not this one. You shouldn't believe everyfink you read, but this one, she's still goin' strong in Calcu'a. She looks after little kids with leprosy, an' she's s'posed to be the loveliest person on earf. Every few years the locals try to kill 'em all by burnin' 'em out and she stops 'em. Once though, the kids all got burned, and she was *so* pissed off." She paused, but never stopped staring into Robin's eyes. "I've got a cousin in India an' she writes me every coupl'a monfs. She wants me to look after this book for ya. I promised."

Robin by now was frowning and wondering what she was talking about. But the eyes held him tight.

"You don't believe me, do ya. Don't blame ya really, but it's all kosher, mate."

"How old are you?" he asked.

"Eigh'. We're all eigh' years old." She pointed to her friends.

"You could pass for two hundred and eight." They both smiled. "Do your mates know about India?"

"Yeah. I tell 'em loads. We do work togever. I'm a wri'er an' they help me by getting stuff for me, like this book cos Neil saw it earlier an' he didn't wanna ask you cos he didn't 'ave the cash an' he didn't think you'd let him 'ave it anyway. But we'll look after it an' you can 'ave it back whenever you want or if you wanna read it again, you can 'ave it back any time. You can trust us, we're yer mates." Catherine bit her bottom lip and frowned. "Can I get the book now?"

"Of course." He couldn't stop looking at her eyes. The more he looked the more beautiful they became.

Catherine carefully tiptoed through the books, making certain to stand in open areas to avoid any damage, and then dropped the forty eight pence into one of the collection tins. Then, with stealth and deliberation, she used some empty floor space to perch by her new acquisition. As she pushed some books aside she picked up a hard-backed book, with a very scruffy dust cover. She was very careful with it as she moved back out of the books, still avoiding damage to any other goods.

Robin realised that even if the book was not special, the little girl was. The pretty little Catherine then stood in front of Robin with the widest of smiles, and boomed sheer excitement through her beautiful grey-green eyes. They were still staring deep into Robin's mind, but now he was beginning to feel a warmth, which had previously been hostility and mistrust. He did not know what to say. During the short silence the girl turned to her mates and put her thumb in the air in triumph, and they all grinned like a litter of Cheshire cats.

"So what's so great about this book?" he asked.

She held up the old book to show Robin the front cover. The dust cover was scruffy, but had done its job by protecting the hard cover of the book, which read "Unknown India".

"Is the book valuable?" he asked.

"It is to us, an' to you. Ain't you read it?" She stopped smiling. "If you wanna give us our forty eigh' p back, I'll give you back your book. But you can always 'ave it back anyway, whenever you want. We're guarding it for ya, that's all an' me cousin said it's yours, so it'll always be yours."

Mixed-up Robin sighed. "No. I haven't read it. I didn't even know I had it. It came from a church jumble sale in Boxted. If I'd known that I had something so special I might have taken it to auction." He could not look at the book, she still had him captured. "But you've bought it. You've given your entire wealth to Polio Children, so it's your gain."

The girl giggled. "Saint Caferine said somefink lovely once. She always does, but this once she said, 'Those who give the most often have the least'. Do you understand it?"

"I think she was referring to what you've just done, given everything you have."

Catherine nodded and tried to wink at him. I wonder why children can't wink.

He said "I hope your parents are proud of you. And thank your cousin, whoever he is. I only know one man in India but doubt it's him; he's not really a wise man." They laughed together.

"Me cousin's a girl. She's only eigh' like us lot. She's Gayla. She told me you'd be nice." Her smile was almost motherly, and she was only eight, honest gov'. "I bet you're mixed up now." She started grinning again. "An' we ain't got a proper mum or dad. I lost mine, a long time back, but we're still looking for them, never give up. But right now we ain't got nobody. Just me cousin an' me niece, from India. Oh, an' me uvver cousin in India. Us four here live in a home called St. Phoebe's Garden, and it's for kids who ain't got nobody. It's so 'orrible." She turned her nose up at the thought of the home.

Robin was beginning to feel a little bit uncomfortable. "I'm sorry. I'm sure the home looks after you."

Quite calmly she replied, "No. They keep tryin' to fuck us."

He was horrified. None of the conversation that went previous was expected, nor was it quite day-to-day, but this bit really shocked him. He was lost for words, and just wanted to cuddle his darling Catherine.

"But they don't fuck us. They're scared of us. The uvver kids ain't so strong. They get fucked." She stood waiting for a response, still staring into his eyes. He had not said a single word, but she went on, "No, we ain't told anyone else. D'you wan' us to?"

Everybody knows that things happen in some homes, but when you are confronted with it, what do you do? He asked "What do I do?"

Catherine thought carefully. "Ya don't 'ave to do anyfink if yer don't want. I'll do it for ya. I'll get the home shu' up."

"But if you do that, what'll happen to you? You'll probably be sent to another home. You'll all be split up."

"Do ya fink we should let 'em get on wiv it, then?"

"No. I don't know. No, it's got to stop. I don't know what to say."

She stared so hard into his eyes, into his mind, and still smiling she assured him, "Don't worry, we'll sor' it." She sprung up on her toes. "I know what. You could adopt us all!"

From the next stall Glennys had been listening in. She urged, "Don't listen to her. She's trying to trap you. You've no idea who she is."

Catherine pushed in, saying to Robin "You can do what ya wanna do." She just smiled.

Glennys said "I think you've said enough young lady."

Catherine continued to smile and turned to Glennys. "I fink you're tryin' to do right. That's good." Glennys stepped back. How do you come back against that? Catherine continued, "You're a good lady, I'm sure, but I can't see ya fitting wiv his lifestyle." She pointed to Robin and held the finger there. "Anyway, he's got a lover."

Glennys puffed, "I'm married. What're you on about?"

Catherine said, still pointing at Robin, "Worry about yer old man, then. This geezer'll look after 'imself."

Robin stepped in. "Catherine. Don't be rude. Glennys was just concerned about a little girl like you propositioning me." He could not hide the wry smile while he spoke. He winked at Catherine. "And I haven't got a lover. Honest gov'."

Catherine, with a serious face, continued "You sure? Anyway, I'll always be 'ere for ya. Yer book is safe an' when you wanna read it, just shout me. You can be the first..." She chuckled to herself. "I was gonna say you can be the first man to ever read it, but that wouldn't be true."

"So, which men have read it?" He was becoming confused, but intrigued.

"None." She again tried to wink, and almost succeeded. "An' one day we'll 'ave a proper chinny. You mustn't care about us, we can watch each uvver's backs. Need to get goin'."

"Hang on," said Robin. "we've said a lot here, and you're just running? There's a lot not been said. Glennys is right, I don't even know who you are."

"A proper intro' then. I'm Caferine. I'm Gayla's cousin and Ca'an's aun'ie. And I'm only eigh'! Honest, gov'. And I know who you are!" With a cheeky chuckle she swung round to her friends. Then, just like in the fairy tales, the skies seemed to blacken and open as she moved towards her mates. It instantly began to rain, quite heavily! Panicking, Catherine and the three boys rushed behind the stall, and Robin, realising what they were after, grabbed a Tesco carrier bag and pushed it over the book. The "treasure" was saved from the rain. The other books just sat and drowned and just maybe, that was their destiny. He really did need to find a skip for the books!

As the four children walked away through the rain, they all looked round, their heads turning in time with the leaves, and they waved. The leaves turned back again and they slowly walked down the length of the runway.

Robin turned to Glennys and apologised for Catherine's behaviour towards her.

She quietly said "You've nothing to apologise for, you don't even know her."

A half-smile spread across one of Robin's cheeks. "I do know who she is. She's Gayla's cousin and Ca'an's auntie. And she still didn't take the brief case." The half-smile turned to a frown. "Wonder who they all are."

Colin Hodgson

3 -- THE GINGER PUSSY

The following day Robin awoke early. It was just about daylight outside, the sun shone through the silvery mist making it look like an angel's globe, and the heavenly looking sun-scape fuelled his belief that the strange meeting at the boot sale was not going to be in isolation. He had a real mood of excitement swirling around in his head.

He was hoping to get some development work done at home. The contract on which he had been working was drawing to a close and he was not due to go back on site for a couple of weeks.

"What today?" he muttered to himself while bending and stretching. Once the old body had straightened up, he looked out of the bedroom window and there was his neighbour, a middle aged lady with whom he had previously had some attachment. The attachment had long been broken.

Washed and freshened, he went downstairs to the living room. "Hi Carla. Want feeding?" He gave his ginger cat some attention, before she bit his hand. "*Why* do you do that?" It would have been a bit of a shock if she had answered, but it did at least seem to awaken his sleepy brain, and whilst pondering the laptop and paperwork he had a much better idea, 'Tesco's for brekkie. Yippee!' "Well Carla, out you go. Come on." The postman had been, and there was a letter on the doormat with a hand written address. He thought, 'What does she want now?' But even without his glasses he realised that it was *not* his ex-wife's handwriting, so he pushed it into his trouser pocket, planning to read it with his breakfast.

During the drive to the Highwoods Tesco store he received a call on his mobile phone from his youngest son.

"Hiya Dad. What you doing this morning?" asked David.

"Well, I'm gonna get some breakfast, and then got some bits to investigate. Had a weird day yesterday. Do you know where St Phoebe's Garden children's home is?"

David hesitated. "I've heard of it. Can't think why. What do you need it for?"

"I think there's abuse going on there." Pause. "I'm coming up to the Rapid's roundabout. I'll phone you later," and then Robin rung off, tossing his phone onto the passenger seat.

The cafeteria was quite busy. Whilst standing in the queue for his usual mix and match fried breakfast, he glanced around to see if he could spot anybody he knew. A sharp poke in the ribs made him jump forward almost into the next customer. "Ahh. What....!"

He turned around and there stood an old flame, Tracy, grinning from ear to ear, looking absolutely on fire. Her brilliant ginger hair hung down over her shoulders and the grey eyes, which he once knew so well, glistened with desire.

"Tracy. It's you." He couldn't believe his own eyes. "You're looking *well* fit."

She did not say anything, just grabbed him, and they hugged for a few seconds. Robin really wanted to snog her, but he was only brave enough to give her a peck on the lips. What a coward.

"Hello." She whispered, whilst looking into his eyes with amour. "I'd forgotten how ticklish you were. Haven't forgotten anything else though." She giggled.

He asked nervously, "Will you sit with me? Or are you with Tony? Or anyone else?"

She seemed spell bound. "I want..." She stopped. "Let's skip breakfast, and just have coffee. Like we used to."

They poured their coffees from the machine, Robin paid for them both and they sat down, opposite each other, by the window. They just sat for a couple of minutes looking at each other, without even a word.

Then she whispered "I still love you. After seven years, I still love you. I've wanted to say it for years, now I have." She carried on looking into his eyes. "Please love me." Her eyes were getting moist, and so were Robin's.

He whispered "I've never stopped. You married Tony, but I never stopped loving you. I think it's really messed me up at times." As the injured party seven years ago, he was a bit suspicious. "Why're you here?"

"Because you asked me to sit with you." She smiled.

"Ha ha, very funny. You know what I mean. Where's Tony?"

She paused while considering her answer. "No idea. We're getting divorced. I can tell you about it if you want." She raised her eyebrows and said, "Do you want to talk about him? We could talk about us." Her hand reached across the table and met Robin's hand halfway, where they gently held. "OK, I'll tell you about the break-up." She was so excited, but nervous, her hand shaking a little as it nestled in Robin's. "You know I'm over forty, and haven't got any kids." She seemed uncomfortable talking about it. "I... I can't have any children. Sorry. When Tony found out, he treated me like I was a *weirdo* or something. He blamed me. He stopped wanting sex with me asking 'what's the point?' and just talked to me like shit." Her eyes were watery.

Robin held her hand tighter and said "Let's talk about this later."

"No, now please. You might not want a weirdo." She stopped, and her face drained a little, "Sorry, I know you may not want me at all, weirdo or not. I dumped *you*. Just tell me to fuck off if you don't want me around." She looked down at the table.

Perhaps that broke the ice. They both knew each other very well; the courting was done several years earlier and the chat-up lines did not seem appropriate.

Robin whispered, "I deserved it. Sometimes takes two to fuck up. It did really hurt, but it's fine, now."

She quietly, and carefully, picked her words. "I can't have children, but we could adopt."

That bombshell would have been too much even for the Marauder's payload! Robin was wondering what was going on in his life as he ruminated the second proposition of adoption in as many days. Catherine's suggestion of her adoption was still ringing around his head, and now Tracy's!

"Is that a serious proposition?" he asked. He waited momentarily as Tracy started biting her thumb, then slowly asked, "You want to adopt? With me?" He waited a few moments. "It could take years. We're not even married. We're not even divorced, well you're not. And I'm in my mid fifties."

He raised his eyebrows, as if to say 'say something'.

She did. "I love you. I want to be with you, it's all I've dreamt about for years. Please. I'm not complete, can't have any kids, but I want you. Please." She pulled his hand towards her. "I don't have to adopt, I just want you. Tony's treated me like dirt for years and I know you'd never treat me like that, and when I went off with Tony, I knew I'd thrown so much away. Just didn't realise what. I know now."

The injured party, still suspicious, caressed Tracy's hand as he asked with a slow deliberation, "But *why* are you here? *Why?* You've not given me the time of day for seven years. Why today?"

She shook her head. "Because you asked me."

"I'm not joking now!" He realised he being was a bit loud, and grinned.

"Nor am I! You called me, yesterday. I heard you."

"I *didn't* call you, I was just…………." He stopped dead. His head went back in time, about a day, and he remembered Catherine asking 'You sure?' after him saying that he had no lover. Tracy had flashed through his mind as soon as the question was asked. "I don't *think* I called you." His face was ridged with frowns. "Maybe I did. Maybe." A tray was dropped, and the moment shattered.

Robin pulled her hand towards his face and gently kissed her fingers. He was starting to remember what they had both felt those seven years past, and suddenly just wanted to love. His forgiving nature was again beginning to take command of the control panel of life. The panel must have been set to "grin" as he thought about his next words. "Remember Carla, my ginger pussy?"

"Of course" she replied with a dirty smile.

He then whispered, "Hope you've been looking after my other ginger pussy."

She leaned over to whisper in his ear, "It's on fire, just dying to be stroked, and fondled. I think it needs feeding. Can you feel it purring?"

They suddenly found themselves in a private cocoon, cut off from the surrounding humdrum and Robin was still grinning when he said "Let's go for it. Let's do what we should've done back then." They stared into each others' minds. Neither wanted to break the contact, but suddenly Robin jumped as a hand was firmly placed on his shoulder.

"*What* are you two up to? This is a café, not a nightclub." Phew! It was only David, Robin's youngest son. "You said you were coming for breakfast, thought I'd join you. Didn't realise you were on a date." He winked at his dad.

"Hiya Dave, remember Tracy?"

Dave held out his hand towards Tracy and gently shook hers. "You're looking *well* fit."

She laughed. Her ginger hair waved across her shoulders as she sang, "That's what your dad said."

Dave had a sideways look at his dad and asked "Are you two back together?"

A simple question, but the two lovers exchanged enquiring glances without really knowing the answer, until Tracy spoke. "Yes. Yes, we're together, carrying on where we left off." She was smiling. "Good job you came along. I think we were about to be thrown out."

They all laughed.

After years of barren relationships, some spoiled by his powerful memories of Tracy, Robin found himself with a fully committed partner! A ten minute courtship; how can life change so quickly?

The three of them sat around the table and chatted about old times, and what they had been up to over recent years, especially about what Dave had been up to. As a young teenager he had gone badly astray. With his mum gone and his dad having to work, the poor kid had been stuck in a treadmill of neglect. His choices had been whittled down to going to work with his dad (not a realistic option), going down the truant route with his mates (not a very good option), and following his mum down the sewers to wallow in the shit poured over them by the drugs scene (the very worst option). At fourteen years old he chose the very worst, coarsely blended with the not very good; he became a heroin addict. Now, at twenty three, although he was clean, he was struggling to stay that way, and had been left mentally and physically damaged by the ravage of the drugs. He was a modern product of the international driving force, money.

Tracy knew about Dave's struggles, they were largely responsible for her break up with Robin, and she also knew that Robin had often blamed himself for the poor lad's personal hell. But past is past and you can never go backwards, nor can you ever really make up for past losses so the only way is up, or down in some cases. But David had been up, and down, and down further, and up and down, and....

Partly to change the "trouble" subject, and partly to carry it on, Robin stated, "I met a strange little girl yesterday who seems to be in trouble. She's only eight, but in trouble. I know it."

David put his finger in the air and said "Saint Phoebe's Garden." He leaned forward, just as one might do when spreading a bit of gossip. "It's closed. Shut yesterday by the police and social. I got straight on the net after we spoke earlier and found the report they put out and it looks like you were right, Dad. There's been paedos in the school. I hope your strange little girl's ok."

Robin's face dropped, he was stunned. "But she only told me yesterday morning. She said I ought to adopt them." He was starting to feel sick with guilt. "Did I tell her to?"

Tracy nervously suggested, "Tell us what you mean. We weren't there. Tell her to do what?"

"The girl, Catherine, at the boot sale. She bought my book. She's promised to look after it, because of its value, and I can have it back whenever I need it, or want to read it. But how will I get it if she's dumped into another home? What about her mates?" He was getting stressed and confused. "She didn't have to do it. It was only an idea."

Tracy quizzed, "Do what? You're not making sense. Calm down and just talk about it."

He calmed a little, and then said, "I think I told her to report the people who were fucking them. She just came out with it, really bluntly, that they were fucking them, as *blunt* as that, so I said 'what can I do?' She said 'nothing', she'd do it. I think I've split them up! She said they were being fucked, just came straight out with it."

"Dad, if she's right, she had to squeal. Can't just leave those things. Too late twenty years later when the poor kids' heads start to recall." At least the messed up boy had the street-cred to understand Catherine. "If they're getting abused, she *had* to."

At that point a Tesco worker approached their table and said "Would you keep the swearing down, please, or I may have to ask you to leave."

Embarrassed, Tracy said, "Sorry, we've a few problems. We're going as soon as we've finished our coffee."

Robin took a couple of deep breaths as David and Tracy looked sympathetically at him. "I'm all right. Just a shock. Just hope they're ok, and looking out for each other's backs."

He calmed, and began thinking dreamily of Tracy, wow, good mental therapy!

They had finished their coffee, and Tracy picked up the three mugs. Robin studied her form as she moved over to the dirty crockery trolley. Completely naked, she carefully placed the mugs on one of the shelves, and then turned round to face Robin. Her vivid ginger hair hung over her bare shoulders, brushing the freckles, while her pale breasts stood firm, supporting two erect nipples, pointing at him, and nobody else. Her hair and her pubic triangle were so perfectly colour-coded, and they stood out like beacons on the well shaped, colourless torso. The slightly rounded tummy was like a patchwork of scars! Robin shook his head and came back to the real world.

"Sorry," he said. "Daydreaming again." He smiled as she approached him and they held hands, walking out of the store behind David.

During the next three days the two grown-ups were like sixteen year olds again, making love, laughing, making love, eating, making love and so on, while David spent some of his unemployed time searching out the fate of the children from Saint Phoebe's Garden. It was a lost cause as they did not even know Catherine's surname, nor any of the boys' Christian or surnames. The authorities were rightly suspicious of them wishing to find children who had clearly been involved in traumatic events, and who, on the face of it, where total strangers to the three concerned adults. The authorities would not give anything away.

Sitting around Robin's dining table they all had to concede that the little girl, her mates and the book, were lost to them, probably forever. Robin remained confused, but his life had transformed so much in those three days that the concern began to fade a little and he told himself that it was one of those strange things, and would probably remain an unexplained mystery.

"Maybe she'll find us," he said, just hoping. "I suppose we'll have to just see what life throws up."

"Dad, I'm sorry I couldn't come up with anything. It's really good, though, that you two've found something. You're both like a couple of kids again." He winked at his dad, then leaned over and kissed Tracy on the cheek. "I need to go." He turned from Tracy to his dad and asked, "You couldn't lend me twenty quid, could you?" As always, David left with twenty pounds!

Being alone again, the two lovers eyed each other up and then moved from the table to the sofa and squeezed onto just one cushion. They held each other tightly and kissed. Robin ran his fingers through her hair and then caressed the back of her neck, sending her into a wanton frenzy. She pushed him down on the sofa and straddled him, then pulled up her skirt, but then stopped just as rapidly and sat back on the sofa.

"We've been shagging each other almost non-stop since we got back together. We've got all our lives for that." She pulled Robin up and kissed him on the nose. "Let's go down the pub. First, though, tell me what's so fascinating about my belly."

He bent down to her covered tummy and kissed it. "It's beautiful. Cuddly, white, and perfectly smooth. Not a single imperfection." He sat up and grinned. "Apart from the couple of stretch marks from your puppy-fat." He earned himself a good slap around his bald head, and they went to the Shepherd and Dog.

Robin's drinking-mates were quite chuffed that he was out with a young lady, especially one so stunning. He was pretty secretive about his personal life, so people made up their own summaries about his lonely life style, such as 'swings the other way', and 'too tight to let anybody else get his money', and 'perhaps his todger doesn't work'. It never bothered Robin though; it gave them all something else to talk about.

Excusing themselves, they sat down side-by-side at a bar table to enjoy some private space, as lovers do. He had a pint of lager and she a Malibu with pineapple. Whilst paying for the drinks with the loose change in his pocket, Robin had discovered the letter which he had received three days earlier.

"I forgot about this letter. I received it the morning we met at Tesco's. You put me right off my stroke." He looked at the writing on the envelope. "Suppose I ought to read it."

Tracy looked at him with expectation. Nothing. "Well, go on then."

He smiled and replied "Don't have my glasses. Can you read it to me?"

"No. It might be personal."

He squeezed her hand and said "I've got *nothing* to hide. We're partners, don't forget."

"Right. But if it's personal I'll stop." She took the letter. "It's from abroad, I think India. Not sure. This is quite exciting." She stopped and leaned closer to his ear, continuing with a comical air of mystery. "What if it's the third in the series of weird happenings? The girl, the book, the letter." Grinning, she hurriedly opened the envelope and pulled out the contents. As was the envelope, the letter was handwritten. "*Lovely* handwriting" she exclaimed. "Right, here we go. Hah, hah. It's so exciting!" She shrugged her shoulders high up and giggled.

"Just get on with it," Robin jested.

"Right. It's from Syed. His address is in Calcutta. Here we go. 'Dear Robin, I hope you are well. We haven't spoken for so long and I feel embarrassed that I have to be asking a favour rather than just writing as a friend. But we are good friends and always will be, so how the hell are you? Have you found a good woman yet who can cook for you, wash your clothes and keep you warm at night? I haven't and don't think I ever will, so I might have to share yours. Only joking. Perhaps you will one day make it with your carrot-top girl! I am in Kolkata where the women are plentiful and varied, but I still can't score a relationship, so I'm going to just sit it out. Maybe it's my destination. I hope you are coping with the loss of your parents, in such quick succession. They did have a long, healthy life. My family still live in north London, but my brothers have all left the nest. I think my parents, after 12 people in the house for so many years, are finding the freedom strange. They'll get used to it. I hope David is coping with life. Anyway, hopefully we can catch up face to face some time. What I'm asking for is a big favour, and you might think it is too stupid to consider, but here we go. My uncle is a doctor of some distinction and has been working on isolating a virus which just eats people away. Its place of virulence is several miles outside of Kolkata, where we are based. It is so devastatingly fast when it gets hold, that people are not lasting much more than a few days before the body is just rotten and dead. He thinks he has directly connected the virus with polio, and believes that it is mutated somehow from what's left behind after polio attacks, sometimes many years later, and it then becomes quite contagious. I'm not a doctor, so this is just my understanding of it. But he has got something, and the problem could become an epidemic or something if it's not sorted. So, can you help us? Hope you're sitting down. He has hit on stony ground with the government and also the pharmaceuticals with getting any support or funding, as they think he is a quack. He has not been able to convince them about the potential devastation, but I know my uncle and he is so convinced. I believe in him, and hope you will too. I know you are the best guitarist in the world, again only joking, but if you can still do what you used to do we can capture some of the pop market down here. Kolkata is buoyant right now and guitar music is king. Add to this, my cousin is in the electronics industry where he is developing an electronic guitar which will revolutionise the industry, but he needs somebody to get in the charts with it and show it off. They don't like the idea of what he's doing; they say it's not real music. So if you can still do it we need you to disprove the critics. My cousin can help finance my uncle's work if the guitar can be pushed into a position of acceptance. The industry is different here. You don't have to be the best in the world to make it, just good enough, and get pushed by the right people. It's all pretty bent. An Englishman guitarist would go down really well out here now, even a really old one like you! Can you do it still? You'll probably have to come over for a month, get to know the guitar then do recording. We will have to find a singer to work with. But it's a good, cranky idea. Can you phone my uncle's number, it's at the top, at 10 o'clock in the morning your time, and I will make sure I am in his office at that time. I will be there for several days to give you chance to think about it. I'm getting so excited about it all. We don't have any money, so can you pay your own fares? We'll keep you when you do get here. Can't wait to see you again, love Syed.' That's it."

The pub was silent. They were all concentrating on the letter which had been read out a little *too* loudly. When Tracy looked up from the reading, they all turned back to their beers and talked amongst themselves as if they could hear no evil, see no evil, do no evil. Robin and Tracy sat looking at each other. She broke the ice.

"Is he a nutter?" she asked. "He sounds like one. Sorry, but he was ranting."

"No, he's very sane. Always has been." He was beginning to worry about those recent events. They felt a little bit too tight, and maybe they were all the same event, just different chapters. Superstition was not one of Robin's faults, but imagination was, an imagination so active that you perhaps could have labelled it one of his curses. Kolkata featured heavily in the recent days. Catherine, Syed and the book, Unknown India, all just crashed around inside Robin's head.

"I need a wee," said Tracy. She got up from her seat and walked out of the door towards the ladies' toilets.

Robin looked around at the friends with whom he normally drank his beer and had to wonder if he was being pushed, or pulled, away from them. They were all good pub people and he would miss them dearly if he was to go to India. And Tracy? She had brought light and life into his dull existence, the kind of which he had not known since the previous love affair they had shared. And Syed? He was an old friend who will always be a friend, even if they stayed at home. He felt as though he had to choose between his lover and his mate and so, in his head, the fight began. As he glanced over to the door, there was Tracy punching the hell out of Syed, a middle-aged Bangladeshi man in his baggy, sandy-brown suit. He returned a good left hook, but an uppercut from the fighter in the ginger shorts proved too much for this aging fighter. The bout was hers. Robin's mind was set in stone, he would stay. Nobody would make him change his decision!

Back on earth.…."We'll go!" Tracy stood in front of him grinning like a 'ginger' Cheshire cat. "We'll go, *both* of us."

"What? I've made my mind up." He paused, thought, smiled and continued. "I've made my mind up, we'll *go*. I've definitely made my mind up! This time." They laughed. As she sat down, he asked her "What do you mean, *both* of us?"

"Both of us implies two of us. And there's only you and me here, so me and you, to India. That's what I mean." She gave him a lovely gentle kiss which left his lips wet. "I was thinking while I was sitting down and having a wee. That Catherine girl was just in your head, I believe, and you've just got to forget about her. And the book is part of the same dream. You know, one of those daft dreams you always conjure up. Forget them both. Me? I'm real, I've just read a real letter, maybe from a real person, but India is real, and we've never been to India. It's just for a month." She shrugged her shoulders up as she had a giggle. "You've *never* been any good on the guitar. Has Syed ever heard you play?" Pause. "Thought not. But me? I'm still brilliant, with young fingers that can still find the spot, and I can sing. And anyway, if Syed doesn't even exist we can have a great holiday. I can get a month off, no probs. And you've got hardly any work, you might as well spend your money in India as spend it here for a month. Just use your imagination. No. No, no imagination, just stay with me in this world." She kissed him on the nose. "Can we, please? Please, please, please. I wanna go."

He looked around at his mates and then whispered in her ear, "That must've been a bloody long wee you had." He stood up and walked to the bar with their empty glasses.

One of his mates pushed him on the shoulder with his fist. "You lucky bastard."

Robin showed his appreciation with a smile, saying "We're off to India; we've got this dream. See you before we go," then sat back with Tracy and a new beer.

She said, "We'll be back after a month, so you can still go on the piss with them." She really wanted to go to India.

He was well and truly won over by the idea. He rather cockily put it to Tracy, "Tell you what, Sweet Pea, prove you can still play, and it's a goer. All we'll need are our visas, and we're away. Oh, and some jabs. Got mine." They looked around at the other drinkers.

She said, "They'll still be here when we get back. So will Carla, and the boys. It'll be like our honeymoon, without the wedding. And don't worry about jabs, got mine when I went back to West Indies." She snuggled up to him. "I can't wait. I'll book my hols when we've got a flight date, you tell Syed that we'll be there as soon as we get the visas. And make sure your passport's up to date."

"Yes, yes ma'am. Just slow down. You're gonna have to do more than just play *with* me tonight. You're gonna have to play *to* me, on that guitar and prove you haven't lost it."

They walked out, hand-in-hand, waving to his mates.

Colin Hodgson

4 -- THE INDIAN EXPERIENCE

Surprise, surprise, Tracy passed the audition. They were going to India and nothing was going to stop them, and as they flew towards their Indian destination at a height of about ten thousand five hundred metres, the excitement began to take control.

"I'm gonna be a pop star. Hee hee." Tracy pulled at Robin's arm. "Do you think they'll love me? Well? Do ya?" She poked him gently in the ear. "Do ya? Tell me, Big Ears."

"Definitely. Just stop poking me, I feel sick."

Tracy looked at him as if to say, 'you're great fun, aren't you'. She looked out of the window and admired the clouds. They all looked the same, pretty damned boring after a couple of hours. "When we get there, how hot will it be?"

"Not sure, but it's December, should be coming into the cooler times." He looked at her, reassuringly. "You don't like the sun, do you."

"I'm ginger. I'm northern hemisphere through and through."

"India's northern hemisphere. Well, Bengal is."

"It's a really big place," states Tracy. "Whatever happens, you won't ever leave me, will you? I'm a little bit scared." She looked towards Robin for a reaction. "Please promise."

"*Never.*" He kissed her on the cheek. "I promise that I'll never leave you, for any reason. Put that into your data store, and don't ever forget it."

"Pretty promise?" She grabbed his hand. "You know, I'm suddenly scared. This's all happened pretty bloody quickly. Just one little, distant call from you, from your head, and here we are. I'm a bit scared. Give me a cuddle."

Robin whispered, "I love you. Don't be scared. We're in it together, whatever. Hope you feel the same, cos I'm a bit scared as well." They touched foreheads. With a bit of a sarcastic grin he suggested, "If you get lost, just call out my name, I'll come running. You've got a friend." He kissed his darling on the lips. "I think there's a song there, somewhere."

Syed's uncle had been involved with NTDs, which is an abbreviation for Neglected Tropical Diseases, for many years. There were seventeen diseases which made up the NTD group and they persisted exclusively in the poorest and the most marginalized communities around the earth. That was, in the slums of the world. They had been largely eliminated elsewhere and, therefore, were often forgotten or overlooked. Most of them could have been prevented and eliminated in the right environment, but in places with unsafe water, poor sanitation and limited or no access to basic health care, they still thrived, almost going unnoticed by the surrounding world. I think the World tried very hard not to notice. "Neglected" said it all. The new forms and mutations usually resulted in segregation as the only control measure, rather than treatment and eradication. But Syed's uncle, Doctor Hussain, was one of the individual heroes of the slums. He insisted on segregation to reduce spread, but also championed the development of vaccines to eradicate the disease. Typically, he received little or no support from the major pharmaceutical companies.

The unfortunates who had contracted some of those "neglected" diseases, even if they had recovered, were often ostracized by society, and their families. Young children, if not killed by the disease, would often die through lack of adult support and protection, or would just starve to death. Serious disfigurement was commonplace.

The many slums in and around Kolkata were home to over one and a half million people. They were also home to the NTDs and their partners: poverty; disease; malnutrition; prostitution; slavery; abuse; and death. That was the sort of hell that neither Robin nor Tracy was expecting. A very long haul from the "desperation" of the boot-salers.

Robin sighed and pushed his head back on the seat. "I think he was just jesting me, but Syed told me a story once about his family's move from Bangladesh to London and their really overcrowded home. Where they lived in Bangladesh was a very poor and troubled area. His dad had done his college stuff, but had no work. They had ten young children. When an employer took Syed's dad on board he wanted them to move to London. Anyway, Dad got over there and found somewhere for them to live in north London. Only three bedrooms. That was plenty for ten small children and two parents. Dad thought, 'four out of ten of them will be dead by the time the youngest is ten'. What he forgot was that they'd be in London, not Bangladesh, and none of them died!"

"Really?" Tracy frowned in disbelief.

"That's what he told me." Many minutes went as they daydreamed. "You don't tell stories, do you. Or have you got one?"

She bit her bottom lip and thought. Bravely, she whispered, "I *have* got one." She frowned a little and carried on biting her lip. Then, "It's a very strange story. You remember when we were kids in Boxted, and those children moved into the flats, and all the big cars turned up? You know, the bigger boy and the little crippled girl, who just disappeared? You remember, he was your age and she was just eight, like me." She waited for Robin to acknowledge. "I dream about them. Even now." She stopped and closed her eyes. Many minutes passed.

"Is that the story?"

She opened her eyes, "No, sorry. Well, apparently the little blonde girl, you know, the cripple, well she went into a home. But the bigger brother got killed. I'm sure you remember him, because your mates said that the 'spastic' girl was asking about where you went, the Legion or the Wig, so they could go with you. Anyway the police wanted to speak to anybody who'd seen him during a time. I saw him, but I didn't speak to the police. I was only eight, a real baby, but I didn't want to drop him in it. I don't know why." She again started to bite her bottom lip. "I spoke to him the very same day that he died. I think his name was Peter and she was Katie. In fact I know it was, I dream about them every night. Anyway, it was almost dark, and I was walking along the poplars in the playing field, when I saw him waiting over near the fen, could just see his shape. I wasn't scared, so I walked the other side of the poplars, and then came out almost in front of him. He smiled at me, and I asked him what he was doing, and he said he was waiting for God. I replied, *"You're silly. You won't find God here, this is the playing field,"* and he grinned and asked me what I wanted to be when I grew up. I answered, *"A mummy. With lots and lots of children who will all love me, like a mysterious Queen."* I went home, and have never told anybody 'til now. But I still dream about him, and her." She paused. "Especially her." She thought for a bit, then, "Wish I knew why."

"Why'd you tell him he was silly?"

She screwed her face up. "You have to go to church to find God. That's what we're told." Biting her bottom lip, she whispered, "And something upset me, a couple of years later, and I realised then that God didn't live in a church, just people did." A long sigh. "I was almost eleven, about to leave Boxted School, and old Queeny Sizer took all the ten and eleven year-old kids to the churchyard. I remember standing at the white picket fence looking across the graves, and I remember the lovely flowers. Then she took us to the corner where the old, dead flowers were thrown; the rubbish heap. Right beside the heap there was a tiny wooden cross. Miss Sizer explained that it was one of my friend's brothers who had died, without being christened, so he wasn't allowed to be buried with his family. She didn't say any more, but I'm sure she was getting at something, and I tried to think what the little boy would be thinking, for the rest of eternity, estranged from his family and totally alone. I couldn't understand how God could allow such barbaric behaviour from a Christian society. Then I made my mind up that it wasn't God's will, it was man's. It's always man's." She laid her head on Robin's shoulder. "I suddenly realised that Peter *was* waiting for God, in the playing field, so after that I looked out of my bedroom over towards the fen, every night, to see God. I never did see Him. But a few weeks ago I was visiting my mum, and was sorting some bits out in my old bedroom. I heard a call. It was you." A silent moment arrived. Then, "I looked out the window, across to the fen, and I saw a little girl, with blonde hair, and she looked just like that Katie girl. The cripple. But she went and I didn't hear you any more. Then the next day I went to Tesco's, and there you were. You'd called me there." She sighed. "I know you did."

Robin put his hand to her cheek and brushed it. Quietly he said, "That's almost as rash as Syed's story." They left the subject.

Anyway, it was a long flight and they were both getting seriously exhausted as the plane approached Kolkata. A little bit of their excitement just hung on in there and they chuckled when the Captain announced that the weather on the ground was comfortable and the air temperature was only twenty seven degrees Celsius.

"That's a nice temperature," said Tracy, relieved.

"Syed's waiting for us at the terminal. Can't wait to get off this plane." They were both very stiff from the flight.

As the two adventurers stepped out of their air conditioned environment the sun dazzled them, but did not scorch. Robin had heard the tales about stepping into the "oven" when arriving in India, but that was probably New Delhi or somewhere else. It was a pleasant start to their holiday.

The move through the immigration controls, customs, and baggage retrieval went smoothly. The airport was not what they had expected, very busy but much smaller and quite old fashioned and it reminded them of a typical London train station. Even the people's clothing was typical of what you would expect on a summer day at Heathrow Airport, with the exception of the "military" style police uniforms. It definitely had a cosmopolitan but "fifties" feel about it.

They found their way to the terminal exit and there, behind the metal barrier with the crowd, was Syed. He was a young middle-aged Bangladeshi gentleman with receding, dark hair and bearing his crooked teeth. Just at that moment he looked like the only man in India who did not have a moustache.

"Robin! Over here!"

They swung round to the left and dragged their cases to the gap, where Syed waited. Where were all the beggars and street urchins? Robin had heard tales of them mobbing the foreign visitors, but that may have been in New Delhi, or somewhere else.

"It's fantastic that you're here. And who's this?" Syed shook Robin's hand then turned to Tracy. "Is she really with you?"

"Behave yourself!" Robin grinned as he introduced her. "This's the 'carrot-top' that you mentioned in your letter!"

A little bit of embarrassment broke through Syed's goofy smile.

"And you're not gonna share her. She's mine."

Tracy huffed, "I *am* here! You can talk *to* me, not *about* me." She compulsively gave Syed a hug, but quite coldly introduced herself. "I'm Tracy, Robin's loved one. I take it you're Syed. It's great to meet you at last."

The informal introductions were over and Syed pointed towards the road. "We've got a cab waiting over there. It's a bit of a drive where we're heading. If you want to see any of Kolkata you'll have to come back another day. Sorry." He led the way across to the street, where the yellow Ambassadors, old fashioned looking taxis, were lined up, beside the strange yellow shelters which sat high on yellow metal frames and with 'police' written on the roofs. They looked like elongated chicken coups on legs, with the house in the middle and a wired run on each end. Perhaps they get a lot of rain in Kolkata.

Syed pointed down the street. "That's where the new terminal will be." They dodged a couple of yellow cabs, and then waited as a bus, with no glass in the windows, went past. It almost ran into them as it swung around to the stop. "In some parts of India a lot of the bus drivers are high all bloody day, and bloody dodgy drivers. Not too bad here. But it's ok, the cabby we've got's a safe driver."

They set off on their journey a little bit amazed at how "normal" everywhere seemed. There were many yellow taxis swinging in and out of the rank, and buses came and went constantly. In a small area in front of the terminal were parked some bicycle rickshaws. "That looks fun," said Robin. "Don't suppose they go far, though."

Syed laughed. "A bit further than the hand rickshaws, but not so far as the motor rickshaws. If you're good little children on the journey, I'll let you go in a motor rickshaw." They all watched out of the windows, and the crowds became more Indian in their dress the further they moved away from the airport. Syed suggested they get the business sorted out and then they could look at some of the beautiful sites in Kolkata. "There is the Dakshineswar Kali Temple, the

Victoria Memorial building, that's lovely at night." He stopped and thought. "Saint Paul's Cathedral. The Indian Museum will be good. There are plenty places to see. This's the Cultural Capital of India."

The city was green with vegetation and trees, having been well watered by the recent rainy season.

The cab drove down VIP Road towards the city, but turned off quite soon. The city seemed to have been developed as three distinct layers, the high-rise modern life, the old flat-roofed, shuttered dwellings, and then the bottom layer, the slum. Initially the slum dwellings were few, but as they moved away from the city they became the norm. Lovely old Victorian buildings occasionally broke the ghetto, but they were all decrepit and ill-maintained. It must have been an electrician's nightmare, with cables going everywhere. Political and religious statements were made, sometimes beautifully, through the graffiti, and the colours added life into those dull, dirty conditions. Most of the buildings were eyesores, un-maintained, poorly built, housing many people, and looking like they were sitting in the middle of a refuse tip. The splash of bright colours slightly distracted from the mess.

Away from the airport and VIP Road, the evidence of the millions of slum dwellers grew. Shacks lined parts of the roads, barely more than tents or corrugated roofs. Kolkata must have been where the boot sale was invented! People were selling their wares everywhere. It was sometimes difficult to see the shops through the haphazard pitches set up wherever there was an inch of room. People were sitting down, laying down, milling around, seemingly with little purpose while their peace was constantly interrupted by the motorbikes and mopeds.

The men mostly dressed in trousers and a shirt which was never tucked in. Some men were in colourful "skirts" known as lungis or sarongs, again with a shirt hanging down over the waist. The women were very colourful and most wore their saris over contrasting blouses or cholis. Many were very beautiful but away from the main road, the people were much less cosmopolitan and the dress became more traditional, and more dirty.

"We're going a good way out from the City. There, it's *not* so much the bloody Cultural Capital of India." Syed had not said much about the detail of the visit. "My Uncle, you can call him Akhtar, has a clinic on the edge of one of the largest slums. You mustn't worry, crime is very low." He looked thoughtfully out of the cab window. "You do need to be a little careful, though. It's not a pretty area."

Tracy held Robin's hand tightly as the little pockets and lines of slum "dwellings" became more numerous. The high rises gradually became smaller as they became more distant. Eventually they were gone. The buildings displayed less and less Victorian influence and were even more decrepit, and the louvered shutters seemed to be a statement of colour amongst the grey surroundings. The lovers realized that they were a long way from the city.

"The area we're going to is a fairly new slum area, but has history and great traditions. It originally was the main government and military centre for this whole region, and it managed from the Anglian Fort." Syed pointed out two grand old stately houses. "Those were occupied by the governess and her consort. She's often referred to as Queen Maya of Anglia. Apparently there's no written history about her, just spoken." The houses were well past their prime! "The area's now controlled, unofficially, by a religious group called the Chi Bantri. I think it's religious. They've been here for a couple of hundred years or so. Ever since the Queen went, in fact. They own the local factories which were built in the fifties and that's when the area became a real slum, as thousands of families were enticed into the new factories from the surrounding rural areas. They do electrical and electronics stuff. My cousin with his guitars works there."

Syed pointed to a turning to the right. "Look. You can see the top of the Fort." They could just see a large roof, and it looked like corrugated iron. "It used to be dominant on the skyline but when the workers moved here for work, the slums engulfed the fort. Some people say the group engineered it. My uncle knows much more about the local history." He smiled. "I'm just a bloody Londoner."

Robin and Tracy were intrigued, but frightened. They held hands, remembering the conversation on the plane about staying together.

"Almost there." Syed said something to the driver who then pulled to the side of the road. "We need to change transport." Syed paid the driver as they climbed out of the taxi.

The people were very interested in the two Europeans. The men, women and children all stopped what they were doing and looked. The children soon got bored and carried on with their business, playing and laughing. But the adults carried on looking.

Syed moved round to the side of the taxi, where his friends, the white folk, stood. He waved his hand to shoo the other people away, but they did not stop looking, so he tried again. One of the women said something to Syed. He faltered.

"Let's go," he snapped. "You've been very good children, so you can have a go in a motor rickshaw. I always keep my promise!" That took the heat out from the intense attention.

They dragged their cases around the corner, and there waited a three wheeled, motorized rickshaw. It was simply a metal frame, three wheels and an engine, covered in canvas with open windows. The vehicle was hinged between the driver seat and the passenger seat and there was just about room for three passengers.

"Wow." Tracy pulled Syed over and gave him a peck on the cheek. "Brilliant."

The driver was so polite, and very humble. He spoke a couple of sentences to Syed and they both smiled. "The driver is your servant for as long as you're here. He'll take you anywhere, and be yours for five hundred rupees a day, if you want him. That's only about seven quid."

"It's a bargain," said Tracy. "What's your name?" she asked the driver.

Syed answered, "He only speaks Bengali. His name's Aalap." He used his finger to great effect to introduce everybody.

Aalap strapped the cases to the back of the rickshaw, whilst the people continued to watch. Once the three of them were sitting tightly in the rickshaw's passenger seat, they set off down the side street. It was very clear why Syed had ordered the rickshaw; the taxi would never have fitted!

The group drove away from the street and entered the slum, where it was similar to the street, lined with makeshift dwellings and street traders, but so tight that the people were just an arm's length away. There were very few substantial buildings. The slum dwellers had to move aside to allow them through, and some even had to be lifted from their laying positions if they were too old or ill to move themselves. Sometimes it was even tight to fit the rickshaw through the gaps between the people's homes, and the refuse was a constant obstacle. Children looked wantonly into the carriage and some were saying things but the two English visitors did not understand. Some were asking for food, others just saying hello, but they all looked on the strangers with quizzical interest, while the adults stood aside and just looked.

The atmosphere was one of nonchalance. Although many folk, of all ages, looked so desperately drawn and hungry, many smiled as the motor rickshaw pushed its way through the crowds. Robin wondered if they were pleased to see them, or maybe they really were happy. I very much doubt it. Everything they did they did in the streets: cook; wash; sell their bits; pee; laugh; cry; fight; and die. I wonder where the prostitutes operated from. Probably from those very streets.

The side streets and alleys, as they passed them, looked even worse. Barely a metre between the shacks, and many of the alleys seemed like they were running sewers. The effluent from the "main" street looked to run into these side streets, where people also lived, cooked, washed, cried and died. The stench was horrible. Tracy and Robin did not realize that just yards away, at the other end of the alleys, there were other streets which replicated the street they were in, many, many times. The Anglia slum was one of the largest around Kolkata, home to over one hundred thousand dwellers.

Slightly depressed and a little downhearted, they reached a welcome open area. There were some substantial buildings creating a perimeter around the large arena, which was probably about two hundred metres across. The buildings were all two and three terraces high, with colourful louvered shutters, many of which hung crookedly from one hinge. All those flat roofed dwellings looked like they were about to fall down! Three motor rickshaws and four hand rickshaws were parked in front of one of the buildings.

The slum inhabitants were avoiding the inner area of the opening, cautiously moving around the outside, and it was evident that the open area was not part of their slum. It belonged to somebody else.

"We're almost there," said Syed. His mood was low, wondering if his two friends were regretting their visit. "I hope you're ok."

"Of course," replied Tracy. "You ok, Rob?"

He raised his eyebrows and replied, "Never been better." He was relieved to be moving out from the tight little smelly streets.

Aalap took them around the open area and turned left to drive along a short, roomy street. There were two single storey, modern, maintained, clean looking buildings at the end.

"These are the Uncle's clinics," Syed proudly stated. "Only vehicular access is through the slum as we came but behind the buildings there're services laid on from the Fort. You'll find it clean and the beds are ok." They climbed out of their taxi and had a stretch. It had been a long day. As Aalap released the cases from the rickshaw, the people gathered at the entrance to the short street and watched. Some children came forward towards the visitors and just stood and looked. One boy said something. Aalap gave him a reply and the children quietly turned and walked back down to the end of the street.

Syed turned to Robin and quietly said "Aalap has told them that when he's fed his own child with the fare money, he'll spend the rest on food for them. It'll save them having to steal, at least for today." Syed picked up the case for Tracy. He continued, "Many children around here have no family. Sad. Let's get in and meet my bloody Uncle." He spoke to Aalap, reminding him that his friends had booked him for a few days. "Aalap'll be with his vehicle where you saw the others, whenever you need him. You do need to pay him, even if you don't use him. Please don't forget."

The clinic was sparse, but clean. Syed introduced his friends to his uncle and they spoke about the day's travels. Then his uncle, an ageing, grey Bengali who insisted on being called Akhtar, mentioned the crazy idea of the music.

"If it gets me funding it's not so crazy. You're a very pretty girl with some striking features so if you can play and sing you'll make us some money. Thank you for trying."

Syed stepped in. "Uncle's offered that you accompany us tomorrow into the heart of the slum to collect samples, and help move a leprosy colony which houses a bunch of children. The children who've contracted the new disease have all been sent into the leper colony in ignorance and are putting the poor leper kids at risk. It's been decided that the diseased should stay where they are to die, rather than move them which would unfairly put the other dwellers at risk."

Akhtar added, "They may already be at risk. But we don't know that at present." He studied Syed's friends for a facial reaction. He must have read something because he then said, "Thank you. You're good people." Tracy looked at Robin,

Robin looked at Tracy. Perhaps the holiday was really starting to go somewhere, but they had no idea where.

After eating a rice and bean meal which the maid had prepared, they all retired to their rooms. The visitors were absolutely knackered!

5 -- ALL THE SAINT'S LEPERS

The next morning came far too soon for Robin and Tracy. They were still quite exhausted when they were awoken, but it was a working day for the clinic, and so there would be no rest.

As they finished their breakfast Syed whispered to Robin, "It's a big thing we're doing. The whole bloody world has again neglected a new slum disease, and as these people do not count in the big arena, we must help Uncle to achieve a special result. He's their only hope right now."

Robin smiled at his old mate and asked, with tongue in cheek, "Have you found God?"

Syed frowned, thinking deeply. "I don't think he's there to be found." He looked out of the window at the folk. "*They* think he is. They've been waiting for him, for his return, for two hundred years." He pondered on his next words. "They wait for God to relieve them of the Chi Bantri. We can talk about that later, but don't mention it to anybody. It could get you killed." He sighed. "Just remember at all times, this isn't England." He looked over to Tracy. Maybe he was beginning to worry about his friends.

"I've been wondering." Tracy cocked her head a little. "Why are we going with you today? It doesn't sound like a jolly day out."

Akhtar perked up and accepted the blame. "Tracy, it was mentioned to me that you may find today very interesting. A little bird told me." He scratched his head. "She also told me that Robin may be of tremendous help in my work with the disease."

"So, who told you these things?"

The doctor just frowned and shook his head several times. "I can't remember." He was getting old and forgetful. "I wonder if I dreamed it." He then had a chuckle.

The four of them went outside, to be confronted by a military man with a close cropped beard and moustache. He wore fancy lapel insignia, with a national emblem, over a gold star, over a crossed club and sword. He was otherwise dressed in army uniform with a kaki turban, as were the other five soldiers behind him. The five privates were all armed with rifles, and wore pistols in their holsters, and one of the men approached Doctor Hussain and took his bag from him.

"Good morning Doctor." The decorated man saluted Akhtar. "We're ready, but Captain Batiste hasn't yet arrived."

"We can wait. Please meet my nephew's friends from England. Robin and Tracy." He turned to the two friends. "This's General Dara. He often leaves his grand offices at Fort William to follow his interest in our slum. He's a great support for our work, and for the local people."

"Very pleased to meet you, General," said Robin.

The General shook Robin's hand and then bowed to Tracy. "The local people are intrigued. I keep my nose to the ground and it seems they have a fascination for you. It's the hair. Bright ginger hair is rare around here, and has special significance." He smiled, but said no more.

From between the two clinic buildings emerged another six military men, in a lighter coloured uniform and with light blue berets. They were part of the United Nations forces. The region's ruling hierarchy was finely balanced between the Chi Bantri and the government forces, and serious strife had been threatening for many years. The United Nations had committed themselves by deploying a small force to carry out fact-finding missions and monitoring exercises. Part of their remit was to observe the general social behaviour within the slum, particularly in reference to reported child abuse.

General Dara saluted and then spoke to the UN's Captain Batiste in French, as the convoy prepared to march out. The five Indian soldiers and the General took the lead position, followed by the doctor and his friends, and they were supported from the back by the Belgian troops of the United Nations. The small convoy left the clinics and began the march around the open area, towards the slums.

From one of the houses overlooking the open area, to their left, by the rickshaw park, emerged a small group of soldiers. They were dressed in much darker green, with pleated sarongs, dark green socks and grey turbans. They all stood to attention, showed arms and saluted the small convoy, which returned the salutation.

"That's Sir Kamdar," whispered Akhtar. "He's given permission on behalf of the Chi Bantri for us to move the lepers across to the new colony."

Sir Kamdar was the head of the Chi Bantri security force, a ragged, but much respected private army. It was made up from people local to the Chi Bantri administration, mostly rural folk, and despite the local's mistrust of the Chi Bantri they had always been loyal to the cause. They numbered an estimated two thousand men, policing the slums and rural areas for many miles surrounding the Anglian Fort. The slum dwellers could sometimes escape their misery by being accepted into the Chi Bantri army.

They left the open area by turning down a fairly wide street, into the slum. On foot the stench was worse, and the people even closer, but they never touched the group. I think the dwellers knew the purpose of the expedition, and generally just smiled at the soldiers. But the smiles were wider, and full of intrigue, when directed towards the two visitors, and the children all laughed and giggled in wonderment. They seemed so happy!

General Dara halted. He looked down a side alley, very narrow, very wet and very smelly. His soldiers rearranged the group into single file, ready to pass down the narrow route. As they moved through the alleyway the people who had not already gone to the "main" street to watch the convoy, had to move inside to allow them to pass. The Indian soldiers had to pick up any wares which blocked the way. The group could see inside the dwellings, where there was little more than a few pots, refuse and dirt, and the occasional old person or a mother nestling her baby. Tracy wondered how many people slept in these homes, and she had a tear in her eye as she clung tightly onto Robin's hand.

The end came suddenly. What a relief. The slightly wider "main" streets actually now seemed welcoming after the alleyway. They regrouped into two's and Syed pushed in beside Tracy. "Are you ok?"

She looked at him, and then wiped the tears from her cheeks.

"Try not to touch your eyes or mouth while out here. And you, Robin."

The expedition moved on down the street, carefully weaving through an outdoor "restaurant". The food aroma was a pleasant relief from the smell of raw sewage.

Then from behind a group of children came a little girl, about eight years old, with long black hair. She was wearing a white kurta, like a night shirt, and short, pale blue pyjamas on her legs. She halted, staring with a look of disbelief at Robin and Tracy, and then her face erupted into ecstasy as she shot forward towards them. Syed tried to grab her, but missed, and she flung her arms around Robin's waist.

"Careful!" snapped Syed.

General Dara swung back to the Europeans and as he did, the girl shouted at him. He stopped in his tracks. She exchanged a few sentences with the General while still clinging around Robin's waist, and the General then explained to Robin, "She doesn't wish to let go of your waist. She says she can't believe it." He went forward to his five soldiers and spoke to them in Bengali.

Captain Batiste, standing right behind Robin, touched him on the shoulder. "Sir, we know of this girl. She's known as My Eyes. Many say she's a witch."

Robin put his hand round the back of the girl's neck to comfort her. She looked up and said something.

Syed translated. "She said that she's found you. She said she knew she would."

The girl hung on tight.

Captain Batiste explained, "Sir, the General is trying to persuade his troops to continue, in the presence of this girl."

At that point the girl let go and rushed round to the front of the expedition and faced the troops, legs apart, and bent forward with her hands on her hips. She looked like a cobra, ready to strike. As the snake struck with her screaming outburst, one of the soldiers wet himself! It was not until the General spoke to his men that she returned back down the line, but this time she clung around Tracy's waist. She "gingerly" held the little girl's head to her chest. The United Nations personnel just stood fast, and it seemed they had joined with the dwellers, as captivated onlookers. They all just stared and waited.

Syed whispered, "I think I know what they're saying. You two just keep your bloody mouths closed, please."

The General came back to the civilians and the Captain. He looked sternly at them, and clearly was not sure what to say, but blundered, "My men believe that this girl's a witch. Get rid of her, or my men'll leave."

At that the girl shouted at Akhtar, who then spoke for her. "She wants to know what you said, General. And she also wants me to remind you of your place." Akhtar smirked, expecting a return volley.

But the General remained calm. "Doctor, I'm General Dara. I don't need to answer to a child, particularly a witch." After a very long few seconds he conceded. "Ok, ok." He turned and stood politely in front of Tracy, and the girl turned her head to him. He spoke to the girl, she smiled and nodded, let go of Tracy and took the General's hand. They walked to the front of the convoy to address the troops. The poor soldiers, born of this area and led by superstition, all saluted the little girl! They were either frightened to the bone, or they knew something the others did not, and so they all listened attentively as she laid down some "terms" and advice.

Syed whispered with a smile on his face, "She says she'll look after them, since she's the witch's mother and they'd better believe it. And she'll help them sort the lepers out from the rotting people. She says she's a friend of the lepers, and even more than just a friend to them." He thought. "Not sure if I got that right." Captain Batiste and Akhtar were listening in, over Syed's shoulder.

The little impish girl moved back around the column and threw an arm in the air. Without her saying anything they all knew what she meant, as she silently roared 'yes, I'm in'. At least that's what Robin heard! She spoke to Robin, eyebrows raised.

"She said she wants to sit on your shoulders, Robin. Be careful."

"She's a child." He locked his hands in front of his tummy and gave her a foot up. With a shriek of excitement she climbed onto his shoulders and sat like the king of the castle, and with a smile so wide. She was so excited, and she leaned over and kissed Tracy on the forrid, muttering something.

"My God," said Syed, but he did not translate her mutterings.

The convoy began to move on with Akhtar walking with the Captain, and they both said nothing. The girl spoke to Robin and Tracy.

Syed translated. "Her name is My Eyes. I've heard the name mentioned by Uncle."

The girl spoke some more, still excited.

"She says she's so excited, and also pleased that the locals are so interested. She says she'll reward their undying loyalty to God." They certainly were interested. The dwellers were by then following the expedition, and their numbers increasing, causing the Indian soldiers to become very nervous. She carried on talking to Robin and Tracy.

Syed translated her words. "She's been waiting for many years, but now you're here. She says that they've *all* waited for so long, and now the time has arrived. And she wants to know what we're gonna do about that bloody rotting-disease." He looked round to Uncle. Uncle spoke to the girl and showed her great respect, just as the Indian soldiers had. Perhaps he was plagued with the same superstitious beliefs.

"Uncle, do you know this girl?"

Akhtar said quietly, "Look at them all, they're all enjoying this. Have you ever seen the dwellers so happy?" The following crowd was increasing with every side alley. "Yes, I know her. I've met her with the lepers. She's something very special. If that's what a witch is, then I'm all for witches." They all had a quiet laugh.

General Dara halted the expedition. He stood looking back at the increasing number of people gathering in their wake. "Captain Batiste. My men're concerned. Are you ok at the back?"

My Eyes, still laughing with excitement, leaned back and spoke to the Captain.

Akhtar translated loudly. "The girl says, 'If they were going to kill you, you would already be dead'." Akhtar laughed and the Captain adorned a look of amazement, and then thanked the child. She carried on laughing and swinging about on Robin's shoulders while Tracy hung onto Robin's arm. My Eyes giggled and spoke, then put her hand through Tracy's ginger hair.

"What did she say?" asked Tracy.

Syed stretched his mouth, not in a smile, and said, "She says she'll look after you." He paused, then, "Don't be scared, Mummy." Robin and Tracy were shocked. They just looked at each other, wondering what the hell was going on.

"Syed. Did she mention me?"

"Yes. She mentioned Mummy and Daddy when she first got onto your shoulders. I didn't want to translate it earlier."

The three mates were all wound up and confused. Akhtar was revelling in it all, and the Captain just walked firm with his troops in the face of adversity. General Dara was aloof and unreadable but was certainly chewing a lot of cud.

My Eyes turned and spoke to Akhtar and he was very pleased with the conversation. Akhtar poked Tracy on the shoulder. "My Eyes has promised to get the disease sorted. Perhaps she really is a witch. Or maybe the other stories are true." The Doctor was quite excited.

Syed said with a bit of venom, "Uncle she's a child. A chancer."

"We'll see." Akhtar was like a tiny child who had been promised some sweeties by his little buddy.

My Eyes pointed to an alleyway and then spoke to Robin and Tracy.

"She says that there's one of the brothel areas. She says you can get a little girl or boy, or anything, really. She says that some of her friends are prostitutes. But her sister isn't."

Tracy asked, "Sister? Ask her how old she is." Syed obliged.

"She says she is eight and she thinks her sister is thirteen. She says you'll love your other daughter." Syed raised his eyebrows. "Oh my God." The three of them were becoming puzzled but the old-timer, Akhtar, just took it in his stride.

The group looked into the prostitute alley as they passed, noticing several girls of different ages sitting out in the alley, and they all waved to My Eyes.

As one very young girl waved, a hand swung out from the shack and smacked her hard around the head, then pulled her inside. My Eyes scrambled to the ground and ran up the alley screaming. Two UN soldiers instinctively followed. They managed to catch My Eyes as she reached the shack, still screeching, and just at the time when the pimp jumped out, with the girl, to grab her. Two guns were instantly pushed against the man's head. He froze. Captain Batiste followed behind, and the entrance to the alley was quickly guarded by the remaining troops. The captain could speak enough Bengali to instruct the man to release the girl and in a cold sweat he did, and she cried hysterically on My Eyes's shoulder. She must have only been about six years old. My Eyes screamed at the man. He seemed to apologise, and she let the girl go back to him. The soldiers were sweating as the adrenalin flowed, but kept calm, and they lowered their guns before cautiously returning to the rest of the group. The alleyway had suddenly become deserted.

"That's why we should leave her to her own business," said General Dara.

"Wrong," snapped the Captain. "The United Nations is here to help to police this region. With you and your troops. I've been instructed to take a more embroiled approach and we're learning, almost with every step." He turned to the girl. "Thank you." He saluted the General and looking at Syed he asked, "Could you please ask why she allowed the little girl back with him."

Syed asked the question, and then translated. "She says that the man feeds her. Nobody else does, nor will." He looked around at the crowd. He wondered how, if there was a God, he could desert so many people. My Eyes spoke to the Captain. "She says thank you for the brave support."

The group restructured and started to move on. My Eyes, back on Robin's shoulders, began talking again. Syed relaxed and, like his uncle, he was starting to feel a warm respect for that little urchin.

"She says 'Daddy, Daddy, we'll be going past the Fort soon'." Syed giggled.

"Are you taking the piss," retorted Robin with a laugh. She carried on talking.

"She says that you and Mummy might see her sister." Now, that was a bit more serious. "She says her sister doesn't know she's here and that she'll be worry-guts'ing."

Tracy looked up at the girl. She was wriggling around on the shoulders, still excited. Tracy asked her, "What's your real name?" Syed translated. She did not answer. "Try her again, Syed." She did not answer. A silence hit the group.

Eventually, "She says that the fort'll become visible after those shacks up there."

As they passed the shacks, they entered a large open area, rectangular, much larger than the one by the clinics and much bigger than the size of a football pitch, with one whole side consisting of a high, turreted, brick-built wall. The Anglian Fort. A large set of double doors, large enough to take a lorry, and reinforced, sat in the centre of the wall. It was a well preserved product of British rule, built about two hundred and forty years earlier after the Battle of Plassey, and originally supported its much bigger brother at Fort William. They could not see anything behind the wall apart from a large, corrugated iron roof. The other sides of the "square" were lined with two storey terraced houses with flat roofs and colourful shutters. A familiar view. The group stopped.

Outside the gates stood two Chi Bantri soldiers. They waved the group across. Also a group of children stood looking towards the convoy, but they were too far away to see much detail. They all had white kurtas on, and pyjamas of various colours. My Eyes and several of the following children waved to the other children across the square, who all waved back.

Tracy asked, "Are they your friends?"

Syed asked. Then he said, "She says 'not exactly'."

The group, followed by the crowd, moved along the edge of the square, walking along the opposite edge to the Fort and as they reached the opposite corner, there sped a soldier on a motorbike, emerging from a pedestrian door by the gates. He pulled up in front of General Dara and they spoke.

The General went back to the Europeans and said to Robin, "She shouldn't be here. Look at the crowd it's pulling. The Monsignor wants to know what's happening."

Robin asked, "Who's the Monsignor?"

"He's the High Priest, Monsignor Plassey. He's the president of the Chi Bantri. We can't ignore his question." He looked hard at Robin. "The girl will have to go home to her sister."

My Eyes asked Syed what the General was saying. He explained.

She spoke to the General, he said his bit, and then silence.

Syed translated. "She's told the General that she's going to get proper support for the Doctor to eliminate the new neglected disease. When he asked how, she said that God will arrange it. She said that the Chi Bantri won't. So he should tell the Monsignor just that."

She spoke again to the General. He raised his eyebrows without saying anything.

"She said to tell the Monsignor that any other business was her business. One day he'll find out what her business really is. She said to tell the Monsignor that as well." She sat high on Robin's shoulders and smiled with assurance. Then she began giggling.

The General turned to Akhtar. "We're here to help you with your healthcare issues, not start a war. I'm in consideration of pulling out." He pointed at My Eyes. "*She* can sort your problems."

Akhtar started to laugh. "I'm sure she can. But they've only asked what's going on." He carried on laughing. "The girl's told you what to tell him, that's in *her* opinion, now *you* must make a proper bloody decision and stick by it."

The General's respect for Doctor Hussain was certainly unquestionable. He smiled at Akhtar, saluted Captain Batiste, who was totally confused, and bowed to the girl. The General showed tremendous humility. After all, he was a general in the Indian Army, and probably the highest ranking government official in the region.

The motorcyclist returned with his reply to the Monsignor's question.

"He's told the soldier to report that they've requested the girl as a guide, and also to help them identify the lepers. He'll deliver the girl back safely to her sister as soon as possible. He said to apologise to her sister for keeping her."

My Eyes swung around on Robin's shoulders, still very excited, and then spoke.

"She said that the General used great initiative. She says he's a good servant." He raised his eyebrows.

The girl was eight years old, more like two hundred and eight! Robin was by then thinking about Catherine, but he really needed to keep his imagination under control as this was no time for daydreams! Then, "*What's* going on *now?*" he snapped, as the group was again held up.

"Ninah, Ninah!" My Eyes shouted. She waved her arms, and the large man standing in the middle of the street bowed his head.

He was certainly big, taller than any other in the convoy, with a heavy black beard and wore a sarong and shirt. His clothes were dirty, as if he had been working hard, and around his waist hung a leather carpenter's pouch. Like most of the dwellers he had no shoes on.

Syed whispered, "The General's asked him to move."

The man looked at My Eyes and spoke to the General.

"He says he needs to speak to our visitors. The General's agreed. Here he comes, so be careful."

The giant walked past the General and his men, as they all bowed their heads in respect, and he stood in front of Robin and Tracy. My Eyes giggled, and then spoke.

"She says that this is Ninah. He's a great man and wishes to greet you." She spoke again. "He's the Fort's carpenter and very beautiful. She says the dwellers both fear and respect him." She spoke some more. "She says he's the children's defender."

Ninah's deep set eyes looked piercingly at both Robin and Tracy. He smiled and spoke.

"He said 'so it truly is true'."

The UN soldiers were becoming confused and panicky and as Ninah lowered his hand into his tool pouch one of the soldiers raised his gun towards him. My Eyes almost laughed her head off and swung around on Robin's shoulders, then shouted.

"She says to lower the weapon, please." He lowered the weapon but remained in readiness. Ninah continued to pick something out of his pouch and came out with two very large shiny silver nails. They shone so brilliantly, like the sun, and he held one in each hand, by the clout end, and slowly moved the dazzling nails to Robin and Tracy's heads. He touched the points on their forrids, drawing a little blood. Everybody froze. My Eyes cheered and tapped Ninah on the head.

"She says he will serve you well." She spoke some more to Ninah. "She's asked him to speak to you."

Ninah said a few words. Tracy's eyes just filled with tears and My Eyes leaned down and hugged her round the head. She lovingly kissed one of Tracy's tears as it ran down her cheek, and the girl licked the tear from her own lips.

"I didn't understand," said Syed. Akhtar shrugged his shoulders. "What did he say?" Again Akhtar shrugged his shoulders.

Robin held Tracy tightly as My Eyes sat up straight again. My Eyes spoke to Ninah and he replied.

"I understood that! She's asked Ninah to lead us and protect us. He said it would be his greatest honour." The expedition was back en route.

A bewildered convoy moved on through the rest of the slum where one street was much the same as the last. As they passed, everybody watched them with great expectation, and most of them were laughing and jollying with the soldiers; the big man seemed to be so well known and respected that he brought instant acceptance for the group.

The expedition eventually arrived at a larger building, still a shack but much more substantial, and it had space around it where nobody had entered, like a no-man's land. An old European looking lady sat at the door wearing dirty white clothes, a bit like mother Teresa, but with no head covering, just her grey hair tied back. She stood up as the group approached the open space in front.

The group halted, but General Dara walked on, to address the old lady and she took his hand. My Eyes grabbed Robin's chin and pointed towards the lady, then scrambled down from his shoulders and walked over to her. The old lady released General Dara's hand so as to embrace My Eyes, and they cuddled.

Akhtar said to Robin and Tracy, "*That* is a living Saint. And that girl, she's so special. You must be very proud of her." A very strange statement. He frowned. "Maybe she's the little bird who suggested to me that you accompany us today." Akhtar grabbed hold of Tracy's hand, pointed to the old lady and said, "And she's Saint Catherine."

What? Robin froze, staring at Saint Catherine. What was going on? He tensed up and almost went into shock, but Tracy was aware. "Darling. Stop. It's just a coincidence. Please." She pulled him to her and kissed his neck, whispering, "It's a coincidence, nothing else. Please darling."

Syed asked, "What's the matter?" He held his hand on Robin's shoulder. "Relax, Uncle will introduce you." He looked at his uncle and whispered, "What's that about?" Akhtar shrugged his shoulders.

My Eyes was suddenly there. She pushed between Robin and Tracy, and held one arm around each waist. She spoke quietly.

"What did she say?" asked Tracy to Syed.

"I didn't hear." My Eyes spoke again, but louder.

"She said that Saint Catherine wants to greet to you."

Tracy whispered in Robin's ear, "You need to be strong, and realistic. Do it for Akhtar, that's why we're here. This isn't one of your daydreams."

Robin responded. "Sorry, it just fucked me up a bit." He looked around at the soldiers, and they were all looking and willing him on, like a proper team. "Yes, please, My Eyes, we'd be honoured." She walked them across the no-man's land to face Saint Catherine.

"Welcome." She just looked into their faces. General Dara stepped aside to give them some space. "Thank you for your help."

The couple did not know what to say. Why should they? They had not done anything to deserve thanks. But Robin just had to ask, "Do you know Catherine?"

"Silly. I *am* Catherine." Her weathered face smiled so affectionately at the two visitors. "Please explain your question."

Robin suddenly felt stupid. "Don't worry, I just mistook you for somebody. I'm Robin and this's my darling Tracy." They both shook her hand.

General Dara said, "We must get moving. It's not a pleasant thing, but we must get moved today. Doctor Hussain needs to identify the diseased children from those with leprosy, then we can move the lepers to the new colony building."

Saint Catherine nodded. "If it's agreeable with Doctor Hussain, My Eyes will help him to identify those with the disease." Akhtar walked over and agreed.

My Eyes had gone into the building, and returned with a mischievous smile. She asked Robin a question.

"Sorry, I don't know what you're saying." He looked at Saint Catherine. She just smiled. So he asked Akhtar. "Can you translate what she said, please?" My Eyes then repeated what she had said but added a bit more.

Akhtar, with a serious look, said "She said, if you can give her two hundred rupees, she'll source a lot of help, so that I can cure the rotting disease." He looked over to General Dara. "I don't know what she means."

"I'll pay," said Robin. About three pounds, it was just small change. My Eyes spoke.

"She said she needs it *now*!" Robin took out his wallet and handed over the money.

Captain Batiste added, "Under the circumstances, we should be moving the lepers, not worrying about backhanders to little children."

Saint Catherine replied, "If you have a problem with giving, speak to my angels. They have nothing, but give everything." Robin's mouth gaped open, as he heard the eight-year-old Catherine echoing around his mind.

The Captain bowed his head and apologized.

Akhtar walked to the entrance, holding My Eyes by the hand and two teenage girls met them at the door and welcomed Akhtar. They were locally known as Saint Catherine's angels.

Inside the colony it was very dim and a sickly, sweet smell overpowered making the Doctor heave. There were two groups of children, one at each end of the building, and the larger group, maybe seventy-strong, huddled around some bags. In the centre of the elongated building was a dirty sheet covering something. Akhtar lifted one corner and found three dead children, their rotting flesh creating the oppressive, sickly stench. One of the angels spoke to Akhtar and explained that they had died that day, from the disease, and they were awaiting the Chi Bantri cart for their disposal.

The angels then took the Doctor and My Eyes to the larger group, which comprised the lepers. They had been badly disfigured by the leprosy, most of them facially deformed, and most with distorted, rough limbs. Some had fingers and toes missing. Some were blinded by the disease and two children sat on "sledges", having lost legs as a result of infections. The other children would have to drag them.

Most of those children were cured of the disease, but the society in which they lived would not accept them back, and the colony was all they had left. Saint Catherine and her angels gave them some kind of life, but even this could have been destroyed by the new disease and general misunderstanding. The new disease was totally unrelated to leprosy and to the seventy young lepers.

The angels then led them to the other end. Those children were not disfigured, just rotting. Large open ulcers festered on their legs, arms and backs. The smell was awful. There were about twenty of the poor sufferers.

My Eyes spoke to them, explaining that they were all dying, and Doctor Hussain would take some samples to try to save other children from the same sad fate. The faces on those unfortunate children were totally expressionless; they just conveyed an air of death. One of the angels went outside and collected Doctor Hussain's bag. As he took blood and tissue samples, My Eyes spoke quietly to one of the victims. The boy that she spoke to was not very far advanced and had an ulcer on one calf.

She looked up into Akhtar's eyes. "This little boy's a friend of ours, and will help us do our job. He'll do God's work before he's lost from us forever."

Akhtar raised his eyebrows. "What're you saying?"

One of the angels went up to the leprosy end and returned with a dirty old pair of trousers. She handed them to the boy, who put them on, hiding the ulcer and My Eyes handed him the two hundred rupees.

"You must hurry," urged My Eyes. "You know what to do."

The boy went to a corner of the colony, and pushed open a small door.

"What're you doing?" snapped Akhtar. "Stop!" The boy stopped.

"He's going out to get a cure. Please don't stop him." My Eyes looked over to the boy, and he went.

Akhtar did not know what to say. He just looked at her and wondered, *'I hope you haven't done anything bloody stupid.'*

The little boy ran his heart out, back to the open area in front of the clinics and from there he hired a motor rickshaw to take him into the city.

Meanwhile back at the colony, as the Doctor took many samples from the rotting children, the angels led the lepers out of the colony.

Saint Catherine announced to the convoy, "They're perfectly safe. Just don't kiss them." She walked out to the front of the group, accompanied by one of her angels and ordered the convoy to move out.

Ninah had left the expedition and returned to the Fort. With a bunch of lepers walking with them, they did not need protection! The followers had all gone home.

Ahead of the convoy one of the angels shouted out in Bengali, "Lepers coming!" She repeated the announcement every few yards, and the way ahead became deserted. Slowly the group moved towards the new colony which had been purpose built by the Chi Bantri. It was situated on the edge of the slum.

"This'll be better," said Akhtar. "Much more accessible from our clinic."

Saint Catherine dropped back to accompany the visitors. As they walked, she spoke to Robin and Tracy. "Why're you here? This isn't a holiday destination."

Tracy thought a bit, then said, "I think we were conned into it. Didn't know where we were gonna end up." Syed had a giggle, and Tracy looked round and gave him a 'and you might laugh' look. "I hope we don't regret coming."

"The whole slum is talking about you two. It's your hair, and Robin's face. And My Eyes is certainly taken by the both of you."

My Eyes was helping the angel and two boys to pull the sledges.

Tracy pleaded, "Please tell us about My Eyes. She's called us 'Mummy' and 'Daddy'. It scares me a bit. And that friend of hers said something. What's going on?" Tracy spoke with a little stress in her voice.

"You must just see it through. I've been here for about thirty years. It's crazy sometimes. These people are so superstitious and are just waiting for something. They say that God has deserted them, and is walking the earth looking for something else, maybe his Mother. I've never seen any evidence that God even exists. Well, not in a form as we're led to believe."

Tracy was surprised. "Aren't you a catholic nun?"

"I used to be. Early on I lived in the shadow of Mother Teresa. She was a wonderful woman. But I found myself very alone here with these poor children. The Vatican wanted to build a church for me, but I was *refused* any other help." Her face grimaced with a hint of sarcasm. "As you can see, a church would really help these children. Whatever. Unless, of course, we could use it as a leper colony." She chuckled. "I told them to stick the church. The Chi Bantri may have had something to do with the Vatican's attitude towards me after that." They quietly walked a while.

Tracy began again. "But My Eyes, what's her name?"

Saint Catherine replied, "She's really spooked you, my dear. She's a clever little girl, don't let her corner you."

"I really don't understand. Why's she attaching to us? How could I be her mother? I was in England eight years ago."

"Look at her. She lives in the Fort with her sister. They're totally dependant on each other and she wants to get away from here. You're a rare opportunity for her. Meanwhile she gets rid of her frustration by helping me, stealing some food for us, frightening the neighbours away, and whatever. I very much appreciate her work."

"But what about Catherine?"

Robin joined in, "Yes. When I asked earlier, it *was* a serious question." He held Tracy tightly. "A girl called Catherine told me about you. You had your children burned some years ago."

Saint Catherine sighed. "Yes, but that wasn't a secret. Lots of people would know that. What else did that Catherine say?"

Tracy was beginning to concede, maybe Robin was too. He said, "You're making a lot of sense. I should forget her, and the book."

"The book? What was it called?" Maybe a glimmer of interest.

Sarcastically, Tracy said, "It's called the same as My Eyes." A sudden guilty plea hit her. "Oh, sorry. That was unnecessary, please forgive me. It was 'Unknown India'. Wasn't it, Rob?" She looked at Robin. He nodded.

"Really? That book's very rare. It's a very old book and very special. Don't tell anybody around here about it." She got a little closer to them. She spoke very quietly. "Have you read the book?" Robin shook his head. "Such a pity. I'd love to read it. It's rumoured that *nobody* has read it. This lot at the Fort would probably like to get hold of the book. It allegedly tells of some history which they'd rather forget, history past, present and future. I think it's all a load of superstitious twaddle, but just be safe. Keep quiet."

Robin closed his eyes as he recollected. "It's bugged me ever since, but she said that if I read the book, I *wouldn't* be the first man to read it, but that no other man has read it."

Saint Catherine just shook her head. She looked around at the convoy and spoke aloud. "It's marvellous to be able to talk to some Europeans, even if you *are* obsessed with the girl. Oh, and really, I don't know her name. Never have known it."

Up ahead of the group the angel stood in front of two brand new "shacks". They were spacious, each about twenty metres wide, and looked like they were going to offer more accommodation than the old colony. They faced the slum, but backed onto some open jungle, and sat well back from the end of the street. The exclusion zone was ample and the quality of building was decidedly poor!

Saint Catherine walked into one of the buildings, arm in arm with the two angels. "This is home."

My Eyes hugged Robin around the waist, then Tracy, and spoke.

Syed translated. "Goodbye Mummy and Daddy," he chuckled. Then she ran off.

Colin Hodgson

6 – THE GARDEN PARTY

Robin and Tracy, next morning, were eventually woken by the noise of the clinic. There were dozens of slum dwellers waiting outside, and they were being hustled by three members of Sir Kamdar's private army. They were questioning the people about their ailments.

The two visitors rested in the sitting area of the laboratory building, watching the people outside, some of whom were being placed aside by the soldiers. The two soldiers handled the sick folk very sympathetically.

Syed came out from his bedroom and sat with them. He looked out of the window and said, "I'd better get moving. Uncle'll need my help today. Did you sleep well?"

Robin gave a wry smile. "Like a log. I was totally shagged. Think I'm getting too old for this." They all had a polite laugh about it. "What're the soldiers doing?"

"They're separating the people with the new disease from the others. Once Uncle has checked them they'll be taken to the old leper building. It's like a bloody death sentence to them." Syed hesitated. "Uncle was very lucky to have agreed the evacuation of the lepers from the colony. Uncle thinks they'll burn the old colony, to control the disease but please don't talk to anybody about any of it. This's a terrible situation which can only get worse. If only the world would care enough to help."

Tracy wondered if Robin's donation of two hundred rupees would make a difference. She very much doubted.

They all sat quietly, staring out of the window. Robin looked over to a group of young, naked children who were just playing. They burst into flame, running in circles, and their parents just held their hands out towards them to get warmed.

"Darling, come back down to Earth. We need to talk." Tracy whispered, but knew that Syed could hear.

"I'll be off to the bloody treadmill again, then." Syed knew when to leave "We'll talk tomorrow about guitars. The guitars might make it seem a bit more like a holiday." He paused for thought. "And I know what you're thinking, the disease, remember, you only get it as a result of past polio attacks. You mustn't worry; but always remember to keep your hands out of your mouths and eyes." He suddenly remembered, "Oh, and never sit down on bare soil."

"Thanks, mate. Wish your uncle luck." Tracy took Syed's hand. "You *really are* into this." She released his hand, and he slipped out of the door.

Robin then grabbed Tracy. "Let's get a day out with Aalap. We can talk then. These walls are like paper and I don't feel private here."

The two adventurers sorted themselves out and walked out of the building. The crowd all stopped what they were doing as they emerged, staring in expectation. They both felt very insecure as one of the Chi Bantri soldiers approached them.

"Good morning sir. Good morning madam." The soldier shook Robin's hand. "Don't be scared of these people. They all love you." He turned and continued talking to the dwellers.

That made them even more scared!

A teenage girl ran over to them. She was so brightly dressed in a dashing red sari, and clean and very pretty. She stood out from the rest.

"You please stay here. I'll get my father." Her English was very clear. She ran off around the end of the street and into the open area. After a short wait, with the folk still looking at the visitors, the sound of a hooter raised above the crowd. It was Aalap in his motor rickshaw. He carefully avoided the people as he thread the rickshaw down the short street, and he then pulled up in front of Robin and Tracy. He jumped out of the vehicle and smiled as he put his hands together in front of his chest to greet them. He took Tracy by the arm, leading her to the passenger door of the motor rickshaw. She climbed in.

"Oh!" She was surprised to find the young girl in her red sari, who was already in the back seat.

"I'm Aalap's daughter, my name is Dilshad."

"Why're you here?" asked Tracy as Robin climbed in beside her. "Sorry, didn't mean to sound rude."

"That's fine. I'm here because my father can't understand a word you speak. I'll interpret. We're a team." She waited cautiously for a response.

Robin spoke. "Hi, I'm Robin and this's my partner Tracy. I didn't catch your name."

"I'm Dilshad. It means 'happy'. Where would you like to go?"

Ah, good question. They looked at each other and both raised their eyebrows, and then looked at Dilshad.

She obliged, "Would you like to go to Saint Catherine? All the people are saying you are true good friends of hers."

Robin nodded. "That's a good start. We really just wanted to get away from the clinic, so we could talk."

Dilshad instantly sat very upright and proud. "You can talk without caring about me. I will *not* listen. And my father doesn't understand. We're very professional."

The couple both felt uneasy, but maybe they could get used to it. Dilshad directed her father and they set off to visit Saint Catherine.

Robin broke the short silence. "I've been thinking ever since I woke up. You know when you watch some of those horror movies, and you get to the point where you think *'why the hell don't they just go away to where there aren't any ghoulies, somewhere else'*. Yeah? Know what I mean? Well, what're *we* still doing *here*? I feel like we're at the start of a cheap horror movie." He snuggled up to Tracy a bit to give Dilshad some space. "Shall we just go? I don't think the music industry is ready for us, and I doubt the guitar is either."

Tracy responded with a look of disappointment.

Robin continued, "So what're you thinking? Don't you feel like you're in another world? Weird. Those people outside the clinic. The soldier said they all loved us. Why? And all the goings-ons yesterday. What about what Ninah said? I heard it as well."

"Oh, I don't know. Catherine from the home started all this. She's part of it. We need to find out how. And what about Syed? We can't just walk out on him. I'm so impressed by his commitment. I never knew him, but you must've noticed how he's so dedicated to these people, just like Akhtar. We should give it a bit of a chance to find out why. Please." She thought a bit. "You heard Ninah? Did you understand? The others didn't." She frowned.

Robin sighed. "You're just obsessed with My Eyes."

"That as well. Why not? Why shouldn't I be? She says we're her parents. And that Ninah bloke. He said even more. We've got to find out what this's about." She was very serious but very confused and looked like she wanted to cry, but bravely held out.

"Ok, we'll speak to Saint Catherine. She knew a lot more than she was letting on. But as *soon* as I feel we're in any danger, I'm taking you home."

They watched the people doing their business in the streets. Robin asked, "Are we going a different way?"

Dilshad replied, "Of course, we wouldn't fit through those streets that you would have taken yesterday. My father told me about the colony moving. This way is much longer though."

Robin struggled behind his bottom to pull his wallet out, and took one thousand rupees. He handed the money to Dilshad, for her to pay her father for yesterday and today. She counted out two hundred rupees and handed it back to Robin.

"You've already paid two hundred in advance, yesterday. The little boy paid us. We took him to Kolkata for you. We dropped him off for his meeting, and he said not to wait for him, he wouldn't be coming back. I don't think he was very well." She nodded. "The children ate last night, thank you."

"But...I gave it to..." He thought better of it, stopped and they sat in silence. The plot was thickening and neither of them could see which direction it was taking. They knew nothing about the child and nothing about him leaving the colony. Maybe they should have asked My Eyes exactly what the two hundred rupees was intended for. Whatever the consequences, they were partly to blame. "My Eyes." Robin said no more.

As for the boy, he had had a meeting arranged for him with the Deputy Mayor and his council in the Municipal buildings in Kolkata. The meeting had been graciously honoured by the council, but the boy was quite soon ejected into the streets where he mingled with the crowds, until finding a suitable place to rest his rotting limbs. The disease had spread very quickly from his calf. He just waited to die.

"How old're you?" Robin asked Dilshad.

"I'm thirteen. How old're you, Sir?"

"I'm fifty four, and I'm Robin, not Sir. This is Tracy." They were warming and some trust was growing. "You talk very well. And dress beautifully."

"Thank you." She looked at her lap, hiding her teenage blushes. "I've been to school. My father's a rich man, he has a rickshaw, and we eat. That's rich in the slums. I'm very proud of him. Most of the pretty children become ugly with age and neglect, but many are recruited into the Fort and escape the misery of the slum. My older cousin went into the Fort and supposedly has done well, but we've not heard from her since. But I'll never go there. My father needs my help in his business, and if we're to escape the slum it'll be into the real world, not to the Fort." She sat with her head in the air, but it slowly turned to look Tracy full in the face. "They say you're the mother of My Eyes. Is that true?"

Tracy did not answer, but played with her fingers.

Robin said, "We don't know. But why do *you* think she is?"

"I didn't say that *I thought* she was. But the others do think it. There's a Princess, a very important person. Tradition has it that the Princess's mother is lost, but will return. People don't talk about it, they concern themselves that they'll be heard by the Chi Bantri and be crucified. They just wait for her to come back. Might be you. It's the right time for it. Anyway, that's what *they* are all thinking, and they're many thousands, not just from the slums."

Dilshad seldom smiled. Her name may heave meant 'happy' but there were no signs of it being an accurate description of her disposition.

She continued. "We don't really know who My Eyes is, but apparently she's the Princess's sister. That means that if you're the mother and father of My Eyes, then you will be the mother and father of the Princess. Now that's *big stuff*." She raised her eyebrows as if to say 'wow'. "They say that the princess never grows up. When she gets a bit bigger, she's replaced by another thirteen year old girl. I think it happens at each year's Festival of Life." Dilshad paused, and then continued. "That's when I think she's changed over." She again paused for thought. "Hmm, but I don't know how they change My Eyes over." So there *was* a leak in her fountain of knowledge!

"But do the others think the same as you?" Robin asked.

"No, *they* think she lives forever. The Princess, I mean. Stupid, most people don't even live to thirty round here, and lucky to grow up at all. Anyway, she always wears a silk hood with a hole where her mouth is, so nobody ever sees her. But then one day My Eyes turned up and nobody knows where from. She's been there loads of years. She's allowed out of the Fort, and Ninah looks out for her and he's *always* close to her. Bet he's watching *us* now. None of the other Fort children can walk freely, only My Eyes."

Dilshad paused for thought. "The people fear them both, but have great respect and would follow them anywhere if they were beckoned, even though most of them think she's a witch. My father thinks otherwise, but he *is* more educated." Aalap looked round and spoke to Dilshad. "Father's asked me to speak quietly."

"So what does your father think?"

"He doesn't believe in witches, so she's not a witch. That's what he thinks." She actually smiled. "My Eyes' sister, the Princess, is an icon. They say that if she goes, they'll all die. And the Chi Bantri will not then crucify any more. We *all* wish she would die!"

Dilshad was getting emotional.

Children had to grow up quickly in those slums, or die very young, and it was evident that Dilshad was a thirteen year old survivor. She was an extremely intelligent girl with an uncanny understanding of people's fears. In the right environment she could have grown up to be a great leader.

"Do people *really* get crucified here?" Robin asked.

"Yes. There're two sites for crucifixion. The small open area where we have our rickshaws, near the clinic, and the large open area in front of the south entrance to the Fort. The minor criminals are done near the clinic, and the special ones in front of the Fort. It's said that really special ones are done outside the main fort gates and are conducted by the Monsignor himself. But that hasn't happened for over two hundred and twenty years. Everybody fears the Chi Bantri for good reason. And the carpenter, Ninah, is the man who nails them."

Robin was starting to think about the horror movies, where the people just stay there and take it all. As he looked out of the rickshaw his mind saw a wooden cross with Tracy nailed to it, her tummy being skinned by a priest-like torturer. She had a big silver nail through her neck.

"I'm beginning to get scared," he whispered. "Maybe it's time to run away."

Dilshad interrupted. "We're just getting to Saint Catherine." She pointed to the colony. It was too late to run away, but maybe later.

Saint Catherine heard the rickshaw arrive and went outside. She welcomed them with a smile, spoke in Bengali to Aalap and Dilshad, and then helped Tracy out of the rear door.

"What a *lovely* surprise. Please sit with me." One of her angels laid down a plastic sheet where they all then sat, cross-legged. "We have milk today. Please have a drink."

Dilshad replied, "You mustn't give us the children's food."

"Thank you, Dilshad." Saint Catherine showed great admiration for the young girl.

The two angels sat down by the door, and the children then began to emerge and join them. Soon all the leprosy children were outside with the 'party'.

Tracy carefully asked, "Are your angels apprentice saints? They're so committed."

The two young girls looked and listened, but did not smile.

Saint Catherine, aware that the two girls were present, replied, "They're blessed with a little bit of God in them. They give everything. That's what I believe God is. I'm afraid that around here God is very much suppressed and they say that he's gone missing from his throne, wandering in search. Just wandering and wandering."

Robin responded, "We've heard that before, but searching for what?"

Saint Catherine suddenly snapped, "We've all been very rude. Ranting on about bloody God and stuff without even asking how each other are. Not very European, I must say." She laughed. "How are we all?"

Aalap replied in Bengali, as did Dilshad.

Robin replied, "We're really well, and looking forward to seeing some of the lovely sites in Kolkata."

Tracy nodded. "Hope you and the children are settling in."

Saint Catherine smiled, and then looked across the no-man's land towards the onlookers. She said nothing, then waved one of the angels over and whispered to her. The girl went into the building, and returned with a bottle.

"Captain Batiste's a nice man, he brung me some whisky. He always does. We must all drink." The angel brought some metal mugs out and the wily old saint poured the drinks. "Cheers!"

Dilshad said to Saint Catherine, "We've brought your friends to visit, and to see the new home. You've very special friends."

She thought carefully then chuckled and responded, "When I'm dead, you must apply for my job." That made 'happy' smile.

The group talked and laughed for a while, with Dilshad wanting to know all about the western ways and opportunities, and Tracy wanting to know all about the local ways and opportunities. Perhaps a life swap was in order. Who knows? But Saint Catherine eventually got fed up with being called Saint Catherine and made her statement.

"I'm Catherine. The saint bit is nonsense! Why'd you call me a saint?"

The group looked around at each other, wondering who should represent them. Robin took up the stand.

"The world calls you a saint, not just us. And not all saints have to be dead."

"The religious groups don't agree with you. I used to be a catholic nun. You have to be dead for years to have a chance of sainthood." She supped her whisky.

Suddenly, one of the children was standing in front of the group, disfigured and blinded by leprosy. He spoke quietly in English. "You *are* a saint." Saint Catherine stood up, moved to the child and hugged him tightly. She was emotional, maybe close to tears, but composed.

"I love all you children. Please love me, that's all I ask. You're my family." She needed them as much as they needed her. I suppose that's how saints are made.

There was no conversation for a while. Everybody took sips on their whisky and made funny faces as they forced the liquor down. Dilshad really struggled, but drunk it to be polite.

The lull was eventually broken by Saint Catherine. "So, you two. Who the hell are you?" Nobody answered. "Come on, they're all talking about you, but *they* don't know who you are, either. Do *you* know who you are?" She looked into Robin and Tracy's faces. "I've been told who you are, but have you?"

Tracy took the bait. "Yes." She hesitated. "Yes, we've been told. You know we have. We told you yesterday what we were told."

"Hmm. You told me that you'd been told that you were My Eyes' mother and father. That's ridiculous. This's all about rumour, myths, superstition and fear." Maybe the whisky was beginning to work its miracles, or maybe Saint Catherine really wanted to stir the shit, but she continued, "The Princess is supposed to be over two hundred years old, and My Eyes is supposed to be her sister, and you're supposed to be her mummy and daddy, and you're supposed to be from England, and the Princess's daddy was supposed to have lived in the Princess's mummy's tummy. Complicated, or *what*!" I think she had run out of breath. "Can you see how this doesn't fit in with reality?"

'Mummy and Daddy' looked at each other, and then back at Saint Catherine.

"Look at me," pleaded Robin.

Saint Catherine and Robin looked into each other's eyes. Saint Catherine's stare was intense. Big grey-green eyes pierced his defences. He was under attack, and felt vulnerable. He asked, "Then why did you bring us here?" He saw Catherine, the lovely little girl from the boot sale, looking back at him. "I've decided that Tracy and I are leaving tomorrow."

Tracy was also beginning to feel the ghoulies creeping up on her. It was time to leave. But she still had a suicidal urge to know. She had to know. That ex-nun had just done her best to frighten them away, and yet she was the one who had brought them to the slums from Boxted Airfield, allegedly. And truthfully even *that* idea was just as ridiculous as was the Princess being their child. She looked to Dilshad. "What part are you in this farce?"

The poor child was hesitant and nervous, but to her astounding credit she responded. "I'm sorry, but that's not what I believe. Saint Catherine is wrong. Why can't you be the parents of the Princess and My Eyes?" She had laid the bait.

Robin took the hook. He put his hands on his hips and play-shouted, "Because the Princess is over two hundred years old!"

Dilshad started giggling, and could not stop, she just got worse. She was in uncontrollable hysterics, and the others could simply look on in amazement. Eventually she calmed enough to talk. "Robin. Don't be stupid, *nobody* can be over two hundred years old." She still could not stop giggling. Perhaps her naming was apt, after all. "Look, just look." The little girl was getting tiddly. "If you can believe that the Princess can be over two hundred years old, then you can believe that *you* can live in *Tracy's* tummy." She just carried on laughing.

Well, the child had all the adults beaten. They had to start considering that either it was *all* a load of rubbish, or that it was *all* feasible. Either way, Dilshad was having a great time!

Saint Catherine spoke. "That's why she should apply for my job when I'm dead. Here's to Saint Dilshad! Hoorah!" They all raised their glasses to a potentially great leader of people. "I love having company. Even better when it's the Queen and Lamma! Three cheers! Hip hip…."

Well, was it the whisky, or did she love stirring the shit? All the good work that Dilshad had done to relax the party seemed to be just as quickly undone.

Tracy was never a hysterical or a violent woman, but people can change, especially with alcohol. "What the *fuck* are you on about *now*?"

"Don't get shirty, Tracy. I'm just a bit tiddly, but still in control. The people around here are believing things about you two, and it's probably healthy for you two to know what those things are." She stopped to regroup her thoughts, but I think she had forgotten what she was about to say.

"So, go on then."

"Oh yeah. Well, we've established that if it's possible for the Princess to be over two hundred years old then it must be possible for you to be her mother. Yes? Or no? Right, that means that you *could* be Queen Maya of Anglia. She was, or is, the Princess's mother. We think she was, maybe, but at least that's the consensus. What do you think?" She was loving the moment every bit as much as Dilshad was. It was turning out to be a proper party.

Robin shrugged, "That is, it's, well, I don't know." He held his hands in the air. "I think you're getting pissed."

"I'm a Catholic, I have to get pissed." She waved her mug, and the angel refilled it. "But can you see what we're trying to tell you. The people in these slums, and in the surrounding countryside, and some from right across the world, are suddenly thinking you may be Queen Maya of Anglia and Lamma. Fuck *knows* what's made them think it." She began laughing with Dilshad.

The angel brought another bottle of whisky out and she refilled all the mugs. It was becoming a little bit like fun. Why not, they were on holiday? Dilshad checked with her father that he would be ok to drive home, before allowing him another drink. She allowed him to have just one more.

The group sat quietly for a while.

"Joke," said Robin. "What's pink and wrinkly and hangs out your pants?"

Dilshad went red, and then translated for her father, while the children discussed the question amongst themselves. One of the boys came over and stood in front of them. As he started giggling he put his hand down his trousers, and poked his thumb out of the front. All the children laughed and chuckled naughtily.

"That's brilliant, but it's not your thumb out your flies. Any other ideas? Saint Catherine?"

She was half cut by then. In an air of innocence she very slowly and deliberately stated, "I'm a catholic nun. I cannot say. It's *far* too rude."

Aalap laughed and shouted at her. She immediately struggled to her feet and playfully slapped him around the head, then almost fell over before sitting down. Everybody roared, and even the children were having a lovely time.

"The swine. He said, 'only when it suites'."

Robin pushed her on the shoulder. "Don't think it suites at the mo'. Well, the answer is…." He looked to the children. "It's your good old mum!"

Oh. Silence for a few moments, then they began to realise what the word play meant and the giggles started up again. As the children explained the joke to each other they laughed and pointed at Robin who said with a wry smile, "At one point there, I thought I'd died on stage."

"At one point there, I was gonna shoot you on stage!" Saint Catherine had a wicked sense of humour. "Thank you all for coming today. It's been a rare treat for us. Fun is hard to come by round here, especially when you're a leper and the world has turned its back on you." Saint Catherine became very thoughtful. "I know I'm drunk, but I want to say this. If you become the big rock star that you could be, Tracy, or even if you just make the Queen Maya bit, will you buy some tall benches with very slippery legs for the children to sleep on? The woods behind us are plagued with rats. Last night we awoke to one of the boys screaming. A rat had eaten the flesh off his affected, numb ankle." Pause. "Long, slippery legs, that they can't climb." She put her head down and began to sob.

The angels went to her, spoke in her ear, and then one of them gave her a cuddle. The other went inside with three of the children to prepare somewhere for the saint to lie down. What a beautiful example of dedication and love. The whole group was inseparable.

Tracy was also very tipsy by then and so she was feeling brave. She stood up, wobbled a bit, and then walked into one of the Colony buildings. A corner had a hole in the roof to allow the cooking fumes to escape, but the oven had no coal or wood to heat with. There was a bag of rice, not big enough to feed the whole colony, and some lentils. A stone container probably held the milk. The rest of the building was almost bare, just some blankets set out around the floor; they slept on the bare ground.

"Will she be ok?" Tracy asked the angel.

"Yes. We'll look after her. Her sleep will be a welcome escape for a few hours."

"Do you have food?"

The angel looked to the cooking corner. "We have some coming. If My Eyes can steal some, we'll be fine. She's our most good friend. Thank you for asking." She continued laying the bed out for the saint.

"Do the rats really eat the numb flesh?"

"Rats eat everything. *We* have to eat almost everything, even the rats. They're just like us, starving. But we'll have a guard each night to chase them out."

Tracy went outside and the angels helped Saint Catherine to her bed. The others were just about ready to nod off, so she poked them all on their arms. "We've just drunk enough money to feed these children for several days. I feel ashamed."

Dilshad, the thinker, comforted her with some teenage wisdom. "We've given a saint a welcome break from the reality of poverty. She's asleep, dreaming of somewhere lovely, and the children have enjoyed watching their hero laugh, and they've laughed with her. We're not bad people, never think that."

Aalap started the rickshaw engine. The children were still outside, ready to say goodbye, and the two angels came out to thank them all. And then the same blind child, who had earlier comforted Saint Catherine, moved to them and stood in front of Robin.

"My friends have asked me to ask you. Please Lamma, will you find God?"

Robin looked over to Tracy for help. His eyes began filling with tears, and then he tried to speak to the child, but he faltered.

Tracy came to the rescue. "Lamma will help us *all* to look. But we must all continue to pray. The little bit of God that we all have in us mustn't be wasted." She looked at the angels.

Following the voice trail of one of the other children the blind boy walked back to the group.

Tracy held Robin as he cried. It could have been the alcohol, but I think his heart had been touched, even scarred, by the children's plea. He wondered why people follow religion. He thought as he watched the angels, *'God is all around, just waiting to escape his confines and do battle with the evil with which he shares his bed. He's not religion, he's God.'*

Perhaps God really had turned his back on the area, but the four visitors to the Colony that day had witnessed two teenage girls who were doing open battle, as God would surely expect. They fought a never ending war against misery, then death, a war which they could never have won. But they carried on. Tracy wondered if they had seen a vision from God?

The rickshaw set off towards home.

The day had been full of intrigue, but all they had really learned from it was that the Princess was somewhere between thirteen and two hundred and thirteen years old, and Tracy could be a two hundred and forty year old queen, and had to put up with Robin sleeping inside her tummy at night. Or maybe the Princess was killed off every year and replaced with a new model. Then her sister, who may or may not be her sister, runs around the slums helping the poorest of the poor to survive, and is followed around by a relative giant called Ninah.

The biggest lesson, though, was the realisation of just how poor, desperate and neglected the world's poorest people really were.

They slowly drove towards home, half asleep.

Tracy asked, "Do you still want to go home?"

Robin thought. "I'm scared. But *now* I'm scared that I'm going to get hooked, like Syed."

Tracy smiled in agreement and asked, "D'you think we should ever tell anyone about what Ninah said to us?" She looked at Dilshad who was taking it all in. "Please Dilshad, understand, I don't think we can speak about it with you here."

The young girl showed her astonishing qualities by saying, "The world has its own business, best keep yours to yourselves." She put on her 'happy' face. "But what'll you do about the children's request?"

Robin asked her, "What's my name, I've forgotten?" He grinned.

"It's Lamma. But it's a title, not a name. It's the spiritual protector of the Queen. It comes from the old language which was spoken around here a long time back."

"Thank you. Thanks for everything today. You and the saint twisted us around your little fingers to get your points over. You were a phenomenal team. I think we're a lot more relaxed now. Thanks."

She giggled and looked at Tracy, who was almost asleep and said, "Tell me that tomorrow, when you've sobered up."

Colin Hodgson

7 – THE BURNING OF THE BEAUTIFUL

Morning number three arrived with a bang! Robin and Tracy almost went through the roof as somebody started thumping relentlessly on their door. He jumped out of bed and pulled the door open. It was Syed.

"Get out of bed, now! And get dressed!" He went over to the open front door. Aalap was standing at the door with Dilshad, and the rickshaw was parked outside, engine running. "Hurry, Robin."

As they grabbed some clothes and money, soldiers from Sir Kamdar's army approached the clinic and spoke to Akhtar. One of them went inside the clinic with Akhtar.

Robin was dressed quickly and went outside. "What's happening?"

Dilshad pushed into him. "They're burning the old colony, with the diseased folk in it. And they're isolating the whole slum." She looked back towards the open area. "I think they're coming for you."

He looked down the street, and yes, the crowds were growing. He could see some of Kamdar's militia guarding the entrance to the street from the open space, and then the officer who had gone into the clinic with Akhtar came out and approached Robin.

"You must go. These people have an issue. Go in the rickshaw." The officer turned and ran to the soldiers who were containing the dwellers.

Tracy came out and the four jumped into Aalap's rickshaw and Syed waved them to get moving. They set off down the short street, but where were they going? The militia stood aside to let them through, and guess what, they were straight out into the open area. The dwellers approached, several hundreds of them, and Aalap stopped the rickshaw. The four of them froze.

"Lamma, Lamma." A man shouted at them. The mob smothered the rickshaw and reached through the windows, to touch them. They just wanted to touch them! As each hand touched Robin or Tracy, it retracted to allow another the privilege! Suddenly the hands withdrew.

"Robin!" Syed arrived at the rickshaw. "Are you alright?" He looked at him. "Thank God."

Robin slowly got out of the rickshaw. He was surrounded by Sir Kamdar's men, who were all set away from the rickshaw with rifles pointing at the dwellers. There were hundreds of dwellers, and just about twenty of soldiers. They were very brave soldiers, some of Kamdar's elite.

"Syed!" Robin grabbed his arm. "Look!"

"Robin, you must go."

"No. Didn't you see? They just wanted to touch us. They don't wish us *any* harm at all." He let go of Syed's arm and turned to Tracy and held her hand. They walked to the soldiers, pushed a way through and stood in front of the dwellers. One of the dwellers moved towards Tracy.

"We're ok." Robin reassured the soldiers behind him. "We're ok."

The dweller reached out and touched Tracy. He smiled, bowed his head and walked away. Suddenly the whole crowd was politely taking their turn to touch one or other of the visitors, bow their heads and then walk away into the slum. Only the slum dwellers knew why. The soldiers bravely maintained their positions.

The stream of dwellers went on for some time, watched closely by the soldiers and Akhtar. But it just stopped and they were all gone. No more people came from the slum.

"I was just starting to relax," said Tracy. "What's happening now?"

The open area was again deserted and back to normal with just the soldiers pointing their rifles into an open space. The officer ordered them to fall out.

"What's happening, Akhtar? *You* must know." Robin waited for a response.

"The old colony is being burned today, with all the poor sufferers inside. That's what I know." He looked to the ground in despair. "I'm days away from the answer."

Dilshad listened to her father, and then spoke to Robin. "Don't forget, you're Lamma."

"This is *not* the time." He was not amused.

"No, listen to me. In the initial panic, they were calling you. Lamma, Lamma. Didn't you hear?" She listened again to her father. "Father knows some of the people who touched you. They wanted some of your spirit to give them strength, because they have loved ones who're now to be burned in the old colony."

That was why there were only a few hundred people, just the relatives of the poor folk afflicted by the disease. They were so desperate for the spirit and strength of leadership, to help them live through the hell of watching their family members burn. And Lamma was their choice! It was religion, not God.

As Robin looked to the ground, a motorcycle approached from across the open area. It was a messenger from the Fort and he delivered the message to the officer in charge.

The officer spoke to Akhtar in Bengali. "Doctor Hussain. We must go. The building must be incinerated as per our instructions from the Fort. I'm sorry. And the visitors can't be present. They'll cause too much disruption. Please explain to them."

"*You* can explain!"

"I cannot. I'm merely their humble servant. You're their friend." The officer saluted the doctor and bowed his head to Robin and Tracy then went over to his troops.

Akhtar spoke to Robin and Tracy. "I'm becoming a believer." He put his hand to his head in despair. "You can't come with us to the burning. Sorry." He looked towards Aalap. "He'll look after you. You must leave the slum for a while until the disease is halted."

He turned towards the soldiers, but then turned back again. "They all love you. Some *very* big news is spreading across the slum right at this moment." He looked at the laboratory building. "Let's go inside for a few moments." Akhtar, Syed, Aalap, Dilshad, Robin and Tracy all entered the building and sat down. Akhtar thoughtfully prepared his statement, and then began. "You've found a cure and immunisation for the new disease. *Don't* say a word, please." He waited to make sure nobody else spoke. "It's moved on from being a Neglected Tropical Disease to an international emergency."

Robin tried to speak, but Akhtar managed to stop him.

"The disease erupted in the Municipal Building in the city." He was looking hard at Robin, willing him to be quiet. "I can only guess at how it moved from the slum. But it's resulted in big company investment, and Sensar Pharmaceuticals came in yesterday and I gave them my results. They've guaranteed a fix within four days. I've got the credit for my work. You, Robin, must accept the credit for yours. We'll have to leave it at that, for now." He went outside to the soldiers. They regrouped and the Officer and Akhtar led the trek, on foot, to the old colony building. The executioners were on their way, towing a small bowser of petrol.

The little boy who fled to the city, financed by Robin's rupees, had had a very successful meeting with the committee. Two of the councillors, big political names, had contracted the disease! The neglected disease could no longer be neglected!

"Robin." Dilshad stood in front of the visitors. "That was a very tactical move. If you don't want to be Lamma, why'd you do it?"

Robin just shook his head in disbelief. He heeded Akhtar's advice and said nothing.

They walked outside where the messenger was still waiting, with another message in his hand. He beckoned Aalap over and gave him the message. He handed it to his daughter to read out.

"The message is direct from the Monsignor. It says it's to be delivered to his European friends. My gosh, it's from the Monsignor. It reads 'It is considered from within the Chi Bantri inner court that you should not be left inside the slum area when it is isolated. The disease must be contained until it can be eradicated. Until that time you will stay out of the exclusion area. Failure to do so will result in the court taking further actions. We do not, under any circumstance, wish to jeopardise our special relationship.' That's it." She handed the message to Tracy. "The messenger'll expect to take a reply. You can't ignore the Monsignor, he's a world leader."

Robin whispered to Syed, "Never heard of him."

Dilshad snapped, "I hope you don't wish me to write *that* for the Monsignor, Robin." At last she smiled.

Tracy took control. "Please thank the Monsignor for his gracious concern. Tell him that we'll not give anybody reason to doubt our 'special' relationship. Tell him that we'll uphold the request of his inner court, God willing." They were all amazed at Tracy's willingness to lead.

The message was handed to the messenger, who bowed his head in respect to the visitors, then sped off.

Tracy continued. "Syed, where're you going?"

He grinned and answered, "No bloody where. I live here now."

"Then Robin and I'll find some rooms outside the area, and Dilshad and Aalap will accompany us." She looked at Dilshad.

"My father has nodded. Will you still be paying the five hundred rupees per day? A lot of children eat from that income."

"Of course we will."

The four of them went to their rooms and grabbed some clothing, and then met back at the clinic before driving off to leave their good friend Syed waving bye-bye.

The rickshaw turned right to drive round the perimeter of the open area but Aalap pointed towards a small child running towards them, straight across centre of the open part. She wore a white kurta and light blue pyjama trousers.

"It's My Eyes!" exclaimed Dilshad. "She's shouting."

They all climbed out of the rickshaw and moved to meet her. She was shouting hysterically and Syed joined them, just as she reached the group. She screamed at Robin and Tracy and grabbed Robin's shirt, tugging for him to follow her.

"Calm down. What's' happened?"

She drew breath, pulled a nervous smile, and explained carefully.

Dilshad translated. "She says that we may be interested to know that the Monsignor has ordered the burning of the colony. Going to happen very soon."

"Tell her that we already know. Thank you." Dilshad passed on Robin's answer.

Instantly, My Eyes took up her cobra stance, legs apart, knees slightly squatting, hands on hips and her head bent towards his face, then *screamed* at him! She was mad!

Dilshad stood bolt upright and momentarily froze with shock. "She says the *new* colony!"

"No. Ask her again." Tracy could not believe it.

My Eyes screamed again, then grabbed Tracy by the hand and pulled her away. They both sped off across the open area.

"Wait!" shouted Robin. "Get in." The rest of them jumped into the rickshaw and Aalap raced off to the colony, horn blowing.

The girls ran their hearts out in the blind panic. It's so amazing at the extra strength and stamina that can be born of panic and desperation. My Eyes shouted as they ran, and the people moved aside realising their real mood of desperation. Some of the younger dwellers started to follow, and there was soon a massive migration towards the new Leper Colony building. The crowd carefully made sure that they stayed behind the girls, and more and more joined the race.

By the time they reached the colony there were two or three thousand people behind them. The exclusion zone was filled with Kamdar's soldiers, all armed. Smoke rose from behind them. My Eyes pushed into the soldiers but was expelled from the line but instantly the soldier who had pushed her out was thrown to the ground from behind. It was Ninah. The other soldiers' bottles broke and they stood aside, and the girls rushed in.

Ninah shouted at My Eyes and pointed at the door. There was smoke beginning to seep out. She rushed forward, dribbling past Ninah's lunge, and went inside. The door closed behind her.

"No! No!" Tracy rushed forward but Ninah held onto her. "No, please! Gayla! Gayla! No….!"

She fell to her knees in despair, with Ninah still holding on to her. She screamed, "Fucking cunts! Fucking killers! Please, Gayla! Please…..come home." She broke down, sobbing uncontrollably, and then Ninah got down onto his knees and held her tightly. "Please God," she begged.

The rickshaw arrived. They all jumped out and the soldiers by now were losing their nerve with the crowd, and just stood aside as flames suddenly roared from the building. Everybody had to move back from the seething heat. Ninah picked Tracy up, carried her back from the inferno to meet Robin where he took her into his arms. Ninah bowed to Robin.

As she sobbed on Robin's shoulder, Ninah spoke to him, explaining that Saint Catherine had chosen to stay with her children and that My Eyes had entered the building. Robin understood every word.

Syed, a little confused, asked Robin what Ninah had said. He told him that Catherine and My Eyes were inside. Tracy sobbed in Robin's ear, "Our Gayla went inside."

The mood of the crowd was fraught. They were uncomfortable about the burning and, like the visitors, their grief was beginning to turn to anger. They mumbled amongst themselves and threatened to move forward towards the soldiers, who responded by shooting some rounds into the air, which set the crowd back a little.

Over to the right side of the buildings, which had by then begun to collapse, the crowd hustled. Some shouting began. The mob started to move towards the front of the building, but stopped short of the soldiers. A gap opened and, with the crowd shouting in support, My Eyes shot out. She flew over to Robin and Tracy and flung her arms around Tracy's neck.

"You're alive." She was still sobbing, but her face lit up. My Eyes just laughed as she kissed her mummy's wet cheeks, revelling on the flowing tears and then let go to hold Robin around the waist. As she clung onto Robin, with Tracy sandwiching her, she turned to Ninah, and spoke very seriously to him.

Dilshad translated. "She says that Saint Catherine said she wanted to be with her children and her angels wanted the same. She said that Saint Catherine was too old to start again. She wanted the angels to leave but they wouldn't. She says that they've all gone home together. She says that's lovely. She says that she's so…, happy?"

My Eyes then listened as Ninah spoke privately to her. She turned to Tracy. Her face was a bit dirty from the smoke, but she was very happy, with no run-marks from the tears and no red eyes. She pulled Tracy down, and kissed her ear as she spoke.

Syed translated. "She said, 'thank you mummy'." This time he did not laugh. "She said you shouldn't have worried about her, and that she got out of the back. The others wouldn't come with her."

My Eyes looked round at the group and thanked them all and then took Ninah by the hand, who spoke to Tracy in the old language. "Thank you, Your Majesty. The Princess now needs us." He bowed to Robin and he and My Eyes walked through the crowd.

"What did he say?" asked Syed.

Tracy stuttered, "It was a bit like 'thank you mummy', but not quite." She was still sobbing when she put her arm around Robin's waist, and looked at the crowd. It was, by then, quiet and the soldiers a bit more relaxed, but what could they have been thinking? If they were just half as confused as Tracy and Robin, their heads would have been spinning out of control.

"I think we should leave," suggested Syed. "This crowd could still get nasty."

They moved to the rickshaw and the soldiers moved aside to allow them passage, but one stepped in front of them. He laid his rifle down. Slowly he went down on one knee and said a short prayer for Tracy, and then several of the crowd followed.

Without speaking all five of them squeezed into their vehicle. Aalap was careful as he approached the crowd, but they parted their way to allow the rickshaw to pass down the street. Many people were bowing lowly to the group. None of the four knew at the time, but it was Tracy who they were bowing to, because if it was the Lamma they would have been kissing his foot.

Aalap and Syed spoke about the "request" from the Monsignor for Tracy and Robin to leave the site, and they decided that, on the way back, they should detour to the arena in front of the Fort. Tracy was still in shock from her experience, and Dilshad was beginning to sink into the realisation that her friend had burned with her children. It had been a terrible day for all of them. Maybe a sight of My Eyes in front of the Fort would help. They at least felt that it could do no harm, and they could then leave the slum before it was closed off.

The rickshaw took a different route in order to pass the Fort and it was dirty, full of open sewers and rubbish. The children were skinny, with scabs and sores, and the old folk sat on the ground as if they were just waiting to die, it was getting worse. Syed apologised to Tracy for bringing them to the slum, but she was in shock, and she did not know what he was saying. Poor Dilshad had begun to cry as the loss of her friends slapped her, and then the narrow street turned into the open arena at the Fort.

"We're at the Fort." Syed announced.

The soldiers in front of the gates held up their hands, saying 'no further'. They halted.

Across the arena there stood some children. They could only make out that they were dressed in white kurtas and various coloured pyjamas, very similar to My Eyes' dress. But they were too far away to see any detail. Tracy stared at them. She spent some time just looking, with nobody else talking, but she did not see anything. Her mind was blown.

"Should we go?" Syed said to Robin. "She needs to recover from this trauma. And Dilshad's stressed."

Robin was also stressed, but was handling it well. He looked into Tracy's eyes. He knew what she was looking for, My Eyes, but she was not there.

Syed discussed the situation with Aalap. They spoke that the Monsignor had 'requested' the visitors to leave the slum, and that they were still there, in the slum. They thought that the fire was sufficient excuse for them not to be leaving until later. They did not really think it through about *who* had burned the colony, and why, and perhaps that the request to exclude the visitors was *because* the new colony was to be burned, by the Chi Bantri. Foreign witnesses were not welcome. Syed and Aalap were not quite as intelligent as Aalap's daughter. Lovely people, but…

"We must go." Dilshad had managed to calm her grief enough to be realistic. "We shouldn't even be here. They'll kill us all."

Robin was also quite calm. He suggested, "You go, but leave us here. They're murderers and we have things to discuss."

"And they'll murder *you*."

Dilshad was right to be concerned. If the Queen and her Lamma had stepped out of the rickshaw, they would have been taken into the Fort and possibly crucified. Who knows? The inner council were reputed to be vicious dictators who administered cruelty liberally to control the common populous. Not an uncommon trait amongst many of the World's powers. But Robin and Tracy were not common people, and the Chi Bantri knew that, and in the wise words of My Eyes 'if they were going to kill you, you would already be dead'. But however you weigh up the options and consequences, sometimes a safe retreat is the top option.

"We're going." Syed poked Aalap on the shoulder and he set off around the perimeter towards the clinic. They never said a word during the drive home.

There were soldiers at the clinic when they arrived and Akhtar was back in the sitting room. They had achieved their burning in a more clinical manner, and the old building area was satisfactorily cleansed. Akhtar had heard about the other fire.

"I'm devastated," he said to Syed. "Why? There was no disease as far as we know, and there were only fifty two children. It should've been at least one hundred before they burned. What is Saint Catherine going to do?"

Syed put his head in his hands. "Uncle." He sat for a moment. He looked at the floor, then at his uncle's feet. He stared in *horror* at his uncle's feet. "Uncle. Are you ok?"

"Of course I'm bloody ok." He then put *his* head in his hands and looked at the ground. "You can see my ankle. My poor ankle. The one with the bloody ulcer." That bloody disease had struck.

Syed knelt down in front of him and put one hand on each of Akhtar's shoulders. They both wept. After a few moments Akhtar snapped out of it.

"I'll have to wait for the serum, or whatever. It'll be here in a couple of days. I wish they'd got him out sooner."

"What do you mean, Uncle?"

"Nothing." Akhtar asked, "Where're your friends?"

"They're in the lab building, sitting. They've had a terrible day. Just terrible."

"Where's Saint Catherine going to stay while she develops another leper refuge?"

Syed looked out of the window at the soldiers. "I think she's gone home at last."

"Good, get away from this bloody disease. You must help her when she returns. I won't be able to help her. Did you know I had polio as a young child? My left ankle is deformed a bit, the one that is beginning to rot."

Syed somehow knew that his Uncle was dying. He had got to know the smell of death, as some animals do. And Akhtar had another ulcer higher up his leg, close to his groin. It had spread very quickly.

"I've told Captain Batiste. He was here earlier. He's going to arrange for me to be isolated here, in my clinic. I might be able to still do some work. You'll still be able to stay in the lab. I heard that your friends were moving out for a while, for the best. Why didn't they go earlier?"

Syed did not say a word.

"I never had chance to tell you about our hell in Chuknagar. That was when we all left East Pakistan more than thirty years ago. I believe that your father never spoke about it." He was morose. "I'm sorry. We just wanted to get to Kolkata and then London, out of that fucking Pak land. Your father and you kids, his children, had crossed the Bhadra river, and were safe. We were meeting you in Kolkata, but were a few days behind you, and that fucking Bihari wouldn't let us over the river because we couldn't afford the new fare. It was put so high, several times what it should have been." He sobbed a bit.

"Uncle, you don't have to tell me."

"Will you listen, for me? I've never told anybody. Please, before I'm dead."

Syed comforted him with a smile and nodded.

"Well, we had some local friends, well, probably a couple of miles away. So I went to see if they'd lend me the money for the river crossing, and your auntie and your two little cousins stayed near the river." He sighed. "When I got back I went to the place where they'd wait, I searched and, like all the other thousands, they were dead. Just fucking dead. Chopped up." He sighed and waited for his strength to build. "Many of the young women had been taken, but your auntie and lots other women were left there, dead. They'd cut their breasts off and pushed sticks into their vaginas. Why?" He looked so confused. "They could've just killed them. I wanted to kill the Paki soldiers, but I didn't. I was too scared. I was disgraced by my cowardice, but even more disgraced by my religion, but I was let go just because I am Muslim. I went with some local Muslims to help clear up our family's bodies, but your little cousin was being eaten by two dogs. I just ran away." Through his tears he looked Syed in the eyes. "Do you know where hell is?" No, he did not. "It's right here. Where there's life, there's hell. Please forgive me, Nephew."

Syed held his uncle tightly as he wept. He whispered, "You can now be with them again, and be happy."

Uncle sobbed, "If they'll have me. I should've died with them."

Next door, in the lab building, Robin and Tracy sat. She was still in shock, constantly sobbing and mumbling. "She's ok." She kept rubbing her eyes. Robin tried to stop her, since they had been told not to put their hands to their eyes or mouth.

"Come and wash your hands." He walked her to the sink and washed her. As he sat her down he looked into her eyes. She had grey eyes, as ginger people often do, but not so grey that day. He pulled his reading glasses from his pocket and looked closer. Her pupil was white, and there was a small bubble, or ulcer, beside the pupil. "Can we just pop to see Akhtar, darling?"

They stood up together and walked very slowly from one building to the next. As they walked in, the doctor and his nephew were composing themselves.

"Ah, our good friends're here. This's a pretty shit place to be right now. You must go for a few days." Akhtar stood up and asked Tracy if she was coping.

"She's got something in her eye, could you please take a look."

Akhtar looked into the eye, and then spoke to Syed in Bengali. Syed fetched a swab. The doctor took a sample and moved over to the bench, then after several minutes he put his head in his hands and said, "You and me, Tracy, are infected with this bloody disease." He sat down and began to cry.

Robin held Tracy in his arms. Neither of them cried, they just stood there, arms around each other. He whispered, "I promised I would never leave you. I love you too much."

Akhtar stressed, "You must understand. Please understand." He was panicking. "You must understand what this means. Syed you must tell Captain Batiste to shut us in these buildings to die. You must get out now. I was wrong." He was wilting very quickly. "You haven't had polio, Tracy. But you've got the disease." He held his head and cried. "What're we going to do?"

Syed took his friends by the arm and walked them into the lab building. "Stay here. I'll see what I can do." He took a long look at his life-long friend, Robin. "I wish I'd never got you out here. Please forgive me." They both just looked at him. Then Syed left the building.

Robin sat by Tracy and held her head on his shoulder. Life for them had tumbled down from a comfortable, carefree life, to come to rest at the bottom of the pit. They had actually seen the bottom of the pit in recent days, but had never even dreamed that they would be down there, with the slum dwellers, rotting. They sat for a long time saying nothing.

The door opened and it was Syed.

"I have Captain Batiste with me." He turned. "Please come in, Captain."

The Captain stood in front of them. "I must perform the unhappy duty of locking you in the building. Sorry." He waited for a response. "D'you need anything?" He again waited. He turned to Syed and reassured him, "We'll ensure that your friends and your Uncle are not disturbed. We'll return in two weeks time, when Sensar've completed their duties, and we'll make arrangements. Robin, do you need me to inform anybody?"

Syed answered for him. "I've all of their details. But we must now speak to my Uncle. He's some very bad news for you, and for everybody. He's beside himself."

Tracy raised her head from Robin's shoulder. She looked at Syed, who was grieving, and whispered. "I've been thinking about what he said. He was wrong."

Syed humoured her, "Yes, we know that now. Uncle is devastated; he'll die as a failure."

"No. No, I mean he was wrong. I *have* had polio, as a young child, when visiting the West Indies. I had mild polio, in West Indies. Please tell him not to fret." She actually smiled, as did Syed. His uncle had not misled the world, after all.

Shortly after Captain Batiste had left the building there was some banging, as the doors were sealed. It was frightening for the two lost souls as the windows were boarded up; the world just disappeared from their lives.

8 – THE SIX GOOD FRIENDS

Tracy sat silently considering their situation with her head still rested on Robin's shoulder.

"Why did I come here Rob?"

He thought for several minutes without answering. Then, "To find your family."

A further few minutes passed.

"Did I find it?" She frowned. "I don't know if she's our little girl. I think she is. I hope she is. I always wanted my own family and children." She lifted her head from his shoulder. "My eye doesn't hurt much, but I can't see through it." She shivered. "I'm cold."

He went into the bedroom and returned with a blanket. "I don't think there's very much food here. We've got drinking water, though. Don't really know how much water we'll need."

Tracy began to shiver constantly as she sat with the blanket around her so Robin fetched another and wrapped her up tighter.

"I wonder if I'll know when I'm dead." She looked into Robin's eyes. She could only see a blur through her one good tear-drenched eye. Her left one was whiting over as the disease crept outwards from the nucleus of the ulcer, and Robin began wondering how long it would be before it went into the rest of her head.

She whispered, "When I'm dead, you should break out. Please. Take Gayla home." Her face was begging, desperately trying to make Robin take My Eyes home to the safety of England. She had not even thought about the Princess, but Robin had.

"I couldn't take her without her sister. Would you mind?" He stroked her sweating forrid.

"Silly Billy. She's not her sister, remember?" She was taking on a serious fever. "But you must take her home as well. Don't fret over me." Her breathing was getting very slight. "Perhaps the children will come to us." She closed her eyes and went to sleep.

He laid her down on the floor and covered her up to keep warm. She was sweating profusely.

"Water. Lots of water." He was talking to himself. He went into the kitchen area and lifted down one of the large bottles of drinking water. The light was limited and he felt a panic set in as he wondered if the power had been left on. It had, and the lights worked. "Thank God." He carried the water over to Tracy. "She's gotta drink. I'll let her sleep a bit, first."

The laboratory was directly off the sitting room. He had not been in that room before and was surprised at the size. It was well equipped, as you would expect from a doctor of Akhtar's dedication and standing. Robin never even knew a spatula from a test tube, so all the equipment would probably be of very little assistance to them, but he decided to search for some paracetamol or similar. He was amazed at the contents of one corner, which seemed to have come out of a torture chamber, and had many bone-cutting tools. One was a sprung guillotine with an extended handle to enable a fast, clean cut. He found some paracetamol tablets. He also grabbed a bottle of dettol and some sterile bandages.

As he stood looking at his beautiful partner, tiredness set in and his head began to wander.

"Go to the toilet."

"Who's that?" he asked.

"I'm your daughter. Go to the toilet."

He looked around instinctively, but nobody was there. "Where are you?"

"I'm here, with you. Your girls are here with you. Go to the toilet, Daddy."

He walked into the toilet. There was a hand basin and western style toilet pan. Nothing else. "Where are you?" he asked again.

"We are both here with you. Look out of the window."

It was boarded up, but as he looked hard at the window he could see two girls standing the other side of the plywood. They were ghostly, but even in the dark they became clearer as he concentrated harder. One was a teenager and she wore a white kurta and red pyjama trousers. She had a fine young figure. Her head was covered by a white silk hood which had a round hole at the mouth area, but there were no holes for her eyes. She whore a thin sword in a blue-and-gold decorated scabbard. It hung from her waist. Also hanging around her waist was a smaller girl, in a white kurta and blue pyjamas, and a massive smile. It was My Eyes. Robin's imagination was becoming clearer as he continued to stare at them.

"My Eyes!" He was so relaxed in his dream. The nightmare around him was temporarily put on hold. "Why're you here?" The bigger girl translated. My Eyes giggled.

"She says that you must already know that. Don't you remember us?" The bigger girl then spoke for herself. "We're here for you, Daddy. And for Mummy. We love and have missed you both."

My Eyes continually whispered to the big girl. Then the big girl spoke, as if she was talking on behalf of My Eyes.

"I'm Ca'an. This is my sister Gayla. She's my eyes. I'm her spokesman." My Eyes, Gayla, giggled, and then carried on whispering. Catan continued, "It's pronounced Ca'an, silent 'T'."

Robin just looked at the two. He had momentarily forgotten about Tracy.

"Daddy, you must remember us. Mummy does, she's thinking of us right now, in her dreams."

Robin awoke to reality and waited for them to go. They both stayed. He looked around to remind himself where he was, and then went through to the sitting area. Tracy was still asleep.

He returned and asked, "Is she in a coma?"

Gayla whispered constantly.

"Yes," replied Catan. "She's dying very quickly. She'll be able to go home if we allow her to. But we don't want her to. We've so much work to catch up on and you can both help before going home. Please, will you trust us?"

A confused Robin replied, "Why should I trust you?" With a shudder he suddenly recalled 'I'm Caferine. I'm Gayla's cousin and Ca'an's aun'ie. And I'm only eigh'!' "I don't believe it! You've conned us both into coming here. That fucking Catherine. She did my head in, now she's killed us. And you've killed your own mum, why?"

Gayla continued to whisper to Catan. "We haven't killed her, but the disease will if we don't stop it. You came here of your own free will, but we can talk about that later. We right now need to keep you *both* here. We don't want to kill either of you, you're our mummy and daddy, and we worship you both. Kill you? That's *silly*, and it's not God's will."

"God? Why does everybody here think that God has deserted them? Was he *ever* here? And Ninah. In that weird language when he called Tracy the Mother of God." He looked towards the living room, and thought of his Tracy. "I want to wake up now. Piss off and leave us alone. If you know God make him help us all, otherwise get out of my dream." He held his hands across his eyes and rubbed them.

"Mustn't keep touching your eyes," advised Catan.

"Are you still here? I'm going to wake up. Now!" He opened his eyes.

Gayla giggled and pulled at her sister. "You're awake. Look, and we're still here."

He looked at his watch, then walked all around the inside of the building and returned to find them still looking at him through the plywood shuttering.

"We're not going to go away. We've found our Mummy and Daddy, after all these years of failure and anguish, and we won't give you up easily. When we go home we'll *all* go home, and that is *our* decision."

"Wow, hang on. I'm your father, now go away, and *that's* an order. And that is *my* decision."

"No. You can spank us later like naughty kids, but right now we have to help you to save Mummy."

A realisation suddenly came to Robin that this was not a dream, and that either he was fully awake and alive, or he was already dead, and this must have been what heaven and hell would have been like.

Catan said, "Don't be silly, you mustn't think like that. You're alive and so is Mummy, but not for long if we don't get on with it." She spoke about his thoughts as if he had shouted them out to her. "You'll learn to love us. Gayla says you will."

Gayla then spoke through Catan. "Please love us Daddy." She paused. "Just do as we tell you, and Mummy can be saved, and then you can fight with us later. But right now you must trust us." She carried on speaking through Catan. "You're my daddy and you've just proven it to us, and to yourself, by seeing what you're seeing right now. And you understand Ninah's language. You're one of us." She hesitated. "We'll now hurry to save Mummy from going home early. We need her here."

Robin looked at Gayla as she grinned at him. He wondered if she ever stopped laughing and grinning, even through what seemed to be a day trip to Hell.

Gayla pulled a small package from her kurta pocket. It was thin, several inches long and was tightly wrapped in plastic. She poked it into the end of the overflow pipe which went into the cistern, and then Catan said, "Take the top off the cistern and you should be able to reach the end." It was long enough to poke out of the overflow pipe inside the building. Robin pulled it through.

"What do I do with this?" He inspected it carefully. "Why didn't you just poke it through the plywood?"

Catan replied, "The package is real and so is the plywood." Did that mean that they themselves were *not* real. Not sure. Gayla carried on whispering to Catan who went on, "You must find a plastic funnel and cut it down so that it fits closely around Mummy's eye. You'll have to hold the funnel tightly so that they can't get to any other part of her body. You *must* keep them away from her nose and mouth. Understand?"

"No. Keep *what* away from her nose and mouth?"

"The worms. They're our friends when used properly. They're inside the tube and you must have a glass jar ready to put them into when they've done their job. You'll need them again later, so please don't hurt them." Catan pointed to where her eyes might be. "Don't let them get out of the eye and they must *not* get into the other eye. You must remain vigilant right through while they're working. Keep putting them in the eye when some more rot appears, and take them out when they start trying to get out, and keep them unharmed in the jar. Disinfect your hands after you've removed them from the eye socket, and before you touch any part of yours or Mummy's body. They're *very* poisonous."

Gayla looked hard at Robin as if to ask, "Do you understand?"

He smiled and nodded. "I'll have to trust you."

Catan nodded her hooded head in appreciation. "We must go now. We can't save Mummy, but *you* can and so you must do it for us, all of us. The rewards will be very colourful." Robin did not know if it was Gayla or Catan speaking, but he nodded his head, and they were gone.

Robin had awoken from his dream, and was totally lost. He just stood and looked at the boarded window, wishing them to return, but they never did and so he was alone with his dying lover. As a tear developed he held his hand up to wipe it, but then remembered what Catan had reminded him about, not touching his eyes. But anyway, he could not rub the tear away with his hand since he was holding the tube full of friendly worms. Was it a dream?

Dream or reality, he was left alone to save the life of his darling Tracy who was failing quickly. He pulled himself together and ran around collecting glass jars, funnels and disinfectant and set about cutting the funnel down to size. There were plenty of scalpels in the laboratory, and he soon cut the funnels so that they tightly fitted around the eye socket without obscuring it. She was restless as he tested one of the funnels for size and then she spoke, but he could not understand.

"Our family came for us," he whispered and kissed her sweating forrid. "I need to sort your eye out. Please be brave for me."

The moment of truth had come. He had no option but to trust those dreamlike apparitions, and as he pulled the end from the tube there were worms! He could not see how many.

He put his reading glasses on. "Here we go." He spoke to himself in an effort to comfort his fears. "Funnel. You must be still, sweetheart. Right." He pulled her eye open. The ulcers had grown and almost completely filled the visible part of the eyeball. He placed the funnel over the eye, which held the lids open, and then tipped the worms into the funnel. There were six, light brown, and about the thickness of a small knitting needle, and they hastily slid into the eye. He was horrified as they attacked the eyeball, and he could see that they were eating it! They had no visible mouths but they homed in on, and began attacking, the ulcerated part of the eye. It was amazing, they were natural cleaners. The smell was pungent and he had to set his head back a little to avoid the full force of the fumes that they were creating, but still diligent in his maintenance of the funnel's position. "They're *very* poisonous." He repeated what Gayla and Catan had warned. It was as though he was explaining to Tracy why he was forcing the funnel into her face.

The worms slowed and then seemed as though they were trying to escape from the eye socket, and attempting to reach up the sides of the funnel.

"Keep putting them in when some more rot appears, and take them out when they start trying to get out," he said to himself. He grabbed one of the jars and placed it beside Tracy's head, then gently picked one of the worms out of the funnel. It was soft, but dry and seemed quite content to be handled. The others came out very easily, and once he had counted out the six, he put the jar aside. He watched to make sure they could not reach the top of the jar. "I won't shut you in. You might panic." He could not afford to risk losing those little friends.

Robin poured some disinfectant over a piece of bandage and thoroughly cleaned his hands and the funnel. He then inspected Tracy's eye. As he held the lid open, he could see holes in the eyeball where the worms had eaten the rotting matter. It was a sad realisation for Robin to know that she would never see through that eye again, but she at least could survive. Her staying alive was something which Robin had not even considered a little while ago, but he suddenly felt positive and thankful. The power of the family unit had so far shone.

He fed Tracy some water, and then drank a little himself. "I'd better watch the water." There were plenty of bottles in the kitchen, gallons, but he was single minded about keeping Tracy alive and felt the need to economise. He looked at her and smiled as he said, "Thank you God, if you're listening."

They lay on the floor together for a while, but he found himself nodding off and he panicked. "I must stay awake." He checked the eye, and it was turning white again, and it was ready for some more cleaning. The length of time since the first clean was about one hour, so the eye ball was clearly rotting quite quickly. "I hope they're hungry." He followed the routine again but this time the worms took a little longer before trying to get out. They had more to devour this time. After that clean the eye was visibly disappearing, by then leaving a void behind the lids.

"Mustn't sleep." He began to close his eyes but awoke with a jolt. "Alarm clock. My alarm clock." He collected his clock from the bedroom and set the alarm for one hour ahead. He fell fast asleep.

The alarm woke him up and he performed the third clean. The eye was by then disappearing quickly. He thought to himself that the next one will be the last, but how would he know when to stop?

But it turned out that he performed a further five cleans and the eye ball had gone, the eyelids sinking into the socket and working sporadically. On the final clean the worms instantly wanted to climb out from the socket. They were not interested in the cavity which by then showed some blood, but no white ulcers. "Have you finished?" he asked his friends. "You're a bunch of little miracles." He carefully put them into the jar, then disinfected.

The eye had completely gone. As he peered into the socket some blood sat where the muscles and nerves had been severed. The worms had left such a clean job, and it was a natural phenomenon which could easily have been described by many as a miracle. "Perhaps there really is a God." He cleaned the bloody patches with Dettol. "Maybe we can *both* take Gayla home to England. And Ca'an. And then find that bloody Catherine."

Despite the empty eye socket distorting her face and the eyelids flicking out of control, she looked so beautiful, and alive. After admiring her for a while Robin dressed the eye with a sterile bandage and when he kissed her forrid he realised that her temperature had dropped, and her breathing was smoother. She had survived. But had she? What about the rest of her body? Robin desperately un-wrapped her from the blankets and undressed her. He then made an inch-by-inch inspection of her entire body for signs of ulcers. He found none. She was clear of the disease and, unknown to him, the body had been practicing its own private miracle by creating enough antibodies to ensure future immunity. I wonder if the girls could have helped Akhtar a lot more than by just spreading the disease into the city.

He set his alarm for an hour ahead and they lay down together and fell asleep.

When the alarm went off, Robin carried out another clean, but the worms found nothing.

"What do I do with you now?" he asked the worms. "Better leave you in the jar, and Ca'an can take you back." Would Catan and Gayla be returning? Their visit seemed a lifetime away from that peaceful scene which had replaced the earlier nightmare. A new day was dawning.

"I'm hungry." Tracy had woken up. Robin hugged her tightly and looked into her eye.

"Guess what. You're alive."

She looked dazed. Her left hand slowly moved up to her left eye.

"My eye hurts."

Robin gave her some water and paracetamol. "I'm sorry, but you've lost it."

"Get me a mirror." Her voice was feeble.

He got a mirror from the bedroom and she sat up and held it in front of her face and touched the bandage with her other hand. "Can I see it?"

"Can you wait 'til I check on it, in about an hour? Don't want to encourage infections."

She was exhausted from the fever and did not seem able to move very much. She laid back down.

They were both exhausted so Robin gave Tracy a drink of water and they again went to sleep, but this time the alarm was not set. They slept for several hours.

Colin Hodgson

9 – THE WORD ON THE STREETS

The South Gates of the Anglian Fort.

The children stood quietly outside the gates of the Anglian Fort where they were waiting for somebody. Catan was still wearing her white kurta, red pyjama bottoms and a silk eyeless hood, but she was not wearing her sword, and Gayla wore her white kurta and blue pyjamas. As she hung onto Catan's left arm Gayla constantly spoke, commentating whilst Catan looked around the open arena. The sun was pleasantly warm.

There were six young children standing with them, five boys and one girl, all wearing light grey kurtas and matching pyjamas. The six young children were all eight years old. Only three boys looked to be of Indian origin. One boy looked very European as did the girl, and another boy had Nepalese features. There was a sheet of plastic laid out on which they could play.

Catan was not often seen outside of the Fort walls, so it was not surprising that the local slum dwellers were standing on the other side of the green, looking on in expectation. The slum had been put into isolation and so they were not allowed to cross the square towards the Fort. So they all just watched and waited.

All the talk and gossip going around was about the two Europeans and how they had been mistaken for the Queen and her Lamma. "They are certainly now dead from the disease. They could not have been the ones," they were saying. "The Lamma would have protected her, if he was truly the Lamma." When there is hope, there is future, but on that day there was none. They all looked to the 'Princess' for solace.

Catan was referred to by the locals as the Princess. They knew very few facts about her except that she was a truly special member of the Chi Bantri. The rest was myth, gossip and superstition. She was reputed to be over two hundred years old, and the daughter of Queen Maya and her Lamma. It was said that when she eventually walks the earth without her hood, she would bring happiness and security for the millions of unfortunates within the world. She would banish torture, child prostitution, neglect and even cannibalism and they said that her freedom to walk the earth without her hood would herald the return to the throne of Queen Maya of Anglia, the one they had all been waiting for, for over two hundred years. But at that time the promise of the Queen's return had been short lived, and all hope disappeared when the two visitors, like mere mortals, died in the clinic. They would have to carry on waiting, and believing. That was the word on the street.

The locals were divided in their beliefs.

Most believed in the two hundred year old Princess, but some of them were cynical, as was Dilshad, and believed that the 'mortal' Princess was eaten every year at the Festival of Life and then replaced by another mortal. That was why she wore the hood and always remained at just thirteen years old. They believed that, along with her 'children', she was eaten by the Chi Bantri's higher members. The higher members consisted of many of the world's most powerful individuals and it was believed that they maintained their positions and status by feeding on the children of the Qeervi. The Qeervi, pronounced 'Curvy', was an ancient race of people which included Queen Maya and her descendants. Many, like Dilshad, believed that there were no descendants of the Qeervi people remaining, and that the Princess was just a consumable real-life effigy of the Queen. The high members would eat the effigy in order to banish the possibility of the Queen's return.

But most were not so cynical and they worshipped the Princess in the belief that she really would bring their beloved Queen back to lead them again.

The language which was spoken by Ninah, when he called Tracy the Mother of God, was Qeervi, and it was firmly believed by most of the World that the language had completely disappeared. That was the point at which Gayla and Ninah believed that Tracy was the Queen. Why else would she have understood and with Robin also understanding, it was a double whammy. Of course, the other slum dwellers did not realise the consequence of that exchange.

All known literature about the Qeervi people had been destroyed by the Chi Bantri over the past two hundred years, and their obsession with the eradication of *everything* Qeervi confirmed just how frightened they were of the Queen. They must have been secretly celebrating when the doors and windows to the laboratory building were boarded up! The Queen and her Lamma were to die! And what a result it was for them that it was the rest of the world who were to be their executioners.

The Chi Bantri could never themselves kill the pretenders in case she *really was* the Queen. They believed that the barbaric treatment of the Queen and her family by the Chi Bantri, two hundred and thirty years earlier, would one day spawn her revenge, and so they had to bestow her the respect of a deity, constantly praying for her forgiveness.

The destruction of all literature about the Qeervi people was probably one of the Chi Bantri's (many) greatest mistakes. Actual history was replaced by superstition and far-fetched beliefs. Long before Robin and Tracy had arrived, the lack of factual history had caused fantastic myths to have been developed about the Queen's reign. It was said that the Qeervi people had ruled this part of the world for many years, and had propagated wealth and justice through good management, humanity and tolerance. They were so successful that it was conceived that the Queen and her family were immortal beings, sent to Earth to stabilise mankind. But the Chi Bantri, for personal gain, had driven them out of their human bodies and banished them from Earth leaving the poorest folk to the mercy of the dictators and fundamentalists. Those poor people prayed for her return. The Qeervi had become legendary deities and Gods.

In the meantime the Chi Bantri had themselves become compromised by those superstitions and myths and had become dedicated believers in those legends, and thus their enemy had become their idol. The fear of the Queen was their driving force.

But what about Gayla? She had not been at the Fort for very long. She just turned up a few years earlier, in 1972, a year or so after Ninah. He was looking for work and so was employed by the Chi Bantri as a carpenter. He was very well respected, and after a spell away he returned from the Bangladeshi War of Independence proclaiming the imminent return of his auntie and the Princess's mentor, Gayla. The witch.

When Gayla arrived the Princess was housebound, unable to see through her hood and could not get around, but Gayla became her eyes and she could move around freely. She referred to her as 'my eyes', and the nickname stuck. All the slum dwellers became to know her as My Eyes and she was such a wild thing, full of energy and always laughing and smiling, and intensely intelligent. Everybody soon built an astonishing respect for her which was worthy of a queen, but most still thought of her as a witch. Maybe it was because she never seemed to get any older than eight. She became a great pal of Saint Catherine and the lepers.

It was believed that Gayla was the younger sister of Catan, and that her father, the Lamma, lived in her stomach. The story seemed to be mixed up with another story which put the Lamma at home in her mother's stomach, possibly that of Queen Maya's. Nobody knew where those stories came from! Apart from that, very little was known about Gayla.

Most of the slum dwellers did not believe what Dilshad believed. They were convinced that the Princess was genuine, and that she was the two hundred and forty year old daughter of Queen Maya. One of the main reasons for that stubborn belief was that the three of them, Catan, Gayla and Ninah, were all reputed to speak Qeervi. It was not the most concrete of reasons, but those poor people had little else to believe in and their various religions had delivered little or no relief from their stress. I wonder how they would have been feeling on that day if they had known about Ninah's Qeervi exchanges with Tracy.

From the crowd across the square appeared the giant figure of Ninah. As he moved towards the Fort two soldiers emerged from the service door but retreated back inside when they realised who it was. Gayla constantly spoke to Catan as she clung on to her left arm and the six children ran towards him and met him halfway.

"When we've sorted our business, we'll play," he promised the children. He heralded a fatherly air, and the children were clearly very fond of him. He turned to Catan and spoke Qeervi. "We need to be very careful. The people are uptight about the deaths from the disease and are now talking of the visitors bringing plague to the slums. They're talking about burning the clinics with the 'devils' inside. Their mood has changed towards the Queen."

Catan and Gayla spent a few seconds thinking. The tiny Gayla suggested, "We may need to get them out, secretly. Burning the clinics, without them in there, could be good for us; we could then court the world with their resurrection." She giggled as they stood pondering the idea. "We can make them look the part. The eye, the leg."

"Hmm. I don't like what you're suggesting," grumbled Ninah.

Gayla chuckled as she spoke. "I'm suggesting that we build on the myths, and exaggerate the facts, just like any other good story. She's already lost the eye, just leaves the leg." She wriggled with excitement. "It'll be the start of the modern scriptures."

Ninah asked, "And how will we remove the leg? *They* believe that he cut it off to feed the Queen, while he was intoxicated by desperate devotion." He pointed towards the dwellers.

Little Gayla pulled at Catan's arm and looked into her hooded face. "Then that's what will happen. We'll give the world what they want. And besides, the same applies now as it did last time."

Catan at last spoke. "It'll be cruel towards Daddy. Just like last time. And you never have told us why." Her voice was subdued. "I don't want to hurt him."

"None of us want to hurt him." Gayla moved away from Catan's arm. "We've a job to do, and we're on the eve of achieving it. We can't mess up worrying about human suffering, else they'll *all* carry on suffering." She looked towards their six children. "We'll all have to make personal sacrifices, as we've had to since time began, and nothing's changed."

Catan lowered her head. "Sorry." She then lifted her head up as though to look at Ninah. "I can't see." Gayla moved to her side, held her left arm and began whispering. "Thank you. Ninah, how long could you keep them away from the clinics?"

He shrugged his shoulders. "Maybe a couple of weeks. I'll need some help."

"What sort of help?" asked Catan.

"Your Highness, they need the medicine. They need to stop suffering while the outside world is being cured. The disease can help us, if you can get the Monsignor to get the bloody medicine inside the slum. They can then believe that the Lamma *has* delivered the cure which they'd been 'promised'."

"Were they promised a cure from Daddy?" asked Gayla, grinning.

Ninah laughed. "They know about the boy going to the city. *You* told them, but they still believe it was Lamma who sent him. If the world can, at least on this occasion, administer the inoculations they'll again believe in Robin and Tracy. That'll give us some working space. Maybe a couple of weeks."

Gayla stopped smiling and pointed at the crowd across the square. "They'll riot if they don't get the inoculations!" She then pointed at Ninah. "Make sure of it. Tomorrow afternoon."

Ninah went down on both knees in front of Gayla and Catan, clenched his hands together and whispered a short prayer. He stood up. "It will be done." He walked back to the crowd across the square.

Catan turned her hooded head towards the children and spoke Bengali. "Sorry, but Ninah has work to do." They sighed and then sat down on the plastic sheet which lay near them. "I'll play guitar for you later. We can sing. Ok?" She then looked down towards Gayla. "I'll tell the Monsignor to get the drugs into the slum by tomorrow."

"What you gonna tell him? They may not have enough."

Catan replied, "We'll have to hope they've got enough. Any ideas?"

"Yes, tell him the disease will be in the Fort if he doesn't get the inoculations out there. He can take it as a threat if he wants." She turned her nose up and grinned. She was definitely making a threat! "I'll be there with you. We'll be as one."

Catan asked the children if they would like to stay outside the Fort while she carried out some business. She spoke to the soldiers inside the gate and they promised to look out for them.

With Gayla on her left arm she passed through the service door at the gate. The Fort was spacious, with a parade ground in front of the gates, quarters to the left and a large single storey building to the right, with a reinforced roof and access to a helipad. A military helicopter sat on the helipad. Straight ahead was the back of a large whitewashed building, three storeys high and with a corrugated metal roof. It was the main building. Dotted around the parade grounds were several groups of children and a couple of groups of soldiers practicing their drill. Many waved to the girls as they approached the large double entrance doors to the building. The two guards saluted the girls as they approached.

"We need to speak to the Monsignor. It's urgent." Catan waited for a reply.

"I'll speak to his secretary, Your Highness." The soldier picked a phone from the wall. He replaced the phone. "Sorry he has a visitor with him. He can't see you until later."

Catan became a little agitated. "Who's the visitor?" Gayla was whispering to her. "Is he as important as me?"

The soldier stood to attention, then again picked up the phone and spoke to the secretary. He handed the phone to Gayla, who held it to Catan's head.

The Monsignor was on the phone. "Princess Ca'an, I have His Eminence, Cardinal Mateo with me. Could you wait a little while?"

She snapped, "No. This is urgent." She waited for a reply while Gayla continued to whisper. "I can speak to you with His Eminence present, if you wish."

The Monsignor spoke to the Cardinal and then, "You may come up now."

The soldier could hear the conversation and so opened the door to allow them entry. Inside was a small entrance lobby with some benches, very sparse, and a staircase leading up to the offices. This was the working part of the main building and the whole atmosphere was cool and clinical. A very cold atmosphere. They entered the double doors which led into the Monsignor's suite.

The secretary welcomed them. "Good morning, Princess. Good morning Gayla." She led them across the room to another large door and showed them into the Monsignor's office.

His office was large, with two fine mahogany and leather desks and leather chairs, and the walls were lined with bookcases. Very little of the structure of the room could be seen behind the thousands of books. It was a fine collection and I wonder if there was anything about the Qeervi in that extensive private library. Behind the desks were large double doors, glazed to display the rooftop gardens and marble patio area.

"Good morning, Monsignor," said Catan.

The Monsignor sat behind one of the desks which had little on it, except for a writing pad, a pot full of pens, two laptop computers and two un-smoked cigars sitting on a brass ashtray. He was dressed in a dark grey suite, and was quite splendid with his greying hair. He was of European-cross-Pakistani origin.

Seated opposite him was His Eminence the Cardinal Mateo with his scarlet skull cap, or zucchetto, and a white cassock with scarlet piping and buttons. A magnificent gold and emerald-studded pectoral cross hung from a long chain around his neck, exalting his senior position within the Catholic Church.

The Monsignor stood up and introduced the girls to His Eminence.

"You Eminence, this is Princess Ca'an and her young sister, Gayla." He turned and, "This is His Eminence, Cardinal Mateo. He's an important member of our court."

Catan stood for a few seconds without saying anything, with Gayla whispering constantly. Then Catan said to the Cardinal, "The Monsignor doesn't speak Italian. What else do *you* speak?"

The Cardinal seemed a little surprised that she had spoken at all. "I speak good English. And you?"

"I speak many languages. I've had a long time to learn. So we'll speak English and I'll translate for my sister when required." A smile showed through the mouth hole of the hood. "Are you enjoying your visit to the Fort?"

The Cardinal did not answer.

"Your Eminence, aren't talking to me?"

He stood up. "I was waiting for you to address me properly." He sat down. "I've only been here for a few hours, but yes, thank you." He looked away from the nubilous face of Catan.

She retorted, "And *where* did you receive your basic training in good manners?" Catan smiled beneath her hood.

The Monsignor intervened. "Ca'an, please be polite. The Cardinal is here to make arrangements for the Pope's visit."

She turned to the Monsignor and bowed her head in apology. "I'm waiting for him to properly address *me, and* my sister. He'll not look down on us. Doesn't he know who we are?" Gayla was still whispering, and getting excited. They turned to the Cardinal. "Your Eminence, I'm Princess Ca'an of Anglia, and this's Princess Gayla of Anglia. You must address both of us as 'Your Highness' when speaking to us. Or we can come to an arrangement and be equal in a more relaxed manner. If you've a problem with either of those options then leave us while we sort our business with the Monsignor."

The Cardinal had become used to his lofty position, looking down on the world from a height. "I am the second highest ranking member of the Roman Catholic Church."

"What does that make you, in the eyes of God? Would you like me to ask her?" Catan waited for an answer from the stunned Cardinal, but it never came. "Right, we'll make an arrangement. You can call my sister Gayla, and me Ca'an. And you don't' pronounce the 'T'. What should we call you?"

The Cardinal looked across to the Monsignor for support. No chance, the Monsignor had learned the hard way. The Monsignor asked, "Your Eminence, do you have a Christian name?"

He faltered, but replied "Yes, Louis. You may call me Louis. And you don't pronounce the 'S'." Perhaps he was more intelligent than they had realised, using humour when up against it. "I'm sorry Ca'an. You take a man by surprise, you know. Please call me Louis."

The Monsignor stepped in and asked Catan, "Why're you actually here? The Cardinal and I have business to discuss."

Catan replied, "I would like to talk to Louis if that's ok with you. I know of his membership, but have never met him." She turned to Louis. "Do you know anything about this sect, or in your language, cult? I would guess that you know enough, else you'd never have been accepted into it." She waited for his reply, but had to prompt, "You must be sufficiently powerful to be of any use to them."

The Monsignor interrupted. "You don't have to answer these questions, Your Eminence."

"I think I probably do need to. Yes I know about the Chi Bantri, after all I'm part of it. I'm one of the higher members and sit in the inner court. The Pope is being considered higher member also." He smiled and nodded his head sideways. "I've heard a lot about you and your sister, and much of it has reached my ears from the other side of the World. The rumours and stories speak a lot about your mystique, but nothing about you. And your sister is described as a witch, being a 'mobile home' to her own father. I can't see anything wriggling inside her." He looked into Gayla's face and asked, "Is your father not at home?"

Gayla covered her tummy with her hand, in jest, and then continued whispering.

The Cardinal observed, "Ca'an, you've not yet translated for your sister."

"It's currently *her* that you're speaking to and she understands the gestures of a clown. I don't need to translate. But she wants to know why the Chi Bantri burned Saint Catherine and her children."

The Monsignor began to panic. "Ca'an, you cannot be rude to His Eminence."

The Cardinal interrupted the Monsignor. "No, carry on, please. What do you mean? Saint Catherine is one of the Fourteen Holy Helpers, venerated by the Roman Catholic Church amongst others, and was beheaded by the Romans because of her undivided faith in Christ. She was *not* burned."

"Louis, yesterday Saint Catherine of Kolkata was burned alive, with her angels and her children, in their new colony. Her children were lepers and she had tended the poor leper children for over thirty years, as a saint would. It's not the first time that the Chi Bantri have cleansed the area of the lepers. But it *is* the first time they've been stupid enough to turn a living saint into a true martyr. But you already know all this." She paused. "It was rumoured that it was because she harboured the diseased people, but that's just rumour, and not believed by the people who live here. They're plotting against the Chi Bantri as we speak. I've been reliably informed that tomorrow afternoon the slum dwellers will be inside the Fort. And so will the disease."

"Ca'an, I must stop you. His Eminence doesn't need to hear about this." The Monsignor was beginning to take the bait.

The Cardinal pushed in, loudly. "Before we talk about rebellions and uprisings can I just say something? This lady and her children, they may have been burned, I don't know, but she was *not* a saint. If she has not been canonized then she was not a saint."

"Louis. Veneration of saints is primarily a Christian thing; it's not necessarily a God thing. Very few people here are Roman Catholics, not many are Christians, so the rules are different and more tolerant, and so, in a divine meaning, a living saint is encourageable. In the eyes of God, and there *is* only one, when somebody consecrates themselves to others as would a saint, God's children must be allowed to recognise that mortal as a saint if they choose. Saint Catherine of Kolkata was a saint and now a martyr. Who're you to question the spirit of God? Or the immaculate intent which may be spawned of other's beliefs? *People* make saints."

The Cardinal was a little dazed but composed. "That is touching on blasphemy."

"No. I've not been irreverent towards the Catholic Church, but *you* have been irreverent to the people of the slums. Your intolerance has been noted. Within these slums lived and worked our Saint Catherine who was loved by the people, and hailed as a living saint. She's now a dead saint and will probably be forgotten about quite quickly, but for a while she'll be missed and her generosity and selflessness will continue to influence. She'll carry on touching people for some time."

A silence fell. The Cardinal fidgeted and the Monsignor lit a cigar.

Gayla whispered then Catan spoke. "Now tell me why you burned her. You're a member of the inner court so you must know why."

The Cardinal sat back and sighed. "I wasn't part of that decision. Monsignor Plassey, maybe you can shed some light?"

The Monsignor puffed on his cigar. He was a clean upright man, with a cold composure which seldom warmed, and he thoughtfully stated, "Your Highness, the children were believed to have been infected, and so they had to be treated in the same way as the other unfortunate victims."

"There was *no* medical indication. It was murder." Gayla was still excited, but the smile had gone. Catan continued to say, "The plague which the two Europeans delivered to the outside World will be with us all by tomorrow. You'll not be privileged, Your Eminence. *You* have had polio."

Catan turned her covered face towards the Monsignor and spelled it out. "Monsignor Plassey, Gayla has been to the slums yesterday and today. She's carried the disease to us, as the Lamma carried it to the World. You'll now do what is right."

"Your Highness, I have to carry out instruction from the inner court."

"You'll carry out your duties as the Monsignor of Anglia. Have you forgotten who you are?"

The Cardinal stood up. "I think this has gone too far for me. I must leave, please ask your secretary to advise my team."

"You're a carrier, Your Eminence, or is it Louis? We can be friends or enemies." Gayla stopped whispering for a while, and Catan stopped talking.

Then Catan stated, "As Her Royal Highness Ca'an of Anglia, I hereby declare this Fort to be in a state of emergency. Nobody will leave the Fort until the slums have been inoculated against the plague. *Once* the slums have been inoculated, then this Fort can be done the same."

She turned to the Monsignor. "Under the terms of your position, and taking that a state of emergency exists, you'll arrange for the vaccines to be made immediately available. You don't need to call a meeting with the court, just do it." Gayla was still not whispering. "If the vaccines aren't available by the morning, the thousands of poor people left out there to rot, will be mad. They'll be right here, in this Fort."

The Monsignor stood up, acknowledged Catan's declaration, and then bowed to the Cardinal. "This is unfortunate, Your Eminence. As Her Highness has reminded me, I have to deploy the rules of the Fort. You'll have to stay."

"But Monsignor, I've had polio, I must go."

The Monsignor picked up the phone and asked his secretary to call Sir Kamdar.

"Sorry Your Eminence, we'll make you and your team comfortable, but we're closing the front gates. The south gates, which lead out to the slum, will remain open. Please be careful where you wander."

The Cardinal was very calm about it. Despite Gayla's grilling earlier he was a good, strong man and carried a presence which you would expect from a World leader. "Gayla, we must talk further." He turned to leave the room, just as Sir Kamdar was shown in by the secretary. He turned back to Gayla. "That was a clever move. Thank you. Ca'an, could you please translate for me." He grinned and left the room.

The Monsignor showed Sir Kamdar to his seat and turned to Catan. "As soon as I've arranged the securing of the Fort, I'll call Doctor Wise of Sensar Pharmaceuticals. I believe you know him."

"Yes, another of the paedophiles who attend the Festival. I know him well." She looked towards Sir Kamdar and changed the subject. "Your brother is doing a fine job in the slums. When will *you* begin?"

The Monsignor intervened before Sir Kamdar could speak. "Please Your Highness, could we have some space. You've already destroyed one of my meetings today." He reached his hands towards the door as a request for them to leave, and smiled.

He had the greatest respect for the two girls, as they had for him. But they all three knew that they were precariously perched on opposite sides of the fence, the good side and the bad side.

Colin Hodgson

10 – THE CARDINAL'S SINS

The two girls walked out of the building and onto the parade ground. Up to one hundred soldiers were assembling in the centre of the ground as they had received early orders from Sir Kamdar. They were to prepare for the closure of the Fort.

"We need to get hold of Ninah."

They walked out of the South Gates and onto the open area, where the dwellers were still grouped on the opposite side, waiting for word about the disease. From the crowd appeared Ninah. He waited for Catan and Gayla.

Gayla suggested, "You should go and talk to them. You know Cat', you've never done that before."

"Are there enough of them? We can't waste the opportunity."

They stood silently for a while, Gayla holding onto Catan's left arm.

She looked up to Catan and confirmed, "Ninah will tell the slum that you'll address them at four thirty, about three quarters of an hour. That should bring a lot more of them here."

They turned and went over to their six children.

"Gayla, is it true the people are going to kill us all?" asked one of the boys.

Gayla laughed and jumped down onto the sheet with them. "Don't be silly, they're our friends. The Princess will talk to them soon."

"The soldiers said that they'll kill us all."

Gayla, for once in her very long life, had to stop for thought. She looked at the soldiers at the gate and they were agitated. She said to the children, "We'll all die one day, but it won't be today. But don't tell the soldiers that." They all giggled.

But the boy was not satisfied. "We *will* die when the Festival comes. I would rather die today." He was full of tears. Gayla pulled him to her and held his head to her chest. The poor boy, who was bigger than Gayla, cried as his friends looked on sympathetically, and then the mood spread. They all cuddled together and cried and sobbed. Catan stood by like a rock.

Gayla pulled herself free from the cuddling children. "Maybe we can do something about the Festival." She had no tears and still wore that pretty smile. "You know kids, this year could be different." The children wiped their tears from their faces, and sobbed. She continued, "If you can keep it a divine secret I can give you an option." The children began to smile. "Instead of dying for the vile Chi Bantri, you could choose to die for God. It would help us to find God who has gone missing again and you could help to afflict God's return. You can be revered as 'God's Six Catalysts'. What do you think?"

The little boy who began the conversation stood up. "What does God look like?"

Gayla giggled. "You can't see God at the moment. God is everywhere, as a spirit in people and in things. You know kids, there was a lot of God in Saint Catherine and her two angels and that's why they gave their lives for the good of the poor leper children. There's not very much God in Sir

Kamdar and that's why he is such an arsehole. He used to have God, but he replaced it with opium, which destroyed his conscience."

"But you said God is missing."

"God is searching. God cannot do things, just help others to do those things by instilling the spirit, and while God searches, people aren't receiving God's spirit. Instead of having God, they have the depraved Chi Bantri whose spirit breeds greed and conflict. But when God has finished searching he'll be seen, and that's my promise."

"But what is God searching for?"

"Lots and lots of questions today." Gayla looked towards Catan who was standing firm, staying well out of it. "God gets lonely and needs His family. We'll talk further tomorrow." She stood up and hugged the boy. "But don't say anything about this to anybody."

She took hold of Catan's left arm.

Catan asked, "I take it you have a plan? If not you shouldn't have said those things to the children." She was a little annoyed.

"Yes, I do, as you well know. We need a catalyst, something the sect will never expect. It'll need great personal sacrifice."

They looked over towards the crowd. It was growing rapidly, beginning to break out onto the square and Ninah stood in front of them.

Catan asked, "How many are there?"

The little girl stretched her head around and estimated, "About seven, maybe eight thousand. They're deep down the side streets. Could be more."

"Then I think that's enough to spread our word to everybody. Seven thousand should be able to tell one hundred thousand. I'll address them now."

Gayla ran over to the soldiers at the gate and told them that Her Highness was to address the slum. The soldiers instantly got on the phone. By the time Gayla had got back to

143

Catan's arm there were a hundred or so soldiers around the gate.

Catan and Gayla walked slowly towards Ninah. The crowd began to shout and cheer. As they reached the centre of the square, a motorcyclist caught them with a message from the Monsignor. Gayla read it.

"What the hell are you doing?" is what he asked. She laughed.

Catan sternly told the messenger, "Tell him, 'Addressing my people. What the hell d'you think I'm doing?' Tell him exactly that."

They continued walking as the messenger retired. They approached to within about fifty yards of the crowd and stopped. The noise lowered and the crowd began kneeling. Soon they were all kneeling, heads down and clenching their hands. They all prayed. Ninah stood firm. He then walked towards the Princess before kneeling and praying.

"Please remain kneeling, but look to me." Catan spoke very loudly and clearly through her hood. "I've never spoken to my people since the killing of my family. This is an historic day for all of us. I hope not too many are missing due to the disease." She paused for thought. Gayla whispered continually. "The plague which has hit us will soon be controlled. The Lamma forced the World to care. The Lamma has now made them deliver the serum." The crowd began to whisper and mumble. "Please give me the respect of silence while I speak to you. Thank you. Tomorrow morning the serum will be delivered to the Fort. You'll be immunised against the disease." They were taking a big risk, not being certain that the Monsignor had sourced the serum. "I understand that you're disappointed by the death of the Europeans. You must not lose your faith." She deliberately stopped and the crowd were visibly begging her to continue. As they began to mumble she stepped in. "I *will* deliver the Queen." The crowd started talking to one another and smiling. "I'll deliver *your* Queen. And I'll deliver the Lamma."

The crowd was getting excited, maybe too excited. "But *first* I'll deliver the serum."

They bravely walked towards the crowd who all began praying. As Catan and Gayla reached them, they shuffled aside on their knees to allow passage and so the Princess and Gayla very slowly walked through most of the dwellers. It was such a moving occasion that many of them began to cry. An eerie wailing began.

As the girls left the crowd and returned to the open square, the wailing continued. The two revered children turned to walk back to the Fort and the wailing developed into loud shouting and cheering, like a war cry. They followed the girls across the open square toward the Fort gates and Ninah hurriedly caught them up to defend their backs, but they never looked back.

The soldiers at the Fort gate had taken up their defensive positions, guns loaded and ready. Many more had joined the force, but it would never have held the thousands for very long.

"Stop!" shouted an officer, but the crowd continued to walk towards them at the same pace as the Princess. The soldiers kneeled and aimed their guns.

The Princess stopped fifty yards from the gate. The crowd stopped behind her.

She demanded, "Put the guns down! That's an order."

The officer replied, "We've instruction from the Monsignor. None of them will pass."

"They don't intend to. They'll wait here in the square for the serum. It'll arrive tomorrow." She turned to the crowd, who immediately went onto their knees. "Believe in me, and believe in your Queen, and believe in God."

They turned, and then walked to the gate and the soldiers allowed the girls to pass. The guns were lowered, but they held their positions. It was going to be long night for all involved.

Inside the gates the Monsignor waited. He was with Cardinal Mateo.

"What're you doing?" snapped the Monsignor.

"Saving your butts." Catan was enjoying the game. "If the serum isn't available tomorrow they'll be in the Fort. They'll kill you all. Perhaps it's now your turn."

The Monsignor was not going to lie down easily. "Your Highness. You are a guest in this Fort, you always have been, a welcome guest, and a working guest. Don't spoil it."

"Is that a threat, big man?" I do not know if that was Gayla or Catan.

"I cannot threaten you. We all need each other, if we die, you die, if you die, we die. It's not acceptable but that's the edge on which we have to balance."

"Is the serum on its way?"

"Yes. It was difficult, many other important people want it and they can only make a certain amount each day. They didn't want to use it in the slum."

Catan laughed, and then slowly said, "This is a day of historic events. The slum will come first. Has that *ever* happened before? I'll not forget the part that the Chi Bantri has played, with its fingers in every government and conglomerate pie. My sister and I thank you, Monsignor."

The Monsignor bowed his head.

Gayla looked at His Eminence and she rubbed her tummy. He smiled and said to Catan in English, "It seems that your daddy is at home today. Please translate to Gayla."

Catan smiled through her mouth hole. "I like a sense of humour. Let's see how much you're laughing if the serum doesn't arrive."

He responded, "Ca'an, I'm gaining higher respect for you both, as every second passes."

She grinned. "Then take what you've learned back across the World with you. Tell some truths, and they'll compliment the myths."

Gayla looked around the parade ground. The soldiers had rounded up all the children and placed them in front of the quarters to the left, so the girls collected their six children and retired to their room where Catan played the guitar for them, as she had promised.

A few hours later it was dark. The girls needed to get to work again, back to the job of preparing their Mummy and Daddy for their long awaited return. Ninah had called to Gayla that the clinics were clear and all talk about burning them had stopped. So far, so good. The rear Gates were congested by the soldiers and the slum dwellers, and so they needed to find another way out and into the slum.

Catan had been around for long enough to know where the escape routes were. The cellars below the staff quarters were quite extensive and, as with all buildings of war, harboured a tunnel to the outside. They crept out unnoticed. The exit took them into the correct part of the slum, not very far from the clinics, and they managed to creep through the smelly streets unnoticed, almost. An old lady bumped into them, but fled when she realised who they were.

Standing in front of the toilet window, Catan called to Robin.

"Ca'an!" Robin had heard her, and rushed through to the toilet. "You've come back." He was overwhelmed. "She's still alive. It's a miracle."

Gayla laughed with excitement. She whispered.

Catan asked, "Are you ok, Daddy? We've been worrying about you all day."

"Yes, I'm good. Tracy's still cold and shivery, but she's alive. I think she still has a fever. We owe her life to your miracle."

"Where are the worms?"

Robin looked down. "They escaped. I'm sorry."

Gayla poked Catan as she whispered.

"I know. Robin, don't sit or lay on the floor, the worms might harm you if you do. Otherwise, don't worry about it, we can get some more if we need them."

"Tracy is on the bed and I'll make sure she stays there." He hesitated. "What can we do now?"

"You'll need to feed her. She'll not get better if she doesn't eat. Give her some substance and she'll mend *very* quickly. The worms will have left the wounds clean and sterile, so long as you look after them they'll heal very quickly. But she *must* eat."

"We haven't got any food, just gallons of water and salt. We had some rice which was left here, but that's gone now, and we're out. We're getting really hungry. Can you get us anything?"

Catan shook her head. "This plywood is real, we can't get anything through it. You must feed her yourself. Keep her watered and she might be ok for a few more days."

"But there's nothing. I've searched everywhere."

"And what did you find?"

"I found this grey powder, but it tastes like shit, and might be poisonous. I'll show you some." He went into the laboratory and returned with a jar full of grey powder. "Look."

"That's really good, but you can't eat it, it *is* poisonous. Good job you didn't try very much." There was a label on the jar which was in Bengali. Gayla strained to read it and whispered to Catan who said, "When you need it you should mix it with one part water and one part powder, easy. Keep it in a sealed jar so it doesn't dry out. It will keep when mixed up, so do a load soon, just in case."

"When will I need it?"

"We'll see how you are tomorrow. Meantime give Mummy lots of water, and keep her eye dressed. It should heal quickly, the worms are very efficient. Oh, and is there any ranar plant in the lab? Search it out and we'll see you tomorrow."

Gayla smiled and blew Robin a kiss, and then they were gone. He was so dejected by their sudden exit from his dream. He knew that they were keeping him hooked on a line, slowly playing him in, ready for use, but he could not make out, though, whether they were divinely good or just plain evil. Sometimes there is such a fine line between the two.

Catan and Gayla crept their way back to the Fort unnoticed.

The next morning there was a lot of activity throughout the Fort. The dwellers were still crowded into the square and the soldiers were standing firm, but seriously tired. The girls went outside with their children to see a truck moving past the main building towards the parade ground. It was a Sensar Pharmaceuticals vehicle!

"They've come!" shouted the Cardinal from across the parade ground. He put his thumb into the air in salutation and walked over to the girls. "You've succeeded, Your Highness. Congratulations." He was very pleased for their success, and I do not think it was totally selfish. He needed the serum, but he was content to wait his turn, and to allow the slum to be immunised first. "I hope there's enough for us after those poor folk are done."

They followed the truck which was shepherded out through the gates. The crowd was elated. They began chanting and dancing. This was not just a load of medicine, it was a delivery from their Queen and her Lamma, and it was the dawn of new hope for them. General Dara stood in front of the crowd with ten of his men. Sir Kamdar stood with him.

"Your Highness, may we have a word?" called General Dara. Catan and Gayla approached them. "We've a difficult project on our hands. Sir Kamdar and I must ensure that the inoculations are carried out quickly and efficiently. We've over one hundred thousand people to administer to. We must ensure that law and order doesn't break down, else the work may never be completed." He bowed to the girls, and then saluted the Cardinal. Sir Kamdar did likewise.

Catan spoke to General Dara. "D'you need us to do anything? Between you, you have thousands of soldiers."

"Yes, we have the soldiers, but as our eyes can witness right now, *you* have the people. We need to split the people into two groups, those who've had polio and need innoculating and those who have *not* had polio. We must conserve the amount of serum and use it only on the polio sufferers as they're the ones at risk." He looked for a response from the Princess.

Catan and Gayla walked further away from the crowd, to ensure privacy. The General and Sir Kamdar followed.

With Gayla whispering, Catan replied, "That's a fact, but these people may not understand that. If many of them aren't to be inoculated they may feel dejected and at risk, and therefore most will claim to have had polio. Your serum will quickly be depleted." Gayla whispered while Catan stood silent and the General and Sir Kamdar awaited further input from the girls. Catan spoke to Gayla in Qeervi, and then returned her head towards the General. "How will the inoculations be administered?"

The General called one of the pharmaceutical workers from the truck and asked the same question. The worker replied, "They'll be injected under high pressure, straight into the blood system and hence no needles will be used, no contact and no cross-infection. It's very economical and very fast."

Catan asked, "Will you be able to administer one hundred thousand, or so, today?"

He replied, "One hundred thousand can be done in about fourteen hours, if the people are properly presented to the nurses, without any break. We've eight units, and with a change of staff after seven hours we could do it. But, big but, we may have a problem; we only have serum for about sixty thousand. Sorry."

"Not a problem," replied Catan. "Only about forty percent have had polio. About forty thousand, that's all the serum required for the slum. The others without polio can have sterile water. Don't tell anybody, and that way they'll believe they've all been immunised, and so won't all claim to have had polio. That means that there'll be ample left for the Fort and the soldiers." She turned to Sir Kamdar. "This's your chance to shine, and help your people, Sir. Don't fuck up!"

The worker nodded to Catan. "That's a good idea, it'll work. I'll instruct my staff and urge absolute silence. The others will be here in about six hours." He had obviously carried out this type of work many times before.

The crowd were sympathetically moved back away from the gates to allow the immunisation stations to be set up. The two stations, each with four units, were split with one to the left of the gates and one to the right.

The Princess and Gayla slowly walked towards the centre of the arena, and the people bowed their heads and moved aside to allow them access and space. When the girls stopped the crowd all got down onto their knees and prayed. Catan allowed them some time, and then she demanded, "Now you must all listen carefully. Remain on your knees but look to me." She spoke loudly and clearly through her silk hood. "The Lamma's promise has been delivered." General Dara grinned in appreciation of the girls' cunning. He was a devoted supporter of the Princess, but wary of her little sister. She continued, "There are two types of serum, and it's important that you offer yourselves up for the correct one. There's plenty, so take your turn without greed or disrespect, and any person found to be fighting or pushing will be put to the back of the very long queue. Help the old and the young and then we can all receive the inoculations today. 'Obey the soldiers', *that* is my order." She deliberately stopped to judge the mood. It was good. Catan pointed to the station which had been set up to the left of the gates. "There are two types of serum. That side is for those who've had polio during their life. *Everybody* who has had polio should start to move to that side. *Everybody* else should move to the other side. If you think you've had polio, go to the polio side. Any of the children who don't know or don't have anybody to speak for them, stay in the middle. Some of the nurses will help those children to decide." She again waited for a few moments, this time while the murmuring died down. "We will, though, first pray for our Queen and her Lamma, whose love, from beyond the immortal, remains with us." Catan and Gayla kneeled and prayed for their parents. The crowd prayed and were joined by the soldiers and nurses. There fell a frightening silence which held for about three minutes before Catan and Gayla rose from their knees.

Catan raised her arms into the air. "Your silent prayers will be answered!" They turned to move back to the gate as the crowd burst into life. They all hurriedly started moving to their selected sides. The children who stayed in the middle of the square were led by soldiers to an area where the nurses assessed them, for polio or not. When in doubt they sent them to the polio side. The others moved themselves, herded by the soldiers, to their sides, many helping old or infirm, and the flow of inoculations began in earnest. The nurses worked so hard, and the majority of the soldiers handled the people firmly, but fairly and sympathetically. Any who did not were sent to Sir Kamdar to face his wrath. Maybe he was becoming infected by God. Maybe not.

The logistics of herding one hundred thousand people through the stations and back into the slum was a potential nightmare, but everybody behaved impeccably. The work took only thirteen hours and a proud team of nurses and aids stood in front of the gates, totally exhausted. The Fort would have to wait until tomorrow!

Night fell, the crowd had returned to their hovels, and the medical team had gone home for the night. It was time for the girls to go to their other work. Catan hung her sword around her waist and they escaped through the cellar and entered the slum, unnoticed. The route through the smelly streets to the clinic was all clear.

"Robin, we're here," Catan called. "Are you there?"

Robin ran into the toilet. "Thank God, I thought you'd given up on us. Please, we need food." He stared through the boarded window at Catan and Gayla. "Have you brought food?"

"We can't give you food. The clinic is boarded up. We bring you cheer." Gayla whispered at Catan's side.

"Ca'an, I'm your Dad. Please help us, cheer won't do. Mummy's starving, I think she'll die if she doesn't eat." He was desperate. "Mummy might die."

Catan held her hand on her sword and slowly said, "You might have to feed her yourself."

Robin fell to his knees. "What d'you mean? I'll do anything."

Gayla tugged at Catan's left arm. "Gayla says I'm wrong, but I think there's only one way to save Mummy. Feed her!"

"How can I feed her? There's no food!" Robin held his hands to his face. He was on the point of breaking down. "I'll do anything. Anything!"

"She can eat you." Catan grinned as she spoke. "You're the food of the Gods." She watched Robin shrink even closer to the ground. "But Gayla says no. She doesn't think you should." The two girls stood in silence.

Robin began to pull himself together. He stretched up, still on his knees, and said to Catan, "How can I feed her?"

Gayla whispered, Catan said "Gayla says there's no way, I think there is. Gayla says you should save your own life, and let Mummy die. She's wrong. You're the Lamma, the Queens' protector. You must protect her." They all thought. "I think you should feed her your left leg. Gayla doesn't agree, but you can live without your leg. Gayla says not to do it. I say do it."

Robin sank down to the ground. He was crying in despair as he tried to comprehend what his two children were telling him. There is a very fine line between divine good and pure evil, and the two were playing one against the other. Robin broke.

"Ok." He lay down on the floor.

Catan shouted, "Daddy, get up from the floor or the worms'll get you!" Robin suddenly awoke from his despair and jumped up.

"The worms. They're our friends, aren't they?"

"Only when it suits. But what're you going to do about Mummy?" Catan asked.

"I'll do it. Will it save her?"

"Maybe." Catan lowered her hooded head. "Gayla says maybe not. It's your call, Daddy. Only *you* can make the decision."

He looked at the two sisters, one smiling as always, the other hidden behind her hood. "I'll do it for Tracy. I love her, I want to do it." He put his hands to his head. "How will you do it?"

"Do what?" asked Catan.

"Cut my leg off."

Catan hesitated. "We can't do that, we're outside and you're in." She looked down at Gayla. "Gayla says you shouldn't do it, anyway. She says it'll kill you, the pain. I think you should at least try. If you die, you die. But Gayla doesn't agree." Gayla waved her arm towards Robin to attract his attention. "Gayla says she loves you more than anything in the World. She says you must do what you think is right. She'll still love you whatever you do." Catan's voice showed a whisker of humanity. "I think you must do what the Lamma would do, Daddy. We both love you, but Gayla has a different type of love for you than I."

Robin was starving, distressed, and now confused. "What should I do?"

Catan scratched her head through the hood, then said, "You must cut your leg off and feed it to Mummy. Or you must leave your leg and hope that she survives." She hesitated and shrugged her shoulders. "You know what we both think, opposites. It must be your choice."

Robin held his hand against the window. "Can I think about it?"

Catan replied, "Don't do anything silly. See you tomorrow." Gayla blew him a kiss.

"But….."

They were gone. The desperate Robin was left alone with Tracy to make such a decision, one which was to be prejudiced by hunger and solitude. He moved to the bedroom and lay with her on the bed.

The next morning the Fort was buzzing. The medical crew was back administering the vaccine to the more 'worthy' members of society, including the Cardinal. He was waiting on the parade ground when the sisters emerged with their children.

"Good morning, Ca'an and Gayla. I hope you slept well." He bowed his head to reveal the top of his scarlet zucchetto. He was also wearing his white cassock and a scarlet sash. His pectoral cross shone out over his sash. He smiled, "Please say hello to your daddy."

Gayla returned a smile and rubbed her tummy.

"Good morning Louis," replied Catan. "You're well dressed on this hot day. Are you planning on going somewhere?"

"Yes. I've been inoculated. So has my team. We'll be leaving, soon."

"You may need to dress down a bit." Gayla was whispering.

The Cardinal quizzed with a frown, "How do you know what I'm wearing?"

"My Eyes tells me everything." She smiled through her hood. "We spoke with the Monsignor yesterday about the quarantine. Although you and many others have been inoculated, you can still be carrying for a while. The disease is

155

not well studied yet. The Fort and the slum will continue the isolation for a further ten days. You're still quarantined."

His Eminence was disappointed.

"Louis, you're a high ranking Cardinal, a man of the cloth as they say, and you should be pleased to be part of such a humanitarian decision. As a member of the inner court, you should've been privy to all such decisions."

"Ca'an, as you know, you were instrumental, the Fort is currently in a state of emergency, remember? Monsignor Plassey is free to make all decisions without the guidance of the court."

Catan bowed and smiled. "Perhaps the Fort should continue in emergency. The Monsignor's a good man, now. Unusual within the Chi Bantri."

"I think you're talking out of hand. We're the biggest and most powerful sect in the World. We live to help others. Just check out the history."

"I could write a very different history, it could be called 'The Truth'. You cause a disaster and then you resolve the disaster and then you reap the personal gains. You're the biggest funny handshake club anybody has ever known. And you spread the word of 'God', I don't know which God, but it isn't the one I know."

The Cardinal seemed frightened. He shuffled his feet. Gayla laughed, and then carried on whispering.

"Ca'an, I'm a leading member of the Roman Catholic Church, and you question my faith in God. I've earned my position through devotion to God and his children. You're insulting me."

"Just trying to save your soul, before it's lost forever to the Chi Bantri. You can still walk away from this evil."

"I don't understand quite what your problem is."

"What about the earthquake in the Daiktara region?" There was a moment silence. "A region which was governed by democratic process. Buoyant, moral and just. A model community where everybody was given their chance in their one, single life."

He butted in, "They were recovered and re-established by the Cambodian government."

"And who's a member of the Chi Bantri? In the Cambodian government?"

The Cardinal snapped, "Exactly, and he was assisted by other key members from Thailand." The Cardinal was becoming aggressive. "Our influence restored the area's industry, and the rebuilding still continues."

"But who now owns the industry? Was it donated by the previous owners, or was it taken from them?" She waited for a reply, it did not come. "And why did it take over three weeks for the aid to arrive? I need an answer from you, the high flying church-goer."

He scowled. "The routes were cut off by the Khmer Rouge forces. The aid couldn't get there!"

"And which Chi Bantri high member, in the Khmer Rouge, organized that, for long enough for the region to be completely destroyed? And during that time over forty thousand people died. The key leaders who didn't die from the disaster were removed by the Khmer Rouge, clearing the way for your take-over. And it was all an act of God. An earthquake." Gayla watched for Catan as he sank his head. "You're part of the movement which took away the region's democratic status and replaced it with a dictatorship, killing over forty thousand people in the process. That's not the work of good people. You all now own the rights to the mineral deposits in the region of Daiktara and it only cost forty thousand lives." Catan remained calm, as always. "You *can* renounce your membership of this cult."

The Cardinal breathed heavily and looked around. "Are these children reliable?" He was looking at the girls' six children.

"They are the adopted children of God. Based on your own beliefs, they might strike you down, but they'll not tittle-tattle. They're the revered 'God's Six Catalysts'."

"I don't understand what you're saying."

"You will, soon."

The Cardinal was relaxing a little. "May I trust you?" Catan nodded. "Could I walk away from this without being killed?"

"Of course not." She listened to Gayla for a few seconds. "If you leave this cult you'll be killed. But remember this, if you stay in this cult you'll be killed. How the fuck do the Chi Bantri recruit people into such a quandary? Powerful, intelligent, *stupid* people."

The Cardinal gave some thought, then, "People are paranoid about losing what they have. That's how they recruit, by guaranteeing your position for life. We all scratch each other's backs, from the presidents, to the chairmen, to the bishops, to the generals and right down to the governors and care workers in the children's homes. There's not an area in the World which isn't touched by the Chi Bantri." They all stood in silence.

Gayla whispered and Catan said, "We already knew all of this, but we wondered if the high members knew it. It's been good to find the truth, it'll help to justify our actions." They began to turn away, but Gayla pulled back. Catan asked, "Would you cut your own leg off for your loved one?"

The Cardinal stood silently whilst he thought. "I've never loved to that extent. But I believe it would take a very special person to make such a personal sacrifice. I don't believe that it would be normal human behaviour."

"Thank you, Your Eminence. Daddy needed to know." Gayla rubbed her tummy with a grin. "You've been interesting company. You must, though, consider your true devotion."

"Ca'an, I've been honest with you. Will you be honest with me? I only know what I've been indoctrinated with.

We're brainwashed. But who are you?" He held his hands together is if to pray. "Please tell me. Help me."

Catan looked down at Gayla and spoke Qeervi. She looked up at the Cardinal then carefully picked her words. "I'm Princess Ca'an of Anglia. I've been trapped here for two hundred and forty years, since my family went home, without me. I'm the divine blood which runs through the veins and arteries of the Chi Bantri. I feed their spirit. They'll die without me, but when I'm beckoned I'll go home with my family. They will *all* then go home, to somewhere, or nowhere." She stood motionless. "My mummy's been searching for many years. She's at last found what she seeks. We are one, almost." Maybe Catan should have cried, but she never cried.

The children were subdued as they moved to Catan, and they all cuddled, but Gayla continued to smile as she soothed the children.

"Louis, these children are on the menu for the Festival of Life. Will you be there?"

The shocked Cardinal fell to his knees. "Please forgive me, Your Highness. I'm your servant. I beg forgiveness. I'll do anything." He held his hands together as he kneeled.

"Louis, you can't do anything for us, but we like your company." Gayla giggled as she ruffled his zucchetto about his head, and that made Catan smile and the children chuckle.

The sisters walked back to their room with the children, leaving a lost soul to fight with his conscience.

Colin Hodgson

11 -- A PERSONAL SACRIFICE

The Isolated Clinic

Robin and Tracy were getting seriously hungry. The isolation, hunger, depression and confusion were really closing in on poor Robin. Tracy was still drifting in and out of coma or sleep and her strength was rapidly draining.

The two had not eaten very well since arriving. Apart from a handful of rice, the last food they ate was the breakfast before leaving for the party with Saint Catherine. It was just lentils and rice and that was five days earlier. The belly full of whisky with Saint Catherine probably did not count for much.

As night fell, Robin desperately strained to see the girls outside the toilet window. They did not arrive. "Darling, we might be alone. What should I do?" He looked lovingly into her damaged face but she did not respond.

He walked to the toilet, but nobody was there. In desperation he went through to the laboratory. The large window which looked out along the street to the open area was partly obscured by boxes. He moved some of the boxes which held bandages and there was a crack where the ply boards had been butted up. His hands shook as he pulled his eye to the crack.

"I can see out. It's dark." As he stared out, an area lit up and there sat Saint Catherine, glass of whisky in her hand and being tended by her lovely angels. "Saint Catherine!" he shouted. She looked happily towards him and raised her glass. Then she was gone. What could he dream about now?

"Daddy." A soft voice beckoned him. "Daddy."

"Is that you, Ca'an?" He strained to see through the crack. "Where are you?"

"In the toilet."

He scrambled from the window and sped into the toilet, and there they were. He had a tear in his eye. "Thank God. You've come."

"Hello Daddy. We've been so busy, sorry we're late." Gayla held onto Catan's arm and smiled. "Have you been looking after Mummy? She's our life you know." Gayla whispered constantly. "You must make a decision about feeding her."

Robin, confused, thought hard. "I want to speak to Gayla. I don't want Ca'an."

"This is Gayla." Gayla looked constantly at Robin. "Why're you thinking that?" Catan continued to speak for Gayla. "You must understand who you are. You're my daddy, and you must save my mummy from going home early. If you *don't* she will just go home before us, and we'll catch her up later, that's all. But the World is waiting for Mummy and they expect the Lamma to bring her to them, in *this* World." Catan paused as Gayla whispered more. "And if you send Mummy home, she'll be alone. She doesn't want to be alone."

Robin thought to himself about life without her.

"And *you* don't want to be alone. If you wish, you can both go home together. You can be happy." Gayla whispered loudly. "But *we* don't want to be alone, either. So please stay here, for us."

Robin realised what she was saying and asked, "What are we all, if we stay together?"

Gayla answered through Catan, "We're a family. We're *the* family, like no other. Make your decision, Daddy."

Robin left the window and went through to Tracy. He asked in her ear, "D'you want to stay here?" She said nothing. "I understand, sweetie. Please forgive me for what I'm about to do." He slowly got to his feet and returned to the girls. "Tracy said to let her go." He stared at Gayla. "But I'm going to do what I feel is right. She'll feed on my flesh." He was so calm about the decision. "It's only a leg, a bargain if I get my darling's life in return."

Gayla and Catan jigged with delight. Catan said, "Thank you, Daddy. The World will owe you one."

Robin sat down on the floor and Catan shouted, "Get up! The worms are still about." He jumped up. She asked, "Did you find any ranar plant?"

He went to the living area and returned with a bottle of clear liquid. "Is this it?"

Gayla studied the label. "Yes. Good. We'll tell you what to do. We can't help you."

Robin was tired, so he fetched a chair from the living area and sat.

Catan began. "First you must prepare. The grey powder has to be mixed up and ready. Mix equal parts powder and equal parts water. Do it now."

Robin fetched the powder and a large jar.

"That's a good jar, your leg will fit in the top."

Robin mixed up some of the powder with drinking water, and whisked it to a cream. He put the lid on the jar.

"The mix must be applied to the open wound. As soon as the leg is off, you must put the jar over the stump to engulf it with the mix. Leave it on for about half an hour, and the mix will fuse to your wound, then you can remove the leg from the jar. There should be no more bleeding and the mix will accelerate the growth of skin across the wound. Doctor

Hussain has used this method several times in *very* special emergencies. You must leave the grey covering alone. It'll harden and you'll be able to touch it, but don't interfere with it. And remember it's very poisonous. Are you ok?"

"Yes, I've got that."

"Next the ranar plant extract. You must make up several swabs with bandages. Put several drops of the plant extract onto each swab and put them into a jar to prevent drying out. When you need one, remove it from the jar and it'll last for several hours. Make them up while we're here."

Robin collected some bandages and tied them into knots, then cut them apart. To each knot he put four drops of plant extract, and placed them into a jar. He put the lid on.

"Good, they're sufficient. They're needed to prevent you from fainting or going into coma during the operations. You can use one of them to wake Mummy. She'll stay awake long enough to help you with the guillotine but don't wake her until you're ready for her, and allow her to go off when she's done. It'll seriously tire her. Is that ok?"

"What do I do with them?"

"You smell them. Every few minutes have a sniff and you'll not go off unless you're dead. Powerful stuff." They broke for a few seconds. "While you're operating, it may be a good idea to tape a swab below your nose because if you go out with the pain you could bleed to death. You must stay awake until the poultice has sealed the wound. Are you with us?"

"I think so." He was afraid. "I'm scared. How do I get my leg off?"

Gayla spoke to Catan in Qeervi. Robin was able to understand some of it. She said that he may not be able to think well enough with the pain.

"Daddy, what if you forget what to do?"

"I don't know. I don't even know what to do now."

Gayla giggled, and Catan said, "Silly us, we haven't told you yet." They both chuckled like a couple of children. "We'd better tell you. You're happy with the prep's so far?"

"Yes, the poultice and the plant."

Catan began again. "Well, we don't think you'll be able to stitch the flesh over the wound in the state you'll be in, that's why you must use the poultice. It creates a sort of cancer which results in the flesh around the wound multiplying at an accelerated rate, very fast. The skin'll be growing over the wound in just a few days, especially for a young stud like you." Gayla chortled and blew him a kiss. "That means you can just chop it straight off, in one go. Much quicker and more possible for you to achieve. And the leg will be clean and fresh, ready for eating." Pause. "You and Mummy will soon be up and away with the Gods."

"Not sure what you mean by that. But don't tell me now." He at last smiled at Gayla's pretty face. "Who's telling me this?"

"It's Gayla, she's a mine of knowledge. She must get it from her dad." They all laughed. "Back to business. You've been in the laboratory and have noticed the cutting tools in one corner."

"Yes. How did you know that?"

"You don't need to know. Later. There's a guillotine in that corner, on which you can fix a leg clamp. You've been quarantined in the best place in the World." They all laughed again. The fear was intoxicating Robin. "You must put a polythene sheet on the floor to keep our friends away, then lift the guillotine down, then fit the leg clamp. Once your leg's in it, Mummy can push down the handle, and hey presto! Your leg is off. Then you put the stump in the jar and half an hour later you can dine. There are burners in the lab, gas is still there, and there's salt. How does Mummy like her steaks?"

The three of them really giggled like a bunch of school kids. Those girls were accomplished players of mind games and they had actually convinced Robin that he was enjoying the challenge. His fear had completely gone.

"Right, we must go. You must make sure everything is ready before you cut. The poultice, the swabs, the guillotine and leg clamp, and Mummy of course. She must push the handle down as fast as she can, with power. Ok Daddy? Good luck."

Gayla held her hand on the ply, and Robin placed his opposite. She spoke Qeervi. "I love you Daddy." She blew him a kiss and they were gone.

Reality again hit Robin hard. He sat on the chair, poultice and drugs at the ready, and his lover still dying on the bed. He had to be brave.

The two girls found their way safely back into the Fort and rejoined their children.

One of the boys asked Catan, "Have you found your Daddy?"

She smiled through he hood. "Why d'you ask?"

"One of the soldiers looking after us earlier said you had."

"Hmm. What did you tell him?"

"Just said we didn't know anything."

Catan pulled the boy to him and gave him a cuddle. "You're very good children. Don't tell anybody anything. But my Daddy? I might've done. We'll know tomorrow, after a very special test, and then I'll tell you. I'm so excited."

The boy waved his arm and the other five gathered around in the cuddle.

He asked, "When will we die for God? We've been talking. We don't want to go to the Festival to die. We know God is back, and we want to die for Her."

Gayla pushed in, laughing and playing. "We've still gotta sort that one. Come on, Ca'an can play to us!" They all sat in a circle around Catan, and Gayla passed her the guitar. Catan was a splendid guitarist.

Once the children were asleep, Gayla said to Catan, "I need to see Ninah. I want to make sure that they're keeping clear of the clinics."

"You could do that from here." Catan was suspicious, being cut off from Gayla's thoughts.

Gayla bit her bottom lip. "I want to see him. D'you mind? It's nothing serious."

Catan said nothing.

"I won't be long. I love my little girl, and I'll be straight back to you, promise." She removed Catan's hood to reveal such a wonderful looking girl, dark and clean. An absolute beauty, with black shiny hair beyond her shoulders, and perfect features. She closed her eyes as Gayla kissed her gently on the lips. "I won't be long."

She left the Fort through the secret exit and moved like a creature of the night into the slum. She dodged the few people still about, but as she turned round one corner there stood a large body. It was Ninah.

"Where're you going?" he asked. "The Princess's been left alone."

"She's ok for a while. She's with our children. I've a meeting, please step aside. I'll speak to you tomorrow. Come into the Fort and we can discuss the way ahead."

Ninah bowed his head and stood aside.

Inside the clinic Robin had the guillotine set up and ready. The poultice was positioned beside where he would be laying. The top was loose. The swabs had been placed beside the poultice. "I think I'm ready." He was trying to convince himself. The intoxication had worn off and the fear had returned. "Don't know if I can." He went through to Tracy. "What do I tell her?" He sat on the bed and looked at her eye-patch. "They got it right that time, perhaps they're right this time. Please help me Trace." He took a deep breath to try to hold back the tears.

Suddenly he could hear some other breathing from behind him, at the bedroom door. He turned around, and it was

Gayla! It was like a gift from above. He stood up and began laughing. "Gayla!"

She ran over to him and he picked her up. She wrapped her arms around his neck, and kissed him, full and long, and then kissed his neck. In Qeervi she whispered, "I love you Daddy. I'm scared for you." She pulled back to look him straight in the face. "I *will* help you. Do you understand?"

He just grinned in astonishment. "How'd you get in? Can we get out?"

"Speak Qeervi. I know you can." She looked like a child, but kissed like an adult. She pulled his head to hers and kissed him again, as he squeezed her tiny body to his chest. "I will *help* you, but *you* and Mummy must do it. If you want you can leave it, and Mummy can go home. But she can't go home on her own, that would be so cruel." She raised her eyebrows. "You *could* go with her."

His Qeervi was rusty, but he explained, "We'll stay. I'll cut off my left leg to feed the Queen. I'm beginning to understand."

Gayla let out a screech of delight. She kissed him again, but this time a peck, much more suitable for a father and child. "I'll tell you what to do," she promised.

She dropped down from Robin's grasp and fetched a swab of ranar extract. "Wake Mummy up with this."

He held the swab below her nose. After about two minutes she began to stir and Gayla wriggled as her mummy came round. Tracy opened her eye. It was damp and she squinted, trying to focus on Robin.

"Darling. I need your help. Just for a while," he whispered.

"Are we still alive?"

"Of course. And so is Gayla, look." He pulled her head up a bit so that she could look at the grinning daughter. He asked, "Will you be able to help me? We've an urgent job to do."

With Robin's help she sat upright, and stretched her neck. "I'm stiff, and hungry. And thirsty." Gayla ran out and filled two mugs with water. Robin helped Tracy to drink the water, then with some prompting from Gayla, he drunk the other one. "What should I do?" Tracy asked.

"You need to push down on a handle when I tell you to. Then you can go back to sleep." He put the swab to her nose again. She was becoming quite high from the drug.

Gayla spoke in Qeervi to Tracy. "I'll help you into the lab' Mummy." She kissed Tracy on the lips and they both smiled at each other.

Tracy spoke directly into Gayla's face, in Qeervi, "I've been dreaming of you. It was nice. Where's the little girl?"

Gayla laughed. "Ca'an's looking after our adopted children. She's at the Fort."

Robin was beginning to return to fear mode. "Can we get this done, please?" He went into the laboratory and sat down in position, with his left leg in the clamp.

"Ah, Robin. I forgot. The tourniquet! You *must* have a tourniquet." She left Tracy sitting on the bed and ran around the laboratory in search of a suitable tourniquet. Without it he could bleed to death before he could seal the wound. She found a tapered cuff tourniquet. "This'll do for a leg." She helped Robin to fit the tourniquet and tighten it. "Don't tell anybody that I helped you, please." That made Robin smile.

She ran out to the bedroom, where Tracy was waiting, awake but in a half-trance. She helped her to her feet and led her by the hand over to the laboratory, and to the guillotine where Robin sat, ready and sweating profusely.

"Mummy, do you understand me? This is Qeervi."

She looked at Gayla with a quizzed expression. "Of course. Why?"

"Just checking. Can you do what I ask? You must press that handle down right to the ground. You may have to lean on in. I can't help you. Tell me what you've got to do."

She pointed at the long lever. "Push that to the ground."

Gayla looked at Robin, for once, not smiling, and he nodded to her.

"Now do it."

Tracy pushed hard down on the lever. She was finding it very difficult, but it was moving down. As the handle lowered, some gears wound behind the knife, compressing a massive coiled spring. The gears clicked and clicked. She had to almost lay on the handle to keep it going but with her bloody determination it kept lowering. Gayla was willing her on.

Bang! She reached the bottom, and the spring released. The razor sharp blade swung down and the leg was severed!

Silence. Then a scream exploded from Robin's mouth. It was chilling, and Tracy began to cry. Gayla rushed down to Robin and put her hand on his forrid. "Quick! The swab. Quick!"

Tracy calmly leaned down and offered a swab to his nose. He stayed with them, and the screaming lowered. He was shuddering.

"Mummy you can help him, I can't." Tracy was still in a daze, so Gayla stuffed a swab under her nose. "Quick, put that jar over his leg and push in onto the wound."

With Robin shaking and grinding his teeth, she pushed the jar onto his stump. She then released the leg from the clamp. It shuddered as she rested it on her lap.

"Don't take it off for half an hour. Can you do this?" She looked into Tracy's face and kissed her. "Please help him." Tracy was a very fast learner. She held her swab to her nose and smiled at Robin.

"You silly boy, why'd you do such a thing?" She gently stroked his thigh. "You *are* silly." Tracy was still smiling at her hero. "I hope you didn't do this for me."

Gayla pulled at Tracy's shoulder. "I'll stay 'til the jar is off, then I must go."

Tracy suddenly woke up dramatically and was beginning to realise the magnitude of this personal sacrifice. She was no longer smiling while she stroked Robin's forrid and asked, "Why? I'm not *that* hungry. This happened in my dreams." She looked at Gayla through her one eye. "I know what you've done." She stared as Gayla dropped her head. "I'm your mother, explain yourself. Now!"

Gayla looked at the ground, then bent over and kissed Robin, who was half awake. She put the swab to his nose. "He can go to sleep when the jar is off. You must keep him warm"

"Answer me!" Tracy demanded.

"You're my Mummy, you know almost as much as me. I'll say no more."

"Then why doesn't Robin know as much as you?"

"Girls know different things to boys. Bloody obvious, innit?" Gayla sighed. "That was rude." She looked up at Tracy with a face like a little stray kitten, and it was saying 'please take me in'. "Sorry, Mummy." They left Robin for a few seconds and cuddled. "Please don't leave me again. Please."

Tracy's one good eye flowed with tears as they held each other. "I'll never leave you again. Never deliberately. I promise on the Lamma's life."

Gayla released her hold a bit and spoke into Tracy's face. "Sorry, I've made you cwy." She greedily kissed the tears from the side of her face. "I never cwy any more. Not done for many years. When I cwy, the World will change. And if you ever leave me again I'll then cwy forever."

The half hour was up. Tracy carefully pulled the jar from the leg, and then loosened the tourniquet. There was no bleeding. The grey covering just had to harden off.

"I don't need to tell you anything, do I?" whispered Gayla. "But there's something you may not know." She snuggled up to Tracy, who put her arm around her shoulders. "I've been saved by this before, while I was searching. I learned it from a friend, many miles away, when I didn't have the inner strength to get home. When a God is willingly given the flesh of another God they share their strengths. These bodies are

171

weak and prone to damage, but your inner self will gain strength when sharing this bodily flesh. It'll bring you back to me, Mummy. You know the rest."

Gayla kissed Robin goodnight and said, "I'll see you soon." Then the little girl kissed her mummy and went. The poultice quickly hardened so Tracy held Robin against her breast and allowed him to go to sleep.

Gayla sped through the slum, but was stopped dead by Ninah who said very sternly, "I heard the scream."

She looked up at his smiles. He knew what had happened, he was her personal aid and they seldom hid their thoughts from each other.

"I'll serve the Lamma well, as always." He held Gayla's hand and walked her back to the Fort, through the back Gates and to their room.

"I found Ninah. Everything's fine, now."

Next morning Ninah was back at the fort, banging on Catan's door.

"Your Highness. The dwellers will leave the clinics alone, but Sir Kamdar has been ordered to burn the dead bodies. It's important that they're burned, as they'll infect others with all sorts, but they include the Europeans in their plans. I spoke to some of the soldiers and the collection route'll take them to the clinic by late afternoon. We only have about nine hours to resolve this one."

Gayla jumped in. "That's great. We need to speak to General Dara. He must be ready with a secret retreat for Mummy and Daddy. Get one press team to show the world exactly what has returned."

The un-hooded Catan frowned. Her eyes were closed as she looked towards Gayla and asked, "Is this really the time? After all these years, we are presenting our family to the World? It'll be a time of bedlam and uncertainty." She pulled her hood over her face.

Gayla was excited. She wriggled as she said, "I'll sort out Mummy and Daddy. They must look good for the cameras.

The battle's about to begin, brace yourselves, World!" She almost exploded. "YeeHaaaaa!" Ninah laughed. She continued, "Ca'an, darling. You'll have to work without me for a bit. The children will help you. You must get hold of the General quickly, to give him chance to arrange a safe haven. He *must* be able to get them there unchallenged and without any trails. Ninah, organise a representative group from the slum to see the resurrection; these people are important, they're our believers. We'll meet back here at midday. Any questions?" She looked at the others. "Children, you help your Princess. Do exactly as she says."

Gayla and Ninah sped off to do their duties, while Catan stood silently thinking about her own instructions from the 'little girl with the smile'. "Peter, please fetch the phone. The secret one. Please, all do as I ask, and our time of redemption will arrive." The boy went to the corner of the room and lifted a loose floor stone. He pulled out a mobile phone and a charger.

"It might need charging," he whispered.

"As soon as it's charged, could you call the number listed as 'Room Service' and hand the phone to me."

While the children were sleeping Tracy had woken up to her soul; she had eaten the flesh! Her spirit had returned, both physical and inner, as she began to recall her origins. Her inner strength had been fertilized with the food of the Gods and it grew, and her daughter knew that Tracy, her mother, had returned, and most momentously, so did Tracy.

She pulled Robin's sweating head up to hers and she whispered, "You must eat, my treasure." She put his head back on the pillow, and sliced a small piece of muscle from the amputated leg, inspected it carefully, then put it into her mouth. She just loved it. The taste, the feeling of warmth, and the wisdom that it was her darling's, given to her without pressure or influence. She remembered Gayla's words, "When a God is willingly given the flesh of another God they share their strengths." She ate the meat of her God, and she returned. "You must eat."

She collected the jar of poultice from beside the guillotine, and a long-bladed scalpel. With one fast swipe she cut a large slice of muscle from her own calf, and then smothered the wound with poultice, finally wrapping a bandage loosely around the leg. Her lover would eat the flesh of a God! "Eat, my darling." She cut small pieces of flesh from the joint and carefully fed Robin, until it was all devoured. "You can grow with me, my Lamma."

Out in the slum Ninah worked hard, using his influence to gather a representative group of dwellers to witness the resurrection. It included Aalap and Dilshad. They were expecting a blessing of the bodies and so the mood was very mournful.

Catan spoke to the General through their covert phones. They made arrangements for him to meet with them at the clinic at three o'clock, where they would agree the finer details of the plan.

Gayla went to the clinic. She had to get in without being unusually noticed. She made it, after explaining to some interested dwellers that she was searching for Ninah. They went off in different directions to help her search.

There she stood, looking into the bedroom as Tracy ate.

"Mummy!" She let out a loud giggle. "Oops, better be quiet."

Tracy looked at the little girl with a confidence that had not shown before. "Thank you. I know who I am. I know who you are. I know who my Robin is." She stood up and they embraced, pulling Gayla's head hard into her bosom. They stayed like that for several minutes.

"Have you fed Daddy? He needs your strength."

"Yes. He's almost awake, stirring and talking in his sleep."

"I hope he hasn't incriminated himself." Gayla smiled as she said that, but Tracy did not! "You're leaving today. It's great, isn't it? We're back together, Mummy. We can get on with our work again." She pushed away from Tracy, and stared hard at her bosom. She knew that they were her mother's covered breasts and she longed to hold them. "We've got so much to catch up on. I can't wait."

"You've waited for more than two hundred years, what's a few more?" Tracy pushed her away with a giggle. "Let's get on."

They pulled Robin up to a sitting position and spoke to him, to wake his conscience. He stirred and opened his eyes. "Gayla." He kissed her on the cheek.

"Right, everybody'll be here at about four o'clock. We've about six hours left to make you two presentable to the World." Gayla jumped back. "Daddy, you should wear a kurta, like us. I'll get you one before they all turn up. And Mummy, a sari over scarlet cholis, hair flowing around your head, and your eye socket empty and uncovered. Daddy, a lungi, to show off your leg. Ok? But if you're not comfortable, just wear what you like. It's you they need to see, not your clothing."

They all looked at each other. The whirlwind was still smiling but the other two were still chewing the cud, a little confused even with their new inner strengths.

"I'll be back at about three with some others. We're going to have a blessing of your dead bodies, so make sure you're ready."

Gayla fled out. As she crossed the slum, some elated young men shouted her over; they had found Ninah for her. He walked Gayla back to the Fort.

"Everything's arranged with the people. They're very sad." He grinned as he considered the local quake which threatened, at about four o'clock.

Catan, Gayla and Ninah stood on the parade ground with their six children. It was one o'clock in the afternoon. The walk through the cleaner streets to the clinic would take over an hour, so they were waiting to leave. As they impatiently shuffled about, the Monsignor and the Cardinal approached from the main building. They were followed by the Cardinal's team of four, and Sir Kamdar and one of his top ranking generals.

"Good morning Your Highness," said the Monsignor. They all acknowledged each other. Ninah nodded his head towards Sir Kamdar.

The Monsignor had been instructed by his inner court to attend the blessing, just as a precaution. They were playing the situation down, and really treating it like a jest. Their main concerns at that time were the Central American coups; they needed their oil!

Despite the inner court's materialistic faith the Monsignor was concerned at the rise in activity around the Princess. So he decided that he would make history by *walking* the slums. And the Cardinal was so fascinated by the aura which surrounded the Princess and her myths that he just had to go along. And so the group all agreed to walk to the clinic together. They were all looking for something.

"Monsignor," asked Catan, "are you afraid?"

He looked at her, Gayla hanging around her waist along with the ceremonial sword, as he quietly answered, "I'm apprehensive. I rarely feel fear, and I'm sure that these people appreciate the support and protection that they've received over the many years. I do remember, though, that our sect has not always been so humane towards them."

"I wasn't referring to the slum dwellers, they'll not harm you unless I order them to. I was referring to the return of the Queen." Gayla whispered away. "There're two possibilities. You know what they are." She smiled through her hood. "And Cardinal Mateo." He was very conspicuous in his white and scarlet, with his team in their western suites. "You must understand your place in my entourage. Understand?"

"Not exactly, Your Highness. Do we follow on with the carpenter and the children?"

"No. You follow on *behind* the carpenter and our children. This's a family in mourning. Respect us."

He was not at all pleased. He was not used to taking second place to anybody except for the Pope himself. But he fell in behind the family group with the Monsignor and Sir Kamdar. The Chi Bantri general and the Cardinal's team walked at the back. As they set off, out of the Fort's South gate, Ninah looked back and nodded towards Sir Kamdar who returned the acknowledgement.

The word on the street, that they had left, soon spread across the slums. Thousands gathered to see their Princess and her group pass, and they all kneeled down to demonstrate their ever increasing faith in her, and in her family.

The colourful Chi Bantri members were overawed. They felt quite small and exposed, and the realisation of total subordination crept into their bodies as they believed, for the first time in their lives, that one instruction from one other certain person could mean certain death to them all. They had spent their entire lives on the other side of the fence, but now they felt the fear.

The walk was slow. They had to return the crowd's respect by waiting for them to move aside to allow their passage. They all wanted to kneel down to the oncoming Princess, and they patiently took their turns. The girls had been extremely cute with their handling and manipulation of the recent events, and they had established total command of the local people's persuasion or faith. The people felt something special that day.

Finally they arrived at the short street which led to the clinic.

General Dara was already there, and the collection team had just arrived, with their curtained truck to carry the bodies away for cremation. The crowd stopped at the end of the short street. Most of the slum were out, just the old and infirm staying at home. Children jumped up and down to see the royal family, and their support totally filled the open area. They constituted many thousands.

There were two trucks, one for the collection of the dead, and another with an open back which was manned by two Indian army personnel. General Dara stood in front of the open truck, accompanied by Syed, and about twenty representatives of the slum, including Aalap and Dilshad. Standing between the two clinics was Captain Batiste from the United Nations, and he was heading his five personnel, with their blue berets. The BBC film crew were set up behind General Dara.

Catan and Gayla stood in front of the first clinic, the day-centre where Doctor Hussain was interned. One of Sir Kamdar's officers ordered the opening of the clinic and his soldiers pulled the plywood shuttering from the door. The collectors went into the building with a stretcher and after a few minutes returned with a body, covered. Syed slowly walked over to the stretcher and lifted the cover, and his reaction confirmed that it was his uncle. Syed's face filled with grief, and although he already knew the harsh reality, it still hit the spot. One of the representatives from the slum said some words and then walked to the end of the street to inform the slum dwellers that their beloved doctor had gone. The mourning spread right through the crowd and into the slum.

The officer then moved to the laboratory clinic. As he ordered the removal of the shuttering, an eerie hush spread round the entire region and the air chilled. General Dara stood to attention and saluted, whilst the men from the United Nations showed arms.

"Wait!" ordered Catan. She stepped forward and bowed her head. Gayla then looked to the BBC news crew to make sure they were ready. "Does anybody have anything to say, before we raise these two bodies?" Nobody said anything. "Carry on." She stood back with Gayla.

As the soldiers jemmied the plywood from the doorway, there was heard a knocking from inside. The soldiers stopped. Sir Kamdar ordered them to continue, as they did and the plywood was soon removed to reveal the double doors of the clinic. They stood back, a little frightened by the knocking, and overawed by the occasion.

Syed stepped forward. "May I open the doors to my friends?" Catan nodded her approval. As he pushed the doors open, he fell to his knees in shock. There stood Robin and Tracy.

Robin was supported by Tracy, as well a crutch and many sniffs of ranar extract. Wearing a kurta and just boxer shorts, his lower left leg was conspicuous by its absence, just a grey-covered stump. He was so white and stressed. Tracy held firm, propping him up and proudly displaying her distorted, empty left socket, while her hair flew around her head like a flaming red beacon. She wore the colours of the Queen, a white sari over a maroon choli. All but the family stood in total shock, and as the two struggled out of the building and into the view of the World, the crowd went hysterical. The noise from those thousands must have been heard from many miles away, and heralded the return of their beloved saviour and her Lamma. Gayla just giggled and giggled.

"It really is the Queen and her Lamma," said the General to himself. He shouted to his men in the truck. "Help them on board!" His men jumped down and placed some steps to the back of the truck. They then rushed to help them onto the truck.

"Just a moment, please." It was Catan, or was it Gayla? But Catan spoke. "There's no hurry. Please hold me, Daddy." She held her arms out and they embraced, then, despite the noise, she spoke to him quietly. "We're again together. We'll serve our God well."

Robin looked into her hooded face and asked, "Are you crying?"

He could see her mouth through the hood as she replied, "When I cry, we'll fight. Look after the Queen, like a good Lamma." They hugged.

Gayla pulled Robin towards the truck. Tracy was already sitting in the back, but Robin could not manage with his newly missing leg. Ninah rushed over, apologised, then picked him up and placed him in the buck.

The Monsignor asked, "Where're they going?"

General Dara replied, "To your clinic in the industrial area. I'm sure the Chi Bantri will look after them well. But first they'll say a long awaited hello to their people."

The truck slowly moved towards the open area, and the people screamed even louder, moving aside as it crept around the masses to ensure total exposure. The BBC cameras never stopped rolling, and Robin and Tracy never stopped smiling at their minions.

The Monsignor and Sir Kamdar desperately tried to raise support through their phones and radio system, but the General had set a block over the area, and no wireless communication was possible.

Catan, Gayla, Ninah and their children all stood so proud as the truck returned to the clinic, but they never had chance to stand with them because the General waved them out past the UN soldiers and between the two clinics towards the industrial area. They sped away with no goodbyes and no more ceremony.

"I need to warn our clinic!" screamed the Monsignor over the roar of the crowd.

The General walked over to him and said, "I've already arranged for their reception. Your people in the clinic are expecting them."

The Monsignor grumbled about something, which the General could not understand, but it did not matter, the Queen was away. General Dara was ahead of the game.

Catan and Gayla approached the BBC news crew, who had behaved exactly as was contracted, in silence.

"I'm Princess Ca'an of Anglia. You may tell the World of the Queen's arrival with her Lamma." Catan waited for a response. "What's wrong? Not a big enough story for you?"

"Sorry Your Highness, but we're not sure what the story is. Apart from two people leaving a boarded up clinic, who should've died from the plague, and a large number of Indian people getting very exited, and a hooded princess and her little sister."

"That sounds like the start of a *very* good story." They all smiled politely. "You may wish to interview the Monsignor, or His Eminence Cardinal Mateo. They are *full* of good stories." The two girls moved away from the camera which had continued filming during that short discussion. Gayla called Ninah to her.

"We're walking back, now," stated Catan.

The family of nine left the others at the clinic and walked down the street towards the crowd, and as they did Gayla ran over to greet Aalap, Dilshad and Syed, and then rejoined Catan. The noise was too much for them to talk, they all just smiled as their regenerated following began to light up with the promise of hope. Nobody was sure quite what they expected from the family, but they certainly expected. The people all laughed and cried, and the roar heightened as the atmosphere trembled. It was not even possible to hear the engine noise from the helicopter which flew overhead.

They eventually arrived back at the Fort gates, leaving the chanting thousands outside. The reception was not good. It had taken the family two hours to get back to the Fort, during which time the Monsignor and the Cardinal had to be collected by helicopter, as they were so frightened, poor dears. They stood on the parade ground waiting as the family approached them.

"Your Highness. There've been problems." The Monsignor was calm and collected. "I have to speak to the inner court about the television reports. But first I have to speak to you." He looked at the other children. "We should speak in private."

Catan retorted, "We *are* in private, apart from the Cardinal." She looked at her children. "These are my children, this is our cousin, and this is My Eyes."

The Monsignor sighed and looked at the ground. "The Cardinal is with me. He's a higher member and I shouldn't wish to say this without a witness." He shuffled his feet in the dust. "Something has happened to the Europeans."

"Do you mean Queen Maya and her Lamma?"

"Yes, if that's what you call them. They're missing. On the way to the clinic the vehicle drove down a side street, but never came out the other end. The clinic contacted General Dara and they searched the route and the truck was found with two dead soldiers, but no Europeans. The soldiers had had their throats cut." He looked at the Cardinal. "His Eminence will pray for the safe return of your friends."

Gayla spoke to Catan and Ninah in Qeervi, and then Catan said, "Thank you for your concern, Monsignor Plassey, and thank you, Your Eminence for your prayers. We hope you'll also pray for the souls of the two soldiers who lost their lives, and for their families. They died for their Queen and they'll not be quickly forgotten."

"Ca'an." The Monsignor sighed heavily. "The two Europeans, especially with the amputations and the hair, resemble what we know the Queen and her Lamma to have been." He looked at Catan trying to read her response. "I'll report to the inner court just that, two people who looked like the Queen and her Lamma. And they're now missing, presumed dead. Sorry." He had little conviction in his words.

Gayla spoke for herself. "You're afraid. That's the beginning."

The two men looked at Gayla, then at Catan. "What does she mean?" asked the Cardinal.

"I'll ask the children, they might be able to help you." Catan looked to the eight year old children. "Could one of you explain?"

One of the boys, Peter, stepped forward. He chose his words carefully and slowly stated, "If you're afraid, you must confront your fear. If you confront your fear, then you must believe in your fear. If you believe in your fear then you must have a fear, even if you had nothing to fear to begin with."

Gayla gave him a lovely hug. "Well done, Peter. That's exactly what I meant." She laughed and went back to Catan. The girls and the children bid Ninah goodnight and they all retired.

Colin Hodgson

12 – THE GREEN EYED QUEEN

The World outside was buzzing with the news of the Queen's return, followed by the Queen's disappearance. Most disbelieved it, some questioned it, but a small few revered it. The Chi Bantri hated it!

The majority of the World had previously known so little of the legends and myths about the celestial Qeervi culture and how, on the last occasion, they were banished to the heavens by the Chi Bantri. But humans are inquisitive things, continually looking for something of interest, more amusing or more just, or more evil, and what a story this was developing into.

And the main man who featured in the abduction of the again-risen Qeervis was under pressure. General Dara's unquestioned high standing in the Indian government, coupled with pure good fortune, was just about keeping him alive. Catan had been able to supply him with a complete list of every higher member of the Chi Bantri, almost twenty thousand of them, so he was able to take evasive action as the plots to kill or take him developed. But man, it was hard. The Chi Bantri were massive, just everywhere, and the only real saving grace were the Chinese who worshiped the spirit of the Qeervi queen, and supported the General's plight, using threats of nuclear action. The World was going mad!

The news mongers were coming up with thousands of stories and fantasies about the couple, with mountains of literature, none of which stood up to scrutiny. The World was moving into information overload and it was forcing the paparazzi and reporters into the Anglia region of Bengal. They swarmed around the Anglian Fort, pouncing on the two giggling girls at every opportunity. Catan and Gayla were loving it.

"Your Highness. Tell us about your life." A BBC correspondent was at the front of the crowd and called to Catan. "They say you're a pretender, and your position is refilled each year. Is that true?"

She turned her hooded face to him and waited a few seconds. "What do *you* think?"

He replied, "I'm asking *you*."

She smiled through the mouth hole, and as Gayla hung on to her, whispering, she said "Faith is all about belief and many believe that I am *not* a pretender. So to them, I am not. There's half your answer, and I don't have a position, and there's your other half."

"But you claim to be a princess. Isn't that a *position* placed upon you by the Chi Bantri?"

"No. I'm merely a guest of the Chi Bantri. You see, this is an arm, that is a camera, you are a human being, but I am a princess. I will always be a princess."

As others shouted questions, the BBC man continued. "Your Highness, are you saying that you are *not* human being, but princess?"

"Yes, and no." The girls giggled. "No more talking. Goodbye World." She twirled her hand in the air and the soldiers pushed the press back. Catan and Gayla went back inside the Fort.

An Underground Industrial Installation, West Bengal

In the secret rehabilitation suite, Robin and Tracy were getting bored. She had been practicing with her new eyeball but you can only do so much of that type of thing. Robin played with his stump which was healing miraculously quickly but that became annoying for Tracy.

"Why've they all gone mad?" asked Robin whilst flicking the news channels. "I could understand if we'd actually become big pop stars." He sighed. "Even that's not gonna happen now."

"It's because they think we're Gods," she answered.

"Yeah." Robin chortled, "and I'm a hippopotamus," and playfully punched her on the arm.

"But *I'm* starting to believe that we are, *really*." She was wearing a serious face. "Robin I know. When I was out cold for those days I saw it all, in my dreams. It all came back to me. I *really* believe we're divine beings." She carefully pulled out her eye. "Look I've healed in two weeks. Look at your leg; it's almost healed after two weeks. We *ate* each other's *flesh*." She was convinced. Gayla had worked her mental magic very acutely. "Tell me what *you* think, then. Come on, hippo-brain!"

"Well. I..." He suddenly realised what Tracy had said. "Hang on, I can't remember eating your flesh." He frowned. "You're kidding me. Anyway, I've got it," he said smugly, "Natural cures which end up being labelled as miracles. And I suppose they are miracles, but natural. The real miracle is about knowing what those natural things can do. And that's what it's really all about; Gayla's a witch and she applied her dark craft on us. Her spells put you into a three day long trance while she brainwashed you." He had his tongue in his cheek. "Pull that one to bits, big ears."

"That's plausible, but one big question, hippo-brain." She pushed him down on the bed and straddled him. "*Why* are we talking *Qeervi*?" And they were! She bit his nose and he just looked confused. "Another question, big boy, what's Qeervi for 'gonna shag your balls off'?"

The two were feeling seriously better, and seriously randy. The trauma had not done anything to quell their urge for each other's bodies so they just made passionate love, all afternoon. What a fantastic way to forget your troubles!

That evening the door bell rang. They could spot General Dara outside with some other soldiers.

"Robin, let us in please, it's the General."

Robin opened the door and let the three men into the spacious, windowless room. The General bowed to Tracy. "Your Majesty." He turned to Robin and bowed. "The Queen's Lamma." He then turned to the two soldiers. "May I present two most loyal servants, they'll be your personal guards, until they die." The soldiers dropped to their knees, clenched their fists and bowed. They were Nepalese and were dressed very smartly, but in combat gear, and they had left their hats outside the door. But they kept their pistols and kukris on their waists.

The Queen felt uneasy and so instructed the men to relax.

General Dara carefully said, "The phrase is 'at ease', Your Majesty. They've been well trained as Ghurkhas with the British Army and have some special qualities. They'll protect you both."

Tracy, The Queen, just stared at the General. She eventually slowly asked, "Why do we need them?"

The General bowed his head. "You are Queen Maya of Anglia. You are accompanied by your Lamma. *He* is your spiritual protector, but *these* are your physical protectors. They're two of the best, hand-picked from many millions, possibly billions."

The two soldiers were still kneeling.

Robin said, "At ease." The soldiers stood up. They both had tears in their eyes. Robin asked, "What's the matter? You can speak to us. D'you speak English?"

The soldiers both saluted the Lamma. One spoke. "I am Sergeant Baba, and this is private Alapat. We are your servants."

The General explained that the two men were to sleep in the adjoining rooms until they all moved out, and that they would be discretely guarding the doors at all times. He had briefed them in their basic duties and commitments. He then left them to it.

"Sergeant Baba, and private Alapat. Sorry, just reminding myself what your names are." Robin looked at Tracy with a wry grin. "Where's this all going?"

Tracy ordered the soldiers to sit with them for a while, to get to know each other. They drank tea. The men had been with the British army for several years, and it turned out that they had had their names down for those royal duties since they were school-children, back in Nepal. They were trained killers, with experience of underground and protection work. Their credentials seemed to be very good.

Robin asked, "What special qualities do you have? The General mentioned them."

The sergeant answered. "We're from a village in the Kali Gandaki valley. They are today celebrating, and the celebrations will last for several days, and they celebrate our achievements in being assigned to our God and her Lamma. They also celebrate the long awaited return of our Queen." He grinned with pride. They both struggled to hold back the tears as they sat in front of their living Goddess, and of course her Lamma. They were in ecstasy.

Tracy looked to Robin, and then held his hand. She very slowly asked the Sergeant, "Why do you think we're your Gods?"

"Your Majesty, you have always been our God. We have temples in the village and your immaculate spirit is honoured there. Your many effigies depict a beautiful Queen with red hair and an emerald eye which shines pity and tolerance onto her loyal subjects." He shyly lowered his head. "You are even more beautiful as an entity." A moment's silence. "This is the greatest posting we could ever have dreamed of; we are like kings to our folk. We will not fail you."

"Is the Lamma depicted in the temples?" asked Tracy.

"Yes. He is hairless and has his lower left leg cut off, and the scriptures say that he fed it to his queen to save her from eternal loneliness. The scriptures say she will return. And she has returned." He bowed his head.

They all sat in silence for some time, pondering the thought that some of the World was treating them like Gods, but the rest was probably depicting two pretentious freaks.

"Any other special qualities that we should know about?" Robin asked.

The sergeant replied, "Yes, we are prepared to *die* for you."

Robin felt a bit of a shiver crawl down his spine.

The sergeant continued, "But a much more cardinal quality with which we pride ourselves is that we are prepared to *kill* for you."

Robin's shivers turned to sweat. He attempted to forget about their special qualities, asking, "You mentioned scriptures. A friend of ours told us that there was no literature remaining about us, or the Qeervi history."

The sergeant smiled. "Maybe our village has been overlooked, by the enemy. Please let us keep this secret to ourselves, Your Majesty."

The soldiers were dismissed to discretely carry out their duties.

The television showed a more volatile World crisis; General Dara's mates. The Chinese, headed by President Li Jinpeng, the paramount leader of the People's Republic of China, were threatening to move into India to protect the freedom of the Queen. As the hunt for the icons hotted up the Indian government spiralled into turmoil. The supporters of the Qeervi movement were jealously protecting the location of the couple, whilst the less devoted Indian leaders insisted on revealing them to the threatening World, and take their chances with the Chinese.

Luckily the Chinese were a big enough threat to matter. They insisted that the Indian government should leave their Queen alone, and to allow her to reveal herself when the time was right. And if they did not leave them alone, there would be war. They were already massing troops just north of Arunachel Pradesh, and very close to the Indian border. The threat of China moving into India was real, and nuclear, and the US government sat back, not daring to step between those two giants, India and China. But, to their credit, the Indians agreed to allow the Queen her freedom to recover in peace, and they pledged to her their protection.

The Chi Bantri? Well they had their fingers in *all* the pies and had become the controlling factor. The Chinese stood lonely with the Indians in support of the Qeervi Queen and her Lamma's freedom to exist, while the rest of the World ran scared, controlled from within by the Chi Bantri. The world was a dangerous place right then.

There was a knock on the door. "It is Sergeant Baba."

Tracy quickly let him in. "Shouldn't you be addressing me properly?" she snapped.

"I pray forgiveness, Your Majesty. When outside of this room we do not want people to hear your names."

She smiled.

"Your Majesty. Quick I have a message that her Highness has spoken. BBC news. I will be outside."

They found the BBC news and there was Catan, with Gayla hanging on, zealously courting the press.

"My mummy and daddy have returned, as you all now know. They don't yet wish to discuss matters with *any* of you, not just yet. I thank the Chinese, and President Li, for their loyal support, and the Indian people for respecting the Queen and her Lamma, and for the Chi Bantri for protecting us from the *nasty* press." She stopped for Gayla to have a giggle. "But you must all now leave us alone and stop talking about war.

You'll not like the consequences of World war." She hesitated. "If that time comes, I'll make sure of it. Thank you."

And that was it. "What a strange statement," noted Robin. "It's like a threat. Who's she threatening?" He frowned. "And who's making that threat? Was that Catan or Gayla's message?"

Tracy held her left eye. "I have a pretty good idea." She raised her eyebrows. Her speech was slow and deliberate. "D'you know who our daughter is? I do." She grabbed Robin around his waist and snarled, "Darling, we might not get much chance after this so, fuck me baby. Fuck me hard." He did just that.

Over the next couple of days, the press slowed down. Perhaps the threat from the girls did have an effect on their activities, I thought it may have had the opposite effect, or perhaps the Chi Bantri were dispensing their influence through their members. But for whatever reason, the World became bored with their stories. However, the Chinese maintained the concentrated force just over the border and the threat of nuclear exchange between those two giants remained.

General Dara turned up on their doorstep.

"Your injuries are healing almost miraculously." He bowed his head to the royal couple. "I have something very sacred." He had an old but ornate box in his hands. "Your Majesty will know what this is when you see it. The council has been guarding it for many, many years." He reached towards the Queen and offered the box.

She hesitated. "D'you want me to open it?" she asked.

"Only if you so wish, Your Majesty."

She took hold of the lid with both hands and slowly lifted the lid. The inside was lined with scarlet silk, which nested a false eye, pure green and crafted from a giant emerald. It shone and she just stared at the magnificent jewel. She did not speak nor move for a couple of minutes. Then eventually she asked, "What is it?"

Robin began laughing.

She sighed, "Sorry, I guess it's an eye, for me." She removed the eye which she had been practising with, carefully picked out the emerald and, after applying some oil, fitted it into her socket. It was a perfect fit. She was beautiful, the ginger hair, the green of the emerald and the pure white complexion were a perfect compliment. They all just sat in silence.

"It fits me well, General."

"As I expected, Your Majesty. It was hand ground to perfectly fit you, thousands of years ago."

Tracy raised her eyebrows and fluttered her lashes, just for the hell of it. "How was it made for me? When?"

The General shrugged his shoulders. "Nobody knows." He paused. "It's been in safe keeping for over two hundred years. Since then it's never left the vault, until today. We all have absolute belief in you."

Tracy felt her new treasure.

"Your Majesty must only show it to the World during official events. You must wear dark glasses at all other times. I have some pairs for you. And your servants will kill anybody who removes your glasses without your specific instruction to do so."

Tracy was beginning to realise that she meant something. She picked her words carefully. "And who, precisely, are you, to be telling me what I can and can't do? I'm your Queen!" She hesitated. "If I'm Queen Maya, and a revered deity, then treat me as one. You tell me nothing, I only want your advice."

The General was wonderfully surprised. He gave a massive grin, before he kneeled down in front of her and clenched his hands together, while bowing his head. He then moved sideways and kissed Robin's vacant left foot. "Thank you, Your Majesty, I'll not show disrespect again."

She desperately tried not to laugh as she dismissed him.

"Wowee Trace! Perhaps this isn't a dream. He kissed my missing foot, and he's a high flying General."

She wriggled her shoulders and head and asked, "What d'you think of the eye, darling?" and then held him by the waist. "Well?"

Robin smiled, kissed her on the lips and said, "You're beautiful, my Queen. Now show *me* some respect, and cuddle me to death." He whispered, "And that's an order."

The next four days really dragged for them and the boredom became intolerable.

"Sergeant! Sergeant!" Tracy screamed for her servant. He quickly turned up at the door and she let him in. "Sergeant Baba. We have to get out. Take us somewhere, that's an order. Now!"

He bowed his head before suggesting, "I'll get hold of the General."

"Why? Do we need his permission?" She was not amused!

"No Your Majesty, but we are locked in. We are several metres below the ground, and nobody will get in, but we won't get out either." He looked very apologetic. "I understand your frustration. I will get hold of the General." He bowed to them both and went out of the door.

They played chess, again, and watched some television, again, but after about three hours somebody was at the door. Tracy looked through the spy hole and could see the General. As she opened the door, something grappled her around the waist, and yippeeeee! it was Gayla.

"Gayla. Robin, look!" They clung tightly to each other before being joined by the hopping Robin.

Gayla spoke Qeervi. "Mummy, Daddy. I've missed you." She laughed hysterically. "You're healing really good. It's bloody good stuff."

"What, the poultice?" quizzed Tracy.

Gayla chuckled as she said, "No, your legs, silly. The best cut of meat you could ever dream of. Yummee, did you save some for me?"

The General made his excuses and left them for while, so they went onto the bed and all kissed and cuddled and giggled, like little children at a sleep over. It was a vision of innocent beauty and love, and they were all falling back in paternal love.

Robin asked, "And where's your big sister?"

"Oh, Daddy. You're speaking the language really well now. Have you been practicing?"

He smiled. "Well, we found ourselves speaking it, and didn't even realise. Weird. Why do you think that happened?"

"Daddy, it's bloody obvious. You're Qeervi." She jumped and hugged him round the neck. "I love you, and you Mummy."

"Stop!" insisted Daddy, err, Robin. He almost sang as he said "asked you a question, where's my answer?"

"Ah, my sister. She's not here. Couldn't come." She released his neck and pushed down between the two grown-ups. She had her usual grin on her face. "Do you wanna know why?"

Robin took a deep breath, and then with a smile he put his hands around Gayla's neck and pretended to throttle her. She carried on laughing with them.

"Ok Daddy, if you're *that* desperate I'll explain. Now that you accept that you are my mummy and daddy, I'll tell you what you need to know. I can tell you the good bits later. Are you cuddling comfortably?"

She looked at Robin, then at Tracy, her big brown eyes glistening. "Ca'an can't come because she's tagged, like all the higher members. There are nineteen thousand four hundred and fifty eight higher members, including Ca'an, and literally many millions of networked associates. The associates don't know of the religious or political principles which are quite rigorously followed by the members, often enforced, and they're just servants of those members. They're all controlled by one or more of the higher members. When the member disappears, you know, dies, and he's not replaced by another member, then the associates below that member become un-associated, just carrying on as normal. Millions of people in the World unwittingly work for the Chi Bantri cause. The Chi Bantri runs the World, without even being noticed." She took a breather.

Tracy asked, "What's their cause?"

"It's to protect each other from all risk of loss, and to increase their personal fortunes, at *any* cost to others." She grinned, "And Ca'an's one of them. Hee hee. But, *big* but, she's not a real member, but a most revered guest; she's their spirit. But she's voluntarily tagged like all the others, so she can't come to see you. You know what Daddy, if she could cwy, she would've done when I left her today. She loves you both and longs to hold you."

"But why would that stop her coming?"

"Daddy, you are *so silly* at times. She's *tagged*, they would know where you are if they know where she is. Huh." She shrugged her shoulder back in despair.

Robin and Tracy just looked at her smiling face. Life was a little bit alien to them at the time, but some of it was just beginning to feel like it was part of them. Robin quietly said, "Yeah, I'm *very* damned silly at times." They all lay down and chilled for a while.

The door knocked. It was the General. He was let in by Gayla, and he presented a false leg to Robin.

"It's great. Hurts a bit, but I think I'll get used to it. I reckon it's a bit like riding a bike, when you have to get used to the saddle."

"Your Majesty. Has Gayla told you about the invite?"

Her surprised look told him 'no'.

"Her Highness the Princess Ca'an has the right, as her enviable position at the Fort entitles her, to invite two friends to the winter ball. And it's a very special year for the Chi Bantri."

"General, I've a recollection that this coming year is special, why do I think that?" Tracy frowned a little.

"Your Majesty, it's the two hundredth year since the inception of the inner court. It was forty years after the murder of your family. There are many myths about this coming year, but nothing written. Anyway, Her Highness has invited you and your Lamma."

"Hmm, that sounds dangerous." The royals looked at each other. "But at least it'll get us out of here."

"It's at the beginning of the year. Six days away. Perhaps the young Gayla can help you to prepare. As long as we're careful with her movements she'll be able to visit a couple of times before then."

They concluded the get-together and said goodbye to Gayla and the General. Robin was always sad when she left him. He never really believed that she would return, so Tracy consoled him in the best way she knew how.

Over the next six days most of the World settled back into normal life. Christmas and the New Year took front seat for many, and they had almost forgotten about the resurrection. The news crews were concentrating on the two military coups in Central America, which had been fuelled by the might of the Chi Bantri membership, under the guise of the United States of America and their newly found allies, Brazil. The oil deposits were just too much for them to resist. Of course it was all fought in the name of freedom and democracy.

But life inside the hidden retreat was becoming so boring. Robin asked Tracy, "D'you remember the aphrodisiac?"

"Hmm. Remind me."

"When we worked together down the Village. Dick had just de-scaled the water heater and hadn't flushed it out properly. I made a coffee, with dried milk, and the de-scaler made it smell like pure fanny. Beautiful. Soooo beautiful."

"I do remember. We never did reproduce it. Could've been rich now." She stood up and poured herself some water. She looked at Robin. He was sitting at the table, playing with the chess men and so she moved behind him and put her arms over his shoulders. "Close your eyes, darling, I have something for you."

He obeyed, with a quizzical smile. She gently slid her hand down inside her knickers and pushed her forefinger around in her vagina, then placed it under his nose.

"What's this?" she taunted.

He had a good sniff and then his face lit up. "Wowee. I don't believe it. It's Nescafe and dried milk!"

"You bastard!" She pulled him from his seat, and threw him on the bed. And they passed some more time.

Gayla managed to get to them twice during the six days, and that was a wonderful relief; they all had great fun dressing up in their new outfits. Little Gayla was great company; she never stopped laughing.

January 2009

At last! The day had come. They were to escape, never to return to that comfortable but claustrophobic dug-out. Robin wore a plain white shirt and a maroon bow tie, beige trousers with turn-ups, and brown, plain slip-on shoes. Maybe that was how a Lamma should look, played down. He had no jacket to wear. I suppose he actually looked pretty cool for an oldish man, it all went with his bald, shaven head.

Tracy was a knockout. Her hair shone with health and bounced down over her shoulders and upper back, held back from her face by an exquisite diamond studded, platinum tiara. The bright ginger and diamonds were a beautiful compliment to her emerald eye, and a little bit of powder and lipstick completed the look of a queen. She would knock them dead, and she knew it.

The clothes had been carefully chosen for her. She wore a low cut maroon choli with short sleeves, tailored around her breasts and cropped high to reveal her faultless tummy, and it was made from a subtle soft silk. Wrapped around her waist and over her petticoat was a pure white silk sari, which was then diagonally draped across her choli and over her left shoulder to bear her midriff. She wore a simple platinum and diamond necklace which matched the tiara and the stud in her belly button, and the sari at the waist was separated from the midriff by a wide, loose belt, of maroon silk, studded with pearls. She was finished off with dainty white soft leather shoes, with low heels. What a sight. Lucky Robin drooled as he looked at her.

The girls had chosen for them the clothes and the colours of the Qeervi royal family, and which the Queen and her Lamma would have worn in past times, maybe on the day of their deaths. And somehow they had been able to hang on to the royal tiara set, which had not seen the light of day for many, many years.

"I still don't understand where we are or what we're doing," sighed Robin.

Tracy just looked at him and sympathetically stroked his cheek. "We'll have to take it as it comes, my little poppet. Could be just like the old village hall bashes we used to go to as kids." They managed to force a couple of laughs.

Colin Hodgson

13 – THE FIRST CASUALTIES

The knock came on the door. At last, they were going outside. Sergeant Baba and his private very proudly took the two out of the room, up some stairs and into a large industrial building. And there awaited their chariot to the ball; an army truck with a canvas covered buck! Things could only get better. For some reason the two began laughing and giggling and for a couple of minutes were totally out of control. But they did calm down and, with their Ghurkhas' help, got into the back of the truck.

"We will pick up your limo' very shortly, Your Majesty," reported Sergeant Baba.

And what a lovely surprise when they eventually set eyes on the limousine; it was Aalap's rickshaw!

The two were hurried into the rickshaw where Dilshad awaited them, and the Ghurkhas climbed into another which followed. Dilshad's stern face suddenly smiled. "This is a great honour, Your Majesty. My father's the proudest man alive. Thank you for choosing us."

Tracy relaxed a bit, and avoided the embarrassing laugh. "We couldn't think of anybody more deserving. Don't let us forget to pay you."

Dilshad giggled and replied, "Good job My Eyes already paid us. Cos I thought royalty never carried money." They all had a laugh at that one; neither of them had a brass farthing on them.

"Hey, good point." Robin suddenly panicked. "I haven't got any money. I need a beer, desperately."

"Please don't panic, Robin. My Eyes asked me to tell you that you don't need anything, it's all there for you. And she asked me to tell you that the ball is to be a televised propaganda event going out live to the World. It'll celebrate the charitable and philanthropic Chi Bantri, who always extend peace and friendship across the nations. And that you mustn't be afraid," she stopped for breath, "and that you must remember her good advice, 'Stay calm at all times'. And remember that 'you're amongst your own people, and the higher members are the foreigners'." She thought a bit, "I think the television is really there to record the concert. It's Jennifer Bush. Don't know who she is."

Robin quietly asked the young lady, "Do you miss Saint Catherine? We do."

Dilshad forced a smile, "The whole region misses her. I'll later arrange a memorial service for her. I hope you'll be present."

They approached the Fort along the main road through the industrial area, straight up to the main front gates. They were impressive, with a red brick guard house on each side, and enormous wooden gates decorated with carved elephants. It was very different from the 'slum' gates at the back. Two helicopters landed inside the fort as they approached.

The two motor rickshaws were halted by the guards so Sergeant Baba got out and showed the guards the invite, and they were waved through the gates. Once inside, the massive limousines with their diplomatic plates and flags made the rickshaws look like little toys. Robin and Tracy felt a warm sense of humour.

Quite menacingly, the drivers and security men stood around like the Mafiosi while the covert security operations of the local militia passed unnoticed. It was a well managed operation.

"You can't park those there," called one of the soldiers. He walked slowly down the marble steps towards them and so Sergeant Baba jumped out of the rickshaw and presented the invitation. The shocked soldier returned the invite and ordered his troops to leave the guard room and assist the Queen and her Lamma.

The mood was mixed as our beautiful Queen emerged from the rickshaw. The soldiers looked on in awe of her mythical reputation, while the Chi Bantri higher members and their personal security staff laughed, but Tracy held her beautiful head high.

"Welcome, Your Majesty." The Chi Bantri soldier went down on both knees, and the other soldiers followed, clenching their hands to their chests. "So it's true. Only the true Queen herself would travel among her own people in a lowly rickshaw."

"Please relax," ordered Tracy. "Thank you for your kind welcome. My men'll remain with us throughout the celebrations." She had an idea. "There may be something that you can help me with."

"Anything we can do for you, we will. My men are at your disposal, Your Majesty."

"I can't see through these sunglasses in this light, so could you please locate an eye patch, for my left eye?"

The soldier proudly saluted his estranged Queen.

During their few minutes in front of the steps other stately vehicles had arrived with their higher members from all the corners of the World. Many were dressed in their traditional costumes, and there were statesmen, military leaders, religious leaders and industrialists. It was clear to see just how the Chi

Bantri had become the most influential secret society that the World had ever known. But then there was the Queen and her Lamma, definitely in a class of their own!

"We must move into the hall, Your Majesty. We're causing a hold-up."

Led by two soldiers and closely followed by the Ghurkhas, they began the climb up the ten steps. That was like climbing a mountain for the Lamma, having never climbed steps with his new leg. He managed three and had to stop. To the Lamma's embarrassment a large soldier walked down the steps, bowed, and picked him up. The other soldiers watched in awe as the legendary spiritual protector was placed at the top step, and they then all stood rigidly to attention and saluted the couple into the building. The press camera in the splendid marble reception area carried on rolling, reporting to the World that the Queen had left her safe haven, and was now on the loose.

"Your Majesty," from behind. The Chi Bantri soldier bowed. "We've found an eye patch." It was light coloured leather, well worn, but finely decorated around the edges with dark brown markings. "It's not a good one, we're ashamed to have to say."

"Thank you. It's wonderful. It'll tone down the glare from my tiara." She smiled gracefully. As they had taken a little time to climb the steps, a bit of a queue had formed behind them. The vice president of the United States of America and his wife waited patiently, while a large gentleman dressed in Arabian clothing was becoming impatient. More stood behind him, grumbling about the hold-up, rather like a bunch of spoiled kids who had been used to stepping to the front at all times.

The master of the door approached them and bowed. He was a higher member, and traditionally one of the older members is given the honour of the master, this year being a very special honour. "You're not members. May I see your invitation, Sir?" he asked Robin.

"My Sergeant has it."

The master inspected it. "It's only for two people. And it's not for you two."

Robin looked at the Sergeant who interrupted. "Her Majesty and her Lamma will be passing, with her loyal servants." There was a stand-off coming. "I believe you are General Laring. Your dictatorship does not extend beyond your own borders and while you are in Her Majesty's domain, you will gracefully respect her." The Sergeant's authority surprised Robin and Tracy.

From behind came, "Let them in so we can *all* move. Or take them away. Do something intelligent for once, Laring." The American vice president was impatient.

Robin and Tracy had earlier been given some advice from Gayla. *"Stay calm at all times. You're amongst your own people; the higher members are the foreigners."*

"Sir," said Tracy to the master, "I'm going to the loo. When I come out, I'll be going into the ball." She walked towards the corner where the ladies room was situated. The Sergeant spoke rapidly to his private, who then raced into the room before her to check that it was safe. He beckoned her in and guarded the door. The Sergeant and the Lamma stood aside to allow the other guests to pass through and they were all escorted in without showing any invites; their implanted tags were their passes. When the Queen returned from the ladies room she was wearing the eye patch. It quite suited her, making her look a lot harder and maybe a little frightening.

"Now the bloody queue's gone, we'll go to the ball."

But the master was still being a prat. "You are pretenders. The Chi Bantri do not recognise your position, and I have had my orders from the inner court. I'll not allow you to pass." Typical bully, stamps his feet, but still does as he is told.

Tracy thought about Gayla's advice. "Sir, stand aside, or show us to our table, do one or the other. *That* is an order." He did not move. Tracy clicked her fingers, and guess what, the soldier who had delivered the patch emerged from the guard room with six armed soldiers, and one put his pistol to the master's head and ordered him to stand aside. He quivered, began to sweat, and did as he was told. The covert security must have been more than just covert, totally invisible.

The soldiers delivered the two guests and their Ghurkhas to the waiters, just inside the entrance to the hall. Robin sighed deeply as he noted how much Tracy had changed!

They were in the hall and man, what a hall it was. The room was enormous. It was not at all like the drab working accommodation at the back of the building. Marble columns held up the lavishly carved, lofty ceiling, which itself supported beautiful chandeliers made up from many thousands of glass crystals and drops. There was a large wooden dance floor and that was surrounded on three sides by tables of various sizes, which seated maybe a thousand higher members. In the centre it looked like there was a special table for, tongue in cheek, special members, including the Monsignor and Cardinal Mateo. On the fourth side of the dance floor, a stage was lavishly decorated with draped silk. A small orchestra played from the back of the stage and were dressed in green suites with gold trim. Overlooking the hall were two boxes, one opposite each end of the stage and they were home to the production crews who were there to record the Jennifer Bush concert.

It was probably a coincidence, but all the waiters were dressed in white suits with maroon collars and lapels, with maroon bow ties.

"I hope they don't think you're waiting, Trace." They had to giggle.

The head waiter did not seem at all confident, but he at least spoke good English. "Your Majesty. Please forgive me, but I'm only following my orders. The Monsignor has placed your table over there." So what was Laring's problem? The waiter pointed towards the dance floor, but all they could see was a very small table positioned on its own, and it jutted out onto the dance area. The head waiter was sweating. "There are only two seats. Please forgive me, I beg you."

Her Majesty nodded to the soldiers who, visible to the Monsignor's table and to the cameras, stood to rigid attention and saluted, before leaving them with their own Ghurkha security.

"Waiter, that looks perfect. We'll be able to dance."

As the orchestra played some unrecognisable piece of background music, they were led to their seats, and had to almost walk the entire length of the building. The buzz calmed, then stopped. The higher members stared at the great 'pretenders'. It was like four strangers walking into a British Legion club, with everybody wondering 'who in the hell do they think they are, in *our* club?' But the couple held their heads high, arm-in-arm, with their two Ghurkha servants proudly following.

They sat at their table, exposed on the edge of the dance area, and discussed the quality of the carvings, and some of the oddities. Towards one end, away from the main entrance and way up in the ceiling, hung a giant copper fire hood. It was quite clean, maybe only used once or twice a year, and could be wound up and down. "Wonder what they do with that. Not the type of hall for a barbeque."

Monsignor Plassey had deliberately attempted to humiliate them by isolating them in such a conspicuous position but, like so often, he had again got it wrong. The members and the cameras were almost drawn into looking at the unwelcome guests, discussing their royal claims, and wow, did they discuss that tiara. Was it genuine? Genuine or not, it looked so beautiful on Tracy.

The waiters were attentive, and the food was superb, but where was the beer? "Waiter." Robin called a waiter over. "I'd like a beer please. What sort do you have?"

The waiter replied, "Queen's Lamma, we don't have any beer." He thought. "How desperate are you, Sir?"

The Lamma smiled and replied, "*Absolutely* desperate. Haven't had a beer for weeks."

The waiter grinned, bowed and left them.

Everybody seemed to forget about the two intruders for a little while, and carried on with their ball, but when the Canadian singer came on, some began to dance, and things became a little more intimate. Many of the dancers deliberately danced as close as possible to get a better look at the intruders.

Robin quietly spoke Qeervi, saying, "I'm beginning to know what it feels like to be a magnificent tiger in a zoo."

Tracy replied in Qeervi. "Yeah, I know. But Gayla said not to speak Qeervi while we're in here. Let's be careful." She frowned. "Wonder where they are."

The waiter returned, and such a look of pride. "Queen's Lamma, these are with the compliments of Captain Batiste." He grinned from ear to ear as he placed four bottles of Abbot Ale on the table!

Robin stood up and shook the waiter's hand. Although the waiter was not comfortable touching the Lamma, he proudly took his hand. "Is the Captain here?" Robin asked.

"No, Lamma. I sent out for it."

"You've made my night. I'll always think of you when I go home, and drink my Abbot Ale."

Once he had sat down, Tracy reached and held his hand. "Robin, dearest, I don't think we'll ever go home, not to England." They stopped talking.

A little later the waiter serviced a table nearby. When he left the table Robin called him over. He was very nervous, and could not look Robin in the face.

"What's wrong?" Robin asked.

The waiter hesitated, slyly looked around, and whispered, "The seven soldiers on the door have been executed for mutiny, or something." He looked at the floor and asked, "Can I get you anything, Queen's Lamma?"

The two were horrified. They were responsible for seven deaths, seven of the Queen's loyal subjects, and began to wonder when it would be their turn? Tracy was aware that the nearby tables were listening and so spoke very quietly. "Waiter, be careful what you say to us, but thank you for the terrible news. Please contact Ninah." She spoke louder. "Please bring me some fresh water, with some lime slices."

The waiter bowed and went off.

She stuttered as she whispered, "Darling, this isn't a dream." For the first time Tracy began to understand the magnitude of the game that they had been drawn in to. Those girls had placed them right on the front line, with the enemy looking down their necks, and had left them to fight the battle unsupported and unprepared. They were canon fodder. She broke the rules and spoke Qeervi. "We are the enemy and we have just experienced our first serious losses. We need some reinforcements. I hope Ninah contacts us. And where are those girls?"

As the waiter returned with the water, the Canadian singer stopped singing. She announced, "I hope you're all enjoying the centenary night. I'm very proud to be able to present a very special guest singer, a young lady of international mystery. Please give her a big hand." From behind the stage walked a pretty young Indian girl, about fourteen years old with black shining hair which hung below her shoulders, and wearing sun glasses. But she was dressed in the royal colours of the Qeervi; maroon choli and wrapped up in a pure white silk sari and belt, exactly as Tracy was, but without the tiara. The singer continued, "We're going to sing MacArthur Park." The crowd clapped in anticipation. They sung very beautifully together, sharing the lyrics, sometimes individually and sometimes as a duet. The young girl was excellent, magical, and the crowd loved her.

Robin and Tracy were enchanted. It helped to take the focus away from the night's killings, but what helped even more was the next surprise, Gayla! She sprung from behind and clung around Robin's neck, constantly whispering, and with her usual smile. Tracy gave her a hug, but Gayla gently pushed her aside, so that she could still see the girl on the stage. They then realised what it was that she was whispering, Catan's sight! It was Catan singing! Why? Nobody else had realised, they had never seen her without her hood, not even the Monsignor. But why was she making such an entrance to the ball? Was it for the television, or was it a surprise for her mummy and daddy? It must have been included in their meticulous planning, as they did nothing by chance.

The song finished and the members gave them voluptuous applause. The Canadian singer then spoke to her, to encourage her to say some words to the audience, but she gracefully declined. As the applause settled Jennifer Bush spoke to the ball. "I believe that this is the highlight of my career, accompanying such an esteemed individual, my legend, in song, so please join me in thanking Her Royal Highness Princess Ca'an of Anglia." She held her hands up for the applause, but none came. The hall just died.

The silence was broken only when Robin clapped and shouted, and was then joined by Tracy and Gayla, and three Chinese gentlemen sitting across the hall. *Nobody* else applauded. One of the Chinese gentlemen wolf-whistled, but still no response from the crowd. The members seemed like they were looking death in the face.

The un-hooded Catan at last smiled, then under the silence of the crowd, walked towards her right, and carefully took the steps down to floor level. Gayla jumped in front of Robin to keep her in her sight. She whispered her eyes to her, and directed her stealthily through the crowd, as she weaved her way towards a pre-planned destination. Some of the crowd politely moved aside to allow her through while others refused to move, forcing Gayla to guide her around them. The crowd seemed hypnotised, suspicious, aggressive and spoiled but watched in fascination and silence. Even the singer sensed that she ought to wait a bit before her next number and that was confirmed when the Monsignor rubbed his forefinger across his throat, signalling to kill the music.

Catan came to a stop by a table at which sat the three friendly Chinese gentlemen, wearing light grey Chinese tunic suites, or Mao suites. One of them was quite huge, probably about six foot six and with a similar build to Ninah. Gayla had placed Catan directly in front of the big man, as everybody watched on in suspense, and he politely stood up and bowed his head.

She spoke very loudly to him in Mandarin. "You know who I am. Who are you, big man?" She just smiled at him for a while.

He replied, loudly, "I am President Li Jinpeng. I am the paramount leader of the People's Republic of China. I am your servant, please call me Jinpeng." He bowed his head. "I believe this is the year of the slow worm."

"Yes, Jinpeng, and next year, the year of the bumble bee." She hesitated. "My hands can carry the World." She held her hand towards him, and he gently took it.

"The strongest hands in the World can sometimes be the smallest, Your Highness." He released her hand.

The introductions were over and they were both satisfied with each other's credentials.

"Welcome to our special year of celebration." Catan continued to speak Mandarin. "Are you coming to the Festival this year?" she asked.

He seemed to hesitate. "I have been selected. I don't know if I will be coming."

Some of the members began murmuring, but a swift wave from the Monsignor quietened them. He showed a concerned interest in the meeting.

"Sir, if you are considering the Festival, then my mummy and daddy would not approve of you. They don't like paedophiles." She watched for his reaction through Gayla. "And they don't approve of heroin or cocaine users, either. They are the foods of the tyrant." She watched him as he nodded in agreement. "And you have threatened to nuke the Indians, using my parents as your lame excuse." She stared up at him. The room was still silent. "If you wish to carry out the will of God, first ask God what his will is. To do otherwise will fuel the spirit of God's enemies. I've warned the World, especially you." Her strange television statement a few days earlier had clearly been aimed at the Chinese.

The President nodded in acknowledgement and replied, "I heeded your warning. Thank you." He looked around the hall and at the film crews. "So many of my people have worshiped the Mother of God for countless centuries. You have discarded your hood." He bowed his head. "Your mother has surely returned?"

"Your studies serve you well. She *has* returned. Honour her. Worship her." The members watched while the cameras rolled and the atmosphere sizzled. The Monsignor was totally helpless, the seven soldiers could easily be disposed of, but those three Chinese leaders could not. "Honour the Queen *and* her Lamma." She held out her other hand and he gently took it. "Come with me. Show the World how big you really are."

The President, so big and so powerful in both stature and position, was being tossed around like a rag doll by the little girl in sunglasses. With the crowd in a trance, she walked him back through the maze of people, but this time they all moved aside. You could almost smell the members' fears.

The President stood in front of Robin and Tracy who had risen to their feet as they approached. "Mummy, this's President Li. It's pronounced 'Lee'. President Li, this is Queen Maya of Anglia and her Lamma. They are my mummy and my daddy and this's My Eyes, Gayla."

The President stood in front of Tracy, staring straight down into her face. He was the most powerful leader in the World but that did not give him any authority with the Queen. He moved his hand towards the eye patch, but he had not reached anywhere near to the eye before private Alapat had pushed his pistol to his head. He had threatened the servant's Queen. The World must have been in wonderment as the paramount leader of the People's Republic of China was held at gunpoint by a Ghurkha private.

The Chi Bantri members discretely began to move towards the exits but were quickly stopped by the incoming soldiers. The poor soldiers had just lost seven companions and momentarily did not know whose side they were on.

Tracy remained calm in the silence. She allowed the situation to progress to absolute boiling point, for maximum return, before turning down the steam. "Sergeant," she quietly ordered, "Pop over to the Monsignor and tell him to assure his members that they're in no danger, and to relax. Get straight back here."

The Monsignor stood up and asked the members to relax, and they did so.

"Sergeant," she paused to look towards the film crews, "please ask the President what he wants with my eye patch. Do you speak his language?"

"Yes Your Majesty, it's Mandarin." He asked the question and the President answered. "He said he would like to see the eye. He thinks you may be a pretender."

Gayla continued whispering at Catan's side.

The Queen ordered the Sergeant to ask the President, "and who are you?"

He had a gun at his head, and billions of viewers were, by then, tuned into this live fly-on-the-wall episode. Sweating profusely he simply said in English, "I no longer know, Your Majesty."

The Queen smiled and then turned her head towards Catan.

"Ca'an, who is this man? Please tell your mother."

"Mummy, he is President Li, he is the paramount leader of the People's Republic of China. He's also a higher member of the Chi Bantri. He's a *very, very* rare man indeed because he's Chi Bantri *and* a good person." She grinned.

The Queen relaxed. "Thank you. Now tell President Li who I am."

Catan faced the President and bluntly explained in Mandarin, "This's my mummy." She then turned to the Queen and said, "Done." Gayla broke from her whispering to make space for some giggling.

Tracy knew what Catan had said to the President. She asked him in English, "Do you believe my daughter?" He carefully nodded and she ordered her Sergeant, "Instruct your private to lower his gun."

The private lowered his gun, expecting the other soldiers to move in, but they remained at a distance. He stepped back with the Sergeant.

Catan spoke to the President in Mandarin, "You may now honour the Queen and her Lamma."

But before he could do anything Tracy pulled the patch away from her head to reveal to him the emerald which shined and glistened below the lights of the chandeliers. It just looked like an emerald false eye, but the President lowered himself to his knees. "Your Majesty." He clenched his fists together and said a prayer to her, then pledged his life-long support for her. He moved sideways on his knees, and kissed the left foot of the Lamma, the false one, which the Lamma had cut off to feed the Queen in her time of need.

President Li's two compatriots joined him, and they also honoured the Queen and her Lamma with their pledged support. The sisters had successfully recruited the massive following from the People's Republic of China, and it had been witnessed by many billions of television viewers from around the globe. Isn't technology wonderful!

But what about the ball? Monsignor Plassey had to bring the ball back into the Chi Bantri's court. He mounted the stage to address the members.

"Higher members. The watching public. We have tonight witnessed the union of the superpowers. The Chi Bantri and China have offered their mighty hand of friendship to the legendary spiritual leader, Queen Maya of Anglia. We must now all relax and enjoy the opening ceremony to our bicentenary celebrations, and show the Queen and her family our real hands of friendship. At the conclusion of our toast, we will all continue with the celebrations. Please raise your glasses to Queen Maya of Anglia and her Lamma."

The toast was half-hearted. The Monsignor had quelled the immediate threat of war but the members all knew that the People's Republic of China had just agreed to share a bed with the mythical enemy of the Chi Bantri, the Queen. The atmosphere was so tense but the Chinese demonstrated a level of excellence in diplomatic behaviour, just calmly returning to their table.

The Monsignor went to the Queen's table, where she and her family sat in isolation. "May I offer Your Majesty and your family a place at our table? There is much more space, and some privacy."

The Queen replied, "Thank you for your very kind offer, but we like sitting in the middle of the dance floor. I thank you for your kindness in placing us here, where everybody can see us." She did not have the finely honed skills of the Chinese leaders, but she could bite.

The Monsignor, and most of the inner court, where pious admirers of Her Highness The Princess, and they believed that they could not survive without her divine spirit. That violent and covetous sect had been built with the Princess as their spiritual foundation, but they had never been able to understand why. Their blind faith taught them that whatever happened they would not continue in business without her.

"Your Majesty, putting our differences aside I must convey my admiration for your daughter, The Princess."

She interrupted him, with a playful smile, "No sir, you can't have my daughter's hand." They all laughed.

"I was about to say that, despite the World laughing about you, the inner court venerate your spirit. You've proven to be the mother of our divine Princess and I wish that, right now,

I was *not* a member of the Chi Bantri. We're all living very dangerously." He looked at Catan. "I do though hope that the genocide to follow will not be on the scale of some of your earlier mythical attempts to tame the World. Please enjoy the evening."

At last Robin spoke. He had become the strong, silent type. "Monsignor, genocide has been plundering life from the Earth for thousands of years, and remains rampant today. The past two hundred years, though, have seen the very worst. I believe that is due to your funny handshake 'club' operating totally unchecked."

The Monsignor looked towards the cameras. "We have a long proven history of diplomatic solutions, aid, support, and benevolence. Nobody will listen to your defamation."

Catan suggested, "All that is needed for evil to triumph is that good men do nothing. I believe you've heard that before."

"Haven't we all? But many a good man has *tried* to do something." He was becoming too smug.

"Who's talking about men?" Catan watched the Monsignor through Gayla. "You really need to be concerned. I've removed my hood, and it'll not be going back on." Catan held Gayla's hand. "The World has witnessed the hands of friendship; they'll be watching intensely. You may wish to discuss our friendship in depth, sometime."

The Monsignor shrugged his shoulders in an effort to stay cool and returned to his top table.

The ball never really picked up again, and it seemed that Catan had spoiled the first of the bi-centenary celebrations. But at last the family were together.

They were sharing a communal feeling of triumph over the minds of the Chi Bantri. The enemy were running scared and they had not at that point even fired a shot. And the girls were so satisfied with the progress so far, particularly that they had convinced the important sceptics that the Queen and the Lamma were back, the most crucial move so far. Yes,

Robin and *Tracy* at last believed that the Queen and her Lamma had returned! Well, Tracy did.

The tiny table forced an intimate family group, which was still under the scrutiny of the members, and Robin felt a little uncomfortable. "Perhaps we should go," he suggested. Nobody spoke. "Where shall we go when we leave? We've got to stay together." They all shrugged their shoulders, but no other response. He then spoke Qeervi. "Sorry, I've been shutting you out, Gayla." He smiled at her, and she looked back forcing a weak smile and biting her bottom lip. "What's up? No giggles. Ca'an, you ok?"

Catan was sad. She peered across the table towards Tracy, the reflections of the lights glistening across her dark glasses. She uttered, "Please Mummy." Gayla cuddled up to her. "Two hundred and forty years." The girls were never shy with their words. She whispered, "Two hundred and forty years."

"What is it? Tell me, darling," urged Tracy.

Catan needed to cry, but she could not. Gayla whispered to Catan, who took a deep, deep breath, and then slowly apologised. "Mummy. I can't remember. I can't. Sorry." Gayla moved from her side to allow her to stand, and she felt her way round the small table to stand in front of her sitting mother. Tracy remained perfectly still while Catan raised both her hands, gently placing them on Tracy's face. She touched her entire head, feeling the beauty which she had forgotten many years before. Her fingers explored Tracy's eyes, first the emerald jewel, then across to the good eye, which had tears developing. "I remember you, Mummy." Smiling, she kissed her mother's cheek, taking in the sweet tear drops which, to her, tasted like the nectar of the Gods, and then she kissed her on the lips. "I remember you, I love you."

Tracy was crying. She brushed Catan's hair back to see more of her unblemished face, and then removed the glasses. The entire hall strained to see more of the Princess. Catan's dark face, black hair and very long, black eyelashes contrasted with her own white complexion. Then Catan opened her eyes!

Fantastic. They were pure, almost white, like pearls sitting in black satin pockets, and they shone like the moon. Tracy gently touched the eyes, and Catan squinted. "They're real, so beautiful." She pulled Catan to her and sat her on her lap, and they cuddled. Tracy muttered, "Two hundred and forty years. Where've I been? Please forgive me." Her tears fell onto Catan's cheeks and they loved together. Catan shed no tears of her own.

By that time, Gayla had crept round onto her daddy's lap, and they cuddled as they watched the two beauties reuniting as one. Gayla giggled and laughed with her father at her sister's long awaited fulfilment. The poor girl had been alone with the Chi Bantri and her own 'disposable children' for almost two hundred and twenty years before Gayla and Ninah arrived, bringing love and companionship into her desolate, sightless world. She deserved some happiness. Her happiness, and her freedom to walk the earth without the hood, was to add persuasion to the myths, and was to herald the return of the Mother.

"Excuse me, Her Majesty's Lamma, I've a message for her Majesty." It was the waiter.

"We mustn't disturb the girls," whispered Robin. "I'll take it." He took the envelope.

The waiter quietly said, "The World's a more beautiful place right now, Your Lord." He smiled as he looked towards the girls. Everybody was watching them.

Gayla read the note which was in Bengali. She whispered it to Robin. "It's from Ninah. He couldn't contact me for some reason. He must talk to me in the entrance hall." She spoke to the Sergeant who posted his private closer to the table, and went off with Gayla as she held his hand.

"Gayla's just gone to the toilet."

In the reception hall, the master was making sure that Ninah did not enter the main hall. Gayla spoke to Ninah, and then the little girl said to the master, "We're going in to speak to the Queen. You've already had seven good men killed. The next one'll be you." The master stood aside and the three walked back in, each man holding one of Gayla's tiny hands. Gayla pulled a waiter and asked him to tell the Monsignor that they needed to speak, urgently.

"Mummy, are you well enough to talk to the Monsignor?"

Tracy smiled and wiped her cheeks, as Catan sat up. "Yes, of course." The Monsignor arrived at the table.

Gayla told of Ninah's news. "The news is out, as we all know it is, that The Princess has fulfilled her eternal promise to return the Qeervi Queen to her people. They now wish to return her fort into her command as a thank you, by overrunning the fort and killing all the Chi Bantri members. They will burn the Chi Bantri bodies before honouring the seven martyred soldiers who tonight died for their Queen." She looked very pleased, but concerned. "Well? Got anything to say?"

They all looked around at each other, then at the other members who were oblivious to their fateful situation.

Back to Gayla. "Well, I *do* have something else to say. The Chi Bantri are our friends and we'll save their necks. We're passionate people." She laughed, as Robin and Tracy just kept quiet. "If Ninah can hold them off, me and me sister can speak to them tomorrow. What about it, Monsignor Plassey?" She looked to Ninah, who nodded, and walked off towards the reception hall.

Monsignor Plassey, knowing that his army was almost certain to turn coats, agreed to keep the news from the other members to allay worldwide panic, and to meet with the warring factions in the morning.

Catan announced, "Tonight our family'll all spend the night in our room with the children. We need to let the General and Aalap know." It was not quite what Robin had imagined royal life to be like. "And we can discuss the way forward, when we get home."

Colin Hodgson

14 – I'VE ALREADY BEEN TO HELL

Under instruction from the Monsignor, Sir Kamdar arranged an army escort for the family, around to the back of the main building. The escort left them at the girls' rooms, with sergeant Baba and his private posted outside the door. The young children were all very excited to have visitors, especially ones of such position.

One of the boys asked Tracy, in clear English, "Are you going to change the World?"

Tracy looked sadly at the boy. She suggested, "Perhaps we should wait to see what comes in the morning." The children pulled a sheet over the floor, and they all sat down. The boy asked Robin and Tracy to sit with them.

He grinned at Robin. "We hear the soldiers talking and they're afraid. They say that God is with us. And also that they're scared of you. It's great." He carried on grinning. "I think they're scared of even us, they're all running scared." He spoke to the other children in Bengali and they laughed. "If they knew what we're going to do, they'd be *really* scared."

Tracy and Robin were a little confused, but that was the theme for the day, total confusion. She looked at Catan for some explanation, but Catan just sat down with them on the sheet.

Gayla joined them. She whispered into Catan's ear, who then passed the English version onto the group. "The children are going to be God's Six Catalysts, and will be revered. They'll be remembered in the modern scriptures."

Robin frowned. "I think we're lost. Sorry."

Catan replied, "Gayla has a plan, and part of that plan is to destroy the Festival of Life, to drain the spirit from the sect. The children wish to be part of that achievement." Catan's eyes were closed as she spoke. "We may have to talk about this tomorrow. The children need to sleep."

A little despondent, the six children were put to bed. They were tired.

The language then changed to Qeervi.

"We'll not sleep," stated Catan. "If you need to sleep, you'll need to sleep on the floor." She waited for Robin and Tracy to respond. "Do you sleep?" Catan asked.

Robin looked at Tracy and raised his eyebrows. "We haven't slept for several days. We can't, and don't get tired."

Gayla giggled and hugged her daddy. "Daddy, you're finally with us. We almost *never* sleep. You've gained your strengths back after sharing your meat." She playfully bit his shoulder and feigned eating. She was very happy. "We can talk all night in preparation for the morrow's negotiations." She jumped over to hug her mummy. "We'll talk about what we're all going to do."

"Hang on," jumped Robin, "before we talk about *what* we're going to do, let's talk about *why*. Your mother and I need some explanation as to why we've been transported into this weird World of yours."

"Daddy!" snapped Gayla, "this is *our* World. Mine, yours, Mummy's, Ca'an's, and our cousins'. You're in *your* World."

"Ok, so let's accept that I'm your long-lost daddy, and Tracy's your long-lost mother. You can help us to accept that in time, but this thing we're doing to the Chi Bantri, why? What's wrong with this Chi Bantri lot?"

What was wrong with them? The family spent all night discussing that question, and the public face of the cult certainly told of a story very different from reality.

The West Bengal region, which lies in the north-eastern part of the Indian sub-continent, had always attracted chancers and profiteers from around the World. Powerful governments and traders had fought for thousands of years to control the area and glean the riches, and the local people subsequently died in their millions from warfare, in-humanity and natural disaster. European traders had continued to grow in influence since the fifteenth century. But the British East India Company gained the taxation rights in the Bengal Province after the defeat of the last independent Nawab, Siraj ud-Daulah, at the Battle of Plassey in 1757. They claimed part of their prize by plundering the Bengali treasury.

That was when the Qeervi family moved into the area and quickly gained the total support of the country people. They developed enviable relationships with the governing British, the Bengal Presidency, ensuring tolerance and justice and the people became devoted servants to their protectors, Queen Maya and her Lamma. The protection offered was not military, but spiritual and democratic, and life for the local people was enviably just. The Qeervi 'royal' family was delicately accepted and respected by the British rule.

As the Queen quietly and unofficially ruled the area from behind the British façade, scholars and religious students moved in from the Himalayan regions and the Mughal Empire to learn more about the rumoured resurrection of one of their mythical Goddesses, the idol with the ginger hair and emerald eye. They studied the art of the meek and they knew her as Maya. Queen Maya of Anglia was surely their revered God who had been worshipped throughout Asia for thousands of years as the Gentle Protector.

Her influence in Bengal was becoming more powerful than the British rule. Even many of the British were metamorphosed into dedicated followers. The Queen did not differentiate between religious beliefs, and did nothing in the name of God, but did as God would. To harm somebody in the name of God was considered the ultimate crime, and to believe that one of God's children was a lower being than oneself was *absolute* blasphemy. The students were beginning to spread the word.

The relationship between the East India Company and the Queen deteriorated in the run-up to the 1770 famine when the Company caused the death of ten million people through starvation. Land tax was increased to over thirty percent of the crop value, leaving growers unable to continue, and losing their land and crops to the Company. The Company took ownership of more and more land and as it did it raised the land taxes for the remaining owners even higher, to over fifty percent. Food crops were further decreased when the Company put over much land to the cultivation of opium poppies for export, and also the hoarding of rice by traders was banned, preventing traders from laying reserves to tide over lean times and famine. To compound the risks many farmers were ordered by the Company to grow indigo instead of food products. Eventually the Company and its agents had an almost complete monopoly over the grain trade, managing it to achieve maximum profit from export, with no regard for those outside of the Company. When the crop failures arrived in 1768, followed by drought and more serious failures in 1769, the people began to starve. Millions died in 1770 as the famine hit, assisted by smallpox, but the British East India Company refused to help the people. They had to maintain their drive for financial profit. The Queen was unable to persuade the officers to act in a Christian manner; they just left the people to die, and over ten million of them did.

After the famine Bengal had lost about forty percent of its population, due to the millions of deaths, and to the migration of entire communities who went in search of food. The East India Company continued to strip the lands of everything profitable, whilst increasing their reliance on the violent methods of tax collection. But the Queen continued to push them into a religious dilemma. It is reputed that in a letter from the Queen, which was delivered to the customs house at Fort William in 1772, she suggested that the 'Company' had behaved in a blasphemous manner in considering that the local people were of a lower order. She stated that the belief in lower orders was the belief of God's enemies, and that the mass murder of, and total disregard for, God's subjects was worthy of eternal eviction from His empires. She accused the East India Company of being in conflict with all of the principles of the Christian faith and that they should leave Bengal. That communication was reported across the World through the students' networks and very quickly stories of the Gentle Protector's ultimatum were raising hopes amongst the poorest communities. Maya's apostles were proliferating!

Queen Maya was ordered by the Governor General, Warren Hastings, to leave Bengal along with her family as neither the British government nor the failing East India Company could afford any sort of uprising in Bengal. The Queen refused. She claimed that uprisings were not part of her ideology, but justice and respect were, and after some long discussions at Fort William, Hastings agreed a truce with the Queen. It did not last long, as the new civil service and British tax collectors administered even more violence as part of their day-to-day routines.

The loss of the many millions of folk during the famine had left much of the area barren, destined to return to jungle, and the East India Company did nothing to protect the remaining farmers from the marauding gangs of thugs. The thug culture had developed through 'necessity', fuelled by hunger and desperation. It was a dangerous place to live.

The Queen, in anticipation of the British and the Company not *giving* a damn, appointed a nephew to raise a police force to protect the area's people from the gangs. The nephew was a well respected soldier of fortune, and a good commander of troops. He was Sir Bruce Kamdar. He raised an army of over three hundred from the farming community, and first trained his officers, then his recruits. They were kind, respectful and loyal to their own people, and their remit was of the people's servants, not their dictators. The people worshipped their Gentle Protector. The British did not.

By 1776 the first Mahratta wars were under way. Warren Hastings was concerned that the ever growing 'friendly' army in the Anglia region of Bengal could become a serious distraction to the Mahratta war efforts. He detailed two Company officers to resolve the problem.

The officers were explicitly detailed to remove the Qeervi family, but to retain the private army, in tact. The battle plan was to remove the army to a location far enough away to enable uncontested removal of the royal family.

During the summer of 1777 it was reported that some of the marauding groups had joined forces to raid some villages to the north of Kolkata. It was also reported that the villagers had suffered heavy losses, and the thugs were still holed up in the area. In response Sir Kamdar took most of his troops to the area to investigate, leaving the Queen and her family almost alone in their colonial house, just a short distance from the Anglian Fort. A group of soldiers, dressed in Chinese style armoury, arrived at the house, asking the Queen to surrender her position. The soldiers had been engaged by the British East India Company to remove the Goddess Maya in an operation seemingly unrelated to the British Company. The mercenaries had been recruited from Nepal, and consisted of a group of religious intellects who did not revere Maya, but traditionally scorned and mistrusted her spirit. They had studied at the Chi Bantri temple close to Khatmandu.

In front of the Anglian Fort's main gates, which then consisted of open farmland, the Nepalese soldiers displayed their captors to a few hundred frightened onlookers. The British soldiers remained in the Fort. There the Queen and one of her daughters were crucified, while another of her daughters was kept alive, to be ceremoniously cannibalised. The Chi Bantri ate the spirit of Catan.

Robin asked, "Is that our only grievance against them? And, why were *we* there?"

Maya's family had moved into the Anglia area to test the theory of the meek. Could the meek survive in the midst of the greedy and powerful? Man had constantly proved that they could only rule with kindness and justice for relatively short periods of time and with the worldwide acceptance of currency the focus had changed from religion to wealth. The British East India Company was, arguably, the most powerful financially based company the World had ever known. But it was driven by profit, greed, and strove to take *everything* from the billions, to line the pockets of a few. A great many millions of people were left dead or destroyed in the wake of the British money machine.

The Company's appointed executioners from Nepal remained in the area after the crucifixion and, as a reward for their gruesome work, were given the responsibility for policing the area. They were given command of Sir Kamdar's troops. The troops were not so just in their policing as they were when the Queen was alive. The Chi Bantri eventually took over the lease of the Anglian Fort.

Nobody, apart from God, knows why, but the Princess Catan remained with the Chi Bantri. She never died. But that was almost certainly the main ingredient in their phenomenal success. The group took spirit from their captor; she cleverly fed their urge to know more about Maya, and she gave them the pointers to selectively lead them to certain knowledge. The cult began to develop its own internal beliefs and prejudices, covertly guided by the Princess Catan. The Chi

Bantri was certainly becoming a cult, with benevolence as their foundation stone, and the deceased Queen Maya their icon, and they were everything that Catan designed them to be.

As they studied they influenced some of the officers of the Company, who were then recruited as members, and who then recruited other further flung members, who then recruited more, and so on. The secret society had begun. Their righteous desires were to help others, improve life for many, influence political and religious action, and to quietly run the World. And after a couple of decades the group had established a membership of many thousands from around the globe. They were even more powerful than the British East India Company, but still mysterious and private. In some areas they *were* the British East India Company. The members were from all religions and races, but all had one thing in common, their supreme prestige and influence. The members often found themselves on opposite sides in negotiations or even military engagement, and wherever possible the court's advice would be considered in an effort to reduce unnecessary barbarism and cruelty. Violent conflict was often averted in favour of contracts and treaties. The sect had become the ultimate philanthropic society with the weak and poor non-members as the beneficiaries. Business was allowed to carry on, but with the minimum of devastation to others. Just as God would have wanted.

But as with all human groups, it changed. The main focus moved from benefitting others, to benefitting themselves. Deals were made between the members which began to increase the barbarism associated with the acts of money making and profiteering, and those early underhand deals led to the sect becoming money-orientated. The inner court declared that profits from the members should be shared with the Chi Bantri, as a form of membership subscription, and in return the member would receive the support of all other members, and a guarantee that their position in life would be protected. The benevolent society had evolved into the malevolent society.

The first hard evidence of malevolence came in 1814. During the lead up to the Second Kandyan War, Chi Bantri members were involved in trading negotiations with Sri Vikrama Rajasingha's representative, of the Kingdom of Kandy, when the inner court deemed it to be not in the interests of the Chi Bantri. Through their network they ordered the members to cease negotiations, as higher profits were forecast through outright war between the British and the Kandyan nobility. The members refused, stating that peaceful negotiation could be profitable for all, without loss of life. Those members were mutilated, made to suffer beyond belief, and eventually killed, as they arrived in Kandy, following orders from the inner court. The teachings of their icon, Maya, had been violated, and Princess Catan warned of the Queen's condemnation.

The general membership had learned about the horrific results of disobedience, and, over the years, they received regular reminders of their fete should they not toe the party line. The human cost of the cult's moral migration still remain untellable. Their undisputed influence in all political and religious powers has caused death, mutilation and humiliation amongst hundreds of millions of innocent people. They had grown into a monster.

"I remember," sighed Tracy. "I do remember." She was disappointed. "They're not good memories. But it was a successful experiment." She sighed. "Our failure is that we've let them carry on for too long, causing intolerable suffering. We've been so fucking irresponsible."

"Mummy," whispered Gayla, "I could've killed them off years earlier, but we had to be together to do it. And we've still got to choose our moment." She thought deeply. "There are other considerations, but they're almost spent, and when they are, we'll make our final assault." The little girl snuggled up to her mother. "But we're together now."

Robin looked over into Catan's closed eyes. "You have a plan?"

"Gayla and I have planned our attack on the Chi Bantri. Our first priority is to keep them all alive, particularly the members who frequent this Fort." She opened her pearly eyes. "We must be their friends and protectors today. We'll meet their representation, but please, Mummy and Daddy, you must be careful what you say. You mustn't know what our exact intentions are."

They all sat thinking for a while, and then one of the children awoke. It was dawn. He climbed up from his bed, and kissed Catan and Gayla. The other children still slept.

He asked Tracy in English, "Have you seen what today has brought, yet?" He carried a quizzical smile. "Are you going to kill the Chi Bantri?"

Tracy was uncomfortable with the little boy's questions. "We mustn't talk about killing so glibly. Come here." The boy moved to her and she put her arms around him. "Where do you come from?"

He raised his hand to Tracy's false eye and gently touched it. "I come from England. The others come from other places." He stared into her emerald. "I was sent here by my school master. He said it would help me. I think he talked a lot of shit." He seemed very sad. "He told me that it would help them from getting done by the Queen. I think he meant you." He was frowning as he looked into her eye. "I think you're going to kill them."

Tracy looked down to Gayla, then back to the boy. "I can't kill people. I don't know why, but I can't." She looked again to Gayla. She asked in Qeervi, "That's right, isn't it?"

Gayla giggled. "Mummy, you're remembering really well." She then pointed at her daddy, "He's not. But he's a silly boy." She smiled at the little boy. In Bengalese she said, "We can't kill people. We have to get our relatives to do that. Unless Ca'an uses her sword, then it's different. You remember my cousin? She's Catherine." Robin perked up.

"She can kill. She killed Peter's school master in England, because he was fucking the children. That was *after* Peter came over here. Ca'an thinks she is bad, sometimes. You know Mummy, Ca'an was going to kill Catherine and send her home, but I couldn't let her do that, and knowing Ca'an, she wouldn't have let herself do it, either. And as Ca'an should have known, Ca'an's sword is no match for Catherine. Catherine *has* killed many people before, but only in defense of others and as a last resort, but never for personal revenge. She mustn't do that, and *she* set the rules." Gayla had one of her very rare frowns. "That's something which has changed since you were last with us. But Catherine is very good."

Robin asked, "Why shouldn't she kill people if they're really bad?"

"Because we would end up like the Chi Bantri. Bloody obvious, ain't it? We can only influence others, maybe plant some ideas and encourage, but we can't be like people. We have to do what's *right* for our people, not what's right for us." Pause. "Things have changed since you were here. Sorry, but we've changed. For the better, but changed."

Robin just looked at the ground for a bit.

"We have to do God's work, Daddy." She winked at Robin. "That's all we're here for. When it's done, we can go home, all of us. I promise."

Robin looked at Gayla, "This is fucking ridiculous. You're talking like we're Gods. We're not, just mixed up people. They put people like us in the loony bin."

Gayla jumped up, "*People* put people like us in the loony bin." She put her head to Robin's head and laughed. "D'you remember when they put *you* in the loony bin? Don't suppose you do, but you weren't a loony. They just didn't agree with you." She sat down by her mother.

Robin looked at Catan, "You're not saying much, Cat." She opened her eyes as he asked. "Can you help me, please?"

She turned her head towards him and slowly said, "I love you, Daddy. Can you help *me*, please?"

Robin smiled, "Of course, anything."

"Please, when we've done the negotiations, will you show me a Christmas tree, by a church?" She was so sombre. "I've never seen a Christmas tree made up. I've been blind since they began doing that."

He thought about it for a few seconds. "If I can, then I will."

She at last smiled. "Thank you Daddy. It'll help me, and I'm sure it will help you."

"Can you help *me* now?" Robin was becoming more confused. "That Catherine. Why didn't you kill her if she did wrong? She killed a school master without trial. You seem to put human life very low in your valuations."

"For one, she's not human, she's my Auntie. For another, *nobody* can kill Catherine. And for another, because you told her to kill him. Remember? From St. Phoebe's Garden."

"But I only…. This is a nightmare." At the boot sale he had momentarily thought about killing the people responsible, and remembered her saying, *"Don't worry, we'll sor' it."* She had looked into his mind. "I never told her to kill anybody." He hung his head into his hands.

Gayla confirmed, "Daddy, you did. You must be careful with your thoughts. You said in your mind that they should die, and Catherine'll do almost everything, within our rules, that you tell her to do. You are the Lamma. You passed sentence!" Gayla chuckled. "And you know what, that was a milestone in our progress. D'you remember what you thought at that airfield and how you thought it?"

He raised his head from his hands and shook it.

"Well, your mate on the next stall thought, in English, 'What a terribly rude girl'. Now *you* thought very differently. You thought, 'What a terrible *thing* that she's telling me'. The language is just words, it's what she meant that mattered to you, and *then* you thought 'He deserves to die', in *Qeervi*! That's when we knew for certain that you're the Lamma. You thought in Qeervi! We knew who you were even before you ever came over here."

Tracy pulled him to her and they held each other. Poor Robin was out of his depths and could not understand what was happening. He was caught up with a group of people who thought they were deities from a distant past. His beloved Tracy seemed to be one of them; he had cut his own leg off to feed her; the miraculous cures of the poultice and the friendly worms; the burning of a beautiful old lady and her innocent, long-suffering children; the little girls who were hundreds of years old, maybe billions; the reading of minds; the killings; the weird cult which seemed to be running the World; the children who were primed each year for the Festival of Life. And he had been conned into going to India by a little girl who would do anything for him, and by his beloved, and by one of his best mates. And he could not accept that he was one of 'them'.

"So what is Syed?"

Gayla answered, "He's your very good friend, but not a Qeervi. Why?"

"Because I'm scared."

"Daddy, darling, think of your boys in England. Just think of England and you'll be fine."

He looked at the ground. There were the six friendly worms with his two sons, David and Russell. They all waved to him and smiled. Then the worms stuck out their tongues and blew raspberries at him. He blinked once, and they were gone.

The group welcomed the other children as they awoke. The Fort was waking up, and the Monsignor was arranging their meeting. Ninah arrived at the door.

"Good morning, Your Majesty. I hope you slept well, if at all." He knelt down and said a prayer.

"Good morning Ninah. I haven't thanked you for your kindness towards me when they burned St Catherine." Ninah nodded his head.

He said quietly, "Your Majesty, the Monsignor has asked that we attend in the court room at ten o'clock. I've two representatives from the people."

Still dressed in their party outfits, Tracy took Robin's hand and they limped outside into the rising sun. The girls and the children followed. Tracy said, "Ninah, we'll have to hold the meeting in English. Will that be ok?"

"Yes, Your Majesty. Our people can speak good English. And so can I." He had previously only spoken to Tracy in Qeervi and Bengali, probably to test her credentials. "I don't know who the Chi Bantri members will be." He looked around at the empty parade ground. "I think everybody is staying inside, today."

Robin asked, "Are the people really ready to attack the Fort?"

Ninah grinned and Catan answered for him. "They'll never be ready. They would all be killed if they were to attack. Unless Kamdar's troops turn, and that's questionable. And if General Dara and Captain Batiste get involved, then the rest of India will step in, followed by China and then half the World. We must play this whole crisis down, for the moment, and be their friends."

They all stood quietly, taking in the new sun and mellowing. Neither Tracy nor Robin knew what was ahead, and they thought of Gayla's earlier statement that they could not know exactly what the girls were planning.

"Where's Sergeant Baba?" Robin looked around, and began to worry.

Ninah bowed his head. "Lamma, they've been taken into custody, as a security measure. I think we should leave them there while we negotiate. We're all safe."

Tracy, with her newly acquired confidence and knowledge, suggested that they all go for a walk into the slums. Robin was worried about just how far he would be able to walk with his false leg. "Ninah will carry you back if need be. It's part of his job." Robin was not impressed.

They walked across the deserted parade ground towards the South Gates.

"Halt!" called a soldier at the gates. He moved forward from the other five soldiers. He spoke good English. "You cannot leave."

Catan opened her eyes, which shone in the sun, and questioned, "Are we under arrest, soldier?" The soldier did not answer soon enough. "Answer me! No, don't answer me. First properly address me. And my family."

The soldier did as he was told. He saluted the Princess, and kneeled down in front of the Queen and said a prayer. The other soldiers followed suite.

"Thank you," Catan said, "You may now open the gates for us. We're going for a stroll, all of us." The soldier was hesitant. "No point in shooting us, we *will* return. And please give Sir Kamdar a message from the Lamma." She looked round at a confused Robin. "Daddy, think of something to tell Kamdar."

He was really struggling. Then he thought of Catherine. "Yes, please tell him that the Lamma will not allow him to kill anybody." He sighed.

The soldiers saluted them as they walked through the gates. The leading soldier said, as they walked past them, "Thank you, Lamma. I'll pass your message on."

Once they were away from the gates Robin began to worry again. It did seem to him like a big game, and the girls, all of them, were treating life that way. They walked across the open area towards the dwellers as if they were untouchable, and Robin was not entirely sure of who was on whose side in that strange match. And as they neared the people an excitement spread. The sight of the Queen walking with the Princess, and both baring their breathtaking eyes to their people, sent them into jubilation. They had always believed that the princess would herald the return of the Queen when she walks the Earth without her hood.

Suddenly the rapidly growing crowd quietened down, and fell to their knees, praying. Four army trucks, packed with armed soldiers, had sped across the area, stopping just short of the family. It presented a menacing atmosphere as Sir Kamdar climbed out of one of the trucks.

"What're you doing?" he asked Catan in English.

"What does it look like, Kamdar? We're out walking amongst our people. Why?"

He looked around at the people, by now beginning to rise to their feet. "These people can be dangerous, Your Highness. The Monsignor is concerned that you won't be at the meeting."

Catan opened her eyes wide, and the sun lit them up like two splendid stars. "You don't need to worry about us. You know that. But before you go, the Lamma would like a word." She looked to Robin.

Again he was nervous and struggling, but, from amidst the sweat, inspiration ruled. "Sir Kamdar, you'll ask my best mate, Syed, to meet me at the clinic, this afternoon. About four."

Sir Kamdar looked over to Catan, who had Gayla holding around her waist. He growled, "Thank you Your Highness." He turned and went back to his truck. The armed soldiers all looked relieved as they swung around to return to their Fort.

Robin remained in a state of confusion. Maybe it was the effects of the ranar plant which had kept him in that dreamlike trance until now, but if so, he needed another fix. Or maybe it was the succulent piece of Tracy's leg which he had unwittingly eaten whilst still delirious. Whatever the reason, he had been floating along in a dream with that strange band of deities, and was beginning to wake up. He watched the trucks drive back to the Fort, and then looked at Tracy. She put her hand on her tummy, then held it in front of her good eye. It was covered in blood, and the skin hung from her tummy, as if peeled back by a butcher. Blood flowed down her legs to the soil where the friendly worms waited to feed. Before sucking at the bloody streams, they all turned to Robin and blew raspberries at him. "Tracy!"

"What is it, darling?"

Robin awoke, back to normality. He was shaking a little. Gayla clocked it, ran over to her daddy and grabbed him around the waist, laughing. "Can I sit on your shoulders, Daddy, please?"

It was enough to pull him out of the onslaught of panic, and so Robin cupped his hands to give her a leg-up. She sat high, smiling at her family and her people. "Let's walk amongst our people," she chortled.

Robin thought to himself, *"Whose people?"* Whoever's people just watched, and kept quiet. They seemed to be waiting for something to happen. But Robin was waking up. His leg, cut off just a few weeks before, began to feel pain. "I can't walk any further, especially with you on my shoulders. Can we go home?" I wonder where he meant, by home. Before anybody could answer him, an old man walked forward to stand in front of the Queen. He kneeled and said a prayer, then rose.

"What is it, sir?" asked Tracy.

"I'm Satvinder. I'll be representing the people at the negotiations, Your Majesty." He put his hands together to his chest and bowed his head. "What would you like me to say at the meeting, on behalf of the people of the Anglian slums?"

Tracy frowned. "What would our people wish you to say, Satvinder? They must want something from this."

"Your Majesty, we just want to eat, and have medicine. We want the clinics to reopen. And we want you, our Queen, to be treated like a Queen."

At last, a real person. Robin looked over to Catan, who looked up towards Gayla, who looked across to Ninah, and then Robin said, "Her Majesty'll ensure that the clinics are kept open. And we'll arrange food." Still shaking a little he stepped gingerly towards the representative, and held out his hand. Satvinder took his hand and shook it. "Can you please help me, sir?" asked Robin.

Satvinder released Robins hand and knelt down, kissing Robin's left foot. Robin shivered; that was not what he was expecting. He then rose and said, "Thank you for feeding our Queen. What would you like me to do for you?"

He froze. Did Satvinder deliberately put him off his stride? Robin thought so, but quickly manoeuvred into a tactical position. He asked, "If I ask you a question, and you don't give me your truthful answer, could I send you to hell?" The family all looked on in fascination. "I'm the Lamma and I need an answer."

Satvinder was a wise old man. He smiled and replied, "I don't know." That was the honest answer that Robin was looking for. The crowd looked on, with the commentary being passed back from the front, right into the slums.

"So, if you don't believe that I could send you to hell, then you don't believe that I'm the Lamma."

The old man smiled, "No, that's not what I meant, Lamma. We *all* know that you're the Lamma, the Queen's protector. You cured the Queen of the disease from which nobody else has survived. And before you did you laid the eggs to spawn the successful inoculation of all our people. You also cut off your leg to feed our Queen in her hour of need. It's been written for thousands of years, that you will return, and in this way prove yourself."

Robin's head dropped. The whole thing was a set-up and this man had been had, just as Robin and the other billions had been, by the girls. Not for the first time he wondered whether they were divinely good or just plain evil. He took a very deep breath and asked, "Then what did you mean?"

Satvinder was calm. He replied, "I've already been to hell. I know you would *never* send me back there. So I don't know the answer to your quiz." A silence fell. Was the Lamma going to strike the man down for his insolence?

"I must be careful with my thoughts, sir. But despite not knowing what my intentions would be, will you still help me, with honesty?" Satvinder slowly nodded, and then Robin continued, "When I wake up, will you still be here in front of me? And will you still be my friend?"

The old man looked Robin up and down, then looked up into Gayla's eyes, and replied, "Before you wake up, I hope that I'll be with my good friend Akhtar, and with our families, and our children who were gang-raped and butchered in East Pakistan. And when I get there we'll no longer be sub-human." He paused for thought. "Or are we *all* being duped?"

Satvinder was a life-long friend of Doctor Hussain, and was caught in the genocide in East Pakistan with the doctor. They both left the mutilated corpses of their wives and children behind, they thought to seek revenge. They never found revenge, but chose just to wait. He reminded the Lamma, "The Chi Bantri are everywhere, they believe that they're God, the very worst side of God. And they're behind every major act of inhumanity, and many minor acts. They cultivate belief within people that another people are of a different sub-human cast, like animals, and it's ok to slaughter animals if they cause a nuisance. There's much profit in genocide, for a very few." He looked around at the people. "You are the people's and the World's only salvation. Prayer isn't enough."

The family was taking it all in, as were the people.

"Back to your question. If you're not awake, Lamma, then please stay that way until the job is done." He said no more.

"Robin, darling." Tracy held his arm. "We should walk back soon, we have our meeting."

They turned towards the Fort and began walking. Tracy held Robin by one arm, Catan by the other, while Gayla sat on his shoulders. The children followed immediately behind and Ninah took the old man by the arm. "Walk with us to the meeting, sir." The crowd kept their distance but followed the family towards the Fort, at crawling pace. The atmosphere was electrifying, silent, as they moved across the empty space, and by the time the shortest pilgrimage in history had reached its destination, the open area was packed. The soldiers at the gate let the family in, and the people stopped short.

Gayla whispered to Catan, and in response she asked, "Where's the gateman who let us out?"

The soldier saluted her, went onto his knees in front of the Queen, arose, and then replied, "Sir Kamdar has put him on other duties, Your Highness."

Robin imagined that his commands did not hold up with Kamdar!

15 – THE INTRANET

While the girls were finalising their tactics, Robin helped Ninah to muster up some food for the children and Satvinder. It helped to take him momentarily out of his personal nightmare. As he spoke about Akhtar with the old man, Gayla ran over to him.

She had a little giggle, and then put her mouth to his ear. "Daddy, I heard you wondering earlier; yes, we *are* divinely good, honest." She kissed him on the cheek. "That was just a tinsy warning. You must be careful with your thoughts, naughty boy. Put up a screen by thinking of my brothers."

Wow, they really could read his mind. But even more formidable was that it was one of his sons' sisters that had just kissed his cheek! That had never occurred to him before and it suddenly sparked concern, this time for the two boys in England, the girls' brothers.

"Please, Gayla, I'm frightened. I just realised that David and Russell are in danger." He hugged her tight. "I want to go home."

She pushed him away a little and stopped smiling. "Oh, Daddy. Stop it. We're not in danger, neither are David and

Russell." She raised her little eyebrows, "But I suppose you don't know that, do you. What should you do about it? I know, get somebody to look after them." She began to smile.

His eyes were filling with tears. "You don't listen! I want to go home, and look after them." He held back the blubbering, but the tears ran down his cheeks. Gayla kissed them off.

"Yummy! You taste sooo good. I could do this all day." She licked his cheek, and giggled. "I could eat you right now, if you'd only let me."

Robin held his cheek to her. "I know you're making light of it all, but it's not helping."

She thought a little, "What about if you had somebody else looking after them, while you helped us here." Her childish face frowned a little. "Somebody who has already been looking after them, and knows their movements, and their friends, and can quietly protect them without them even noticing it. Well?" No reaction. He was pretty hard work at times. "Somebody who would do anything you ask. Absolutely anything, and everything." She held her eyes wide open and raised her eyebrows. "Come on, Daddy."

"Hmm, you're talking about the little blonde killer." He smiled, at last. "Catherine."

"There, you're not as daft as you make out. Yes, tell her to look after them."

"Don't get cheeky. Anyway, how can I do that? Pop home to see her?"

"Ha, you don't *have* to. You know the internet? Well, we've had our own *sort* of intranet for quite a long time, ever since the first period. Just tell her, in your head. Say something like, *'Catherine dearest, look after my two little boys while I'm away. Cheers big-ears.'* Try it." She jiggled side to side in front of him. "Go on."

He smiled, and thought Gayla's suggested words, but he did not hear anything in return. His head dropped, as he decided that Gayla was probably again taking the piss. But there she was, down by his feet, waving and staring with those penetrating green eyes, and he heard *'Of course, Robin, me ole mate.'* Pretty inconclusive, but it was hope. He was not going to get out of that bloody dream very easily, so what else could he do, but trust his girls? "Thanks, Gayla's cousin." He blew her a kiss, as she melted back into the dry, lifeless soil.

"We're nearly ready for the meeting." Gayla pulled Robin by the arm, and nodded towards Ninah and Satvinder. Tracy carefully tied her eyepiece around her head and Catan donned her dark glasses and sword.

A teenage girl was to look after the children while the Qeervi family discussed the World's issues with the World's self appointed rulers. "The battle must begin," giggled Gayla.

With Gayla holding Robin on one arm and Catan on the other, the group of six began the short walk across the parade ground. Out of the quiet came a putt, putt sound, and from the side of the main building emerged Aalap's motor rickshaw.

"Aalap!" shouted Gayla.

He pulled up beside the group and out climbed Dilshad, smiling with excitement. "I'm to be a representative of the people." She bowed to Tracy and Robin. "I hope I'll be fine." They all nodded their approval. After all, what chance did the World's leaders really stand against three little girls?

The group were shown into the inner court room, where they were set along a table which faced another table of similar size.

The room was not very impressive, and nothing like what you would expect for a regularly used court belonging to that enormous cult. It was just a bare room with enough space for a few large meeting tables, and a banked gallery which could hold about a hundred viewers. The gallery was empty and it was all very cold and businesslike, with the thick, polished rosewood table tops glaring from the lights from the small chandeliers.

At the head of the two tables sat the Monsignor. He stood up. "Thank you for all coming here today. This is an emergency meeting of the court, and we must welcome the Qeervi Royal family and their local acquaintances. We don't have a formal agenda, not that I know about, so could we please break the ice by each introducing ourselves to the court. Could we begin with The Cardinal, and then move round clockwise. His Eminence, thank you." The Cardinal stood up, very straight, dressed in his usual zucchetto, sash and pectoral cross.

"Good morning, I'm Cardinal Louis Mateo. I'm proud to have been an officer of the College of Cardinals responsible for the election of His Holiness Pope Steven the First" He bowed towards Tracy.

"Good morning, I am Amir Al-Kasatan, member of the ruling family from the United Arab Emirate state of Ras al-Khaimah." He just sat down, in his Arabian costume.

"Good morning." The gentleman stood up, in his smart grey suite. "I'm Peter Bowler, from the United States, and I'm recently the Chairman of the Senate Foreign Relations Committee." He held his hand up to Tracy, "Hi," then sat down.

"Good morning, Your Majesty, Your Royal Highnesses." The large Chinese man bowed low, and held his hands to his face in brief prayer. "I am President Li Jinpeng, I am the paramount leader of the People's Republic of China. I am privileged to again have your acquaintance and am forever your servant." He slowly sat down. The others raised their eyebrows.

"Good morning, my friends." A white-haired black gentleman stood there. "I'm President William Smith, from the Democratic People's Republic of Cofur. I welcome you to our court." He bowed low and sat down.

"Good morning." A white-haired European gentleman stood up and bowed. "I'm the Right Honourable James Parfret, Secretary of State for Foreign and Commonwealth

Affairs for Her Majesty's Government, the United Kingdom." He pompously sat down.

The Monsignor stood up. "Your Majesty, I would imagine that you have all heard of our most honourable members present. We'd be very pleased to hear your representatives' introductions." He remained standing, awaiting a response from the Queen. "If you'd prefer, one of you may introduce each member of your group."

Tracy sat firm and replied, "Yes, Monsignor Plassey, thank you." She held her hand towards Catan. "Her Highness can introduce us."

Catan smiled, her dark glasses glistening in the harsh surroundings. She stood up and Gayla moved to her side and hung on. "Good morning gentlemen. I'll briefly introduce myself, my family, and my friends. I'm Princess Ca'an of Anglia. I'm the daughter of God." She paused to allow the members to scoff. "This little girl is My Eyes. She sees everything for me, and she's been lost for more than two hundred years. She's now found what she was searching for." She listened to Gayla's whispering for a few seconds. "My Eyes is known as Gayla and she's reputed to furnish her daddy a home inside her little tummy. She has generously allowed her daddy, and my daddy, to come out to play today. The *Lamma*." As she held her hand towards Robin, the Cardinal laughed quietly. "The Lamma is the Eternal Protector. His children sometimes call him Homer."

President William Smith asked, "Because he's a philosopher?"

"No, they think he looks like the cartoon, Homer Simpson. Moving along, this is Queen Maya of Anglia, who has always been, and always will be, the pinnacle of the Qeervi family. She is The Mother of God." The court members smiled. Robin looked across to them and chuckled as he wondered just what they must be thinking.

"Beside Mummy is Ninah. He's the Protector of Children, but hasn't been very active since our catastrophe back in seventeen seventy seven. He serves the family with devout loyalty.

"This young lady is Dilshad. She represents the people of the Anglia region, and is destined to fill the gap left by your murdering of our Saint Catherine." There was some murmuring. "Please show me the respect of silence whilst introducing our group. Thank you. Dilshad is an ardent scholar and modern historian. And finally, Satvinder also represents the people of Anglia. He's a former academic from the Dhaka University. He escaped the area during nineteen seventy one. His two daughters and wife did not." Catan bowed her head towards the Monsignor, and then sat down with Gayla.

The Monsignor gave a wry smile. "As pointed as ever, Your Highness. Thank you." He stood up. "Does anybody have any questions before we explore our intentions and curiosities?"

Tracy raised her hand and stated, "I've some questions and requests." She stood up, and looked along towards Gayla. "We need to see our servants, Sergeant Baba and private Alapat." The Monsignor did not flinch. "And we need to see the guard which was kind towards us this morning, at the gate." She looked hard at the Monsignor. "Now! The meeting's on hold until we do."

The Monsignor sent a doorman with his instructions. "Sir Kamdar will accommodate."

After an uneasy silence, the doorman returned, and presented Sir Kamdar.

"Sit with us, Kamdar." Insisted Catan. "Where are Mummy's requested attendees? Not dead, I trust."

Sir Kamdar sat down beside James Parfret. He looked hard at Robin, who remembered Gayla's advice, and thought of Peter and Russell.

Sir Kamdar smiled at him as he spoke. "Lamma, your children are safe." The smile turned into a wide grin, his yellow teeth perfectly complimenting the greasy black hair.

Robin thought *'that's twice today, are they threatening me with my children?'* Gayla rushed along from her seat to help her Daddy.

"He can't hurt the boys, Daddy." She kissed his cheek and returned to Catan.

Robin was just beginning to believe in the private intranet. He wondered if Tracy was online. He looked towards her and thought, *'After everything, I still love you.'* She touched her shaggy leather eye-patch and thought, *'If we don't sleep, does that mean we won't share a bed, ever?'* He grinned and thought, *'You've lost your eye, and I've lost me leg. But I've still got me dick.'* They both had a dirty chuckle.

Oh no. Who else was listening? He called Gayla over to him. "Did you hear that?"

"Hear what?" She looked at his thoughts. *'No. If you think to an individual, nobody else can hear you. You're learning. Clever Daddy.'* She playfully pinched his cheek. *'Tell Kamdar that he's a prat. Go on, dare you.'* She pulled her face beside his and they looked to Kamdar.

'Kamdar, where're our men?'

'They're on their way. They're safe.' He nodded his head at Robin.

Without thinking another word, he hugged Gayla. "I feel safer, now. Thanks for looking after me, my little pompom." He suddenly realized that Sir Kamdar was one of them, a Qeervi. Sir Bruce Kamdar, the Queen's cousin, the soldier of fortune.

The door opened, and Sergeant Baba entered, with his private and the soldier from the gate. The Ghurkhas saluted their Queen and the Lamma, then saluted the rest. The gate soldier went onto his knees and said a short prayer.

Tracy stood up. "Thank you Monsignor, and thank you Kamdar. The soldiers can all sit in the gallery while the court is in session."

The Arab thumped the table. "Let's get on with this. It's becoming a farce."

"Right." The Monsignor informally opened the court and then, "Now, the first thing to discuss is that which has arisen from last night's events. The threat of rebellion from the slum dwellers." The other Chi Bantri members knew nothing of the threat. "The threat has been successfully muted, in order to avoid any panic within the members' respective governments and to prevent any unnecessary interference." He gathered his thoughts whilst studying the six court members' moods. "The Chi Bantri *must* be left to manage its own affairs, unallied to government, industry and religion. When the *Chi Bantri* require their involvement the *Chi Bantri* will kindle it, as always. And we must thank the Queen and her family for abating the threats, subject to our discussions, here today. We thank Her Majesty for her kind consideration in the matter."

The Amir stood up. "I could resolve these problems. Just give me the permission of the court." He sat down.

The Monsignor replied, "The court will *not* give that permission. Our constitution would forbid it. Policing, and protection in the Anglia region, the sect's heartland, is the responsibility of Sir Kamdar and his loyal soldiers."

The American stood up. "Hang on, Plassey, the loyal soldiers were, allegedly, executed last night. Some loyalty."

"Senator, the soldiers died through loyalty to their Queen. To *our* Queen!"

"Plassey, you're losing it, old man. We've worshipped the Princess through all the good times, and now she's turning. We'll worship something else. Just crucify them all."

President Li stood up. "You are a little too self-centred to be an active part in our magnanimous sect. The Chi Bantri succeeds because we are an engine, made up of thousands of components which synchronise perfectly, to continually push us forward into ever increasing personal success. Each component is a *consumable*, and when it fails, it is replaced, *never* repaired. I would suggest greater care with your

American-style flippancy." He bowed to the Queen, and then sat.

The other members gently applauded President Li's short reminder.

"Gentlemen, and ladies." The Monsignor was calm. "For over two hundred years we've thrived. The spirit to continue, to grow into the controlling force across our planet, has been sourced from our Princess and her children. She educated the sect in the early days, and developed belief within us all. Without the belief, we're simply many thousands of individuals. And as we all know, and acutely believe, the Queen and most of her family died to spawn the founding of our sect. And as we all know and believe, the Queen will return to reward us for our strength in benevolence." He looked to the Queen, who remained silent. "When the program from last night's ball is broadcast across the World, they'll admire the performances of the beautiful Jeniffer Bush, the Kolkata Orchestra of Life, and the surprise guest performer, Princess Ca'an of Anglia. They'll also briefly witness the return of the Queen and they'll be intrigued, and they'll seek knowledge, and many, or all, will believe. We must be ready."

The American stood up. "Monsignor, I acknowledge the reminder laid down by the Chinese President. We are one." He looked at his notes. "But, we've no reason to believe in this woman. She's a ginger haired woman with one eye, who's turned up from old Blitey. So what?"

There fell an eerie silence, which seemed to last for such a long time. Robin and Satvinder looked into each others faces, momentarily wondering where they were.

Then William Smith stood up. "I've witnessed similar weaknesses in other members in recent years. We must act positively to put such nihilism behind us. It seems to be a problem with the older members. Maybe us."

President Li, "There is a fundamental flaw in our constitution and code of practice."

James Parfret added in his clear English accent, "Yes, the concept of greed both motivates and strangles. While we were all young, the sect fed our greed for success and riches. The established members pushed, lied, deceived, even killed to ensure our individual successes, then we all promised to guarantee each other's position and fortune. We became the established members, in positions able to help the younger members to achieve what we have already achieved. We find ourselves and our families sitting in enviable positions, surrounded by the fortunes of war and connivance, but suddenly afraid. We're afraid of losing what we already have, and wary in risking our fortunes in the pursuit of young members' successes. The more successful we become, the less we can be motivated by greed. That's our weakness. Many members are beginning to question the requirement to behave so divinely ruthlessly towards the weak as well as the strong. They're wondering why they can't follow their religions, and behave as their God would expect them to behave. And I for one, well, I question why we don't continue the teachings of our Princess, from the late seventeen hundreds. We now strive to gain, not to help."

The Monsignor looked around the group. "Does anybody else have anything to say on the subject of constitution or code?"

"Yes." The Cardinal stood up. "I agree that the sect has begun to outgrow its constitution. I've a conscience and it pricks me every time we instigate inhumanities for the sake of profit. I've all the riches I could wish for, but I don't have happiness."

"But Your Eminence," the Amir speaks, "If you're looking for happiness, sex, and every panacea for sadness and frustration, then come with me. I'll show you how to spend the riches earned from your successes. The Chi Bantri has given you *everything* you could ever wish for. Learn to enjoy it, it's only your conscience which prevents it."

"President Li, do you have any further input?"

President Li stood up. "I do. I must air my reservations about my continued membership of the sect. I am, arguably, the most powerful individual on this Earth. I have a responsibility to my long-suffering people. They must be given protection against inhumanity, they must be allowed to believe in things other than the state. And the constitution of the Chi Bantri severely conflicts with the developing constitution of the People's Republic of China. I am sitting between two peaks, and must now choose on which one to leap." He continued, "And the modern constitution of the Chi Bantri severely conflicts with its *own* constitution, the one of seventeen seventy nine."

The Monsignor stood up, then banged the table with his fist. "I'm sorry. This is a dangerous day for the Chi Bantri." He stood pondering. "I put it to this emergency court that we make representation on the subject of modernisation, to the inner court."

They all looked around at each other. The Cardinal stood up and stated, "I'm happy since the Amir's kind offer of help. I'm against the unnecessary breeding of discontent, and against taking this discussion outside of this group."

The Monsignor stated, "The Cardinal speaks very warily. The inner court will consider any talk of internal revolt to be blasphemy. We should accept that the Chi Bantri is bigger than all of us, and we should thank our Princess for the spirit to grow."

President Li stood up. "I can accept that you are all afraid of the animal which we have all contrived to develop. I, however, must do what is right for my people, and that will almost certainly be in conflict with the Chi Bantri. I will abstain from a vote to take this to the inner court."

The Monsignor smiled. "Can we vote on the representation of this issue to the inner court? Who's in favour?" No hands were raised. "Then the issue is closed. Can I, however, remind the members present that you're all responsible for the maintenance of our communal spirit. Any cracks must be sealed instantly. And remember President Li's earlier warning about failing components. We *don't* repair!"

The Monsignor walked out, followed by the six members.

"What happened?" gasped Robin. "Where've they gone?"

Gayla began to giggle. She could not stop, and jumped up in front of Catan with her hand in the air shouting, "High five Cat'!" and Catan gave her five.

Catan in English. "Gayla and I are pleased. We ain't done that for a long time." She chuckled. "We don't have to do anything at the moment, as they're starting to deteriorate into a committee. No committee has ever successfully run a large club, they all end up fighting, then closing." Gayla ran round and hugged her mummy and daddy, then shook the hands of the two representatives. Catan continued, "They don't even remember that we were here at this meeting. And they've agreed to *all* our demands."

Robin looked at Satvinder and then at Dilshad. They were all mystified, wondering what it was that they seemed to have missed out on. He asked Catan, "For the sake of the ordinary people, here at this table, tell us what the hell's happening. We're totally lost."

"Oh, Daddy. Keep forgetting that you're not quite here yet." Catan laughed. "Well, we had our meeting earlier, and they agreed that the clinic would be reopened, with Syed managing the staffing in the early days. They also agreed to a monthly subsidy to ensure grain and rice products, fruit and veg', clean water and other social benefits, even a set of schools. And they agreed to restore the Royal Palace and Lodge back to their original states, as they were back in seventeen seventy seven at the time of the crucifixion. That's good for Mummy, she's a Queen, and I know she quite likes the human comforts, after forty-odd years of practice. And President Li, who spoke so intellectually about Mummy, is taking the news of Maya's return back to his people. They'll be given the freedom to believe in God, if they so wish. He's been a great scholar through his youth. He's also been an absolute bastard on behalf of the fucking Chi Bantri. But he's now on our side, and I believe in him." She paused for breath. "Oh, and we stuck in the idea about their constitution being outdated and cruel. Well, they all know that. And they've all taken the rewards following the removal of entire casts and peoples, leaving fortunes to be scraped up from the bloody wreckage. Hundreds of millions've died, or worse, as results of their profitable campaigns. And they're all now developing a conscience. Thank you, Mummy, that was brill'. They'll all now begin to destroy themselves." She laughed with Gayla, and Tracy managed a smile.

Robin looked at Satvinder and then at Dilshad. They were all mystified, wondering what it was that they seemed to have missed out on. He again asked Catan, "For the sake of the ordinary people, here at this table, tell us what the hell's happening. We're *still* totally lost."

Catan slowed down a little. "So sorry, Daddy. Pratling on a bit. We're pretty chuffed at what we just did." Gayla whispered at her side. "I'll explain slowly, in English, to you all. Well, the meeting which we all came to didn't feel right. So we stretched time by five days. You can remember the start of the first court meeting, which we all attended, and which seamlessly flowed into the end of the second court meeting, and me and Gayla filled in the missing five days. Those days which we inserted between the two meetings. That was hard, but we did it." She was so proud. "You'll all remember the whole in a little while, maybe after you've been to sleep. We came up with an agenda, presented by us, and we rushed it through like a whirlwind. We only asked for very basic things, mostly for the people of Anglia, but as they were fussing over those basic demands, we took the opportunity to influence both mind and time. We left them some interesting little doubts, which they were unable to leave alone, and couldn't help but to come back to a later court to discuss. You know what happened at that meeting, you were there. Your memories will adjust back into line after some sleep. All in all, very successful bit of manipulation. The seeds of doubt always germinate quickly and grow strongly."

Tracy at last spoke in her capacity as the Mother of God. "I think you girls are moving forward without the proper consent from the family. That was a clever move, but it could've been disastrous. It was, the last time you did it. And you both *know* that we have our rules."

Gayla jumped to their defence, in Qeervi. "Ah, but Mummy, it *wasn't* a disaster. It worked. And we didn't break no rules, as we took nothing away, but gave extra. Five days extra." The little girl frowned and very slowly added, "Many people across the World have just lived for five extra days." She looked down as her mummy stared into her face and she realised what her mummy was thinking. "I know, a lot of people have just suffered, some unbearably, for five days longer than was destined." Both the girls hugged Tracy round the neck. They knew that they had done wrong.

Tracy whispered, "We must accept that what is, is, good or bad. You just changed life for billions of people." They hugged for a few moments, as the others looked on in bewilderment.

Gayla pulled herself away and spoke in Bengali. "Satvinder, would you do me a great favour?" He nodded. "Thank you. Would you tell yours and Doctor Hussain's stories of nineteen seventy one to our writer, to be one of the many reminders to the World as to where the kingdom of hell really is? You told a prologue at the meeting, you'll remember later, which would make any reader wish to read." She stood in front of him and quietly comforted him, "I'll help you through it, if you wish."

He smiled, but his eyes were caverns of sadness and despair. He asked, "What should I call you?"

"I'm Gayla, just Gayla. Some call me other things, like My Eyes, but Gayla's much prettier. Don't you think?"

"Yes, most definitely. Thank you, Gayla, but I've heard people call you other things." He looked into her eyes for a few moments. "Yes, I'll do my best to convey the truth, without exception. When'll your writer be available, as I'm bloody old and knackered, with very little time remaining?"

"Don't fret. She won't miss you." The little girl took his hand, and held it for some seconds.

Tracy then snapped her fingers, and almost instantly the Sergeant and his private were there. "I think we need to leave this Fort. It smells of death. Ca'an, the children can come to the house, with us."

Robin suggested, "The house won't be ready, yet. We'll need drinking water and electricity."

Tracy smiled as she took Robin's hand. "They've had *five days* and most of the World's resources to prepare it, it'd better be ready." She looked over to Sir Kamdar, who was still sitting in the gallery. "Kamdar, whose side are you on?" He smiled at her, showing his yellow teeth, but said nothing. The girls unsuccessfully tried to follow his thinking.

He stood up and moved towards the exit doors, and said to Catan, "The Lamma is lost. Poor Lamma."

The group then left the court room, and went outside onto the parade ground in the sun. Lots of people were milling around, some wearing their national dress, and discussing matters in small groups. Something was going on. They were members of the inner court, preparing to meet.

Catan said, "This's when somebody dies, when they all panic."

Aalap was waiting outside for his daughter, and as they approached him he asked Dilshad where she had been for five days. He was rather stressed. She could not truthfully tell him very much.

Dilshad interpreted for him. "Your Majesty, my father's arranged a car for you to travel to the Palace. He's been told that it's ready for you all. The Lodge is also ready for your servants and staff."

Tracy looked around at the dignitaries on the parade ground. They all looked at her, some quite intensely. "How big is the car?"

Dilshad enquired, and answered, "It's a limousine, and will comfortably seat six, plus your two Ghurkhas as drivers."

"Ninah," Tracy waited as he walked over to her. "Would you please take Satvinder safely home, and then meet us at the Palace. But before, get the children here? They'll travel in the limousine with the girls."

"You'll not all fit into the limousine."

"No, I want to ride with Robin, with Aalap." She smiled at Ninah. She was beginning to remember how loyal and caring the giant had always been. "We need some time together." As she looked at him she heard his thoughts, *'He'll soon be with us. This's happened before. Just remember what Gayla told you, in the clinic.'*

The limousine, a shiny, black, stretched Jaguar, appeared from around the main building. The driver parked up in front of the living quarters, and handed the keys over to Sergeant Baba. He and the private drove off through the main front gates with the three girls and the children.

The dignitaries were intensely curious, maybe resentful, as Aalap's tiny motor rickshaw carried the two souls out of the back gates, and across the open area. It was quiet there, and very few of the slum dwellers were to be seen. Maybe it was the heat of the sun keeping them in.

Robin looked at Tracy, and she at him. They kissed passionately for a few moments, and then Tracy put her head on his shoulder. He asked, "What the hell is going on, Trace?" She did not answer. "I was at that meeting for about an hour, but apparently for five days, with three soldiers, an Indian child and a sad old man. I was comfortable with *them*. But I was also there with some other things. And I don't really know what they are. It's not the first time that witch has come to mind."

"As Ca'an says, you'll catch us up. Please be patient."

"Catch up with what? What are you all?" His face was sad. "I think I've lost you. Don't know what to do."

"You'll never lose me." She was thoughtful. "When you were in the clinic you talked in your sleep. After you'd cut your leg off. I know who you are. You're the Lamma." She paused. "Some things you said, hurt me at the time, but not now. You couldn't have known those things if you weren't the Lamma. Please keep with me." She looked at Aalap. Then she thought, *'I wonder if Aalap believes in us.'*

Robin looked at her, and thought, *'I wonder what any of them must be thinking. And d'you know what? I'm using our intranet like I was born to it.'*

'See, you know who you are. It's growing in you. When I ate your leg I felt I was in heaven. I could've eaten every bit of you if you'd let me. It was the most beautiful thing I've ever experienced. It brought me home to myself. And while you were out, and a bit delirious, I fed you a bit of my calf muscle.'

Robin frowned in disbelief. *'Did I eat it?'*

'Yes, you loved it. You almost bit my hand off. But I think you need more, it was such a small morsel. Gayla told me something that I never knew before, so I know how to get you back. I'll give you some more of my meat when we get home. You can grow strong again.' She put her hand on the side of his face, and kissed him, pushing her tongue into his mouth then running it round his lips. *'You can eat me, I want it. And drink my juices as the sweet blood of my ambrosia melts into your soul, pulsating with strength and vitality. Drink my juices and come with me to heaven.'*

Robin was getting excited. "I think we need to wait 'til we get home." They put their heads together and smiled. "And what'd I say in my sleep? Go on, you've wetted my appetite. Was it good, or bad?"

"At the time, I cried. I couldn't understand and it was so painful. But now it's beautiful, now that I understand again about who we are, and how close we are. I'll tell you one day."

The journey to the Palace was slow. The limo' went by the main roads and was probably there pretty quickly, but for some unknown reason Aalap was taking a 'long' cut home. He must have known that they needed the privacy, just enough for them to chill. And, despite not understanding English, nor being logged into their celestial intranet, he knew that they had pulled back together again. It was a good job they did, really, as they had a responsibility to protect the World from their two fiery daughters. Whoever said it was easy being a parent?

16 -- THE TRIP TO HEAVEN

The Royal Palace, Anglia, West Bengal

The old red-brick building had been transformed from what it looked when they passed a few weeks earlier. It was still a bit of a wreck, but clean, with light blue painted shutters in good repair, and flowers hanging from baskets over the small balcony. The tin roof looked like it had been repainted green, and the red brick walls dusted. In a prehistoric way, it looked like home, and the canopied entrance, with its potted flowers, was delightfully inviting. The Lodge was its smaller brother, with a less grand entrance canopy.

The large double doors led into a spacious hallway which then led each side into two large living rooms. The floors were marble, and the walls painted white, with light green coving separating the tall, white ceilings. The lights were all twelve lamp chandeliers.

The two were welcomed 'home' by the children and the Ghurkhas. The three girls were already routing around the several rooms, looking for old treasures and relics. At least sometimes they were children!

"Well, this's home." Tracy was a little excited to be back where she was the last time she was Queen. "It'll do." They were philosophical. "It's not what we've been used to."

Private Alapat approached the Royals and asked if they would require dinner. They had acquired a cook, a personal servant and two cleaners. Tracy removed her eye-patch and looked deep into Robin's eyes. She thought, *'I think we've some business of our own to attend.'* Robin nodded, trying to hide his excitement. "Thank you, Private, but we'll be dining alone, without the family, tonight. Could you please ask whoever to allow us some privacy? We don't want to be disturbed." She remembered. "Oh, and Private, could you please ask Aalap to come to see me, right away?"

He bowed and went off with his list of duties. Aalap soon arrived, and he must have been waiting for them to ask.

In clear Bengali Tracy asked Aalap, "Will you stay with us for a while? We need your help, and we need to talk to Dilshad. And could you drive the Jag'?"

A smile stretched from ear to ear. "Thank you, Your Majesty. I'll be greatly honoured to be your servant. Thank you."

Tracy smiled at the little Indian driver. "I've a job for you. It's very important that you're discreet and fast. First, have they opened the clinics, yet?" He nodded. "I need you to visit the clinic and collect some medicine. If you can find Syed, he'll help you. I need some powder, which's in a jar in the laboratory, grey, and is marked up as 'Akhtar's second batch'. I also need a jar of ranar extract." She smiled as he scurried off to do his duty for his Queen.

The marble stairway and landing led to five large bedrooms. The Queen's was lush, while the others were comfortable, and it was the Queen's room which led to the balcony, overlooking a grassed open area and the road. It was previously used as a platform from which to address her local people.

"We just need to relax, and wait for Aalap to return." She pushed Robin onto the large bed. "You ready to fly? I am." They lay together, relaxing, but neither had slept, nor eaten, for several days and Robin was restless. Tracy asked, "What's up, darling?"

"Don't know. I've found my intranet skills, you even speak fluent Bengali. You know all these things, but I still have a fear of where we're going."

"Oh, honey-bunch. I know what you mean, as I've really enjoyed being human. I'm gonna miss it. Hold me tight." They held each other, lying raggedly across the bed, then she whispered, "Would you rather stay as human? I think it's probably too late to take that option, but we could ask Ca'an."

They called for Catan, and she came up to the bedroom. Gayla and Dilshad were with her.

"I need to ask you something, Cat', but I don't know if the two children should be here."

Catan took her glasses off and sat on the edge of the bed. "We're all family, Mummy. Well Dilshad is almost, she's our good friend."

"Ok. But you must promise to be a real friend, and say nothing of this. That ok, Dilshad?"

"Of course. I'll never tell."

"Ok. Well, Ca'an, if your daddy wanted to stay as a human, what would happen?"

Catan smirked. "Mummy. You must know what'd happen. The same as has happened to both of you in the past two hundred-odd years. You'd live, die, and your souls would be passed in to new beings, and you'd die, and your souls would be passed in to new beings, and so on, until one of us finds you and brings you back to the family. That's all. Why?" She looked towards her mummy and studied her mind. "No. We don't know why you and Daddy became human. We don't know why Ninah got lost. We just don't know why we were split for over two hundred years. It should never've happened, but it did, something interfered. Now we need to be together to carry on our never-ending duties." Her beautiful pearly eyes showed no emotion. "So why d'you ask that question?"

Tracy looked sympathetically at Robin. "So your father could carry on with his two sons, and his brothers and cousins. They'll all be gone in not too many years. That's what humans do. He could be with them until they've gone, couldn't he?"

Catan's sightless eyes turned momentarily towards Gayla. "Hmm, it might be too late, he's already partly joined us. He couldn't go back to what he was, he can't just forget." She looked into Tracy's mind, "No, sorry Mummy. You couldn't go with him. You're the Mother of God, you're no longer in a human state. You'd have to lose him and say goodbye until his family have all died. " She looked towards Robin. "We can't do our work without you. We'd *all* have to wait for you."

Robin took her point. He was sad to have to say, "I can't go back. I can see that."

Catan and Gayla whispered. Gayla spoke. "Daddy, you can still see your family. Would they reject you as a Qeervi?"

He quietly laughed to himself, then pulled Gayla to him and cuddled her. "They wouldn't even know what Qeervi is. Why should they? I don't." Gayla held Robin's midriff very tightly. "Maybe I'll get back to see them soon."

Gayla released her dad, and stated, "We've heard from General Dara, and from Syed. There're some problems. Shall we discuss them over a G and T later, chappies?" The little girl giggled, even though she had a concerned air about her.

The girls left the room, closing the door behind them and Private Alapat stood guard at the bedroom door. Robin and Tracy both realised that their life together would no longer be the human experience into which they had been resurrected, and which they had taken for granted for many years. They also knew from the mood of the girls that things had changed since they went into that meeting. Something was seriously not right.

Anyway, let's lighten up a bit. The powder and ranar extract had arrived. Robin and Tracy were on a knife-edge, saturated with expectation, and trembling at the promise of their immaculate reunion. Robin crept like a naughty boy to the door, and locked it.

Tracy spoke with a husky voice. "Join me, my darling. We can fly. And when we land, you'll be the Lamma, in body *and* in mind."

Tracy slowly slipped her smooth silk sari off to reveal her white shoulders and tummy, radiant under the maroon choli. As the pearl studded belt dropped, her sari slipped down around her ankles, and she stood in her white petticoat. The shape of her legs was silhouetted with light from the windows, and Robin could see her crotch, moulded like a polished stone on a beach, waiting for the wash of the tide. "Help me, darling." Robin carefully removed the necklace, and then played with the tiny buttons between her breasts, until the choli opened up. Her breasts shone, dappled with freckles, and her nipples stood up, waiting. They puffed, filled with the nectar of the Gods. Then Robin bent down to them and kissed each one, gently squeezing them with his lips as his hands slowly massaged the tummy, so soft and flawless, then Tracy whispered, "First we'll eat."

She dropped her petticoat to reveal her short-cropped ginger mound. She pushed his shoulder and chuckled. "This's your larder, your fountain of life. And you'll drink from that fountain." She pushed him down and pulled his face into her pubic area, opening her legs enough for him to taste the lips, but then pushed him away. "Enough, for now." She closed the larder, grinning. Robin took his clothes off, then removed his leg and sat on the bed. He studied his lover's nude body as it manoeuvred across to the ranar plant and as she bent over to pick up the medicines, her vagina revealed, spiking his head with desire.

She chuckled, "We're gonna make a serious fucking mess," reaching to the cabinet to grab a long, sharp knife. She also pulled out a china plate, and a bowl. "I'll mix up the poultice, you can make some swabs for the ranar." The cotton pillow cases tore easily, and then he dripped the extract onto two swabs. They were ready.

The lovers sat on the bed opposite each other, with the plate, poultice, knife and ranar swabs between them and each studied the other's valley of plenty as they plucked up the courage to slice the meat joints from their calves. Robin became erect, and stared at her beautifully formed love-lips, which had started to wet in response to the burning promise of union. Tracy picked up the knife and pushed it into Robin's hand.

"You cut me first," she whispered, and then she put a swab to her nose. Her speech became more emphatic. "I don't want to miss any of it. Just do it." He placed the knife at the top of her calf, on the inside leg, and then sliced! It cut the meat quickly and cleanly, the joint peeling off as Tracy tensed with the pain, and she grunted as her body became taught and her nipples hardened. She pushed her hand between her thighs, squeezing her clitoris, as Robin lifted the meat onto the plate.

He hurriedly scooped a handful of poultice, and moulded it over her bleeding wound.

Panting, she whispering in a husky wheeze, "*That* was fucking good." She leaned forward to kiss him with her sweating lips. "Ready?"

He nodded. A good sniff of ranar wakened every sense in his body. He held his good leg forward, and she, without further warning, sliced the meat. He screamed and shuddered. His eyes rolled as the pain caught hold of his body, and so Tracy pushed the ranar under his nose to keep him with her. She tended the wound with the poultice, and he settled.

"Fuck, that hurt. *Fantastic!*"

They held each other for a few minutes, their senses alive with pain and evil satisfaction. But the pain turned to ecstasy, and their chests held tight together as their organs met, his penis caressing her clitoris and lips. She snarled, "We must eat."

They pulled themselves away from each other. She grabbed the two meat joints, and squeezed and twisted them together, to make them one and then bit into the bloody meal, her eye almost rolling out of site, and she groaned with delight. Robin pulled her hands to his mouth and ate the meat. It was heavenly. He had never had anything like it, except when out of it, and he could feel the strength surging into his veins. They both pulled together and like animals tore at the meat from both sides. Their faces, covered in blood, pushed together and the meal was shared, passing meat from one mouth to the other, and back. And snogging violently between mouthfuls. But then it was gone, and momentarily Robin felt depressed, as if he'd just snorted his last line of coke. "Afters!" shouted Tracy and pulled his head down as she laid back, legs almost up round her neck. "Drink, you bastard." His face was pushed into her vagina which ran with juices. He drank his mother's fluids, sending her into a frenzy, and he ejaculated over the bed clothes. Her body stiffened, her teeth ground and she had an enormous orgasm, and screamed. "Now fuck me, you bastard. Fuck me hard. Now!"

Robin pulled himself up to her, and their bloody faces combined to kiss, bite and lick. He pushed his tongue into her mouth and she bit, sending sensational shudders through his body. Then he fucked her. They went at it hard and furious, trying to hurt each other as their pelvis clashed, her vagina burning and sucking. She tensed her muscles and held tightly onto his glans, refusing to let him slip out as he pumped his manhood. Then he again reached his climax, his vinegar-face screwed up, just as Tracy reached hers. She screamed and tore at his back with her nails, and then they both locked up, like boards. They panted, and slowly the bodies relaxed, and Tracy rolled him off, to lay side by side, exhausted, exhilarated, and regenerated. They looked into each others' eyes, saying nothing.

After a while, they came round, and Tracy stood up, and looked at the bed. "Fuck, what a mess." The bed was splattered and scuffed with blood stains. And so were they both. "What're we gonna do, Rob?" They both started to giggle, and just carried on for a while.

"Lets get a shower. But what about the poultice?"

"How long's it been on?" She looked at the clock. "Think it's about an hour. Let's pull them off." They peeled back the grey covering, and the wounds were sealed enough to shower. "It's a miracle."

After inspecting the shower room, Tracy helped Robin up, and they shuffled across the room. But as their faces came together the blood was too much for them to neglect, and they began to suck and lick each other's faces, until the blood was gone. Their passions were again set alight. He pushed her over the table and took her from behind, pulling her head back to him by her flowing ginger mantle. They bit and kissed violently until she released a rapturous scream and his hands squeezed her breasts so hard that they wept ambrosia. He slipped his penis out of the larder and swung her round, then fed on the Mother's milk. She suckled him as they both floated in a state of divine delirium. They were one.

After the shower Robin replaced the leg and reminded, "I seem to remember Gayla mentioning G and T. We'd better get down there. I need a drink." They had put on their European cloths.

She seemed a little shy. "Did I scream?"

"A little. I can't really remember much, just our pure greed for each other. You know what, you're a fucking animal." He had a sly smile.

She was a little worried. "You don't think I made too much noise, then?"

"No." He kissed her frowning forrid. "No, don't worry."

As they opened the door, the *Ghurkha* private stood to attention.

"Private, at ease. Could you please get the cleaners to change our bed."

He stood grinning, and bowed in acknowledgement.

From the bottom of the stairs they looked into one room, nobody there, and so entered the other. The leather armchairs were arranged around an enormous teak coffee table, and there sat the three girls, with Ninah, General Dara, Captain Batiste and Syed, and with the six children on leather poufs. As the couple walked into the room the three girls began to giggle, and the children joined them. General Dara's pale coloured face turned brilliant red, but the valiant Belgian, Captain Batiste, remained polite. He stood up and asked, "Have you settled in to your new home?" and then lost it, laughing uncontrollably as he sat down.

Tracy was red with embarrassment. She turned to Robin, quietly saying, "Cheers, pal. 'Not much noise'. Just *wait* 'til I get you home." They gingerly moved to their seats and sat down. The silence rang out.

"Right, where's me drink?" Robin broke the ice and the Captain poured him a whisky with a splash of water. "Cheers, lovely to see you, Syed. Lovely to see you all."

Syed smiled. "I was a bit bloody concerned that I hadn't heard from you, until a little while ago. I was just approaching the front door at the time!" They all laughed and giggled, apart from Tracy.

Robin tried to rescue her. "Ok. Let's all act our ages. We've all had sex before." He looked at the children. "They can't speak English anyway. So, we almost fucked the life out of each other. Can we just leave it at that?" He looked around the group as Dilshad translated for Gayla and young Peter translated for the other children. They all roared in hysterics.

Tracy took Robin's hand and with a wry smile begged him, "Please don't try to help me any more. I can drown under my own volition!"

The group settled down, and spent some time with chit-chat. The party was settling into some good conversation, and it brought fond memories back, for some, about their garden party with Saint Catherine. Dilshad was destined, and determined, to fill some of the gap left by their venerated Saint's death.

Catan sat with Dilshad on a two-seater. They were becoming very close, with so much interest and intellect in common, but there was more than that. Catan had spent many desolate years by herself, in a sightless existence, and was enjoying the physical companionship of the little teenager. She was falling in love. Quite how that could ever work out between two different species, I don't know. But I think they both deserved some non-paternal love and happiness, and maybe a teenage crush.

General Dara brought life back down by suggesting that they should begin looking at the current issues. "The past five days've seen the World in turmoil, it's been absolute bedlam. I feel that it's my duty to tell you that you're not the popular Queen that you were before you pledged alliance with the Chi Bantri."

Silence instantly fell upon the group. What was the General talking about? The past five days, that was what he was talking about.

Gayla and Catan sat with calm, cold faces, trying to look in control, but knowing that it could all be beginning to slip. And Tracy and Robin looked at each other, then at the girls. What had they done?

"Right!" snapped Tracy. "Right, you two, say nothing." She scowled at them. They had been really naughty, but how naughty? How far had they gone? "General Dara, could you please explain. I've had a bad period, as you probably know, but I'm now back. Please tell me what you think's happened over the past few days. And Syed, please, you can help." She stopped scowling. "We all need to be friends right now."

The General was wary about saying too much. "I'll have to think where to start, Your Majesty." He fidgeted his thumbs. "The natural disasters've been terrible. Catastrophic. Millions dead." He took a big breath. "The Italian volcanoes. Millions are dead or missing. The cloud is likely to cover the whole of southern Europe, and ash is falling heavily. There were several eruptions, all the main ones, Etna, Vesuvius and Stromboli, Santorini, and loads of smaller releases." He lowered his head. "Weird, but you're getting the blame."

Robin suggested, "That's just the newspapers. Sensations, that's all."

"No, it's not. This lot have claimed responsibility. The Chi Bantri've been telling the World that their combined financial power has been exalted by the return of their God, Queen Maya of Anglia. They're bestowing the Chi Bantri, that is themselves, with the veil of a deity. They're claiming the World."

"That's ridiculous." Tracy wasn't amused, but she wasn't convinced.

"But Your Majesty, you've put your seal to it."

Tracy snapped, "We'll talk about that one later. What about the eruptions?"

"The eruptions were unexpected, devastating, and enormous. Etna went with a VEI of six. That's rather colossal. The Chi Bantri had been very close to waging a private war against China and Russia after both those countries had removed most of the Chi Bantri members from official office. Some are still in custody in Russia. So, with your divine support, the Chi Bantri threatened the World with the Italian volcanoes." Pause. "And then delivered them. They're winning."

Catan spoke. "We have... Sorry, the Chi Bantri have, many volcanologists amongst their scientific members. Those scientists could let their club know very early of any known activities, and also prevent others from having that information. Even manufacture data to confirm zero chance of eruption, just as the eruptions are imminent. They're very resourceful."

"That makes sense, Cat'. What else's happened?" asked Tracy.

The General thought his words carefully. "The Chinese didn't accept that you're sitting on the Chi Bantri throne. I believe you've met President Li, and I believe Ca'an knows him. He's sent a team of scientists to work with a Russian team to disprove their 'act of God'. They can prove that the eruptions were predictable, and beyond the control of any group of people." He hesitated, as though waiting for Tracy to lead him. She did.

"So, that sounds good. Common sense and technology will prevail."

"But the absolute brute-strength of this cult may well prevail. I'm sorry to have to report that this morning saw the bloody assassination of President Li, and six of his fellow government leaders. Your supporters, they've gone, and along with them goes the organised opposition to the Chi Bantri. I believe the scientists've been given a new brief, to *prove* the 'act of God'. The Russians have recalled their team of scientists and probably by now have also relinquished their opposition, at least in principle. You must understand that the Chi Bantri is not a gang of people which could be cornered and knocked off en masse by heavy artillery. They're secret, never all together, with thousands of unknown soldiers, fighting within the enemy's very own camps, maybe even commanding them. They've become stronger than God. That's why they're winning. That's why the World doesn't believe in you; you've allowed them to do what you should have been preventing."

Tracy looked to Gayla and thought, *'Was this the time slip?'* Gayla replied, *'Sorry, Mummy.'*

She continued with the General. "Thank you for your honesty. What else has happened over the past five days, General?"

"The Catholics have denounced you, and labelled you as a blasphemous fraudster. The Muslims are regrouping, and who knows what else. Everybody is panicking. Right across the World they're talking about the new religion, Chi Bantri. And the Hindus are currently discussing your claim."

"Hang on. What claim?"

"That *you* are our maker, and that the hundreds of religions had better sort out their differences, as you're closing in on their control. You say that God has returned to pass judgement, and deal out the punishment. And that there're many other volcanos in your armoury. All very basic and childish, but it hits the spot."

"Stop!" Tracy was beginning to feel angry. "I've heard enough. That sounds like the rantings of a lunatic, and I've not made any of these claims. What else've I done wrong during the past five days? Well?"

"I'm sorry, Your Majesty, but I'm just the messenger."

"You're more than the messenger. You've protected Ca'an, with your family and coleagues, for more than two hundred years. Will you be continuing? Do you still support me? I need an answer, now."

"Of course I do. We all do. And my military support is still at your disposal. But our people will need some explanations." He regrouped his thoughts. "Everything seemed to be out of character. You approved the hanging of four common thieves. You ordered the open area behind the Fort to be kept clear, a no-go zone for all slum dwellers, all those of a lower order. And you..."

"*Now stop*! Don't say another word. That last sentence has convinced me." She ground her teeth whilst looking viciously at Catan and Gayla. "Syed, do you have anything to report, good or bad?"

"Confusion. I've been concerned about my good friend here. Sir Kamdar arranged for him to meet me at the clinic a few days back, but Robin, you never turned up. When I contacted you you told me to fuck off. Why?"

Robin looked into Syed's face and raised his eyebrows.

Syed smiled. "I'm glad it wasn't you. Welcome back old mate." He sighed. "And yes, I've some very sad news to begin. Satvinder has been killed. He was decapitated only this morning by four soldiers out on patrol." He looked at the Captain. "Captain Batiste's men questioned them, and were told that the local policing had returned to the nineteen thirty two rules. We've checked that out, and it's the rule of the gun, basically. The soldiers have unquestioned right to administer the laws and their punishments. Satvinder had upset them, somehow. The soldiers acted within the local laws; they thought he should die, so they killed him. I'm sorry. I'm so sorry." He passed a sympathetic look towards Dilshad.

"What else?"

"The agreed food supplies were cancelled." He looked at his feet.

"Why?"

"I don't know, you didn't give a reason."

Five missing days. How much more damage was done throughout the World during those five days? God only knows, but He wasn't telling.

Tracy was sinking very slowly. "What d'you think, Ninah?"

He bowed his head, "I think we need to regroup. We need to fight this one carefully, and with stealth. We mustn't let anybody see a thing, unless we need them to see it. And when they do see it, we must make it count." The gentle giant held the little hand of one of the children. "Some of us may need to make sacrifices. Do you remember when we had this very same problem with the Zhou Dynasty. Almost three thousand years ago it would have taken a year to deliver a letter to England from China. We had plenty of time to adjust the people's minds. But now the whole World can watch you eating your beakfast, live. We need to play this one very differently." He bowed his head to Dilshad and the General. "This local area is a catalyst for our work, so we must use it to seed the growth of disbelief against the cult, and that will give us some time to plan our attack. Whatever we do, Maya, it must culminate in the total destruction of the offending cult. Nothing must be left." Harsh words from one so gentle. And one surprising word for Robin, as it restored some of his fond memories, about his beloved Maya, his Queen.

Catan was looking very guilty, like a naughty child, but she had found solace in her new soul-mate, Dilshad. She gave her mate a gentle cuddle. Then Captain Batiste poured everybody another drink, and they all tried to relax for a while. The party spirits had vapourised, but they were all polite, and they humoured each other's jokes and stories.

Gayla reassured everybody, "Poor Satvinder, I think he was ready to go. Hope he didn't suffer, like his daughters. And Catherine can still get his story. He can still be part of the modern scriptures."

Catan suggested, "Dilshad's a fine writer, she could help Catherine. She could stay here with us forever." She was smitten. But she had overlooked the truth that humans do not stay *anywhere* forever. She pulled a wry smile. "But she couldn't get Satvinder's story. Catherine'll have to do that."

It had been a strange day. Just the morning before was six days before, and the family had allowed others to control destiny, for only five days. It was five days too many for such a fickle World.

After the guests had gone, the family looked calmly at each other. Dilshad was still sitting with Catan, drinking orange juice.

"Would you like me to go?" she politely asked.

Nobody answered imediately, but Gayla, after not saying much all evening, suggested, "You might be interested in what's coming up. If you're going to help Catherine with writing, you need some inside info about us. The sort you won't get anywhere else."

Robin supped at his whisky and suggested, "Stay and be part of our family for a bit, or forever, well, you know what I mean." He was getting a little intoxicated. "If Cat' wants you to."

Catan grinned at her daddy. That was 'yes'.

Tracy moved seats, to be opposite the girls. "You really fucked up this time. This time slip's done a lot of damage. Bad damage." She was not angry, more disappointed. "What's your part in this, Cat'?"

Catan's eyes were blank. My Eyes was not talking her sight to her, so she was totally blind and isolated. "I've been here for a long time, in this imperfect body. I don't know what my bit is with all this. I helped Gayla plan, and to rebuild the five days. I thought we'd got it right, so that nothing changed." If there was a time to cry, that was it. Dilshad put her arm around the child's shoulders and comforted her, but her eyes never dampened, just stared. "I'm sorry if we've killed so many people. I hope it doesn't spoil your plans, Gay'."

Tracy allowed her to take the comfort of her friend, and moved to Gayla. "Right, as usual, it's down to you. Speak. Tell your family what you've done this time."

The little girl stood up. "I had to do something, and I had to do it on my own."

"That's not true. You've a family, and we have rules. Break the rules and the Earth itself suffers. You've blown a big chunk of the World up, and that disaster will affect billions of people with its initial blast, and the after blasts, and that wide-spreading cloud of ash. There's gonna be loss of light, crop failures and famine throughout the World. And the Chi Bantri are stronger than all others, and will manipulate it, rid themselves of the opposition, and will profit from it. It's the same old story. The really strong always win." She was getting heated. "And what're you going to do about it?"

Gayla suddenly dropped into her evil posture, as they had seen with the Indian soldiers in the slum. She stood like a cobra ready to strike, knees bent, hands on hips and leaning her scowling face towards Tracy. "Some speech Maya, but what do *you* think I'm gonna to do about it? I've got it slightly wrong, so spank me, if you dare. I've had to plan this fucking lot on my own for years, without you lot. I gave up searching for you, so I did what I had to do with Ca'an and Ninah. And if it wasn't for Catherine I'd still be doing it on my own. Now what are *you* gonna do about the consequences of your deserting your whole bloody family?"

"Hold it!"

"No, *you* hold it, I haven't finished!" Gayla was mad. "You went, and never came back. You went against all my instructions!" She suddenly calmed down as if something had got hold of her. She stood a little more comfortably, took some deep breaths and then spoke quietly. "Well, you did. Please Mummy, we've had to fight this one on our own. We knew the European volcanos would go, maybe not that hard, but we thought that they could be used to bring this lot out into the open. So we didn't make them blow, so we didn't kill anybody, and no rules were broken. But *they* really do believe that they made it happen, and so've left the safety of their shells, and are still coming out even further. They'll be totally exposed soon, and for the first time ever, showing their colours to the World. Then we'll be putting down an entity, one which the people can relate to, and to learn to hate, before we return the World to some form of status quo. Most people are now aware of the Chi Bantri for other crimes, as they've publicly threatened leaders, and are known to have assasinated our friends from China. They're feeling big enough to claim responsibility for their own actions. The President and his leaders will be sadly missed, but the results of their deaths will be worth it, trust me." Pause. "And the volcanoes'll prove to have been natural; believe in the strength of the human scientific machine, they *always* come through in the end." She grinned. "Sometimes they're wrong, but..."

"So this is all planned?"

Catan jumped in, "Yes, we've been planning it for a long time. We just need to fill in some detail as we proceed." She still just stared ahead. "Some of the detail isn't pleasant."

Gayla continued. "They're all blaming you. We put a double in place, to make sure they blame you. Before the eruptions, the World saw you as a bit of a joke. A serious joke. And why not? It's hardly believable, is it? The long lost Queen suddenly appearing again hundreds of years later. And you've done nothing to make anybody believe you're real. It's just fairy-tale stuff. Now, at least, they believe in Queen Maya."

Tracy stood up. "This is madness!"

"The end will justify the means! Now that the Chi Bantri are leaving their hideouts, confidently coming out into the daylight, we can encourage the World to accept their existence. We will be able to rid the World of the controlling Chi Bantri dictators, and replace them with lots of smaller, regional groups. You know, gangs. Humans must be in gangs to survive, they're like wolves who need their pack. They must be able to work together, fight, wrangle, steal, and hopefully do what's best for them and their people, and for their region, without being Chi Bantri puppets. The rewards of successful control and leadership can remain in the region to benefit all. That's the idea. Human beings can't be just one big happy, or unhappy, family. They *have* to live in gangs. They have to have a leader who they can see, hear and believe, as well as admire, maybe fear. Sometimes he'll be a prat, but natural selection'll kick the prat into touch eventually, unless he has a Chi Bantri behind him. The secret society is now coming out from its cover, where they can popped off at will. The gangs will be able to see their enemies, and deal with them. Am I making sense?"

Tracy laughed to herself. "Yes. With me as the sacrificial bait!" She pulled Gayla to her and sat her on her knee. "You *must* understand my rather nervous reaction. I still don't see everything."

Dilshad raised her hand, like a school child. "Can I ask something?" Tracy nodded. "If you're going to rid the World of the Chi Bantri, by bringing them out into the open and then, I guess, killing them all, where will it leave you? You're now the Chi Bantri leader and their spirit. Whatever they do now, it'll be your fault. They'll all despise you."

Gayla raised her head from Tracy's breasts. "They'll not hate God, even if they hate us. When I give them a real God to admire, they'll forget all about us. We're not looking for reward, just doing our jobs." She thought, "But if they don't hate us, that'll make our jobs easier, for a long time to come."

Dilshad asked Gayla, "But why does your Mummy have to be on their side? She takes the blame for everything."

Gayla had to admit, "They're very strong, and very intelligent. I think they have infinitely more of Ca'an's spirit that we realise. You have to remember that when we planned this, Mummy and Daddy weren't back here with us. It's gone off in a slightly different direction to what the book originally read, but we're still on line, and the book can always be rewritten. And just like when they held onto poor Cat' for all those years, somehow stopping her from going home, they've kept our decoy, and they've used her far beyond our predictions. There's a lookalike, a human, who's playing Mummy and she's brilliant. We didn't expect them to turn it round like this. But I think it's all gone really well, so far."

Robin spoke at last. "Unless you've some fantastic plan for recovery, it's not gone very well at all. They're winning."

"Daddy, the volcanos were totally natural. They were gonna happen, and the human beings'll eventually prove that, so the plan is following its course. The lookalike, who's now jumped ship, was not expected to live beyond the eruptions, but I'm not gonna expand on that. She'll be gone soon, and we'll all be smelling of roses." She sighed. "But since you and Mummy woke the neighbourhood with your sordid sexual stunts, I believe you're back with us, properly. I'm now prepared to give a *very* brief outline of my plan, if you like. Yes?"

"Maybe you should've done that earlier," retorted Robin.

"No chance, not with you still in that half state. But I can now. First, we court the catholics and the muslims, who all agree that the Queen is a blasphemous fraudster. We can agree to rid the World of the fraudster, and the Chi Bantri. And Tracy will be seen to be instrumental in the removal of the imposter queen. They'll then respect our intentions, and maybe show less distrust in us. In the meantime we'll ruin the Festival of Life for them. They'll not receive the Qeervi spirit which has sustained their mettle for two hundred years. They'll mentally weaken. And when the time's right, we'll remove them from power. The World can then return to its former glory."

Robin stood up, "Where's the whisky? After that, I think I need some spirit of my own. I'm about as much in the picture now as I was before you explained the plans."

"Daddy, you're all just gonna have to trust me. We're too far gone to drop out. Ca'an and Ninah are with me. So's Catherine, so what about you two?"

Tracy looked at Robin and thought, *What do you think? I think we've no choice.'* Robin's answer surprised her. *We have to trust her. She got it right with Hatshepsut.'* His memory had revived.

She spoke for them both. "We haven't been here, so we'll fit in with your plans. Just get it right, and remember that we *are* here now."

They all flopped back into their luscious seats. "Been ok, tonight, hasn't it." Catan had enjoyed it. They all agreed, but she did add, "But I thought we were going to fight. Glad we didn't." She was so at home with her friend, the two young teens finding a different, shared element in their lives; love.

But what comes after love? Hopefully, more love. "Daddy, you made a promise. Remember?"

Robin frowned, "Err, of course I remember." He was racking his memory. "Of course I remember. When d'you want it?"

"Now, right now!" She wriggled with excitement. "Can Dilshad share? Can she? Please Daddy?" She jumped up, pulling Dilshad by the hand, and they squeezed onto Robin's seat, one each side of him. They held hands across his tummy. "You can start whenever you want." She kissed him on the cheek, and Dilshad did the same. "Isn't this lovely, my family together. We're ready, Daddy. Come on."

Colin Hodgson

17 -- FIRST LOVE LAST LOVE

The family retired to their rooms leaving Robin cuddling Catan and Dilshad, their contrasting eyes staring deep into each other's. Dilshad asked, "Cat', your eyes are hypnotic. Can you see me with them?"

"No, but I can feel your eyes. Warm, almost black on ivory pedestals." Catan bit her bottom lip. Seemed like a family trait. "Daddy, could Dilshad have a sleep-over? Just for tonight. Please."

Robin had had some experience of girls' fathers, from his boys' teenage years. "Only if her father agrees." He looked towards the doors. "Private!" Private Alapat opened the doors and entered. "Could you please go to Aalap's room, and if he's there, ask him if Dilshad can have a sleep-over with Catan. And could you mention from me that he can say no. Thank you."

"Now, can we have our treat? I can't wait." Catan was so excited about what Robin was about to give them. Robin looked into her eyes and thought, *'Sorry, poppet, I can't remember what I promised.'* He was a little wary of the answer. Catan, grinning, replied to his message, *'The Christmas tree. We've never seen one.'* That was a relief for Robin.

He began to think. He was home, in Boxted, England, and looking towards Saint Peter's church from the east entrance out of Church Street. The old stone and brick church, of Saxon origin, was a mish-mash of a tower, roof slopes, dormers, and buttresses but was beautiful; it was real England. The low, turreted tower was to the other end of the two-level red tiled roofs, but looking out towards Robin was the ornate stained alter window. Sheltered by the holly, yew and fir trees, the ancient gravestones had gathered lichens and moss, obscuring the names of the folk they remembered. But they had left room on the lush grass for a Christmas tree.

"Is that your home church, Daddy?" Robin nodded.

The sun was shining, and the sky deep blue, but it was cold, and the children who had gathered around the tree to place decorations wore coats and scarves. They laughed and shouted as each one placed a piece of tinsel or a borbal on the tree, then the teachers helped by reaching the higher branches. Catan and Dilshad watched for some time as the children worked and played, scrambling to get their turn in, but then suddenly they had finished. They all rushed to the gravel path and waited. As the vicar handed out the mince pies, four children stood away from the others, just watching the festivities. One of them was a little girl with long blonde hair, a grin which almost went from ear to ear, and beautiful grey-green eyes. She was holding an old book.

"It's Catherine! She's my auntie."

Dilshad answered, "I can see her. She's really pretty."

Catherine and the boys waved to Robin and giggled. Then the sun went out.

"What's happened?" whispered Dilshad.

But, just as suddenly, the Christmas tree lights came on. They shone all around the churchyard, with all the colours of the rainbow, and the reflections glistened on the stained glass window. The children sung 'Away in a Manger' and then they

blushes showed through her dark complexion. "Do you want to see me?" she asked nervously.

Catan stared at the ceiling, smiling as she nodded her answer.

Dilshad took her clothes off so quickly, and suddenly laid there, waiting. She also had a tight, clean, teenage body, darker than Catan's, and her breasts a little more developed. Her nipples were erect and wanting.

"I can't see you. I'll have to *touch* you and *smell* you. And *taste*." Catan felt her way across the bed, and her hand rested on Dilshad's tummy. It slowly felt around, exploring the belly button. Then she moved her hands to Dilshad's face, and touched every millimeter of surface, even putting her fingers in her mouth. Then the smell. She hovered with her nose over her face for several seconds. "That's wonderful." She lowered and kissed Dilshad, properly, with her mouth open, and caressing her lips with her tongue. Catan wanted to see as much of her friend as she had of her, so she moved down her body, feeling and smelling. Working around the breasts, gently fingering the nipples and then gliding her nose across them, she viewed the beauty of the young female form. Then she moved her hand slowly down the tummy to her waist and felt around her mound, pulling at the tiny hairs, and then opening the fold to reveal the vagina. The aroma was like nectar, sweet and sour, and her fingers explored every part of her little friend's pubic area and vagina. She was having a really good look, and she complimented the senses of feel and smell with taste. Her tongue felt and tasted every part of her teenage zones. The legs and feet were not left out. Dilshad wriggled a little when Catan sucked each of her toes. "I can see you now. I think I love you."

Dilshad wasn't too sure about what to say. They were friends, but maybe they were more; she was very nervous.

Catan laid down beside Dilshad, very close, her little breasts pushing against her. "I'd like to look at you again," she whispered. "But I know you didn't look very closely at me.

Not at everything." Her mouth was close to her ear, and she breathed into it. "Do you want to look at me properly? You can close your eyes and look, with smell, feel and taste."

Dilshad said nothing. The little thirteen year old was nervous, but wanted to see more, and smell and taste more. Without any further wooing, Catan climbed onto her, straddling her face, and pushing her own face deep into Dilshad's crotch. They spent some time looking, smelling and tasting, and wriggling at each sensation. They were in heaven.

The two had just experienced young love. They lay together, tightly woven into each other's bodies, and looked into each other's eyes. Catan could actually see her lover, from her memory, and wow, from the smell of her own love-juice on Dilshad's mouth and nose. They kissed and giggled.

"Do you know what Daddy was thinking, downstairs?" asked Catan quietly. "We can see each other's thoughts most of the time, you know, like with the Christmas tree." Dilshad shook her head. "Well, he was thinking that we're falling in love." She smiled. "What do you think?"

Dilshad frowned. "I'm scared, but I think I love you. No, I *know* I love you. What do you think will happen to us?"

"How do you mean?"

"Well, we're girls. This sort of thing's not liked around here." They squeezed each other so hard. "They could make us not see each other."

"Then we must be sure not to tell anybody. My family will know, they'll easily read me, but they won't tell anybody else. They'll protect you. We could be friends and secret lovers. We could do sleep-overs and we could look closely at each other, all night if we want to. And we could keep it all a secret."

"Ok. We can do that." They both thought a lot, but said nothing. Then Dilshad asked, "Have you ever had sex? You know, with a man? You know, him putting his penis in you? Cos you're much bigger than me."

Catan did not really want to answer, but felt she had to. "I have." She said no more.

"Well?" Dilly rolled over to look down onto Catan's face. "Was it good?" She waited a bit. "You can talk to me, we're together."

Catan frowned, and then bit her bottom lip. "It was *not* good. I've been fucked, probably a thousand times." The room seemed so silent for a long few seconds.

"Did you make love?"

"Never, just fucked." She spoke harshly. "They don't make love to children, they fuck them. I'm never gonna use pretty words to describe such dirty shit. But some of them paid for it. I killed them." Dilshad was shocked. "Yes, some of them tried to fuck me at the wrong time, so I killed them. Catherine helped me. That's when they stopped putting me into the Festival." It was again silent for some time.

"Do you always go to the Festival? Some say they eat you and you are a different person each year. I think I'd die if that was true."

"Do they say that? Didn't know that." She was frowning. "But they don't eat me, not me." She took a massive breath. "They eat my children, and fuck all the others." She showed no real emotion. "They used to have me as a special, for special members, until I killed them that year. Now they fear me and they're all scared of me. Right, too. Would you like to know about me, some of the things that none of the others know?" She grinned at her mate. "Our family is not so big now, but we're still in control. There're only seven of us left, we've got rid of the bad ones, almost. Kamdar is our family, but he's bad. I think I'll have to kill him one day."

"Cat', you scare me when you talk about killing."

"Don't be scared, I'd never kill you. I wouldn't even be allowed to; you're good. But it's my job to execute. That's what I do. There're three executioners. Me, Catherine, and Kamdar but I think Daddy's stopped Kamdar, so it's me and Catherine. We're pretty little girls, but have to do a gruesome job."

"Can we stop talking about killing, please? Tell me about the sex."

"Ok, but it involves killing. Just cuddle me tight and you'll be all right." They pulled together. "When the Chi Bantri started, I was like their prisoner. They tried to torture and kill me all the time, but I never died, and I said that one day I would fight back, and then they'd all die. I was called the Dying Princess by the then-current Monsignor. Anyway, this Festival developed early on as a glorified junkies party, which slowly turned into a yearly ritual where they all got bollixed up on drugs, and then fucked a load of children. They thought that it gave them longer life. Don't know why. Anyway, I was one of the kids that they fucked. Some of them didn't like me cos they thought thirteen was too old, and so they just did the younger ones. The children all cried and screamed, often for their mummies, but I never cried. I always said to myself 'they won't hurt me and when I do cry it'll be for my family.' 'And that when that happens they'd all better hide.'" She kissed Dilshad. "You'll be able to write *loads* about me. Anyway, when some of them tried to fuck me in the parade ground, you know, gang rape me, me and Catherine killed them all, very slowly and very painfully, and told the Monsignor that when my mummy comes for me, it'll be even worse for them, all of them. So they were suddenly scared of me, and Mummy, but worshipped me, but they decided that at the next Festival they'd eat my six best friends, as my punishment. They did that, cooked them and ate them, and by pure fluke, after that they experienced the best year they'd ever had. Some prat came up with the idea that it was because eating my friends gave them some of my spirit, and they would get stronger. So then they made me bring six children up each year, especially for the menu at the Festival of Life. It's really the Festival of Death."

"So they really eat the children every year? What, even people like the Cardinal?"

"Yes, the higher members all get their turns eventually; they're all the same. You've met my children, which should be eaten this year. Well, they won't be. Gayla's plan will make sure of it. They've volunteered to die in another way. In just a couple of weeks we'll put the Chi Bantri into turmoil, and *you've* gotta stay out of it. Ten traders died in the Kingdom of Kandy, which began their two hundred year reign of cruelty. They were mutilated, cut into pieces whilst still alive, and eventually killed. Our children and their protector will soon die, but this time it'll signal the *end* of their reign. And, in our own version of the Kingdom of Kandy, the Chi Bantri members will all suffer the mutilation of lingchi, but we'll not make the World share their suffering, they'll be mutilated after their death. They'll join the endless Lingchi Line, and suffer, maybe forever, until the children have the compassion to forgive." She again kissed Dilshad. "I love kissing you. And you smell so sweet. Anyway, I hope you're remembering all this, for your writings." A moment of silence passed. "Back to the the children. They're put onto a thing like a cross. They're winched over the fire, at a height, and slowly lowered, and they cook slowly, and tenderly. They also die slowly, screaming. They think that the child has to be alive when they put them over to roast, else they lose the spirit. They're stupid, eating them doesn't give them anything, except belief. For nearly one hundred and seventy years the children've just burned to death, the flesh is blistering, and smelling, before they're dead. And the little children who're just fucked, well they suddenly think that their lot is not so bad after all." She stopped talking. The two girls clinched, then, "I don't know how, but Gayla turned up with Ninah, and then found me." She was sweating, but cold. "Please don't leave me, Dilly, I need you. Promise me."

Dilshad had tears running from the corner of her eyes. "I'll never leave you." She looked into Catan's eyes and sobbed, "You can cry if you want. I want you to."

"I can't, not yet." She composed herself. "Ninah has got his nails, made from the oxidised bones of Queen Maya's father, and he can do things with them. Somehow, Gayla wriggled her way inside the Fort and under everybody's skins, and got Ninah working there. Or was it the other way round? Anyway, he used his nails, and the children didn't suffer any more over the fire. Suddenly, the only screaming at the Festivals was that from the kids being fucked. The cooking children stopped suffering. You know, Ninah's shiny nails, which he hammers through the neck, and he says it's to keep the head high and proud, but he gets the spinal chord, just in the right place, to totally anaesthetise the body, while keeping the head alive. They carried on eating the kids, but the kids didn't suffer. Not physically. They still knew they were being cooked, but they died painlessly."

Dilshad was only thirteen. She had listened to all the local gossip and legend, but she had never been prepared for the absolute truth. Catan held her tight as she wept. Her older cousin had been drafted into the Fort a few years earlier. She never knew what for.

"Will you believe in me when I do what I have to do?" asked Catan. "You don't have to, but it'll hurt me if you don't." She waited for Dilshad to answer, but she just wept. "You know, I love you, and I think you love me, but my daddy thought earlier that you'd hurt me."

"I won't ever hurt you."

"No. But he's right. You'll die, and I'll live. That'll hurt. I've never been in love. I don't know what it is to lose somebody special, forever. I think when it happens, I might just kill the World."

Dilshad sobbed. "Don't be silly." She asked, "How old are you?"

"I'm thirteen. I'm the baby of the family. Always have been, always will be." She paused.

Dilly took a deep breath to clear her sobbing. "But Gayla's the baby of the family. And what about Catherine?"

Catan giggled quietly, "I'm the baby, and still doing my confirmation-of-suffering period. That's why I have to stick with the Chi Bantri. I think that's why. You'll just have to believe me." She shook her head. "But I'm old. Almost as old as the universe. How can somebody so old, never have loved? But now I do." They were both thirteen, both scared, both learning about life, but only one was young. "What will I do when I lose you?"

Poor Dilshad, who *really was* thirteen, did not know what to think. She was still a child.

Catan, perhaps out of guilt, whispered in Dilly's ear, "If anybody hurts you, they'll go to hell, the long way round. I'll destroy the World for you. Only *you* will stop me."

Dilshad needed to sleep. She lay in Catan's arms and dropped off, while Catan listened to her quiet breathing. She wondered where she was in her dreams.

"Night, night lover." She carefully pulled away, covered her with a sheet, and then felt her way out of the room and across the landing. Private Alapat was the perfect gentleman, and never looked at the naked girl's body. He opened Gayla's bedroom door for her and closed it behind.

"Cat'. What you doing?" Gayla, wearing a big, baggy t-shirt, walked her to the bed where they sat down. "Do you want a shirt? It's not very warm tonight." She helped her on with one of her t-shirts. It was only just enough to cover her privates. "You OK? Thought you were with Dilshad."

"I am. She's right here in my heart." Her head was floating, up high in the sky.

Gayla gave her a very old-fashioned look. The little girl said, "I knew it. I knew you were falling in love. Give me a hug." They cuddled for a few minutes, and then Gayla thought, *'You'll get hurt. You know that. She's human.'* Catan replied, *'I know she's human, what about it? We're in love. I've never felt like this before, ever.'*

"What I gonna do with you? My little girl." The eight year-old fingered Catan's black hair from across her face, and looked into her pearly eyes. "Why do you love her?"

"I just do, don't know why. Just happened." She smiled. She could feel Gayla's warm breath brushing her face. "You're worried about me, I can smell it."

"Cat', we'll always be together, sometimes from a distance, but always together. That's us. You know, think about it, how old will you be when Dilshad is twenty, and when she's thirty, and forty? Tell me."

"I know. I'll be thirteen when she's twenty, thirteen when she's thirty, and thirteen when she's forty. I know. And I know how old I'll be when she dies. I'll be thirteen." Her eyes were void of any emotion. "I know all this. Can't we just be happy for one year, then stop? Maybe two years, or three?"

"Of course." Gayla chuckled. "This must be the worst job you've ever had." They both giggled and then rested together.

The morning came, and the south-east facing palace took the full warmth of the rising sun. It was a glorious morning. Gayla suggested that Catan goes back to her guest before she feels neglected, but before she had, there was a knock on the door. It was private Alapat, who was knocking on behalf of Dilshad.

"Your Highness, Miss Dilshad is wondering if you are all right."

Catan thanked the guard, and he walked her through into her room. This time the private did not have to hide his blushes.

"Catan, I was frightened when you weren't here. I thought you had second thoughts and had dumped me."

Catan grinned, and waited for her to come to her. "Never. It's just that we don't sleep, and you were so settled and content."

Dilshad smiled, and said, "I have to go with my father, to the clinic. Syed has something for us to bring back here."

She dressed quickly, and went off to the Lodge to meet her father. He was very pleased that she had had such a wonderful time with the family and Catan. But he really had no idea just how wonderful her time was.

The trip to the clinic took some time. Aalap always tried to avoid the main roads with his little rickshaw, and so took the slum roads. He felt safer.

"This's for my good friends, Robin and Tracy." Syed handed Aalap a manuscript, and Aalap placed it in his glove box.

Several hours later, they had not returned to the Palace.

Ninah offered to go out and search for them.

"It's ok, Cat', she'll be ok." Robin was trying to reassure her.

Gayla stood by her with her arm around the taller girl's waist. "Ninah'll find them."

Ninah had gone in the Jaguar, with Sergeant Baba driving. They were held up by an Indian Army vehicle and patrol at the entrance to the slum.

"I am Sergeant Baba. I am servant to Her Majesty Queen Maya. Can we pass?"

"Not at the moment, Sergeant. There's been an incident. In front of the Fort."

"We are on Her Majesty's business. We will not interfere with your work."

"Sorry, but General Dara has ordered us to seal off the slum."

Ninah, who was sitting in the back, opened the door. "What's happened, soldier? The longer we wait, the more concerned I become. We *must* get through. Tell the General that Ninah's here."

The soldier got on the radio. He waved the Jaguar through and it squeezed its way towards the Fort's slum gate, to within walking distance. The General came to meet them.

"I don't quite know what to tell you, Ninah. We've a stand-off with the Chi Bantri soldiers on one side and the slum people on the other. Something terrible has happened." He briefly explained.

Back at the palace, "Daddy!" shouted Gayla, "It's Ninah. We've got to go to the west side of the Fort open area. Not through the Fort. And the car's gone!"

As she shouted, an army truck pulled up.

"Where's my sword?" Catan pushed Gayla. "Get my sword!" Gayla held back. "Get it!"

They all got into the truck, with the ceremonial sword hanging from Catan's waist.

The General met them at the edge of the open area. The Fort gate was to the left, and to the right was a large crowd of hundreds of slum dwellers, silently looking towards a small wooden contraption. Some guns were visible. Four of Kamdar's soldiers stood by the contraption. Towards the opposite edge of the open area and in front of the Fort were several hundred Chi Bantri soldiers, their guns trained on the Indian Army soldiers, who had amassed on the near side. An Indian helicopter gunship moved around overhead, and four Chi Bantri canons menacingly peaked through the Fort ramparts.

Ninah had already warned the Sergeant and the General to speak only when spoken to, and he quietly warned the private. The family logged their minds off from their intranet, to protect Catan. By the wooden contraption sat Aalap's auto rickshaw! Catan waited as Gayla described the scene but she never mentioned the rickshaw.

Tracy ordered, "General, send a message to Monsignor Plassey. We must meet, out in the open if he's brave enough." He contacted the Monsignor on the radio.

"He'll be out on the no-man's land in ten minutes."

Gayla almost allowed Catan into her thoughts, as she caught a thought from Catherine. *'Satvinder's told his sad story. The old geeser was done because he was pally with Queeny. Watch out.'* She thanked her, and then turned to her mummy. *'The nineteen thirty two rules have a by-rule added. Kill anyone who's Qeervi friendly.*

I think they've killed Dilshad and Aalap.' Tracy replied, *'That's what I was thinking. Do you think Catan has any idea?'* *'Not at the moment. She will though, she doesn't miss much.'*

Catan pulled Gayla's head towards her. "What's happening? You're cutting me out."

"Mummy's going to meet with the Monsignor. I'll let you know when we know anything else."

The Queen walked out alone to meet the Monsignor in the open. The press had turned up from somewhere, and two more helicopters appeared above, cameras rolling. The World was about to witness the hostilities between the Chi Bantri and the Queen. The disheveled Monsignor had messed up again.

"Good morning, Your Majesty. This is a sad day for all of us." He knelt down in front of her and spoke a prayer, then stood up. "I feel that the past few days have overtaken us."

"No more shit, Plassey. What're you doing?" A refined diplomat, or what? She looked around. "You've a lot of guns pointing, quite a few at me. I hope you're not preparing for another mistake. You won't survive many more."

He raised his hand, and then pointed at the ground. The guns were lowered. The Queen sent a message to Gayla, and the Indian guns also lowered.

"Plassey. You've killed the wrong people. You've killed the good ones, the meak. Why?" She looked through her good eye at a man who was breaking under the pressures. "You've ordered the army to operate the nineteen thirty two capital rule, but with a twist. Kill anybody who supports us. Doesn't make sense while the reports keep telling me that we're now mates, bed fellows, partners in crime. We've blown up Italy together, and washed away a few islands. You've worked hard to achieve a virtual partnership, now you've broken it. You're not very clever."

The Monsignor did not speak. He just looked at the fiery Queen.

"Are those the soldiers who've done this?" He nodded his answer. "Did they also kill Satvinder, the old man?" He again nodded. "What're you going to do about it? Before you speak, I must tell you that she was Ca'an's lover. The Princess's first and only love. Does that frighten you?"

The Monsignor was sweating gallons, and shivering with fear.

"I have to tell Ca'an. She'll decide on what to do. I hope you've studied your own history, particularly the rape of The Princess some hundred and fifty years ago. This could be much worse."

The Monsignor managed to speak. "If you need to, you can kill me. It would be justice."

"It'll prove higher justice to leave you alive, to suffer, until we get tired of you."

The Queen turned and slowly walked towards the rickshaw. But before she got close, she stopped. *'Come to me, Ca'an. Bring your sword.'* Gayla walked Catan across the open area, the troops and dwellers looking on nervously. Robin and Ninah followed close behind.

"Mummy, what's happening?"

Tracy turned to Gayla, and Catan, "Gayla, please be My Eyes." Tracy had tears in hers.

The Qeervi family walked together towards the execution site with Gayla whispering the scene. The four soldiers began to move away, but stopped when several guns from the slum were loudly cocked. They were under common arrest by the people.

Aalap was tied to the side of his rickshaw. He had pins through his eyelids and they were tied back to keep them open. He had been forced to watch his daughter's ordeal. But he was still alive.

"General, medic! Quickly." Robin hopped over to Aalap, and lifted him to take some of his weight from the wires which were passed through his wrists. The medics arrived in seconds. "He's alive." The medics took over.

They moved to the wooden contraption. It was a wooden pallet, and the naked Dilshad was fixed to it, arms and legs nailed at each corner. Her breasts and thigh muscles had been cut off, a piece of wood forced into her vagina, and it was a bloody scene. Catan put on her silk hood, in case she cried.

"Dilly, are you dead?" The celestial answer was 'yes'. "I love you. I always will, and I promise not to cry for you, but will forever remember our love shared." She could be seen biting her lip, through the hood's mouth-hole. "What do you want me to do?" She looked at her body using her fingers, gently moving from her face to the open wounds on her chest, and then down below. She pulled the long piece of wood from her vagina, then moved her nose across the wasted girl to remember her smell, and again asked, "What would you like me to do, Dilly? Anything, and everything." She smiled through the hole in her hood as she received the girl's wishes. "It's a promise." She removed her hood to reveal her stunning eyes and she showed them to the crowd. The area had suddenly turned into a stage, and currently showing was the Return of the Qeervis, co-starring Dilshad and Aalap, and competently supported by the Dying Princess, Catan of Anglia, designated executioner, by appointment to His Lord. "Then I'll do it for my love."

Catan cast her blind eyes around the crowd and then moved towards them. Gayla, clinging to her waist, thought to her, *'What're we doing?'* Catan simply thought, *'Recovering.'* The two of them moved towards the crowd.

She spoke loudly and clearly. "You know who I am. I know who you are. But do you know who my mummy is?" They stood waiting for a response. "I ask a question. Do you know who my mummy is?" The crowd began to murmour, but still no answer to her question. "Then I'll help you and tell you who she's *not*. She's *not* the Queen who courted the Chi Bantri over the past few days. She's *not*. *Now* tell me who she *is*."

Slowly an old man stepped forward, holding a shotgun. He moved towards the girls, and instantly both armies raised their guns towards him. He struggled to get onto his knees and pray, but he did and then rose. "I'm a friend of Satvinder's. And of Doctor Hussain's. Soon I'll join them both, with my sons and daughters."

"Sir, you were a neighbour to my friends, here. Did you know them?"

"Yes Your Highness. Very well. They were good people. Is Aalap alive?"

"Yes. We hope he'll again be strong, to witness, for his daughter, the death of the Chi Bantri. That was one of her dying wishes, the death of the Chi Bantri."

The man had sad eyes. They had witnessed hell. "The sight of that little girl took me back to Khulna. I saw my own daughters laying like that. Why is it happening here?"

Catan thought carefully, then, "It's *not* happening here. *This* isn't genocide, it's murder. The genocide was allowed to happen so openly in East Pakistan because my mummy and daddy weren't with us to prevent it. Nor was anybody else. We're now together, and strong. Will you help us?" Gayla began whispering, but Catan put her finger on her mouth. She stopped. "Will you now tell me who my mummy is, please?"

He smiled at her and looked down at Gayla. "Last week she was the devil. We killed her. Ninah can tell you more about it. She burned to death in a shack, and she screamed like a little pig." The crowd began to get fidgetty. "Now that she's returned, she's standing right there, and we're certain that she's the Mother of God." He returned to his knees, and begged, "Please forgive me my sins."

Gayla placed her tiny hand on his shoulder and said, "She was a bad spirit. There's nothing to forgive," and then giggled.

Catan spoke loudly. "Stand up, and take my sword." He stood up, but did not dare touch the sword, so Catan drew it, and handed it to him. "Take it, and execute that man, standing alone over there." She pointed to the Monsignor.

"Why?"

"He helped to kill your children in East Bengal. He's guilty." She urged him on with her piercing blank eyes. The teenager shouted at him, "Kill him!"

He did not take the sword, but wept for his lost family. "It won't help my children."

She smiled at the old man. "Thank you, sir. I now know that we're on the same side. Please tell your friends who my mummy is. Tell everybody."

She replaced her sword and turned, and they walked back to the family. Tracy looked proudly at the girls. Catan said, "My Eyes, I need to do something for Dilly, the first part of her wish." Gayla smiled and released her waist and Catan began the dark walk to the centre of the opening, to join the Monsignor. The armies became wrestless, their guns pointing all over the place, in panic. Then General Dara ordered his troops to lower their guns, and surpisingly, Sir Kamdar did the same. Suddenly all one could hear was the buzz of the helicopters overhead.

She stood in front of the lonely Monsignor.

"Sir, I've known you for many years. You've been instrumental in the organisation of genocide, in East Pakistan in nineteen seventy one. You've been found guilty by me of the torture and murder of over three million civilians, being man, woman and child. And you have been found guilty of the murder of my friend Satvinder, and of my one love, Dilly. What do you have to say for yourself, Monsignor?" She was cold and emotionless.

He stood there shaking, but did not answer.

"Why did you have my one love killed?"

He stutttered, "In the name of God. After so many years, I've now made my peace with God. And there *is* only one God."

She smiled and quietly asked the Monsignor, "Why does man always blame my mother?"

He seemed to calm down, aware that the inevitable was nigh. "Because she is God." Pause. "I beg forgiveness. But I plead guilty."

"Keep your peace with God. As much as I'm tempted, and as much as it distresses me, I'll not interfer with your arrangements with my mummy." Her pearly eyes burned into his mind. "My mummy can't hear us. Is there anything that you'd like to tell me? Privately."

"I did it for God. I don't know why."

Catan, almost whispering, sympathetically replied, "I know you did." She smiled. "You've been a good servant." She straightened her stance, her head held high. "I can't forgive you for your part in the Pakistani war, I don't have the right to forgive for others. And it would take far too long to ask all of your victims. So it's for them that I have to *forsake* one of my Dilly's last wishes. But at least you can die knowing that she's forgiven you." Her right hand whipped the sword from its scabbard, and it sliced the Monsignor's throat. Momentarily he just stood there, but then the blood spurted out, rapidly covering his chest and legs, and he sank to his knees. After a few seconds he colapsed. She stood without emotion as she thought, *'Kamdar, take your fucking troops home. But leave the four murderers.'* She turned back towards her lost love, as the Chi Bantri army shocked the World by retiring into the Fort leaving the Monsignor's body crumpled, bloody, alone and lifeless. He was no longer the puppet dictator. And the Indian troops remained in position but lowered their weapons, and their heads, as their Princess ambled back to the family.

"Dilly has forgiven the Monsignor. He died for his other crimes." She pulled Gayla to her waist. "I'll now do the second part, the rest will come later, with my family's help." Gayla walked her over to the four soldiers, stood in front of them and Catan spoke very loudly. "You killed my only true love!" One of them wet himself. "She has asked me to convey her forgiveness. I don't know why." She turned away from those fortunate killers and rejoined their family. "Mummy, can we go home now?"

The General joined the group and asked, "What of the four soldiers, Your Majesty?"

Tracy quietly answered, "They're forgiven." She cast a macabre look at the giggling Gayla. "The Monsignor was.... Well, he's gone."

As the family went home to the palace, and the military dispersed the crowds, the press went to work. The horrendous murder of the little girl, the public execution of the Monsignor and the burning of the thespian Queen all hit the headlines, putting our family right back into the hearts of their children. Maya was back at the top. A lucky break? Maybe, maybe not.

18 -- THE CRUCIFIXION

General Dara organised an escort to take The Queen and her family back to the Palace, and despite Tracy's objections, part of his command set up residence around the house to offer some security.

"The Indian Government has committed their support for you, Your Majesty. The mood has completely turned in your favour over the past day, even with the local people, and today's events will only but help to recover the people's reverence. But the public execution of the Monsignor may have some backlashes."

"I've spoken to Gayla about that and let's hope that we get that backlash." The ginger beauty smiled nervously. "We're counting on it. Anyway, my girls never cry, but they are still very sad and in mourning and so I must join them. Please look after Aalap. And get his rickshaw back here. He'll need it when he recovers."

The day was a sad one for the lonely Catan. She had experienced something new, something that had not happened to her for probably millions, maybe billions, of years; she felt deep, rasping, humiliating pain; pain from inside, uncontrollable, undefined and relentless. It was a pain which went hand-in-hand with absolute ecstasy; when there's one the other just lurks around the corner. Robin and Tracy were able to relate to the teenager's moods, they had been plagued with human moods and feelings for forty or fifty years, and by God how they missed them. But it was certainly a lucky break for the World that Catan was not plagued with the human feelings of rage and revenge. Else that day could have been the end for life as we know it, and we may not be sitting here telling the tale.

The news reports went so well for them that Catan began to feel that her lover's life was not taken totally in vain. The pictures and reports of the little girl's raped and murdered body shocked the World, almost as much as the volcanoes had, and many societies frowned upon the execution of the Monsignor, but privately celebrated. Catan's little friend would certainly be a revered martyr in the modern-day scriptures, the ones in which she so fleetingly had the promise of involvement.

The Chinese requested, on that day, that The Queen and her Family pay a 'State' visit to Peking, to attend the commemorations for President Li and his colleagues, those murdered by the Chi Bantri. And then the Pope had requested that they visit the Vatican for an 'in camera' discussion about the way forward. The modern press can be fantastic while you are their flavour of the day. Instant stardom!

The family and the six children sat in their comfortable living room in the evening.

Captain Batiste's whisky was such a comfort for Robin. He did not really need it as he was coping so well since his holy feast with Tracy, remembering things that had happened over the millenniums, and he was feeling more in control. "I wish to raise a toast to our lost friends, Satvinder and Dilshad. They died because they knew us." They all raised their glasses. "Before we get into the party mood, can I ask you something,

Ninah? That old man, he said they burned Tracy, and you knew about it. What's that all about?"

"Lamma, as you already knew the Queen was our own intruder who'd been turned by the Monsignor, hence the Monsignor's absolute fear when Maya met him today. She looked the part, and conveyed Maya's wishes to a tee. She was a real nuisance during those five naughty days, so I made sure the local people were pointed in the right direction. They did the rest. And now everybody thinks that their Queen has come back, again, risen from the ashes, but this time as the good. You can't beat luck."

Gayla hung onto Catan and chuckled to herself. "*Very* lucky."

Catan spoke. "They'll appoint a new puppet leader very quickly, they always do. Wonder who they'll choose."

The children were bored, and so Catan played her guitar for them as they sang.

"Robin, what about our destinies as rock stars? Was it just this lot cheating us to get us over here?" Tracy looked around at the thoughts, and they were all innocent. "I can't believe that Syed wasn't some part of this whole sting."

Catan handed the guitar to Tracy, and she played and sung. A bit morbid, but she put over her version of 'You've Got a Friend' which reminded her and Robin about their flights over there, seemingly a life-time ago. Not at all bad, but not rock-star stuff. I think she made a much better demigod Queen.

Catan wanted to talk about the plan, Gayla's plan. "I want to make sure it achieves what my Dilly wished for."

Gayla was a little annoyed and snapped, "This is about *God's* work, not revenge, and don't you *dare* forget it!"

Catan dropped her head. "I'm sorry. I just wondered. I miss her already." Gayla cuddled her tightly. Her little girl really needed to cry, but she didn't, she just uttered, "I'm sorry M….." She almost said it, which made Gayla smile. "It's just a blip. I'll learn from it." She pulled herself into Gayla's neck.

"I'll explain our plan, Cat'. How's that? Yeah?" Gayla began to giggle. "They really think they stand a chance. They're big men when they're sending in their brainwashed monkeys to kill and maim the innocents, to make way for their greedy campaigns. But now we're back, together again, and they're feeling it already."

Robin and Tracy had not heard much about the plan so they listened intently as Gayla became the centre of attraction, a position which she dearly loved. She sat bolt upright to deliver her plan. "My plan is designed to clear the Earth of the one single power which has risen to a dangerous, unacceptable position, quietly dictating the direction of mankind, and placing themselves above the laws, and above God. Our experiment should have closed down after about fifty years, in the early eighteen hundreds, but we got lost. Something, or somebody, sent it all out of control. Now I'm going to close the file on this one for good. As soon as me and Ninah got here thirty-odd years ago we began the plans. Mummy and daddy couldn't come back until they were the correct ages, so we went forward without them. Before we begin the shut-down, do we need any more information?"

The experiment had been designed to allow a group of basically sound, just humans to become strong enough to make the World a better place for the unfortunate poor folk. It proved beyond all doubts that their original ancient findings still applied to the modern human society, that is, humans cannot handle uncontested power. The first twenty years or so showed kindness, common sense and humanity, spreading social benefits and charity, but as always the curse of human greed poisoned them all. They became cruel, perverted and unnecessarily pagan.

"Well, we've allowed the poor people of this World to suffer for one hundred and eighty years longer than anticipated. This year is when it ends, their own bi-centenary year." Gayla moved and sat down with the children. "They've just below twenty thousand higher members, and billions of unsuspecting minions, doing their duty for that monster. The monster must be killed, every bit of it, leaving them no opportunity to regroup. It must be replaced by new blood, new belief, new opportunity, and especially competition. The World must be made up of a healthy mix of gangs and cultures. Gang culture is what keeps the human race on its fore. That's what I made them into, and that's what's coming back, very soon." She hugged the children. "We've already achieved the first step, with the Chi Bantri openly taking responsibility for things such as the President's murder, and the volcanoes. They've never done that before, but now the World acknowledges their existence and probably their threat. They've exposed themselves. The next step is to gently accustom the World into accepting their demise, and the loss of twenty thousand influential and *powerful* individuals. The people need to be able to carry on with their own beliefs and religions, once this monster's died. But first we must begin to break down the spirit of the animal. Demoralise, weaken and disjoint them. They believe, beyond all reason, in Ca'an. She's their spirit, and they hers. That belief must be used to open the wounds which they are currently nursing, and they must fester. So, the very next step is to expose the Festival of Life to the World. The press are our friends, and they'll be given the bait, and they'll tear the myths apart, exposing the sect's acts of paedophilia, cannibalism and drug abuse. The press's previous efforts have always failed; they need some real help this time, so these darling children have agreed to help."

Robin stood up. "Gayla, people get killed when they help us. These are *real* eight year-old children, and they're not like you. Not like us."

"They know that. We've talked about it and *they* came up with the idea."

Robin scoffed, "Like I came up with the idea of cutting my leg off."

"Daddy, you'll have to accept the children's decisions to be God's Six Catalysts. Ask them what they think."

All the children sat smiling and nodding in support of the plan. Robin allowed Gayla to continue.

"The children's gift to God will enrage the Chi Bantri, because they'll not have any spirit to eat at the Festival. They'll also have to make a show to the World, by bringing the children's killer to justice, and they'll all ask why he did it. That'll bring the press flocking in their thousands, and hopefully witnesses will be brave enough to stand up. The secret society will no longer be so secret."

Tracy clapped her hands and shouted, "You're going to kill the children?" With a smile of disbelief, she raged, "You're worse than them!"

"You've forgotten a lot while you were human. Mummy, these children cannot do what we tell them to do, you know that. They must *want* to do it, and they *do*. What d'you think'll happen to them if they don't want to do it. Well? The same as has happened to all the previous children, they'll be cooked alive and eaten, to the benefit of the devil. They'll feed the spirit of God's enemies. *They* have chosen *not* to do that, and they'll have my eternal love as a reward." They all cuddled tightly around Gayla. Tracy raised her eyebrows, but accepted it.

The cuddles loosened and Gayla continued. "Catan has some good friends in the industrial area. They live nearby and visit her regularly. They advise her on her eyes and her sight, allegedly. They're top scientists, and work for Chi Bantri companies. One works in the company clinic, just outside the front of the Fort. Another works in the Dallet Company, who own four communication satellites. Another is a developer in visual sciences. He is a leader in holography. These men are like the children; they're all aware of what they're doing, and will die for it, if required. We've a winning team. My plan, Catan's team. Me, Catherine and Ninah are part of the team, and we need your support. You're our public face and people believe in you. You've a history and like Marmite, they either love you or hate you; but either way they now believe in you. So you have to help us. What do you think?"

A chilling silence fell. Little Gayla breathed deeply, and as her patience strained, adopted her cobra stance. "You've two choices; you can willingly help, or I can make you help. You'll not fuck us up this time." Then, just as quickly she stood bolt upright, as if she had been scolded. Almost pathetically, she whimpered, "Please stay with me."

Robin shook his head in disbelief at her threat. But it was a revelation for him, drawing back yet more memories of their family, especially of Gayla. "You haven't told us much about the plan. But I think we need to work together, always." Tracy grudgingly agreed. "One thing. Why didn't you do this when you first came back? I can't see how us not being here would stop you progressing."

Gayla got up and went over to Robin and Tracy, pulling them together and kissing them both. "A, because we love you. And B, it's taken twenty years for our human team to get to this point. The program has been slow at times. And C, Mummy, with Daddy feeding you, you're the best shit stirrer the World's ever known. You, without even trying, draw attention with everything you ever do or touch." She wasn't giving much away.

Tracy, although suspicious, stated, "Just tell us what to do. We're here for you." She pulled herself away and resumed the 'Mummy' role. "Cat', your children are tired. Beddy-byes I think."

The next few days saw reporters, diplomats and the return of Aalap. He was in shock. Tracy gave him a loving hug as soon as she met him. "Thank you, Your Majesty. Dilshad told me about her love for the Princess. I was surprised, but very proud of her."

"Your rickshaw is round the back. But you don't have to work until you're ready. Your eyes look very sore so keep away from the dusty places." The lids were stitched and swollen. "If you need to talk, we're all here for you."

"Thank you. Your niece has helped me so much. I wanted to die, and join Dilshad, because I blamed myself for her death, but she helped me through it. She came to me when I was asleep. I thought I was dead, and that she was an angel with her lovely long, blonde hair and big grey-green eyes. When she told me the story of Satvinder's and Doctor Hussain's children, I decided not to die." The poor man was a wreck. But he knew that the two old men in Catherine's tale went on to experience happiness after their dire losses, and so he could too. "Did you find the document from Mister Syed?"

Tracy retrieved the delivery from the rickshaw. It was a hand written account of how to make up the poultice which healed so miraculously. Syed clearly knew of its importance to the family. The original author documented the use of the poultice on 'The Dying Princess', used on her hands and feet. Maybe she should use it on Aalap's eyes, but then on the final page Doctor Hussain had written about his disappointment of how it had never worked on 'normal' people. The doctor, and his predecessors, knew much more about the Princess than they had ever admitted to and he was clearly instrumental in luring the couple to India, probably in cahoots with Catherine.

Meanwhile, the inner court had, after days of maneuverings, elected a new Monsignor. The Queen and the Princess were asked to attend a meeting in his office so in response the entire family went to the Fort, kids and all.

Ninah stayed outside the Monsignor's office with the six children, while Robin, Tracy, Catan and Gayla entered. They were escorted by Sergeant Baba and the private. The secretary showed them in.

"Ca'an and Gayla." What the....? The Cardinal. That wet rag.

Gayla hung onto Catan's side and they both laughed as soon as they heard the voice. "Louis. What've they done to you? They've given you the worst job in the World!"

They all sat down in front of his desk. Catan opened, with mischief in her voice. "We should be informal, like mates. Mummy and Daddy, this is Louis, and Louis this is Robin and Tracy. Mummy, what do you prefer, Tracy or Maya?"

"For the sake of this project, I prefer Tracy. And I would prefer to sit outside in the sun." They moved out onto the beautiful rooftop garden, taking in the midday sun. "Have you heard the saying, mad dogs and Englishmen? Wonder who the dog is?" They politely chuckled.

His Eminence started the meeting. "As you've probably guessed, I've been given the supreme accolade of Monsignor. And we must work together to achieve our goals."

Gayla whispered at Catan's side. Catan asked, "What goals? We're not hungry, we need for nothing, we don't own anything and we don't wish to. We've different goals to yourselves."

"But Ca'an, we've the Festival of Life just around the bend. It's the two-hundredth Festival, and will be attended by the very best from around the World. Two hundred of the World's leading dignitaries for the two-hundredth Festival."

Robin smiled. "That reminds me of a car I had. It was two hundred pounds deposit and two hundred pounds a month for a Rover 200." They all gave him a sideways look.

"Anyway, back to business, the Festival."

Catan snapped, "Don't want to talk about the fucking Festival." She just looked around the garden, through her sightless eyes and Gayla, at the pretty flowers which partly hid the chimney which rose from the hall, where they cooked the children. "I executed your predecessor. What've you to say about that?"

His Eminence shuffled his feet and played with his pectoral cross. "What d'you want me to say about it? Nobody knows why you did it, but we are guessing that it was because of the girl. Tell me if that was not the case."

"Not really. He killed many people, and it was for all of them. But it was very good for you, you got his job, top dog. Maybe top parrot, or even top prat." She grinned and took a deep breath. "And I'm feeling strong as a result of his death, my spirit flourishes." She looked towards her mummy. "I don't know if I can make the Festival this year."

The Cardinal's face dropped. "Why? You *must*. We flourish together, or we die together. You have to attend, and the children cannot go alone. Gayla, talk to your sister." Gayla couldn't understand his English, so she guessed he was asking after her daddy. She pulled her kurta up and displayed her bare tummy, rubbed it, then pointed to Robin. The Cardinal smiled, "I know it's your daddy."

"Louis, I'm only thirteen years old. I'll have to ask my mummy's permission to go to such a seedy, degrading dive. It'll be full of paedos and druggies." She turned her nose up, and her head towards Tracy, "Well Mummy?"

"Of course you can go, darling. Just be home by ten. And take Sergeant Baba with you in case there are weirdoes there. Those dignitaries can be like spoiled brats at times."

"Oh, goody." She rubbed her hands together. "You'll all get big and strong, and be able to terrorise the poor defenseless minions. I wonder what's in it for me? You ever been to the Festival, Louis? Are you a drug-crazed, cannibalistic paedophile?"

The Cardinal looked into his lap. "Ca'an, I'm sorry, but we're not getting on quite as I'd hoped. Maybe your mother and I should carry on the meeting. I think it's worth mentioning that despite having much to offer the Chi Bantri the thing that really swung it was my previous association with yourself and your sister. You're an important cog in the machinery of this massive enterprise. I hope we can see eye-to-eye at least occasionally."

Catan shrugged her shoulders. "If we don't, you could follow your predecessor. I have the permission."

"Can I take it, Ca'an, that with your mother's permission you'll be attending the Festival, with your children? I need to be able to satisfy a very concerned and demanding inner court."

The young Princess thought a little. "First let's see if we can see eye-to-eye. A test. You're a holy man, a Cardinal in the Roman Catholic Church. Now, look very hard into my beautiful eyes. What do you see?"

The Cardinal looked hard, studying the exquisite pearls, then movement came. He could see a mother placing her baby into a hole. The baby was just bone, with a skin covering. Then Catan blinked, and the baby was gone.

"What did you see? Would you like to see some more, some real dead babies? You've walked with us in the slum before, and you were frightened, and that was when they liked you. We can walk the slum again today, and you can see some of the dead babies and children."

His Eminence gave an understanding grin. "Ca'an, Gayla, Your Majesty, Lamma. I know what happened after our meeting. I promise that I will reverse the decisions to stop the supplies and aid to the poor people."

"At last we're seeing eye-to-eye. Make sure it's set up properly, an independent charity with enough capital to feed and serve these people for many years to come. Your hundreds of billions will not miss this small amount, and should you hit hard times, or otherwise, the charity fund will continue to support and feed our people. Get your secretary to start on it, *right now*! Thank you, Louis."

Tracy smiled in appreciation of her girls' foresight. Louis went into the office and detailed his requirements to the secretary. She got onto the job immediately.

"Consider it done."

Robin and Tracy were saying very little, as they did not really know of the relationship between the Monsignors and the two girls, so they just took in what they needed.

But the quiet was suddenly broken by a screaming woman. The sergeant ran into the office, and then came out calling Tracy to follow him. They ran, followed by Gayla, the private and the Monsignor. Robin limped over to Catan and took her arm. "Let's see what's happening." They slowly walked into the office, through the secretary's lobby and onto the sparse landing.

"It's Ninah," whispered Catan.

Ninah stood motionless, tears running down his cheeks and onto his dark beard. He was holding a long knife which was covered in blood, as was his scruffy lungi, and the blood dripped onto his feet. The children. They all lay dead, throats cut, and the blood beginning to run down the stairs. Ninah had killed the children.

The shock waned, and panic started. The Cardinal was unable to move, but his secretary rushed into the office and almost instantly soldiers appeared, their guns trained on Ninah. He was devastated. He looked at Gayla and thought, *'why, why, why?'* She replied *'because they wished it. You know the rest.'*

One of the soldiers checked the children and confirmed that they were all dead and Gayla took Ninah's bloody tool pouch and the knife. As the giant cried, the soldiers placed him under arrest.

"Poor Ninah," sighed Catan. Gayla led her to him, and the Princess gave him a hug around his waist, and then she carefully climbed down and laid in the blood with her children. They spent their dying moments as one, and then the spirits were gone.

The next day the court found Ninah guilty of murder and he was sentenced to death by crucifixion. Despite objections from the Indian courts and religious groups, the decision stood. Monsignor Mateo was convinced that making a stand for justice by executing the killer of children would help to smooth out the waves caused by their public announcements about the Chinese killings. It was just a smoke screen, and would soon be blown away by the prevailing winds.

Tracy was shocked and confused by the killings. "Tell me, Gayla, why. You've lost the six children and Ninah."

"Mummy, the children always wanted to give themselves to God. They asked Ninah to cut their throats, they'd planned it the night before and me and Cat' had said goodbye to them. So Ninah has not done wrong in our laws, and he still believes in our plan."

"But why lose Ninah? He's our family. It could've been Catherine."

"Never! He's just going home where he has loads of work to do. We'll catch up with him when we're done here. Ninah knew what the children were destined for; he's serviced the Festival for twenty years, and has saved them so much pain. You haven't heard the screams of the children when they used to be put high above the fires, and then lowered into the heat. The screaming…. They didn't scream when Ninah killed them, did they? They wanted to die quickly and usefully and they have. We've now got the sect on the run, so they've done their bit, and I love them for it. And will do forever and ever."

"Love? What's that?" She scowled for a while into the little God's face, but calmed. "I know that Robin and I promised to support you, and we will. It's just a little barbaric at times." She held the little girl tightly. "This isn't the nicest of jobs, is it? You know, you're the hardest little girl in the Universe, on the outside." They both pursed their lips and gave each other a peck. "I'll never leave you again. I Promise." That wasn't the first time she'd made that promise.

The cross was built, and then raised in the centre of the open area at the back of the Fort. Objections had prevented it from going up at the traditional spot for major executions, in front of the Fort, where the Queen was crucified over two hundred years earlier.

The locals were mystified by the whole affair. And they were frightened; Ninah was a popular slum diplomat and they felt that they would be much more vulnerable without him. But the Cardinal helped a little by reporting that Ninah had negotiated the return of the food and benefits, before going mad. A rare piece of Chi Bantri kindness.

Late afternoon, and the soldiers led the condemned man over the open area to the cross, following a corridor left by the masses of onlookers from the slum. Crucifixions were not extinct, but rare in the industrialised, accessible countries such as India, (they were illegal in most,) so the press were there in numbers. They had already been given the Chi Bantri press release which showed the condemned man as a dangerous psychopath, who had befriended and killed those poor children. He was a detestable mass murderer, bitterly condemned by the pious Chi Bantri.

Ninah stood up onto the cross, on the small platform, his back to the upright, and held his arms out along the horizontals. He asked them not to tie his arms, he would not move. A cloth tied his head to the wood to ensure that his gaze was forward, and then they nailed him. With one strong clout a nail went through his wrist and into the wood. It was then banged in hard. He screwed his eyes and whimpered, but did not scream. Before they nailed the other arm, a swab of ranar was pushed under his nose to keep him conscious. The other arm was then nailed. The pain was excruciating, his eyes rolled and he breathed rapidly. They then put a nail through his left leg, just below the knee, and he finally screamed. Many of the crowd were weeping for their dear friend. The other leg was nailed, and a sledge hammer used to break away the platform to ensure that his full weight was on the nails. The ranar swab was again pushed under his nose. As if the crucifixion was not enough, his stomach and chest were deeply cut four times and a bucket of citrus placed beside, to be splashed into the wounds should an avenger have the desire. The sergeant and his soldiers stood to attention and saluted the gentle giant, holding back their personal grief while the crowd prayed beneath their weeping.

Ninah ground his teeth for several minutes, but eventually unscrewed his eyes to look over the slum dwellers, his dear friends for many years. But they were blurred and unrecognisable. He managed to ask, "Is Lamma here?"

The sergeant replied, "No, but he asked me to say, 'see you later, we'll all see you later.' That's all, I'm afraid." The soldiers turned towards the Fort and marched.

Beside the cross stood an old hag. She held the stick with the ranar swab on the end, and she had a small paint brush, should anybody dare to splash the citric acid into his open wounds. Her remit was to extend his suffering to the maximum, and to ensure that he stayed awake to endure it, to the very end. Why?

"Goodbye my friend. Send my children my love." It was the old man from Dilshad's murder site. He walked towards the slum, and the crowd filtered around to ensure that they all passed by the cross, some praying, some weeping, but none splashing his wounds. A little boy stopped and asked him, "Was it God's will, that you've been crucified?" Ninah, suffering, managed to smile. He said, "Yes." The boy dropped his chin in amazement.

In the Palace they were quiet. They knew what was happening to Ninah, but chose to stay away. Aalap asked Tracy if he could go to the slum to pay his respects. She agreed, sending the private to look after him.

The crowd was still milling its way past their friend when Aalap arrived in his rickshaw. The private helped him to walk the little way across the area, to take his place in the queue. He waited for a long time.

"Ninah, it's Aalap. Can you see me?"

Ninah moved his teary eyes down. "Yes Aalap. Your eyes look painful." The little man had three stitches in each eyelid.

Ninah's wounds would require hundreds to affect repair, but he still worried about his little friend.

Aalap asked, "Is it true that you can talk to lost souls?"

"Sometimes. Only today I spoke to one. Your Dilshad. She wants you to forgive the soldiers. She wants you to live for her, without intolerance or revenge." Ninah was fading, but it seemed from nowhere that a ranar swab was pushed below his nose to revive him. The hag took her job seriously.

In the Palace the family discussed Ninah's death quite calmly.

"I'm worried about Ninah," sighed Catan. "I'll visit him. Will you come, Gayla?"

Gayla chuckled, "I was wondering when you'd ask. It's getting dark, we need to get going." The others were not invited.

Sergeant Baba drove them in the Jaguar. When they arrived at the closest driving point, Catan told the sergeant to stay in the car. He was not comfortable with the potential risks, but Catan told him to stay put.

She donned her silk hood and ceremonial sword, and the two girls set off in the half-light. The locals all moved aside as they approached. Some knelt in honour, others scurried away, but none came close to those ghost-like apparitions. It was a menacing spectacle! Quite rapidly, the open area was almost deserted. Ninah's cross stood lonely in the middle, with four burning torches lighting up an angelic vision of peace. The vision of the old hag spoiled it. As the girls wandered towards their loved one the few soldiers at the Fort-gate went inside, and the dwellers that had stayed on to watch over the scene hurriedly moved back into the darkness.

"Ninah," whispered Gayla. "Ninah we're here." The old hag pushed the ranar under his nose, and then splashed his wounds. He shivered with the pain. "Is this hag annoying you?"

Ninah opened his eyes. They were red and shot, but he could see his girls. "It hurts. Make me sleep."

Catan turned her hooded head towards the old hag. "Do you enjoy your job, Hag?"

She replied, "It's good when I get one like this." She laughed.

"This's my uncle, do you enjoy hurting him?" The hag splashed some acid over his wounds and he squirmed.

Ninah croaked his words. "Please Gayla. Tell Catan to send me home. I just want to sleep." He was crying, but the sobbing hurt his sliced stomach muscles, so he tried to hold back. "I love you Gayla, please send me home."

Catan moved close to him, and reached her hand up to his lacerated stomach. "Poor Ninah. You must go home now. Be good."

Ninah smiled. "Thank you."

Catan stood close to him, while Gayla pulled herself up to sit on her shoulders, and she gently kissed his dry lips. "I'll miss you. Thank you. We'll have more fun, one day." She climbed down and took her place on Catan's right, she whispered, and then Catan swung her sword through his throat. It split right across, below his jaw, and he choked for a few moments, and then went to sleep. The ranar would no longer work. "Look after our children."

As Gayla whispered, Catan turned around towards the old hag, and without a warning sliced her throat open. She dropped like a log. That was naughty.

"At least we know he'll be at home when we follow." They had a mournful cuddle before leaving the deserted open area.

Colin Hodgson

19 -- THE DYING PRINCESS

The press were doing a marvellous job, chasing like bloodhounds for explanation and evidence, and sensation of course. The Monsignor, still green behind the ears, did not get a moments peace. His position continually cropped up in interviews, and for a few days it was his implied involvement in *everything* that fed the World's lust for malicious gossip; the more gruesome, the better the ratings. Poor Louis' reputation was slipping into meltdown, and every black mark that went against his name was carbon copied against the Chi Bantri name. To add to his torment, the College of Cardinals succeeded in removing him from his prestigious position as a cardinal bishop and for a while the headlines shouted about the Vatican, not the Chi Bantri. Locally, word on the street was that the Monsignor was not going to be in office for very long, and because traditionally the position was for life, the street also suggested that he could imminently be joining his predecessor.

Sitting in the Palace lounge the family laid their plans.

Gayla sat bolt upright and began. "To date we're bang on course. The Monsignor is not clever enough to allay the suspicions which are being fuelled by the press. He'll soon be gone. But we won't have to worry about his successor, whoever he would be. So I suggest we move on."

Catan reminded the family, "The anniversary is close. That's when the people of the World will cleanse their own planet of the canker which is spread by the proverb of the Chi Bantri."

Robin laughed, "You put that rather elegantly, Cat'."

She shrugged her shoulders and grinned. "Thank you, Daddy. But all joking aside, it's only four days away, and I have to sort my end out. I need to get an appointment with my eye specialists and I'll have to meet them in the main clinic in the industrial area. So I'll need to have the Sergeant and the Jag' for a couple of hours"

Gayla giggled, "And then we're almost there. Just need to get a few seeds germinating out there about the real reasons for the children's deaths, that is, the Festival and the rituals. I've spoken to some of me old mates in the slum and a few have agreed to interviews. Once a few have given their stories, others will follow."

Before the girls could make their absolute attack on the sect, the World had to be made to appreciate what they were. Gayla's pals in the slum included workers from the Fort as well as men and women who had been abused by the sect as children. They had witnessed the pagan acts at the Festival of Life celebrations, and their individual accounts, which had been told to so few, would bring credence to the sect's assured punishment, which the World was soon to witness.

Catan went to a meeting with her team. The Jaguar arrived at the clinic ahead of a mob of paparazzi that had followed them from the Palace. The Indian Army escort quickly surrounded the pretty Princess and the Sergeant, shepherding them through the front doors. As they reached the door, the princess turned and waved. Pictures of the little girl in dark glasses and Kurta were clearly at a premium; the cameramen and women scrambled for advantage.

The meeting with her doctor was held in a private clinic room.

"My Princess. We're almost there." The doctor was accompanied by two scientists; one scrawny little old man who managed two communication satellites, the other an expert in laser holography. "I think our parts are assembled. Are you ready?"

Catan smiled. "Yes, we've a couple of issues which me and Gayla need to finalise, but they'll not affect your ends. How many are they?"

The doctor replied, "Nineteen thousand seven hundred and fifty one members. They've increased by about two hundred higher members in not many days. The recent bad press seems to have attracted a lot of new members and our clinics have been very busy with the tracking devices. And remember, for each new bloody member there's probably a network of thousands of un-recruited minions working for them. They're stronger now than ever before."

They spoke quietly about the timing. "Fourteen hundred hours, local time. There's no leeway."

Catan took her glasses off. "You realise the consequences of failure? They'll continue to grow with compound interest. I trust I won't have to call in my mummy!"

They returned to the Palace.

The interviews with the slum dwellers went ahead. And what a result! Ninah swung from evil mass child murderer to saviour. He had saved the unfortunate children from horrifying torture and abuse, and consequential death. He had also spent many years hypnotising the victims' bodies with his 'magical' silver nails, saving them the excruciating pain from slow-cooking. He was becoming a legend, an anti-Chi Bantri icon. And yes, the press can be darlings.

In addition to crowning Ninah the child-saviour, the people were beginning to wonder who the Chi Bantri really were. People from across the globe were going out on their witch-hunts in search of members, and sadly, many people were lynched and killed. In Italy, where they were desperately struggling to rebuild from the volcanoes, a group had accused four catholic priests of membership, and without trial, burned them at the stake. They shouted "An eye for an eye!"

"Sadly, in times of warfare, people get hurt. Innocent people." Gayla was satisfied with the small number of panic killings. "But it shows that the people, the meek, are now turning on the Chi Bantri. The plan moves on."

A press interview was arranged to be held outside the Palace. There were about fifty journalists there, the Qeervi family and the Monsignor. The Indian Army saturated the area.

Queen Maya sat at the centre of the table, with Lamma to her right, and Catan and Gayla to her left. The Monsignor sat with his advisor on a separate table. The Queen and the Princess both had their eyes covered.

The Queen opened. "We're here to answer relevant questions about the recent activities of the Chi Bantri, and maybe a little about ourselves. *Stick* to the agenda." Her usual harsh approach.

Reporter. "Queen Maya, what's your involvement with the Chi Bantri?"

The Queen. "I have only one direct association with them. They killed me and my family. Since then, Lamma and myself, well, we've been on other business."

The Monsignor. "That's pure myth."

The Queen and Lamma smiled.

Reporter. "Some say you're the Mother of God. Is that just lunacy?"

The Queen. "The state of my mental health is not on the agenda."

Reporter. "Lamma, you've kept a low key on all of this. What about the six children killed by Ninah? Will it stop the cannibalism?"

Lamma. "I think the loss of the six poor children will save the suffering of many to come. The children willingly gave themselves to God, in preference to the Chi Bantri. Their spirits will now serve the meek."

Reporter. "But they'll just steal some more children from the homes and slums. Is that not correct?"

Lamma. "To you, Louis."

The Monsignor. "The stories of the Festival of Life are false and malicious. The Chi Bantri don't conduct cannibal feasts, nor paedophilic orgies, nor kidnapping. There's no evidence to suggest we do."

Princess Catan. "I take it then, Louis, that you'll not require my services in the future." She waited for a response. "You've ten seconds to respond."

The Monsignor, sweating. "I think it'd be expedient to discuss that in private."

Princess Catan. "You may not get the opportunity, Sir."

The pressmen fidgeted. One asked, "Princess, you're said to be the spirit of the sect. Has that changed?"

Princess Catan. "Nothing has officially changed, *yet*."

Lamma. "My daughter's been a slave to the Chi Bantri for many years. What began as a benevolent society of scholars has grown into a demon. My daughter will feed that demon no more and the Festival of Life is no longer. That is my decision."

The Monsignor. "I hope you know what you're saying. You know how powerful the sect is."

Lamma. "I do, but do please tell the rest of the World." The Monsignor did not bite.

Reporter. "The people in my country have come to their senses and are no longer blaming the Queen for the natural disasters, the volcanoes and the waves. But they're now turning on the Chi Bantri members. Queen Maya, do you approve of what the people are doing?"

The Queen. "Murder and false-conviction is *never* acceptable. I know that the four priests who were burned were totally innocent of the people's charges as where the others who have died. This type of uncontrolled retribution is never acceptable in the eyes of God or the law. So, no, I don't approve."

Reporter. "You talk of God. Whose God are you referring to?"

The Queen. "Sir, there is only one God. *Your* God, *Our* God. Many people worship Him in different ways and relate to His spirit in different forms, but He is only one."

Reporter. "If you consider the Italians to be wrong to punish the Chi Bantri, then what should they do? Perhaps *you, Queen Maya,* should lead them through the valley of death."

Catan. "The Queen *will* lead the people. And she will now ask for the people's help."

The Queen, after looking hard at Gayla, stated, "I *will* lead you." She then looked to the Monsignor. "But the priests were innocent. They weren't higher members of the Chi Bantri, and as such they were murdered. So I ask the people of the World to hold back. The secret society remains secret, and spurious accusations of membership will only result in the further murder or abuse of innocent people. You must believe in us enough to allow us to deal with the Chi Bantri members."

Reporter. "Our government has identified eight members. Are you saying that my government are wrong and should release them?"

The Queen. "Yes, that's what I'm saying. Answer this. Are the Chi Bantri being held, or is the Chi Bantri holding?"

The same reporter. "I support my Government on this."

Princess Catan. "Then, Sir, you don't know your own government. I know for certain that only four higher members are key players in your government. And *they* have not been arrested."

The Queen. "Governments, industries, Royal families, religions. Sit the next two days out. You can't fight an invisible enemy from within. The day after tomorrow, I will announce verdict on the case of the Chi Bantri. You'll all then know who the Chi Bantri are and I'll punish them. So please be patient, for just two more days."

Reporter. "The whole World wishes you well, but they're running out of patience."

The sweating Monsignor. "We can work together to resolve the recent set-backs. We've organised additional aid to be shipped to southern Italy. Just one of our many aid programs."

The Reporters. "Too little, too late! If the Queen doesn't get resolve, the people will. That's the mood right now."

The Queen. "Please, everybody, save the mood swings for after my verdict. You won't be disappointed."

Reporter. "Your Majesty, you're promising a lot to the World. What should we do if you're no longer alive in two days?"

The Queen smiled, looked down at the giggling Gayla and replied, "Pray to God. To *your* God."

The family retired to the Palace, and the Monsignor was escorted back to the Fort by the Indian soldiers. The next stage of the plan was to make a public press statement on the date of the two hundredth anniversary of the festival, just two days away. The Queen's promised verdict was the main item on the agenda, and her statement had been specially written for her by the family writer. It was to be an historic event with most of the major news channels being invited to attend.

Meanwhile, in the Palace. "Did you hear from Catherine? I did." Gayla sat with Catan on her bed, in their night gowns. She sat between Catan's legs, her back to her, with Catan's feet pulled up around her, as she gently massaged the Princess's feet. "Do they hurt?" she whispered.

"Always. My hands as well." The girls were a little sombre. "Will you do my hands after?"

Gayla leaned back and answered with a kiss. She said, "You know, Cat', Catherine and her mates went to another school, you know. There were some really young children who were being interfered with. Seems it was quite serious, fucking them." She frowned a bit. "Catherine says that she had nothing to do with it, but the children got the bloke who was the main one and tied him up. They cut his penis off and stuffed it in his mouth. He died. And the children've been taken to a mental institution." She moved her attention from her feet and began massaging her hands. "You know, Cat', I'm gonna really miss you. Will you miss me?"

Catan tickled Gayla with her free hand, and they both wriggled and giggled. She replied, "You know I will. It's been lovely for the past thirty-odd years with you back, and now your Mummy and our Daddy. Shame it has to end."

"We'll still talk every day, and you'll soon be back. My plans haven't changed. And you'll be with Ninah for just a little while." The little girls were silent as Gayla worked on Catan's hands. "You know, Cat', I think if Catherine and Ninah were people, they'd get married. They both love children." She continued to sooth Catan's hands. "You know, Cat', I think I'll ask Daddy something tomorrow. He's a bit dumb, but he has some real rash ideas."

"What you gonna ask him?"

"What if you can't hide something? That's all."

Catan frowned.

"You know, Cat', this has been a good project. And I almost never made it back, ever. Wonder what would've happened?"

"Don't think about it. I don't." Catan pulled her hand from Gayla's and hugged her round the neck. "Do you think Mummy and Daddy still love us?"

"Course they do. They've just forgotten a bit. You know, Cat', could've been that time-slip. Promise we'll never do it again. Mind you, it worked out exactly as planned in the end."

They just cuddled for a while, and then Gayla asked, "Can we look at that day? Haven't done that for so many years, I've almost forgotten" Catan did not answer. "Hey? Can we?" Gayla pulled round to face her sister. "Won't hurt, will it?"

"Don't know." She pushed her nose against Gayla's and suggested, "We could look at me and Dilly. The rude bits, if you want. She had some lovely rude bits." They grappled each other and rolled about the bed giggling. "But you want that day, don't you." Quite sombrely she whispered, "All right, I'll try."

Catan sat upright with her legs open while Gayla sat between them with her own legs wrapped around Catan's hips. They held each other's waists.

As Gayla's intense stare searched deep into Catan's pearly white eyes, a vision formed. Her two eyes slowly merged into one, opening up a passage to another time. There were soldiers wearing leather armour, and many Indians watching from the wings, and wailing. Through the flames could be seen two wooden crosses with a woman nailed to each. On the right cross hung Queen Maya, and she had her right eyelids clipped and stretched open, anchored to her cheeks and forrid, by pins. Her emerald eye was missing. She was naked except that her ginger pubic hairs were hidden by a small skirt, but it was not a skirt, it was her skin from her stomach which had been stripped down as far as her hips and weighted, to preserve her decency, and her breasts had been sliced off. A hag dowsed her raw torso of the blood. The nails had been driven through her wrists and lower limbs, and her head was supported from the neck by a single silver nail, the sign of Ninah. On the other cross hung a dark haired woman, about twenty five years old, and the daughter of Queen Maya. It was Gayla. Her eyes were also pinned open to make her see, and she was nailed arms and legs, and through her neck with Ninah's silver nail. She hung naked, with large open wounds from where her breasts had been removed. At the base of the two crosses lay two dead men. The hag pushed ranar swabs under the girls' noses to ensure that they did not miss the show, and they both wept; they were watching Catan! The little girl was chained to a large square metal contraption which had been lowered over four fires, one at each corner, and each hand and foot slowly cooked, blistering and sizzling. Her eyes had been pinned open. A priest of some sort carefully cut some meat from one of the Dying Princess's hands and ate it, ceremoniously holding it above his mouth and then lowering it in, making sure that the wailing crowd could see him eating their Princess. He then shouted with his arms in the air, and the metal contraption was turned upright, for Catan to see her mothers, and they her. Her eyes streamed with blood and tears and she whimpered 'Mummy' as a ranar swab was offered up to her nose.

A large soldier stood in front of Queen Maya, with an enormous horse-chopping sword on his back. He lifted it from the scabbard, then, whipping his body to increase speed, he swung it, slicing through the Queen's body from her neck down to her hips, and her intestines fell out. They were left hanging between her legs. He moved over to Gayla, took his stance, and sliced her from neck to hip. He then turned to the dead men and decapitated one of them. As another soldier pushed Gayla's loose gizzards back into her body, he picked the head up and pushed it into the girl's gaping torso. The head stared out onto the world from her stomach. It was the Lamma. The wailing increased and Catan screamed.

Gayla watched herself in amazement, her big, dark eyes open wide, witnessing their executions through her daughter's memory and sightless eyes. But then the vision blurred, and in the corner of each of Catan's eyes a tear formed. Gayla grinned and lost all focus of the vision, concentrating on those two tiny tears. They grew and they grew and then began to roll down her cheeks. Gayla pursed her lips and then seductively picked each tear from Catan's cheeks, and her body shivered from the ecstasy rush. The tears were heavenly, she wanted more. She whispered sensuously, "My little girl….my baby….. feed me. You can cwy if you like. I won't tell."

The tears suddenly filled Catan's eyes and she started to shudder. Her face screwed and she just could not hold back the crying any longer. Almost two hundred and forty years of pent up emotion exploded from her as the two girls squeezed each other so hard, and she screamed. Gayla kissed her face, feeding on the ambrosial tears, and as poor Catan wept her heart out, Gayla laughed.

Then Gayla screamed, "Mummy, Mummy! Daddy! Quick! Get in here!"

The door burst open and a panicking Tracy flew in. "What's happening?"

"She's cwyin'! Look, my little girl!" Gayla couldn't stop giggling as Catan sobbed. "She's done it. She's cwyin'!"

Tracy held the sobbing girl and said nothing, just comforted her, but Gayla was so excited. Her little girl was crying!

Then Tracy whispered, "Gayla, could you give us some time, please."

So Gayla ran out of the room, bumping into Robin on her way.

"She's cwying! Our little girl! Our baby!" She pulled him by the arm and they went into Gayla's bedroom. "Lay with me, Daddy. Please. I'm so excited." They lay on her bed, and Robin cradling the little girl to his chest. "It's so good. She had to cwy before the verdict." She kissed Robin full on the mouth, and flirtatiously licked his lips. Robin pulled away. "Oh, Daddy, I love you so much." She kissed him again. "Daddy, make love to me. You know, like you used to." He again pulled away, and she calmed, resting her head on his shoulder. "Sorry." She was kissing his neck. "It's this baby body. Sorry." After a silent few moments Gayla whispered, "Our daughter can go home now, peacefully. She's cwied. And I've spoken with Catherine and we've passed her. After all these centuries she's completed her confirmation. She's really suffered, but now she's ready." She chuckled quietly as they lay there as one. "Our little girl, I'm so proud of her."

Robin frowned. "Does she know? I mean, that you're her mother, and Tracy's her granny?"

"Yeah, course she does. So does Mummy. Remember? That's how she introduced us at the meeting. We just don't talk about it. But you already know all that, so why ask?" She looked into Robin's face, breathing into his eyes, and asked, "Will you make love to me when we get home? Do you still love me enough?"

He pondered over something which had not yet fully returned to his memory. "I think I'll always love you, and Mummy. And Catan and Ninah." He sighed. "But you've changed. There's something missing, and something added. I can't explain." He frowned, looking up at the ceiling. "But I really miss the boys." Robin had a tiny tear in his eye.

"It must be brilliant being a human." The tiny little girl didn't know everything, after all. "What's it like?"

"Not so brilliant all the time. But when it's good, it's *really* good. But you've seen them suffer though, you must sometimes feel sorry for them. Poor Dilshad must have suffered. Don't you feel?"

"Nah, not really. If I felt for them, I couldn't do my job. Now Ninah and Catherine, *they* feel sorrow for the children, and sometimes they do the wrong thing because of it. That's why I have to always have the final word, well, sort of." Her pretty eight-year-old face suddenly showed question. "I think I do."

Robin smiled at that. "But I like Catherine's attitude. I almost fell in love with her at a boot sale not long ago." He grinned. "And I think she threw me and Mummy back together. I owe her for that." With a slight frown he mumbled, "But I don't even know her. All I know is that she's Ca'an's auntie and Gayla's cousin."

Gayla sighed with a smile, and then rolled onto Robin, her legs each side of his stomach. "Pity I'm a little girl. You know, Daddy, Mummy's a very lucky old granny." They giggled and rolled around on the bed, and then she gave Robin a long, sensual kiss on the lips. "That was from Catherine."

The sun eventually rose and flooded into Gayla's room. They all got dressed and met down in the lounge.

Tracy asked, "Are we all ready for tomorrow?"

Catan grinned, her eyes glistening in the dappled sunlight. "I am. Especially now." She had shed her chains. "But I'll check with General Dara that our assistants are all ready." She was very happy after her crying. "Daddy, Gayla wants to ask you something."

"Oh yeah. Silly me, almost forgot. Right, we got a dilemma, and me and Cat' can't think of anything. So you're our man." She gave him a high five and jiggered about on the seat. "If we have something which we don't want, but we've got it anyway, but we want to hide it, but can't, what should we do?"

"Ah, a riddle." Robin was a keen quiz player.

"No. Not a riddle really. Hang on. Right." She spoke very slowly. "Something's going to happen and we can't stop it. But we don't want anybody to see it happening, but they'll all be watching when it happens."

"Hmm, Sounds simple enough. If you can't *hide* it, *feature* it. And maybe dress it up as something else. You know, let them see it but *believe* it's something else. Do a con-trick on them."

The girls looked a bit confused, then, "Hey man. Got it!" Gayla had sussed it out. "Daddy, you are *so* clever, you've just saved Ca'an's life." She jumped over to him and hugged him, then hugged Catan. "You can stay!" The two girls jumped up and danced with joy. Confusion reigned.

Tracy's script arrived with the post, and there was a lot of erecting going on in front of the Palace. The road was closed off by the Indian army and a grandstand was built across it to house the press, and some mysterious equipment which resembled rather complicated guns was installed into the two rooms at each opposite corner of the palace, supervised by the holographic scientist. Robin and Tracy didn't even ask! Between the Palace and the grandstand was built a low stage, with seating for the Qeervi family and a strong wooden table set out in front. A large block of wood, like a chopping board, was placed in the centre of the table. To one side a few seats were set out for some special guests.

"Gayla," asked Robin, "What do I have to do?"

"I'll tell you tomorrow, best you wait." She danced around like an eight year old. "Can I ride on your shoulders? Can I, please? Pretty please?"

He gave her a foot-up and they limped slowly around the stage area. His leg was holding up well.

"I love going on your shoulders. Weird, ain't it." She swung from side to side, and waved at Aalap. "We could go for a ride with Aalap."

"Haven't you got work to do?"

"Nah, done it all. Let's go and see Syed. I'll tell Mummy."

As the tiny rickshaw moseyed towards the clinics it had four army escort trucks in front and four behind. They were getting very nervous about the forthcoming press release. Much of the previous day's press conference had been quite correctly reported as a threat towards the Chi Bantri by the Qeervi family, which seemed to have given most of the World a bloody good laugh. Oh, they of little faith.

Syed grinned. "Robin, what's happened to us? We're totally bloody lost." Syed poured a coffee for the adults. "I've a new career managing these clinics. Not sure if I even want it."

"Just gotta do what you want to. You only have one life. Spend some time with your parents. When this conference is over tomorrow, I can come home with you. I want to have a few beers with the boys." In his mind he knew that a few beers with his two boys was never going to be quite the same again. "Fancy that, Gayla? You can come with us."

She giggled. "We can all go. Cat' can go with us now, thanks to your brilliant advice." She kissed her daddy on the lips and then went into the clinic, next door, and returned with Doctor Hussain's nurse. "Nurse Ri is going to be at the conference tomorrow, with two other girls. She's agreed to help us."

Nurse Ri curtsied "Yes, Lamma, we'll be very honoured. We've mixed up the poultice already. And the swabs."

What poultice? Robin's suspicions began to niggle. "I think you need to tell us a little bit more, Gayla."

She fiddled her thumbs. "Well,…" She looked at the nurse. "The nurse must know, she has to plan. But she won't tell, I know that. You know what, Daddy, all the higher members will die tomorrow. Nearly twenty thousand of them. All at once. *All* of them." She sighed and looked at her feet. "*All* of them, including Ca'an."

"Why?"

"I told you before, *she's* a *member*. She has the tag in her left wrist. And so you must do *exactly* as I ask you tomorrow, no questions. You've got to. Promise?" She bit her bottom lip. "Come on, promise, else we'll lose her."

Robin nodded his head in agreement, and then looked at Syed with raised eyebrows.

Gayla continued, "If she'd refused to be treated the same as them, they would be suspicious. Just make things harder. We all have to make sacrifices."

He just had to go along with them.

That night really dragged on. They all sat in the lounge and nattered about something and nothing. Captain Batiste made a short visit with General Dara, and they shared some of his whisky. But it still dragged. They stayed in their comfy seats all night, until the sun shone through the living room windows.

"Well, this is it," insisted Gayla. "Let's all get out and amongst it, shall we?"

The time arrived, a quarter past one in the afternoon, and the grandstand was packed. Reporters and cameramen hustled for position, while the television crews took the places allocated to them. And thankfully, it wasn't raining.

The few guests included Monsignor Mateo, and President Hon who had replaced the late President Li Jinpeng, and a surprise in the President of India, the Supreme Commander of the Indian Armed Forces. He had been instrumental in forcing the closure of the Anglian Fort for the duration of the conference, with all the resident members and the army kept inside. They were at least taking the Chi Bantri threat seriously.

The family sat at the back of the stage, in front of their Palace entrance, and were wearing the royal colours of the Qeervi family, with their loyal Ghurkha guards looking over them from behind. The conference got under way.

The Queen. "We've called this conference in order that we may announce our verdict on four of the charges made against the Chi Bantri, a private sect. The charges include mass murder, genocide, paedophilia, and gang rape. Many other charges, not being considered today, also include cannibalism. Before I announce my verdict along with the punishment, are there any relevant questions?"

Amazingly nobody raised any questions.

"Good. I'm pleased to have the Monsignor, Cardinal Mateo of the Chi Bantri, here with us if we should need any explanation. I'll begin."

"I've kept the list of crimes to a minimum. This list in no way excuses the accused of their thousands of *other* crimes against humanity, which have resulted in many millions of deaths. We seek only to *justify* the execution of the higher members of the Chi Bantri. Monsignor Louis Mateo, do you have anything to say before I pass judgement?"

He said nothing.

"Then I'll begin. I'll first read out the charge, and each verdict as it arises.

"Charge one. In seventeen seventy seven the founders of the sect were engaged by the British East India Company to murder the members of the Qeervi Royal Family. They successfully murdered four of the family members. Although found guilty, those founder members have been forgiven, unconditionally, by the murdered Qeervi family members.

"Charge two. After thirty seven years of successful operation the sect began killing. The Chi Bantri are charged with the killing of ten of its own members in eighteen fourteen, in the Kingdom of Kandy, in an effort to contrive all-out war between the British and the Kandyan Nobility. The deaths successfully fuelled the war machine, resulting in thousands of mutilations and deaths. Ultimately the land known as Sri Lanka became a highly profitable region for the cult, producing vast income from the export of tea. We find the Chi Bantri guilty in the first degree of the murder of ten of its members and of the indirect responsibility for the deaths of British and Kandyan nationals.

"Charge three. The Chi Bantri are charged with the manipulation of the Chinese people between eighteen thirty six and eighteen sixty four in order to gain profit from trade, particularly in opium. With members active within the ruling Qing Dynasty, and within Lord Elkin's administration, as well as in the Heavenly Kingdom of Great Peace, the sect had an enviable opportunity to establish peaceful relationships. But the Chi Bantri profit forecast looked much stronger from the results of war, and hence peace was not on the agenda. The resultant deaths from the Taiping Rebellion and the Second Opium War numbered over twenty six point three millions, nearly all of them civilians. We find the Chi Bantri guilty of conspiracy to intensify discrimination and hatred, resulting in the deaths of twenty six point three million people.

"Charge four. The Chi Bantri are charged with the torturous use of lingchi to achieve the murder of my daughter's first love, Dilshad. She has been gang raped followed by execution using the Chi Bantri's own form of lingchi, being a form of execution also used by the Chi Bantri in East Pakistan in nineteen seventy one, a form which has been so vividly described in Satvinder's story, following his own lingchi murder and decapitation by the Chi Bantri. We find the Chi Bantri guilty of murder, by lingchi, of Dilshad and Satvinder, and many thousands more.

"We have *not* taken into account other outstanding charges against the Chi Bantri such as their involvement in the Holocaust, their interference in the Congo, their direct implementation of events in the war of independence in East Pakistan, the conflicts in Sudan and Ruanda, Collectivisation in the Soviet, and many, many more. The sum of their direct and associated involvement with unnecessary human deaths is high. It is currently running at over three hundred and twenty two million. And you, the World, can judge their individual, as well as shared, involvements for yourselves, once we have published the full list of members."

She was reminded by Gayla that the time was running close to two pm.

"I'm required by my family to pass sentence, and allot punishment, which will result in the total destruction of the Chi Bantri, passing power and competition back to the people of this World. Monsignor Mateo, do you have anything to say before I pass sentence?"

He was shaking, but was able to stand. "I question your right to pass judgement."

"I'm Queen Maya. *That* is my right of passage."

The press murmured but, amazingly, none of them questioned the Queen.

"From their many thousands of acts against humanity, we've found the Chi Bantri guilty of three charges. As a result of those three crimes we sentence the Chi Bantri to death."

The Monsignor stood up, "You're a lunatic."

"Sir, you can call me whatever you wish. But instead, you really should be considering your last request, or maybe considering prayer. The executioner is already sharpening his axe. And for all you Chi Bantri members who are listening to this broadcast I suggest you apologise to God for the misuse of his name over the past two hundred years. You've about five minutes left." She continued, "The sentence will now be administered. Princess Ca'an of Anglia, also known by the Chi Bantri as the Dying Princess, is one of the family's appointed executioners. That duty falls to her today."

Catan stood up and Gayla walked her to the table. She drew her ceremonial sword and held it in front of her chest. From the two far corners of the Palace, the gun operators took aim, they focussed their sights and synchronised, keeping their fingers on the triggers. The nurse and her two assistants stealthily moved from behind the scenes with their bags, and picked out some pieces of equipment. The World waited in suspense.

Catan spoke. "For over two hundred and thirty years the Chi Bantri have fed from my flesh. Now, they are about to go on a very long journey, never to return, but never to arrive." She stood quietly, waiting for the clock and thought, *'Daddy, you must come now. Take the sword and when I say to, use it.'* He rose, and limped around to the side of the table as she offered him the sword. *'I can't do this, Cat'.'* Gayla replied for her. *'You'll kill your little girl if you don't.'* He was nervous, not being sure of what was happening. The time was two minutes to two.

Catan spoke loudly. "The convicted killers from the Chi Bantri will join a never-ending queue for the cross, where the teenagers of Dhaka will be waiting. The teenagers will administer death by lingchi. And the children will not stop the torture until they themselves are satisfied, and ready to offer forgiveness. It could be a very, very long time." She laid her left arm out on the block. "I give my spirit to the children."

The gun operators in the Palace pulled their triggers, and their invisible laser beams met and became one, creating a vision of fire on the stage in front of Catan, and the flames rose. The virtual fire roared. *'Now cut my hand off, Daddy. Quick, do it now.'* Robin raised the studded sword above his head, and sweated. *'Now Daddy, Hurry!'* He swung the sword hard down on the block, and cut the hand off above the wrist. Instantly, the nurse rushed to Catan's arm and pumped a tourniquet around it, and then pushed a bag of poultice over the bleeding stump. She revived Catan with a swab of ranar. Catan managed to stay on her feet, her eyes and face screwed tight, and Gayla led her to the severed hand, which she picked up from the table. The Princess walked around the table and dropped the hand into the hologram of flames.

"Follow the hand of fate. The children are waiting." But as the hand sparked into a bright white flame, a bullet-hole punched through Catan's shoulder. The bullet silently passed through her tiny body, exploding out of the back, and she stumbled. The nurse jumped forward with her bag and pushed poultice into the large ragged hole in the back of her shoulder, then into the tiny hole in the front.

The flames rose higher as the little girl fought to get to her feet. Then, with Gayla's help, she took the sword from her panicky father and moved towards the fire, which by then had begun to take the shape of the Dying Princess, chained to a metal contraption and with her hands and feet in flames. Catan swung the sword and decapitated the Dying Princess.

"Die." Catan's voice was weak, but audible. "They are dead. They're all dead."

The virtual flames engulfed the headless torso of the Dying Princess, and then died down to nothing. Catan collapsed. The Army swung into action, surrounding Catan, and trying to pinpoint the source of the bullet, but to no avail.

Catan wheezed, "Did we do it?" She lay calmly behind the barrier of soldiers and smiled up at Gayla. "Mummy, did we do it?"

Gayla giggled, and then pulled her little girl up. "Look." She pointed between the legs of the soldiers, where they could spot the Monsignor. He looked so peaceful, but stone dead. "One of many thousands." She then, with Robin's help, pulled Catan up further, and they managed to stand. The soldiers reluctantly moved aside as the Queen and her family walked into the open, and over to the bank of excited press-men, and they bowed. As they stood there, General Dara approached them with a little old man, the communications scientist.

He whispered in Catan's ear, "Your Highness. Only six failed." He bowed very low. "We are sorry for this, they'd all lost their left arms in accidents. But we can remove them manually."

Catan replied, "If I live, we'll have a party." She coughed. "But if God has allowed the six to live, then we'll take His lead. Let them live."

Almost an anticlimax, but it was the end of a long, drawn out era.

The Chi Bantri had spent a bit over thirty years as good, followed by over two hundred years as evil. Then suddenly, at two o'clock on that lovely sunny afternoon, they were nothing. The little girls' twenty years of planning had culminated in a total success.

Catan was left without a hand, but, what the heck, she still had another one and her gunshot wound healed quickly; must have been the Qeervi genes. And the Queen was officially decorated by the Indian Government, and so she was recognised as a *real* Human Queen. And of course the World searched for reasons, theories and spoilers about what had happened and why, and how, but they never found the remains of the microscopic carriers which accompanied the tracking devices and which had exploded in the left hand of each and every higher member, releasing a minute amount of toxin, just enough to instantly arrest the heart. They had all died from heart attack, natural, but miraculous.

The communications scientist was relocated with his family with brand new identities, to ensure that it never became known by the World just how he had triggered off the mysterious explosive carriers, from his satellites. And, of course, the holistic scientists retired gracefully to avoid the decapitated Dying Princess from being found out as a fraud. The dedicated small team of doctors whose jobs it was to insert the Chi Bantri tracking devices into the members' hands, just never mentioned the carriers which went in with them; they had only inserted *tracking* devices into each member's left hand, honest Guv'.

And so, the Earth was cleansed of the evil which had grown from good, and it was all achieved through the miraculous powers, and through the inhuman suffering, of the Princess Catan of Anglia. And it seemed like the end of my story.

20 -- THE PASSING OF SAINT NINAH

The project was complete, almost. It just needed a few more years to ensure that the enormous vacuum, created by the deaths of so many dignitaries, industrialists and religious purveyors, could be filled by the thousands of competing groups of humans. They all needed influence from a well meaning leadership, maybe in the form of a religion, and, in the belief that their old established faiths had failed them, they craved for something new. They looked to the Qeervis.

Tracy was the family front, always had been, and her authoritative approach to all and everything attracted the new followers in their millions. Most believers continued to follow their own faith, but those who were new to spiritual belief or had lost their faith looked to their new Queen for inspiration. That was exactly as Gayla had planned, but Tracy was not amused.

"We're not a religion," Tracy told the press. "We won't compete with the established religions for congregation. We only wish to work *with* the established religions, not against them."

"So what are you?"

Everybody was asking that question. Over the millions of years it had been asked so many times but the answer never came any easier. This time it was particularly difficult, since there was conflict within the family as to the way ahead. Gayla's personal current project was incomplete, and she insisted that it ran through to its conclusion.

Gayla insisted, "We ran the Chi Bantri project to assess man's ability to work together, for each other. It proved after a very short number of years that they can't do that. They're too tribal, and too greedy. But my current, long-term project has its own significance, and that is to see if the established religions can accept that there really is a God. And you all know a little about that project."

They all sat on their comfy sofas and pondered the project's aims. A heated disagreement was developing between Robin and Gayla.

Robin questioned the reasons. "Why do we really need to know that? It won't make our jobs any easier by knowing one way or the other. It could just break down the present sets of beliefs, and heaven knows what'll replace them."

"But we need knowledge. That's part of what we do, collect knowledge in order to progress the evolvement of the Earth and everything on it. And it's too late to turn back. They've already been told several times that Mummy is the Mother of God, and her spiritual protector is the Lamma."

Robin was getting heated. "So let's just all go home, and let them carry on thinking it. They'll do the same as they've always done, that is, either develop belief in the Qeervi family or just forget all about us. That's how it's got to be, it's our law."

Gayla started laughing. "You know, Daddy, we did that in the first century AD. Three hundred years later the Christians were still being persecuted, and you know the main reason why? Because they renounced all other Gods, in favour of their own God and their messiah, Jesus Christ. They were intolerant of all others and secretive of their own. So, if this lot choose to worship us, they've got to be led down a route where tolerance is a virtue. If a Muslim or catholic wishes to believe in us, they must be able to do so without discrimination. And they should be allowed to continue to follow their established beliefs. I'm not trying to change those, just compliment them with modern history."

"But we can't preach or convert. We've got our codes of practice."

"We all know that. After all, the Chi Bantri could only be removed by willing humans, and they were. It all fits in the code. We've now got to be here to monitor what the humans make of us and how they develop their beliefs. If they develop an intolerant following of us, renouncing all others, then we've got to do something to stop it. We just need to be here for a few more years. Ninah is keeping an eye on everything else."

"So you think the present religions could continue as is, with this new belief working on another level? Their new belief in the Qeervis would not destroy their inbred beliefs?"

"No, or maybe. That's what we need to find out. You know, Daddy, Mummy has already laid the foundations, when she told the press *'there is only one God. Your God, Our God. Many people worship Him in different ways and relate to His spirit in different forms, but He is only one.'* We know that, but maybe the people out there need to know it, and believe it. The Christians' renouncement of all other forms of God's spirit was wrong, but it's not too late for people to learn to believe in, for example, the Christian church, whilst also believing in something which envelops *all* of God's children. And that's where we're going. Ca'an's confirmation is complete and I'm *not* stopping now."

Robin looked around at the others, especially Catan, who were taking it all in, but keeping mum.

Then Catan spoke up. She looked hard at Gayla, through her sightless eyes, and spoke with some venom. "Monsignor Plassey had my Dilly killed in the name of God, and there is only one God." She said no more, as Gayla squeezed in beside her for comfort.

Robin took the meeting back to the agenda. "What if it goes wrong, as the Chi Bantri project did? Hundreds of millions of people suffered through the Chi Bantri because we didn't shut it down one hundred and eighty years ago." He twiddled his thumbs, and then came up with the most brilliant of ideas. "Let's have a whisky."

"Daddy, that's a *fantastic* idea. Where do you get them all from?" The heat of the moment was doused and they had a laugh. "Can I have a glass of wine?"

"Of course you can, poppet. What about you girls?" They all had a drink.

Gayla continued, "Now, Daddy, the Chi Bantri project showed that the only thing in the World which can successfully group humans into a multi-racial, cross-religion establishment is money. As a rule of thumb, money is everything to humans. But it's addictive: the more you've got, the more you want, and the more you'll fight for it. It holds communities together, but also pits them against each other. It never does what's right for the whole. But Saint Catherine and her angels are proof to me that people can throw away their prejudices and work for everybody, irrespective of colour or creed." The little girl had a passion for her project. "Saint Catherine once said that those who give the most, often have the least. I want to know how far that principle can be expanded."

"Hey, I know how you feel. But not many humans are capable of being saints, not for long, anyway."

"But, you know, Daddy, they can nearly all be saintly for a little bit, and some for a lot. Add that all together and I think that we could come out on top. We could encourage the religions to be more tolerant of each other. Ain't it worth a try?"

There was no reply. After a long, silent moment Gayla searched her soul. She stuttered as she spoke. "Would it help if I told you, honestly, that I don't know what happened with the Chi Bantri project, but that I do know that it was *not* just left to its own directions?"

"I don't know what you mean."

"Nor do I. But it all fitted in with Ca'an's confirmation training." She hesitated. "And I should know what's going on, but I don't. I don't know." The almighty Gayla suddenly seemed a little lost. "You said that I've changed. A bit gone, and another bit added. Well, I'm still getting used to it. Sorry." She was morose, but her eyes never wetted. "I just know that I'm better, more in control. So, I know we're doing right, honest gov'."

Robin grinned, "Ok Catherine." A silence fell for what seemed an eternity. Tracy squeezed his hand tightly before he got the meeting back on course. "Gayla, it could work. But as soon as our presence sparks the usual religious wars, we put a stop to it, if we can, and I'm only gonna go along with it if we put it to the vote."

They all concentrated hard. The Qeervi intranet was opened and a net conference held between all of the Qeervis, including those present, Ninah, Catherine and Kamdar. The only negative vote was that of Kamdar, who suggested they all go home and leave him in peace. But the vote went in favour of staying for long enough to monitor the beliefs which had been developed in the people during the closing stages of the Chi Bantri project. Gayla's project would continue.

The family had been offered accommodation all over the World, some of it so grand and pompous that they would not be able to show their faces again, should they have accepted it. So they decided to stay in Anglia, in their modest little 'Palace' on the edge of the slum. It was their home.

As for the Anglian Fort, it was placed under the management of the Indian Cultural Office, to be established as a museum of ethnic history, whilst setting part of the barracks aside for the army of Sir Kamdar to occupy. His army was inherited by the Indian Government, and so General Dara, with the blessing of the Indian President, placed it under the day-to-day control of the Royal Palace of Anglia. The Queen and her 'Prince Consort', the Lamma, agreed that the private army would be used to police and assist the people of the slum areas, in a similar humanitarian role to that which they carried out in the seventeen seventies. Sir Kamdar agreed to the arrangements.

The family were invited to so many events, from opening new shopping centres, to visiting natural disaster areas, to royal weddings, but they declined most, preferring to spend their time relaxing in the palace. They had come close to the end of a very long journey which had spanned almost two hundred and forty years, so they really needed to chill.

"I want to go home for a while." Robin was missing his sons and friends. "I think Syed wants to go as well. Shall we all go?"

They all sat on their comfy sofas and pondered the idea.

Catan, nursing her missing hand and gunshot wound, bit her bottom lip and then asked, "The boys are my brothers, aren't they?" She thought a little. "I would like to meet my brothers."

"So would I," stressed Gayla. "I've only seen them in Daddy's and Catherine's thoughts."

Robin pulled Tracy to him and flexed his authority. "Right, that's it. We're off to Boxted. Who's gonna sort it all?"

Tracy, the only real adult amongst them, reminded them all, "We'll have to go through the Indian Embassy, or Foreign Office or something, the proper routes and all that. It won't be like when we came here; there'll be minders, military and press, maybe even enemies. Won't be out on pub crawls."

There's always one to spoil it. But she was right in what she was saying, a Royal family, particularly a high-vis' one, cannot just wander around on their own. They couldn't even do that in the slums any more.

Gayla had the right idea. "We could go incognito. You know, dressed up." She giggled. "I could be a little monster. Rahhhhhh."

Catan chuckled, "But everybody would recognise you, then. Go as a young lady and you'll be ok."

"Huh, you can take the piss, but I'm now the only one here with all me bits. So who's the little monster now?" She cheekily stuck her tongue out and blew a raspberry at Catan, who didn't see a thing. The girls were getting bored, beginning to peck at each other, so a trip to England was just the medicine, and they would go in just two weeks time, before the steamy, rainy summer season got under way. The Foreign Office would sort it.

Robin sat looking at the World passing by along the road. And there were his good friends, the worms. Each one of them looked up at him and stuck its tongue out, then blew a raspberry. He waved, and they scurried back into the soil. "Funny little things, just like Gayla." He smiled to himself, but he was brought back to the real world with a message over the intranet. *'Good morning Lamma, this is Kamdar.'* He thought and replied, *'This is a surprise. What're you after?'* The line went quiet for a little time and then, *'I wondered if you'd like to meet up for a drink and smoke. Chew the cud.'* He had never trusted Kamdar, the black sheep of the family, but what the heck, he was family. He agreed to visit the Fort for a chin-wag.

Sergeant Baba drove Robin through the main gates of the Fort where the sentries had been replaced by workmen. The Cultural Office had begun work on the museum. The grand entrance to the hall was also getting a makeover. Around the back, the parade ground was quiet, with no children, just a couple of small groups of soldiers drilling.

The Sergeant escorted Robin from the car to the barracks, where Sir Kamdar was waiting, in his military regalia.

"Good morning Lamma." Kamdar took him by the arm and they walked to a bench under the shade of a large shrub, where they sat. "I was wondering how you were feeling. You've had quite a traumatic return to Qeervi, with everybody dying."

"It's been an experience. Had never been human before. None of us really know how or why me and Trace went that way. Do you have any theories? After all, you've had two hundred and forty years to consider it."

"Lamma, I don't worry about those sort of things. I've had a very happy time down here with the Chi Bantri. I'll miss them." He pulled a packet out of his pocket. "I like the opium. Share some with me?"

"No thanks. Could do with a whisky if you've got some."

Sir Kamdar waved his hand and his batman attended. He quickly returned with a bottle and a glass, and a small paraffin heater and a long necked opium pipe. The pipe was highly decorated, in dark blue and gold, and reminded Robin of Catan's killing tool, her sword. He appreciated the lethal ability of both tools.

"Good health, Lamma." He put a pill in the pipe bowl, held it over the heater for a while, then drew on his pipe, which exhumed a long satisfied sigh. He was big into his poppies.

"All the best Kamdar. But why d'you do that shit? It's turned your teeth yellow. And probably turned your brain yellow as well."

"Hah, teeth, brain, I could get some new ones if I was worried about it. But I love the shit. It makes me feel human. And I like feeling human. Why do you drink so much whisky?"

"Perhaps I drink to forget. To forget about feeling human. I miss it." Robin supped his whisky. "Would you want to be human? They only live seventy years, and that's only if they're not killed early."

"I love what I am, a bit of each, that is, a celestial human." He laughed, and sucked some more shit into his body. "I feel like a selective cross breed. But you're going to spoil my happiness when you start the religious wars. I don't really want you here." He stared at Robin. "Go home. You could be a lot happier there, and you've let your work slip, so go and do some catching up. Leave me to my debauchery; the sex, drugs and sausage role." He suddenly roared with laughter. "And when the fighting starts, your boys won't be safe." He carried on laughing, his greasy mop of hair swaying in the light breeze. "I won't be able to protect them." Now, I think that was a threat.

"No, but Catherine will. She's much stronger than you. And I've stopped you from killing."

"Lamma. Lamma, cousin Lamma. Surely you don't think I'd kill your children. I can't, can I. But I'm just warning you. Go home before the troubles, and they'll be safe."

"I'll go home when I die. Until then, we're in the middle of a project."

"Hmm, it's a wee chilly under this bush. Come and sit in the sun with me." Sir Kamdar stood up and picked up the heater. "Over here, cousin."

Robin followed him to a grassy patch, in the sun. Sir Kamdar sat down on the grass, and arranged his heater and pipe in readiness. "Have another whisky and sit with me."

Robin sat down and they chatted, cross-legged.

"Now, let's be friends. Tell me about your best sexual memory."

Robin frowned. "What, human or otherwise?" Robin did not want to talk about his bomb-blasts with Tracy and the God steaks. "I'll tell you about my human memories. I was seeing this girl for a while, and she was always so wet once she got going, and one night I'd done the business, and she was running and dripping. She decided to give me a massage, so rolled me over onto my tummy, and straddled me. As she massaged my back, the juices ran out of her pussy onto my arse cheeks and she slid back and forth on her clit. She had a massive orgasm, but so did I, just with the feel of her pussy sliding over my cheeks. A strange one."

"Hmm, a bit tame." Sir Kamdar raised his eyebrows. "My strange one was when I was just watching. This girl said to the soldiers, 'come on then, fuck me,' and they took her and tied her to a pallet. They cut off her tits and thighs, fucked her four times, then stuffed her cunt with a lump of wood." He began laughing, out of control.

Robin froze momentarily, then "You fucking bastard!" He climbed up onto his feet and with his good leg, kicked the bottle of whisky. It hit his cousin on the head and smashed. "You fucking arsehole. Dilshad? You're fucking dead, man!" He swung his foot at Sir Kamdar's bleeding head, but missed and almost fell. His sergeant caught him.

"Home, Sir." Sergeant Baba led the wreathing demigod to the Jag', with the other soldiers waiting for command from their General, but it never came. He just sat bleeding and laughing.

On their return to the Palace Robin was still seething with anger. He received a thought, *'consider it done, me ol' mate.'* It was Catherine. Not again. He calmed a little and replied, *'I only thought it. Don't do anything.'* That was a close thing. Kamdar would have gone the same way as the paedophiles in England.

"Gayla!" He called for some help. She arrived down the stairs. "I need some help."

He explained to the little Indian girl what had been said.

"We mustn't bite. The bloke's a primeval prat, but we've gotta stay in control. I'll speak to Catherine, and she'll make it her priority to look after the boys, and *not* to kill Kamdar." She looked at her Daddy, who was at the point of crying, so as always, she kissed his delicious tears away. "I don't know what his motives were, but let's not tell Cat'." She knew what could happen if Catan really lost it over the latest news of her one love, and also knew how fortunate they had *all* been that Robin remained inside his shell when he realised who Kamdar was talking about. He was much stronger than he seemed to realise. It was a delicate situation. "It would, though, be a good test for Cat'." But she decided not to use the situation.

The following day Robin was feeling below par. That was strange for a Qeervi.

As he sat on the bed he laid his head on Tracy's shoulder. "I feel sick. And I hurt around my kidneys."

Tracy decided that she should speak to the new doctor at the slum clinic. She called Syed.

"He's getting worse." Tracy sat as the doctor made an initial check of temperature, blood pressure and a visual. She suggested, "I think the girls might know more." So she called them in.

Gayla and Catan sat by the bed. Gayla asked, "What is it Daddy? I'm sure you know."

He managed a smile and whispered, "Yeah. I passed a worm this morning. The smell. It's the same as Tracy's eye was. Those bloody worms, our mates." He smiled at both the girls, and Gayla whispered to Catan. He continued, "I thought it'd be ok, Kamdar sat down so I did."

Gayla chuckled, "The wily old prat probably had a cork up his arse." They all forced a laugh.

Robin slowly said, "Anyway, our friends've finally got me. But they didn't blow raspberries this time."

The ensuing hush heralded the coming of death. They all just sat there looking at the dying Lamma.

The doctor broke the silence. "What is it?"

Catan answered him. "It's the puri worms. They've got Daddy and we're gonna lose him. The poo they pass has already broken down his organs, far beyond repair." She felt her way around the bed to Tracy, and clasped her arms around her neck. "We're gonna lose him, Mummy. He's going home early." They both sobbed.

Tracy looked at her lover and thought, *'please keep with me.'* He replied, *'I'll always be with you. I'll still be here for you, with Ninah.'* She leaned over and kissed him, and her tears ran onto his blueing cheeks. He smiled, and then went. It was a very kind death.

They all sat in silence, contemplating the loss. Eventually the Doctor asked, "What should I put on the death certificate?"

Gayla replied with a smile, "Liver and kidney failure."

The loss did not hit Tracy to the full until a few days later. She thought about the beginning, the plane journey to Kolkata, when he promised never to leave her, 'for any reason'. And she thought about the God steaks which they had shared, and the primeval sex which had blown their heads apart, and she thought about the love. She began to pine. *'Can you hear me, darling?'* After a little while, she received an answer. *'Yes, I'm here, honey-bunch. Getting back into my work. It's strange without you.'* She smiled and replied, *'I've just realised, you didn't leave me, I've left you. You've gone, and I haven't followed. But I now know what to do. I love you.'* They signed off, and she cheered up a little. She had a plan.

The world took the news of the death rather seriously. The family announced, through the Indian High Commission, that there would be a funeral when they returned from England as they had decided to continue with the visit to the boys, having put the body into cold storage. The funeral would be held on the River Hooghly, not far from the Anglia region, and Lamma was to be cremated on a traditional floating pyre. It all fitted into Gayla's 'revised' plan to hoodwink the people's belief in a celestial body which sat above and outside of the traditional religions. And, almost as if the Indians were in on the act, they had invited *all* the major political and religious leaders. The Lamma's death, just maybe, could have been the catalyst which the people were waiting for, a common feeling of loss felt by all creeds and a respect for something outside of the man-made constraints of religion. Good old Kamdar!

The journey to England was organised by the Indian Ministry of External Affairs and the British Home Office, and the level of security almost made it unbearable.

"Mummy," Gayla whispered as they sat in the armoured limousine outside Heathrow Airport, "They're forcing the World upon us. This's bad publicity and they're gonna all end up either loving us or hating us."

Tracy smiled, "Yes, I know. The only good thing is that they won't find any dirt on us. Whatever comes out will be the truth."

The car journey was long, and they were escorted by dozens of police vehicles and three helicopters. People stood at the roadside hoping to catch sight of the demigods. To the disgruntlement of the security forces, Catan and Gayla gave them their wish and hung out of the windows and waved to them all. The girls found their reception quite moving. The entourage eventually arrived at their hotel in the Essex countryside.

"I think we're going to be disappointed by the visit," grumbled Tracy.

"Don't get down, Mummy." Catan comforted her. "We'll have a lovely evening nosh-up with our brothers, and then we'll see if we can wrangle a trip down the pub. Leave it with us."

Gayla jiggled around and had a mischievous chortle, "I suppose as the Chi Bantri project's over, I can speak English."

"What?" Tracy was mongrelised between shock and anger. "What did you just say?"

"I said I could speak English. I'm speaking English, ain't I?" She giggled, "I almost got confused what I was talking."

With a massive sigh, Tracy calmed down and asked, "Why didn't I know that. You've always spoken English, same as the rest of us. Why didn't I remember that before?"

Little Gayla, the true professional, soothed her mummy by suggesting that maybe a ginger moment could be even worse that a blonde one.

The next day, they had that wonderful (English) evening meal with David and Russell. It was in the hotel restaurant, and they had insisted that the other diners who had booked were allowed their tables. They wanted a bit of atmosphere. The girls fell instantly in love with their two brothers, and vice versa, and the wine flowed and they loosely arranged the trip for the funeral. But they all got a little too tidly, and began to play up, as youngsters do, until a little old lady shuffled over to the table and asked them to think of the other diners. "Who do you think you are?" she snapped. They found it funny, but quietened down. They all went to bed without the pub, after all.

The next day they were going to a service to remember Robin at his local C of E church in Boxted. As they were walked through the crowd, into the old church yard, My Eyes saw for Catan, who gasped, "I remember this from Daddy's thoughts. There was a Christmas tree, and Catherine was here." She faltered. "I watched it with Dilly, through Daddy. Now they're both gone. I miss Dilly."

The family were all dressed in black. The three girls were wearing black silk saris and cholis decorated with mother-of-pearl, hiding their faces with flowing black veils and the Queen wore her royal tiara and necklace. David and Russell had black crombi-style overcoats, more in line with the chilly weather.

"I can't see Catherine. She can't be here." Gayla was looking for her amongst the crowd of onlookers, but she was nowhere to be seen.

The beautiful old church was full to the brim, and luckily the front row of pews was reserved for family members. In an atmosphere of asking eyes and tuts the boys walked the exotic young ladies down the aisle and they sat opposite the pulpit.

The vicar said some nice things about Robin, and everybody prayed and sung some hymns, and then the vicar invited Queen Maya of Anglia to say some words about her 'husband'. She slowly walked up to the pulpit, pushed her veil aside and she shone, with her emerald eye glistening like the stained glass behind her. She spoke loudly and clearly.

"My husband, Robin, the Queen's Lamma, has returned home to continue his usual work. He'll be sorely missed by the people of this World. He'll be sorely missed by his family and friends. But we mustn't mourn him; he's still with us in spirit and as such we must *celebrate* his return to the celestial Palace of Qeervi. Lamma lives forever."

The vicar shuffled his feet about, as the congregation began murmuring amongst themselves.

She continued loudly, "I'm sorry if I've offended your beliefs." She waited while the murmuring stopped. "My husband momentarily ruled the Earth as man. And he'll leave his many children in good hands, in firm hands, hands which are strong enough to be just and fair, but gentle. And consequently the meek will never inherit the Earth. *That* is my husband's will."

The murmuring began again. As she waited for it to settle, the vicar mouthed to her, 'Are you nearly finished?' He was concerned about her content, and about his finely conditioned old folk.

"Yes, I'm almost finished." She looked at Gayla. "But my husband will not sit alone for long. I will, with Princess Ca'an, our *youngest* daughter, join the Lamma on the pyre. We're going home."

Gayla's face widened. "What? No! You promised you'd never leave me, not again! *Ever!*" She jumped up and stood in front of the pulpit, adopting her cobra stance, and screeched, "You're not fucking going! You promised me!"

Tracy tried to continue, "Our daughter, our strength...."

"You fucking liar! You promised. Why?" The church fell silent. The shocked congregation sat open mouthed, in disbelief of the Queen's words, and in her daughter's reaction. And Gayla stood like the cobra who was about to strike at her own mummy, and was shaking with anger. Dust fell from the lofty ceiling as she trembled, but the silence continued as Catan stood up and took the few slow, blind steps towards Gayla, and she took her arm, gently persuading her to sit down. The dust stopped falling and they eventually, to the relief of the vicar, sat one each side of David, with Russell the other side of Gayla. Gayla took a quick look around, pulled David's coat apart, and hid her head inside it. She was safe from the eyes of the people. Catan bent over David, and also pushed her head under his coat. The two little ostriches took refuge.

Nose-to-nose, they shared each other's space. Gayla pushed her hand in and put the veils aside, and then Catan whispered, "Please Mummy. I love you." She kissed her on the lips. "You know, Mummy, if you want to cwy, I won't tell anybody." The little girls at last smiled, and the tears held back. "You'll think of something."

David's coat was getting a bit claustrophobic, so they emerged, with the church still silent and waiting. Gayla sat bolt upright, looked around, and then caught Russell's eye. She solemnly whispered, "I didn't cwy, Wuss', honest." Russell, tears in his eyes, pulled her to his chest and loved her.

Tracy had waited patiently in the pulpit. She resumed, "Our daughter, our strength, will inherit the Earth." She said nothing else.

The vicar took the pulpit and tried to return the service to the norm, with some prayer and a hymn. It didn't go anywhere; the congregation were so preoccupied by the aura of the strange people from the east.

Gayla lay on her brother's chest. *'Gay, a message from your old chap.'* Wow, it was Catherine, at last. Gayla's face lit up as she looked back, and there she was, several pews back, with her three little friends and Syed. Her massive smile and flowing blonde hair was a blessed sight for our Gayla. *'Your dad say's 'if you can't hide it, feature it. And maybe dress it up as somefink else. You know, let them see it but believe it's somefink else. Do a con-trick on them.' That's what he's said.'* The two little girls quietly giggled, and poor old, confused Russell gave her a very old fashioned look. *'Get Cat up in the pulpit,'* thought Catherine.

Gayla thought her instructions to Catan, who stood up and interrupted the vicar.

"May I speak in honour of Daddy?"

The vicar, a weak man, couldn't say no. So Catan listened to My Eyes and found her way up the steps into the pulpit. She stood straight and proud, silhouetted against the bright stained window, and she looked menacing, almost evil. She lifted her left arm. Her stump was hidden by a fingerless black silk glove, and it pushed below the veil and threw it up above her head to reveal her dusky face and jet black hair. As the congregation looked on in astonishment at her beauty, she opened her eyes. They sparkled and glistened, hypnotising the innocent onlookers who gasped, and the church became brighter with the sun flowing through the high windows like beacons from heaven. She was an angel in black, with the stars in her eyes contrasting with the darkness, creating a vision of mystical warmth. She was the most beautiful sight on Earth.

My Eyes handed the controls over to Catherine.

The congregation settled, and Catan began.

"Good morning. I'd like to relate my Daddy's love to you all by reading a passage from the modern scriptures, the Book of Saints. It's called 'The Passing of Saint Ninah'."

The little beauty stood tall, and followed her guide from Catherine who sat with her friends. They chuckled and fidgeted as she passed her words into Catan's mouth.

Catan spoke loud, with authority. "Lamma was a bit pee'd off with his ole mate's lot. The poor bloke 'ad got 'imself crucified for doing in the six kids. God's Six Ca'alysts. So he fought he'd go an' see his ole mucker, angin' on the cross. He said to Saint Ninah, *'Ninah me ole china. Wot's afloat?'* An' Saint

Ninah smiled at Lamma an' he said *'I'm dyin'.'* An' Lamma stood back an' he clocked the bloody great gashes in the tummy. *'Ninah, ole pal, I ain't gonna be able to help yer wiv those guts all angin' out. You'r a gonner. But before yer go, can I ask one?'* But Saint Ninah butted in and said, *'Lamma, word on the street 'as it that you're God. Is it right?'* And Lamma smiled an' said to Saint Ninah, *'you've known me over millions of years, you must know who God is.'* And Saint Ninah said, *'No-one needs to know who God is, cos he's everywhere. But we all 'ave our own Gods to worship, in different places an' different shapes. And they all come from the same roots, they're all part of God.'* And Lamma asked, *'Then who is your God, ole mate?'* and Saint Ninah replied, *'The Muvver of God walks the Earth with her children. God is with us right now. She's me prima donna, an' I mean that in the best possible taste. Well, what 'bout that question?'* Lamma laughed an' said to Saint Ninah, *'Before I cut yer froat and send yer home, tell me, why'd you kill the kids?'* An' Saint Ninah replied, *'Cos they willed it and God permitted it. An' I look after kids, I'm their protector, so I 'ad to do as I was telled. They wann'ed to give their spirit to their God, not the bloody Chi Bantri.'* And Lamma asked, *'But was it not cos they would be cooked at the Chi Bantri festival?'* And Saint Ninah replied, *'No. They would've gladly burned, if only it was for their God. But it weren't so they died wiv me. And now God has become stronger after their gifts of spirit, and is ready to return to the throne. The end is nigh, if ya know what I mean. But best you know, me old mucker. You'll soon be joining me, so keep yer mates on the right side of yer, if ya know wot I mean.'*"

The congregation were silently appalled, but she continued with Catherine's excerpt.

"And Lamma asked his old drinking pal, *'You saying that me friends will hurt me?'* Saint Ninah replied, *'Yes but not on purpose. Some give life, some take it, but God 'as made them all. I know you'll fergive the little devils, as you fergive me.'* And Lamma said to Saint Ninah, *'I fergive ya, me lovely ole mate. See ya soon.'* And Lamma swung the executioner's sword an' cut his throat right open. They both of 'em went 'ome. And that ends me readin' fer terday."

The ghastly silence stunk like festering anger, until David broke it with two claps of his hands. They all seemed to awake from their trance, and the murmuring returned. A baby suddenly began crying which injected life back into the church, and the vicar said one more prayer before the close. Everybody stood, but remained at their pews as the Queen and her daughters walked slowly, arm in arm, down the aisle. Then out popped little Catherine. She stood facing them, biting her bottom lip, and then scrambled down and kissed Tracy's feet, and stood up. Gayla and Catan giggled as they gave Catherine a kiss and thanked her. "It was lovely."

"Your Majesty, I 'ave somefink for ya."

One of the old congregation told the girl to stand aside for the Queen, but Tracy shook her head.

"This's your inheritance. We've kept it good an' clean. An' when yer want me, just shout me and we can 'ave a proper chinny." She held a tatty old book out towards Tracy. It was 'Unknown India'.

Tracy took the book and held it to her chest. She wasn't sure whether she wanted to cuddle it or burn it, but it was part of Robin. "Thank you Catherine. Please visit us before we go home."

She chuckled, her big grey-green eyes burning into Tracy's.

Tracy grinned, "I can see why he loves you. I'd like to get to know you one day."

The tiny god replied, "You already do." She stood back into her pew to allow her estranged family to pass, and they all went home.

Colin Hodgson

21 -- UNKNOWN INDIA

April 2009, the Royal Palace, Anglia

The family returned home to the Palace, accompanied by David and Russell, and, against his own better judgement, Syed had also returned.

They sat in the lounge and drank whisky and beer.

Russell suddenly asked, "Did it hurt? You know, when Dad cut your hand off."

Catan peered over towards Russell. "Why've you suddenly asked that after all this time together?"

"Just been wondering. See, if you were human, it would. Like shit."

"But my body is human, hurts the same. It just doesn't get older. And yes, it hurt but I've hurt a lot worse, when they cooked my hands and feet. You know Rus', they still hurt me. Gayla has to massage them." She paused. "I've had a different type of pain, when Dilly was killed. Human pain." She stared into space.

David suggested, "Rus', leave it. We're all the same."

"Sorry. Just forget I asked."

"No, Russell, you *can* ask." Catan cleared her throat. "We *are* different, and that's why you must stay away from us after the funeral. You'll get hurt, or killed, as everybody else seems to. You remember that little schoolgirl at the church? Well if you see her, acknowledge her, but don't feel offended if she just grins at you, and if she ever tells you to do something, do it without question. She's your minder and will keep you alive." She could see Russell through Gayla. "I can see that you're worried. Neither of you should worry, well not too much. Maybe just a little, well you know… Ooops, sorry. Not trying to frighten you but… Oh dear." Gayla had a private whispering session with her little girl, and Tracy was not amused. *'Don't be rude,'* she thought. Gayla replied, *'But Mummy, we need to stop Kamdar. He'll kill them somehow, just won't do it himself.'*

Tracy nodded in appreciation and demanded, "Enough of this whispering, you two. Syed's coming round for a drink with General Dara and Captain Batiste. We're gonna get pissed. Yeehaaaa!"

The guests arrived, and the drink flowed.

Syed asked Tracy, "What did you think of the reading? Really unusual, I thought. Ca'an spoke bloody suspiciously like that little girl who tagged onto me when I arrived at the church."

Tracy smiling, replied, "I thought it was beautiful. But to others it was probably atrocious, like something from a youth club comedy act, and probably seen as blasphemous by many." She frowned as she thought about it.

The Captain joined in. "I've seen a transcript of the reading and it's being analysed by the whole World. But I think there was no blasphemy whatsoever. I'm a Catholic and there was no hint that I am worshipping the wrong God. And if I were of another religion I would get the same message. It's saying that they're all the same one, in different forms. But it's saying that you, Tracy, are the Mother of All Gods." He also frowned as he thought about it.

Catherine was quite brilliant, not previously known by Tracy and Robin. She could certainly take it on the run, and her 'Passing of Saint Ninah' was straight off the cuff, and had been sparked by the threat of her Niece and her 'Mother' being burned on the pyre with the Lamma. If her tiny piece of literature, read beautifully through Catan, could get the message over to the world quickly enough, they could *all* go home with the Lamma, including her beloved cousin, or whatever, Gayla. That is, of course, if the pyre is big enough to hold them all! But ten out of ten for invention and effort. Apart from that she did have a great laugh over it all.

Syed, aiming at Tracy, "You spoke about the inheritance going to your daughter, and you also said that Ca'an is to be with you on the pyre. That only leaves Gayla. And the reading said that you are the mother of God, and God walks the Earth right now." They all looked towards the little girl.

Gayla jumped up and put them straight. "Uh uh. That's *not* what Daddy meant, and that's *not* part of the plan. I don't do that type of job." She threw herself back into the settee, and huffed.

General Dara quietly said to Tracy, "The transcript of *your* words worries me, your Majesty. You're going to be burned on the funeral pyre, with your daughter. That's illegal."

"Then *make* it legal," she snapped. No change given!

In the meantime, Catan and Gayla had to give Catherine a chance to carry out her duties, without always having the distraction of needing to protect the boys from Kamdar. Tracy had already given them the nod of consent, and Catherine just laughed when it was mentioned to her, so they knew what they had to do. They arranged to meet Sir Kamdar in the Fort, and arrived in the jag'.

"Sergeant, wait by the car, but keep us in sight. You may not want to miss this." Catan wore her ceremonial sword. That very often meant just one thing.

They stood on the parade ground, looking so tiny and the three groups of soldiers who were carrying out their drill were ordered to stand to attention, facing the two little girls. The sun was shining, and it was humid and the sweat flowed from the men. Sir Kamdar came out from the barracks and had dressed for the royal occasion, but his hair was straggly and full of grease, and his yellow teeth flashed as he saluted the girls.

"Good morning Ca'an. I hope we're not going to argue."

"Of course not. We've made our decision, so we've nothing to argue about. Do you know why we're here?"

Kamdar smiled. "Funeral arrangements?"

As Gayla giggled by Catan's side, his face dropped.

"Yes, Kamdar. We've already made the funeral arrangements. Yours." She smiled and Gayla chuckled. "This time you won't be back. You enjoy the company of the Chi Bantri, so you'll join them in their never-diminishing queue. You can share the endless pain of lingchi with your mates, until the children can find it in their hearts to forgive, especially Dilshad. You're to die as a human, and your body will be thrown to the gharials, in disgrace." She took time out to remove her glasses. "Ninah is a good person, and you shame him. Your brother will be written into the scriptures as the Saint who looks after the hearts of the children, and who gave his life to free their spirits. You'll be depicted as the evil one, who succumbed to the opium head, and sank to the absolute low of only having six friends, the worms." Gayla stuck her tongue out, and blew a raspberry at him. "The evil one who contrived with his six gullible friends to deny the Earth of their Lamma, returning him early to his heavenly palace. You'll be remembered as the one not to be." Gayla giggled as she led Catan. Catan slowly stated, "Mummy will *not* send you home, she'll send you nowhere."

Sir Kamdar looked to his soldiers, but they never even flinched. "You can't do this, I'm family. And I didn't kill Lamma, nor the girl." He attempted to move away, but was rooted to the spot.

"The worms were your hands, and the soldiers were your prick. They're all forgiven, you're not, and so I will now, with the blessing of God, discharge my duty." Her hand clenched the sword and it sliced through the air, and then through his throat which gaped open. He momentarily stood, blood pumping from the wound, but then fell to his knees. His black eyes watched the giggling Gayla as he slipped away and she put her hand on his greasy head and, like a vicar, uttered "Bless you my son," and laughed as he fell to the ground, dead. She wiped her hand on her kurta.

"Captain!" Sir Kamdar's captain approached, and saluted. "Don't be nervous. You've just witnessed the execution of an evil spirit. Now take the carcass in the refuse truck and dump it with the gharials. They'll enjoy him. Nobody else has."

Kamdar, Ninah's brother, was only the second of the Qeervi family to have been permanently removed, and on that wretched, sad day, the girls high-fived and laughed.

The family waited and fidgeted as the day of the funeral loomed. Just two days away, and the three little girls were stumped. General Dara had negotiated a license to allow Tracy and Catan to be burned with the body of the Lamma. The pyre would float out into the Hooghly and the bodies of the three demigods would burn, and they would go home. Gayla and Catherine would be alone. They had to do something.

Gayla communicated with Catherine. *'Well? It's getting close,'* thought Gayla. *'I don't want to ask Daddy. That wouldn't be cricket, since he's dead.'* She waited for something back from her. Eventually it came. *'What about those flippin' holo scientists?'* Gayla bit her bottom lip and replied, *'Not enough time.'*

They pondered, Gayla in the steamy rains of Bengal and Catherine in the cold rains of Essex. Catherine asked, *''ow would Daddy have worked it out?'* That was a difficult one, as he was a man. Gayla thought, *'He was a man, so it would be really simple. The last really brilliant idea he had was, let's have a whisky. To be fair, it was a good idea at the time.'* They both laughed like little school children. *'But Dad did say if you can't hide it, feature it. I think he's telling us to make good use of the situation.'* Catherine jumped, *'Go' it. I've bloody go' it. I've been a real berk. We'll use you, me old china. Only you can do it. And under the circumstances, we can bend the rules just a tinsy bit.'*

A plan was developing.

In the palace sitting room, "Can you swim?" Catan asked David.

"Not very well. But Russell's a brilliant swimmer."

Catan nodded towards Gayla who asked Russell, "Would you help us with a little thing? It'll be dangerous for you, Wus. The Hooghly is full of all sorts of poisonous shit." They came to an agreement, and the plans were set.

The site of the funeral was chosen to suit the crowd with both sides of the river clear, allowing many thousands of mourners. A team of ageing volunteers from the slum walked the body in a hand-drawn funeral carriage from Anglia to the riverside. The carriage was pure white, highly decorated with carvings and mother of pearl, with large windows to display the almost naked Lamma amidst a nest of maroon flowers. It was refrigerated to keep the body and the flowers clean during the nine hour trek.

It seemed that millions of people had come out to pay their lasting respects for their Lamma. In just a few months Robin and his family had become icons, particularly in India, and people of all religions and nationalities lined the streets as the carriage slowly wound towards its destination. Gayla's project was showing positive results.

Staging had been erected for the press, and for the many dignitaries, and there were plenty of them. Something was happening. Amongst others the dignitaries included Kings and Queens from Europe and Africa, Presidents and Prime Ministers, the Pope, the Bishop of Canterbury and the Grandayatollah Ali Azari Mioni, Jainist and Hindu scholars, and Buddhist philosophers and the Governor of Punjab. It was a wonderful turn-out!

The army had built a small jetty, and a wooden quay where the closest mourners would stand to see off their loved ones. The local importance of the funeral was reflected in the amount of preparation. The pyre was like a large wooden raft, with flowers placed around the edge, and a wood-fire built up with a latticed platform on top, for the bodies. It was moored to the jetty, with a brazier burning fiercely, ready for the torching of the World's most famous strangers.

The funeral carriage arrived and the throng lulled into a chilling silence, broken only by the ducks who carried on with their busy lives. The body was drawn out through the back doors, and the bearers, old, tired and decrepit, marched very, very slowly down to the quay. David, Russell, Gayla, Catan and Tracy stood at the front of the group, with Syed, General Dara, Aalap and Captain Batiste behind, and they were flanked by the two Ghurkha guards, in full military dress. The girls wore the cholis and sari of the Qeervi family. Catherine was there in spirit.

As the body passed by the family, David and Russell wept, along with many billions of newly found admirers, but the girls stood firm. Gayla received a thought from Catherine, *'Good luck, Cous'.'* Amongst the tears and the respect, the little Indian girl grinned.

The body was carefully placed on the top of the pyre, on the platform, and the World felt something break in their hearts, but then Princess Catan and Queen Maya kissed their family goodbye. The pain could be felt around the World as they stepped onto the pyre and sat on the platform, one each end of the Lamma. They were ready to pass to the other dimension, they were going home. The thousands of local mourners wept and wailed as the fire was lit, and it caught quickly.

As the pyre was untied, and toed out and away from the jetty, Gayla moved. She poked Russell in the ribs and then ran forward, avoiding the lunge of the Sergeant. She picked up speed along the small jetty, and then made her stupendous leap, hitting full into Tracy, who toppled, and fell into the water. Gayla desperately grabbed Catan and they lay with their daddy, cuddling and writhing as the flames scorched the life out of them both. And as the crowds screamed the skies just momentarily flashed. Their spirits were gone.

But the Queen? Russell ran forward, diving into the dirty river-water and quickly got hold of Tracy as she began taking in water. Captain Batiste followed him, and between them they managed to pull the Queen to the awaiting sergeant and his private. After coughing up some water, she screamed, and the crowds silenced, and her pitiful wailing could be heard right along the Hooghly banks, while the raging pyre floated out towards the end of its journey. They were gone, but the Queen remained. She lay on the jetty, joined by David and Russell, and wept. They all wept.

The next day Tracy shut herself in her Palace bedroom. "Nobody is welcome." She instructed her two loyal Ghurkhas accordingly. The boys returned to England, accompanied by Syed who had seen two too many deaths, leaving the only surviving Qeervi known to mankind alone, and distraught. *'Auntie Maya.'* It was Catherine. *'I'm sorry. Will yer talk wiv me?'* Who is this Catherine? Tracy just turned her mind off to her and sat in her room for many days, seeing nobody, eating and drinking nothing, and her Ghurkhas kept all-comers out.

The funeral had shocked the World. But hey, what a result it turned out to be. They suddenly realised, or manufactured, or maybe just fantasised, that the Queen was to inherit the Earth from the Lamma. After all, why else would the Lamma's two daughters give their lives so dramatically to keep their mother here? Really strange, because before the Lamma died they did not even know that he owned the Earth. But allegedly he did, so all eyes were trained on the Queen from all parts of the World, and they awaited her return to the throne. They all had a million questions to ask her.

The Indian government looked after her very well. The whole Anglia area was so tightly policed to ensure that she was never disturbed, and they reported to the World's press and leaders that she was temporarily in private mourning. I don't think she ever again wanted to leave that room, she just wanted to die. "Fucking kids. Spoil everything." Gayla's plans did not allow for the loss of the Queen, nor the loss of the World's favourite Princess, Catan, but since Tracy had taken to making her own plans to get home with Robin, one of them had to go. And since they couldn't hide it, they had to feature it! It turned out to be a brilliant bit of public relations.

Several days passed and she stayed put in her room. General Dara was turned away again, and Captain Batiste's bottles of whisky were accepted, but he himself turned away. The servants would die before they allowed *anybody* to pass.

But one evening, "Sergeant, let me pass." The sergeant instinctively instructed the private to open the bedroom door.

Tracy was lying on the bed, staring with her one eye at the ceiling. She was wearing just a tee-shirt and knickers. "Who's that?" she snapped.

"A little girl."

Tracy just lay there for several minutes without a word. Then, "How old are you?"

"Eight, just eight."

Another spell of silence passed. "You that bloody Catherine?"

"Maybe."

Tracy's head was waking up. She was getting interested. "Why're you here?" She continued to stare at the ceiling.

"To love my mummy."

Tracy shot bolt upright. It was Gayla! The little monster shot over to the bed and almost hit her as hard as she had done on the pyre. They hugged and chuckled, and kissed. They spent ages just rolling around on the bed until eventually Tracy just had to ask, "How?"

"Oh Mummy, I can't tell you everything. You'd be as clever as me."

The return of her little girl did not make her want to head the World. She still just wanted to go home and be with her cell-mate.

"I'm still going home. I've had it with your projects, and this poor Earth isn't ready for you to be down here. Much longer and you'll have killed as many as the Chi Bantri."

"Mummy, it's not that easy. You've got to stay, until I've adjusted my project plan. I'll get you home, but not just yet. As soon as I've finalised my project."

"I'm going home to be with Robin."

"It's not so simple, you know! You can't kill yourself. Right now nobody out there has the nerve, nor the reason to kill you, and you can't ask somebody to kill you. They're the rules. You're stuck here, so let's make the most of it and have a laugh." She giggled and tried to tickle Tracy, but she was pushed away.

"And why do you laugh at everything? Cry, just cry for once."

Gayla sat back and bit her lip. "No." She looked up at her mummy like a wanton puppy. "Please don't try to make me cwy."

Tracy was drunk, and getting worked up. "Just cry! Go on, now. Do it for mankind. See if you can make a whole new project out of it. Go on!" She was pissed, and wild. "Go on, cry. I *hate* you! I wish you'd stayed away. Cry! Cry!" She was shouting.

Gayla curled up with her arms around her head. "No."

"Why not? Tell me why. I cry. Does that make me weak, or stupid?" She leaned over the little girl and shouted in her ear. "Cry for fuck sake!"

Gayla never moved nor answered. She just wrapped her arms tighter around her head.

Tracy let up a little. "Why won't you cry?"

Gayla slowly took her arms from around her head and looked up at Tracy. With a pitiful mourn, "I cwied for nearly two hundred years. *That's* why."

Tracy frowned in disbelief. "When?" She put her arm around Gayla's shoulder, but it was pushed away. "What would make you cry for all that time?"

Gayla turned her head back to look her in the face. "*You*. It was *you*. Both of you. It was only Ninah who cared. So don't fucking talk to me about crying! I've had enough of it!" The little girl had no tears in her eyes. She wasn't going to cry, so she laughed. "How's that, big Mummy?" She carried on laughing.

"Stop it! Stop!" Tracy screamed. "Please stop. Talk to me, please."

Gayla's face turned evil. She sneered at Tracy and scowled, "Every project we do, you mess up. You're too pig headed to carry it through, same as this one." She breathed heavily, "And you pissed the last one up. And you pissed all of us up. You nearly wiped us out. When your dad gave you to me, he said you'd be trouble. He never spoke a truer word!" She stopped, and the World seemed to go on hold for several minutes.

Tracy rubbed her tired eyes. "Well go on. If you're gonna condemn me, lay down your case. Explain yourself, or shut up!"

Gayla relaxed and smiled. "Right. Ok. As you know we were planning on staying here while the Chi Bantri found their feet, and if they went the wrong way, we would shut the project down and go home. But *oh no, you* wanted to go home *early*, so you rearranged the plan behind my back, and we were all executed. And then what?" She pushed her head towards Tracy's in anticipation. "You don't know, do you? Well I'll tell you what you did, apart from inflicting suffering on hundreds of millions of people because we weren't here to shut them down. Apart from that, I went home. Did you know that Mummy? I went *home. On my own! Completely* on my own. You and Daddy went one way, lost for over two hundred years. Ca'an had to finish her confirmation training so stayed here. Kamdar chose his own roots and stayed with his dope. Ninah couldn't find his route and just went round and round." She quietened and almost whimpered, "And I went home on my own." She sighed, and then pulled over to Tracy, and laid her head on her breasts. "Sorry Mummy. I do love you."

Tracy twiddled with Gayla's ear-lobe.

"Do you really want to know about your little girl? About the last two hundred years? Do you care?" A deathly silence hung like a ghost over the room. She spoke quietly, squeezing her head between her mummy's breasts. "I'll tell you some, then. At first I waited for you all to come home, but you didn't, so to sooth my loneliness I began playing with the people. It was amazing. I got so much pleasure from hurting my own children, and it warmed my lonely heart. And the poor people really suffered. In about 1840 I had a crying session which lasted for over 5 years, just non-stop crying for you. As my tears fell they evaporated, never reaching the earth, and the World dried up. In many parts of Africa, the cattle died, and the children withered to bone, and were lost forever. Millions died, and millions resorted to eating their own as desperation took control. But that became boring, so I set about playing some more exiting games, and got an undersea volcano to erupt in the South Pacific, hundreds of years before our schedule. A group of islands were washed away by the tidal wave, and I watched for many days as the people, men, women and children, clung onto life in the seas, slipping away one at a time until there was only a handful of them left. They cried for each other as the sharks began to pick them off, and I laughed. I was laughing, and not crying, and I felt so good. And the people were nearly all gone, but one small group clung onto the driftwood until they were in sight of land, and they found just enough spirit to smile at the little girl who was perched on the wood, encircled by her surviving family. And I thought to myself 'you're never gonna make it,' and I was going to make sure of it. And as they neared the safety of the beech, their hearts rose to the occasion and they began to sing, and the little girl who was their idol, was helped onto the beach. She sat watching the people help each other from the driftwood, and I was so bitter that I couldn't stand the child's jubilation, and I couldn't understand how a child could be so happy, when I was oh so broken hearted and lonely." Gayla stopped for a good sniff. "Anyway, I made these salt-water crocodiles come out of the jungle, and two of them fought over the girl, tearing her limb from limb as they contested the sweet meat, and her screams didn't last long. The adults howled at the sight, as the blood spat all around and the child became dismembered, and eaten by the crocodiles. And I just laughed and laughed."

"Why are you telling me this?"

She took a deep breath and continued, "Because what then happened makes me different. I seemed to explode, and life disappeared momentarily, and a loud noise cracked through my head, and there she was. Right in front of me. She smiled at me and told me, without moving her lips, to save the poor castaways. And I had to. I couldn't fight her, I just had to do it. So I held off the crocs, so that the people could get onto the beach and seek sanctuary. But they wouldn't. Instead they returned to the driftwood, and they were heartbroken, so they went back out to sea, and one by one, the sharks ate them, and they didn't even fight. When I took away their little girl, I must've taken their spirit. I felt so ashamed, but so jealous of their emotions and love that I decided instantly to blow Yellowstone. Fuck the people, why should they have everything? All that love?" She held Tracy so tightly. "That's when I changed. Cos she said 'no' and I had to stop. I didn't blow Yellowstone. She wouldn't let me." She began sucking her thumb.

"Who was she?"

"My conscience. My twin, Catherine, who I ate so many billions of years earlier. She moved out. I was the bad, the creator, and she the good, the conscience and I was becoming too strong for her, so she escaped. And she wouldn't go back. She is me, but she won't go back to me, and so inhabits the Earth looking out for me, and making sure I don't ever again lose it enough to hurt our children. God almighty, the creator, who ruled as one together, now rules as one apart. We are now one apart. No other God has been one apart, whilst also being the creator. I'm the ultimate, living as two, but working as one, with Catherine the good keeping Gayla the brilliant from misbehaviour."

Tracy pulled Gayla's head into her breasts, and the tiny God sucked her thumb.

"But I still cried. I cried for another hundred and thirty years. The crying didn't stop me wanting to blow the Earth to bits, so something had to be done. While me and Catherine were together her strength held me back, and I never let my devil take over, but when we were apart, I rebelled. I know now what happened on your daddy's Colony in 1971. I'd watched the Chi Bantri succeed as evil, greedy humans, and I had really enjoyed watching the games that they played. Their games involved them in many of the black periods. They starved about eight million people in the Ukraine, killed millions of Jews and Gypsies in Europe, the atom bombs in Japan, and they murdered thirty million people in China in the sixties, the Vietnamese war showed some wonderful technical advances in destruction, and I was just getting into the warm-up for the East Pakistani war, after the Bhola cyclone had hit, and she took over."

Tracy whispered, "You don't have to tell me all this."

"I do. It's for *me*. I need to hear it from myself. I wasn't sure at the time, but I now know that Catherine sent me away; she had to for my mental health, and for our children. But we never talk about it." She faltered and took some deep breaths. "Anyway, there was a boy, same age as Daddy, who I really thought was Daddy. I became his little blonde, deformed sister and went with him, looking for you, to the New Bury mining colony where your father ruled. God Edward, who gave you and Daddy to me, and who gifted me the original raw materials to start the Earth living, just wanted to kill him, because he wasn't Daddy at all, just a human boy. But he wasn't just a human boy. He was the most *beautiful* human boy, and I fell madly in love with him. He was Peter and I was his little sister, Katie. And his absolute power to care replaced some of the conscience that Catherine had taken back, and I lived a few weeks in true paradise. I couldn't get back to Earth without Catherine's strength, and I could've died. It was such a beautiful feeling of reality and vulnerability, and just for a couple of months I felt human. I discovered some of what I'd given my children, true love. I've never been happier. But apart from a lesson in human love, Catherine had another purpose for my trip to the colony."

"Is my father ok? Please."

"He is, now. He moved to a safer place. One day, Mummy, we'll get Daddy and go and visit. But, anyway, the other thing which she had masterminded, probably with Edward, was that I needed strengthening. You see, Catherine was so much stronger than me, and we didn't match. So, the other lovely two children of Edward, the last of their kind, became our very best of friends, and to cut a long story short, I took Mo's strength. Stumpy and Mo were twins, your cousins, and had chosen to become one as one at puberty, unlike you and Daddy who chose to be one apart, so, after a night of storytelling around the camp-fire, Stumpy gave up his right as a God. He didn't eat his twin, he gave him to me. I ate Mo. I ate Stumpy's conscience, his twin brother, Mo." She sucked her thumb for a while. "I'm now the most powerful God ever to rule anywhere. I live one as one with Mo, and one apart with Catherine. No god has ever had that level of freedom and diversity." She wasn't smiling.

"So why so glum?"

"I miss Peter and Stumpy. I never wanted to leave the colony, but I had to. I'm the most powerful God ever, but still can *never* get what I want."

Tracy whispered in her ear, "What do you really want?"

She stopped sucking her thumb. "I want Peter. I want to be human. To love. Just love." A wry smile crossed her dark face. "Just like Stumpy wanted. And just like Stumpy, I can't. I'm God."

Tracy thought and frowned, and then whispered, "I met Peter. He's stayed in my dreams all my life while I was human, and I never knew why. I met him in the playing fields, when he was waiting for God. He was waiting for you, the 'spastic' girl. It all makes sense now."

"Yes, but I never turned up. Catherine sorted it." Finally a smile appeared. "And you've got all the children you could wish for, and they all love the mysterious Queen. Peter told me what you said."

A long period of contemplation took over. Eventually Tracy stirred. "I'm sorry. I've been so selfish. Hope at some time over the next few billion years you'll be able to forgive me." They lay down.

Chuckling, "Mummy, if I hadn't forgiven you, I would've killed you both when I found you." That was a bit cold. "That's not true, Catherine would have stopped me. If Catherine hadn't, Peter would've. And now there's Mo in here." She held her hand to her chest. "He would've stopped me."

The two lay on the bed for several hours, motionless and speechless, and eventually Gayla's nose pushed hard into the Queens breasts.

Laid back and relaxed, Gayla whispered. "You know, Mummy. This's all about Ca'an. She's finished her period of confirmation. She's experience unbelievable pain and suffering, she's lived the solitary life without sight for many years, she's loved, and she's lost. And despite her torturous suffering and broken heart, she's forgiven. We've passed her.

She passed with flying colours, as I knew she would all those centuries ago. The World really wants *her*."

Tracy touched her nose against Gayla's and, pointedly said, "You're forgetting something. What they *really* want is their God."

"I know, but I can't do everything myself, and I don't do that sort of job, and besides, the spirit of God is everywhere, *especially* in our little princess. She's the perfect stand-in and has proved her strength and her absolute dedication to the job, *and* her commitment to me. When she was put to the test, she again came out smelling of ambrosia. As long as they believe she's God, then she is; she can carry it off for a few thousand years. And I think the daughter of God is close enough for my people."

They were quiet for a while, while Tracy had a drink of whisky. She frowned and asked, "What test?" She was becoming suspicious. "What test? I hope it's not what I'm thinking."

"Oh Mummy, don't even think about it. It's just work."

"I don't believe it! How *could* you?" Tracy screwed her face up as she looked into Gayla's face. "I heard my Lamma wondering once, if you were divinely good or just plain evil. What are you?"

"What do you mean?" Gayla cuddled up to her. "Let's not fall out again."

"You led your own daughter into love, with Dilshad, and then killed it off, just to test her commitment to her duty, and to you. Tell me how that's not evil."

Gayla put her hand over her eyes and bit her bottom lip. "You know Mummy, if I'm going to put Ca'an into a position of absolute power, representing God Almighty, she can't ever behave like a human. She proved with Dilshad that she's strong, stronger than you, stronger than Daddy, and just think what could've happened if she'd failed the test. Me and Catherine would've had a fight on our hands, I can tell you that for nothing. The avenging Princess could've destroyed this world. But she didn't, and she won't. I know that now, all at a small cost of just one little girl." She pulled herself back into Tracy's breasts. "You must've by now returned enough as a Qeervi to know what's what. Me and Catherine is God, and you *all* support my work. Just remember that next time you piss off." She sighed. "And you must always remember that I don't take chances with my work. I don't work with luck, it's all planned, if not by me, then by Catherine."

Tracy looked hard into Gayla's eyes. "So they all died by your hand? Robin, Dilshad, Saint Catherine and all her children and angels, Satvinder, Ninah, the millions of people caught in the volcanoes?" She squeezed Gayla's head so hard. "I'm beginning to remember an awful lot more."

"It's work. It's what we do, *together.* You're part of it!"

An eerie silence fell. Gayla fidgetted with her teashirt, before pulling herself right into Tracy's face. She spoke so quietly and deliberately. "Catherine's just reminded me. I need to remind you." She again began biting her bottom lip. "You're the Mother of all things. But *never* forget that you're the *adopted* Mother. I can always get another one."

The Queen looked blankly towards the window as a tear rolled down her face. Gayla knew that she needed to change the subject.

"Mummy, please don't leave me again until we're done. I can't do this job without you. Please." At last, she wasn't giggling nor chortling. With a slight stutter, "Remembering Peter and Stumpy has made me realise how much I need you. Is that what love is?" She pushed her face into her breasts. Tracy's eyes continued to wet up as she felt the dampness of tears seep through her tee-shirt and onto her cool chest. Gayla shuddered, and pulled her face harder in to Tracy. She was crying. The tiny little God quietly sobbed. She put her thumb into her mouth and stroked her cheek with her finger, and sobbed. Despite having been back with her Mummy for several months, she had only just at that moment found her, and they reunited.

Tracy whispered, "You *had* to keep me with you. It's not love, it's hunger. You must be getting very hungry."

Gayla looked up at her with tear sodden face and grinned. She was absolutely starving. She pulled Tracy's tee-shirt up and gently put her mouth over her nipple, closed her eyes and suckled. With one hand around the breast and the other gently stroking her cheek, she fed. The Mother of God nourished the Earth as it poured with rain all around the globe and as she changed nipples the thunder crashed and the lightning flared, and the fertile seeds which had lay dormant since her last feed sprung into life, and the deserts bloomed. Just for a day.

Then, as the desert blooms shrank back into their pods the World slept, and so did Gayla. Smiling, Tracy kissed her head and whispered, "I'll wake you up next century, poppet."

Gayla awoke quite soon. She was strong and giggly, back to normal, and her mother was again sober. Tracy hadn't known about the lonely stress which had plagued her little God for so many years, and it gave her a timely kick up the jacksie. They were truly back together, and forgiven.

"Now Mummy, if you want to go home, stick to the bloody plan."

"Which is?"

"Well, you've been pushed into this Queen thing, not unreasonably as you've been Queen Maya since they hung you in Nepal, and they all love you, but they love Ca'an even more. After all, they've not waited for *your* return for all these years, they've waited for the Princess's mother's return and there's a subtle difference. They've awaited the Mother of God. And it just so happens that they believe that Ca'an's mother is *you*. So you've got to be here for a short time longer." She pulled herself into Tracy's face and giggled. "See, it's not *just* because I was hungry." They cuddled tightly. "Apart from that, me and Cat' can stick it out here for a few more thousand years, with Catherine in the aisles. They can revere our little girl as their God, and I'll be right here for her.

And you know Mummy, as soon as we've got Ca'an back in place, you can then go home to Daddy."

Tracy was suddenly elated. "Thank you, I won't let you down again." She solemly asked, "But what about you? I know we share Robin, he unwittingly told me during his coma. So what about you?"

"As long as you don't go missing I can see you whenever I want. You know that. So we can get back to business pretty soon. Now back to the plan. When they all see me, they'll just think I'm some kind of witch, risen from the flames, as they always have done. But Ca'an, they'll welcome her back, restored, as your daughter. She always takes the limelight, doesn't she? So she'll melt instantly back into their hearts, and then I can send you home. Just gotta get her back here somehow. We've recalled the holo scientists, gotta make sure the world takes notice." Gayla jiggled with excitement. "You can cuddle Daddy soon, honest. And he's gonna bring you a present. Day after tomorrow General Dara has organised a trip to that hill, where those poor Muslims were all hanged by the soldiers of the East India Company. And the World'll see Daddy again."

"Hang on, Cat', I'm *not* gonna cuddle a bloody *hologram*."

Gayla was heating up. "You've gotta go with the plan, else the same bloody thing will happen. *Just* do as you're *told* for once!"

Tracy pulled back, and she was a little bit shocked. "Ok, I'll do my best, but I know it'll hurt me."

"Oh, you can do it, and we've got a beautiful present for you. You'll get it day after tomorrow, on the hill, when we see Daddy." Gayla bit her bottom lip, and asked, "Have you ever looked at the book? You know, Daddy's old book?"

She shook her head, "No. Don't know if I want to. I was going to throw it away or burn it."

"Come on, let's look at it." Gayla looked around the room, and there it was, on the dressing table. "I'll get it." She scrambled off the bed, and collected it. "Come on. Let's see what's in it today. You know, I used to read it to Peter, Stumpy and Mo, back on the Colony."

They sat side-by-side and placed the tatty old book across their legs. The title was Unknown India, and the author was Catherine Qeervi. Who'd have guessed? Tracy turned the pages slowly, passed over the bits of little interest, but eventually arrived at a pictorial story called The Bengal Dawn. The colour plates were so beautiful; some finely painted in watercolours and some photographs, and reproduced on a heavy art paper. They almost climbed out of the pages as they told the bloody story of the return of the Qeervis.

The first plate went back to the seventeen hundreds and depicted Queen Maya of Anglia welcoming Emperor Shah Alam II, set in front of two elaborately decorated elephants, donning their impressive castles. She was dressed in the family colours of maroon and white and was fully jewelled up with the royal tiara set. The emperor was flanked by his colourful dignitaries, while the emerald-eyed Queen had the Lamma to her right, and a grown up Gayla to her left, and then the little teenage figure of Princess Catan of Anglia. Supporting plates showed the local people starving, and dismembering the bodies of their dead neighbours, and feasting. The Bengal famine was in full swing.

The next four plates, still in the seventeen hundreds, showed the story of the Nepalese scholars taking the family from the Palace, and crucifying Queen Maya and her adult daughter, Gayla, with the face of the Lamma poking out from Gayla's bulging tummy. They showed the young Princess, chained to a metal frame and being partly cooked, as the Monsignor ate flesh from her hands and feet and poured a white liquid into her eyes. The people wailed in despair.

The story of the Dying Princess was told in graphic detail, showing the mutilated girl with her hands and feet stripped down to the bones and her freshly cooked body still steaming, with the Princess staring into oblivion from her two dead, pearly-white eyes. She never died, and one plate detailed an

Indian doctor applying a grey poultice to her hands and feet. She was then shown as complete, with hands and feet, but with her head and face hidden by a white silk hood. She had shackles around her ankles.

The story of the six children followed, with the Princess standing over them as they play, but then an awful painting of one of them hanging on the metal frame, facedown, and being lowered over a white-hot bed of coals, the child's face displaying absolute pain and fear as his personal hell was administered him by the Chi Bantri. The members could be seen in the background holding their tin plates, and their tongues hanging out, waiting to be fed from their Princess's divine spirit, and all around there were tiny stoves heating the opium pipes.

The next pages touched on the mass murder and genocide associated with human control, often carried out 'in the name of God'. There were a few plates showing dead, mutilated bodies, some piled into wells, some almost blocking the river ways, and some of dogs feeding on partly devoured children. And there were young girls with breasts removed and laying dead, with other young girls looking on, broken and drained of all spirit. It was a sordid reminder of the reality behind the pretty public face of the Chi Bantri.

The death of the Chi Bantri took up just five plates. The mood changed as the media moved from watercolours to photography and the first was a photograph of Robin and Tracy drinking and laughing with Saint Catherine and their friends, with the leper children and the angels looking on. A moody, but celestial photograph of Ninah reminded the reader of the pain of absolute belief and self sacrifice, as he hung on the cross, the sun going down on the shacks, and on poor Ninah. The next showed the Lamma wielding the ceremonial sword and the left hand of the princess separated from her forearm. The photographer had caught the Princess's surreal look of total satisfaction as she sacrificed her hand, her pearly eyes shining like beacons through her dark face. The hand was then shown flaring in the fire, as the headless Dying Princess rose like a phoenix waving her Chi Bantri members to follow, and they did. They followed her to the never-ending queue which was depicted as a dark scene, in watercolours. They were sad, stripped of their riches and positions, and flanked by millions of laughing children. The members were waiting for their turn on the wooden post, way up ahead. They could just about make out one of their fellow members as he hung, whimpering, with large swathes of blood over his chest, shoulders and thighs where his flesh was being cut away, a little at a time, by the lingchi executioners. The members begged forgiveness from the children.

The death of the Lamma was shown as a peaceful scene with the two girls laying in the flames on the pyre, cuddling their beloved Lamma and drifting into the Hooghly. Scenes of the despair of the onlookers began to change the mood of the story. There was no evidence of fear nor pain, just the love of the people for their lost Princess, and the respect of many religious leaders paying their respects for something that they didn't quite understand. The Queen was not featured.

The next pages were photographic records of the return of the Lamma. He was shown naked, hugging and kissing his Queen as he paid her a miraculous visit, and Saint Ninah was pictured handing a brightly shining gift to her. The crowds cheered and celebrated as the Lamma walked a little way with his family, and the religious leaders were shown kneeling and bowing, united in their support for their common God.

And then the final section showed photographs of their magnificent God, first as she descended from the heavens like an enormous, shining angel with pearly-white eyes, and then elevated upon a small hill and silhouetted by the sun which had created a halo of brilliant white light around the black hair and stunning Indian eyes. It was the Princess Catan of Anglia, almighty, beautiful, and perfect in every way.

"And Mummy, this bit's just for you." The next page showed a mangled body, laying in the road after being hit by a car. It had bright ginger hair, and an eye which shone into the onlooking crowd, spraying all with a heavenly green light. It was Tracy, dead. "Just don't mess up, or the book will have to be rewritten, again."

Tracy smiled and closed the old book. "Why is Catherine never featured in the book?"

Gayla, as always, giggled. "This story's all about Ca'an. *And,* as you know, I don't like talking about myself." She rolled onto her mummy's lap and just laughed her pants off.

"But this book, it's a very old book, it was Robin's. When did she write it?"

Gayla stared up into her mummy's green eye and chortled, "Soon, Mummy. She'll soon be writing it."

22 -- THE END OF THE BEGINNING

April 1971, the mining colony of New Bury, around the camp fire.

Peter continues Katie's story, "And on the day after tomorrow the General arrived with their transport, an enormous Indian elephant carrying a magnificent maroon and white castle, decorated with gold trim. It was led the way by the tiny rickshaw of Aalap, to the sacred hill, where Gayla had predicted the return of the Lamma.

"The people cheered as they watched the Queen's castle pass by, but some jeered and shouted 'witch' at little Gayla, who just laughed along with it and waved to the millions of people. When they arrived at the hill the elephant lowered the two royals to the ground, and they walked through their people to the top, where they found a little khaki army tent. It was a tiny tent, just like ours, and the people looked quizzically at it. Then, as the waiting World thought it was just a tent, the flap pushed aside and the massive hulk of Saint

Ninah crawled out. The crowd cheered hysterically, but quietened as the flap pushed aside again, and out crawled the Lamma. He was completely naked, and was without his false leg, so Saint Ninah assisted his Lord to walk towards Queen Maya and Gayla, and the crowds again began to roar. As they stood in front of the Queen she shook with anticipation, because she feared the hurt of holding just a hologram of her lover. She held her hand out, and very slowly he moved his hand to hers. She could feel him! He was real, and the Queen instantly threw her arms around him, kissing him, and crying. She looked down at Gayla and whispered, 'Thank you'. The Lamma said to the Queen, 'We have some presents for you.' Saint Ninah bowed to his Queen and handed her two large silver nails, the sign of Ninah. They had been crafted from the bones of your father, the God Edward, one from his left leg and one from his right. The Queen took the nails and presented the points to Ninah's forrid. Two tiny balls of blood grew from within his soul, the blood of the many children who had suffered at the Festival of Life. The Lamma then held his arms into the air, the holo scientists synchronised their guns, and a beautiful angel appeared from the skies. It gently settled on the top of the hill, its pearly-white eyes shining down onto her subjects who gasped in awe, before the angel melted down into the form of a beautiful little teenage girl, long black hair, and large, dark brown Indian eyes. It was Princess Catan, complete and perfect in every way.

"The Queen held the Princess tightly, as the crowds went crazy. The Lamma stated, 'Only one of us can come back, so I have to go home, but I'll see you soon.' The Queen gifted one of your father's nails to the Lamma and said 'this pair will soon be together again,' and he and Saint Ninah returned to the tent, which was then gone.

"Princess Catan of Anglia, the World's adopted God, was returned and the whole World celebrated.

"The Almighty Gayla kept her promise to her mummy, and with the help of her conscience, she had her mummy killed. The Mother of God went home to her Lamma. The end." Peter closed the book, 'Unknown India'.

Stumpy held little Mo tightly as the tot's strength waned, and said to Peter, "That was a lovely story, Peter. And Mo has managed to hold on right 'til the end. Thank you. But when did all this happen?"

Little Sis', Katie, grinned as she cuddled the book and whispered to Peter, who then replied to Stumpy, "Thanks to your family's absolute love for my little sister, it will all be happening soon. It will be happening very, very soon."

---------- **The end.** ----------